Casino

Bill Freeman

A novel of Las Vegas

by
— ROBERT KIRSCH —

LYLE STUART INC.
Secaucus, N. J.

Queries regarding rights and permissions
should be addressed to Lyle Stuart Inc.,
120 Enterprise Ave., Secaucus, N. J. 07094

Published by Lyle Stuart Inc. Published simultaneously
in Canada by George J. McLeod Limited,
Don Mills, Ontario

Manufactured in the United States of America

Library of Congress Cataloging in Publication Data
Kirsch, Robert R   1922-
Casino.
I. Title.
PZ4.K596Cas   [PS3561.I75]   813'.5'4   79-10936
ISBN 0-8184-0275-X

Casino

one

The dealer stepped back from the craps table and solemnly passed one palm over the other in Pilate's ancient gesture of handwashing. Like everything else in the huge casino of the Mecca Hotel, the move wasn't what it seemed to be. The casino required people who handled chips to clap their hands and turn them palm upward to the mirrored ceiling to show that no chips were being palmed.

The boxman nodded at the dealer's empty hands. Behind him both the pit boss and the floorman watched. Nothing special. It was six o'clock in the evening on a Friday in August in the largest hotel in Las Vegas, the biggest money-earner on the Strip. Four thousand guest rooms. A casino over an acre in size. When it was designed, some of the Vegas know-it-alls called it the Titanic, for it did look like a huge ship set in the tawny desert, the high tower a kind of mast, twenty-six stories high, with a penthouse, the three round towers like smokestacks coming out of the superstructure.

Also like a cruise ship, the Mecca tried to provide everything that would keep people aboard: restaurants and shops, entertainment, sports, the chance to sun, to win money, to try not only the familiar but the exotics of sin. Winning was most often an unborn dream on this ship of fools but it happened and you could hear when it did as a roar went up from the craps table when someone made his number. Losing was more definite, steadier, the determined grind of statistics. But even losing had a kind of masochistic pleasure for many people; it paid for guilt.

The shift had changed at the table but the game went on without pause. The energies in the room began to rise. New people were heading in from Los Angeles and New York, from Rio and Riad, from Columbia, South Carolina, from Paris and Amsterdam.

The new dealer scanned the action: four customers killing time, grinding out craps and numbers: a pipesmoker and therefore automatically a rube to the crap crew. He probably wore brown shoes, was a cheapskate and wouldn't dream of leaving a tip. Obviously waiting for his wife and the early dinner show. Then, the blonde, tanned lady of indeterminate age, her hands embossed with gold rings and bracelets, the glint of diamonds, but someone who knew her dice, took the odds, watched for a run of numbers and went to the back line on them; and, a funny sort of guy, dreamy, maybe stoned, wearing a rugby shirt, hardly paying attention to his bets. Next to him, maybe with him, was a slender looking girl, pale and freckled. Nothing much was happening.

"New shooter coming out," the stickman intoned. "Here's a new shooter, folks." Bets went down on the football green and white of the pass line. The pipesmoker bet the field, which looked like a good bet since it paid off on so many numbers but was for suckers only, a one-shot wager.

To the side of the casino, a jingle of bells and coins, a jackpot rose out of the ranks of the clicking slot machines. The acoustics sopped up the noise.

The dice went to the blonde. The dealer and the boxman talked under their breath. "So how do you like the new house, Murray?"

The boxman answered in a flat sparse voice, his long fingers dangling protectively over the bank of chips. "Two days and the plumbing goes sour. The second bathroom—needs new pipes according to the plumber."

"Plumbers are worse than lawyers," the dealer remarked.

"Well, I can always get Cousin Bruno to break his arms and legs." The dealer smiled. It was an old Vegas joke. It used to be a warning to cheating dealers.

Then, suddenly, something electric coursed through the table. The blonde had rolled four elevens in a row. People began to gather around the table. High-rollers cruising watching for a hot table; voyeurs looking for excitement. Chip hustlers, girls who hung around winners with promises of future fun, gathered.

There was talk and encouragement. "You can do it, Miami," a tubby produce merchant from Passaic encouraged the blonde, talking through his cigar. "Give us plenty of numbers."

Towers of chips went up along the back line, where odds were paid every time the shooter made five, six, eight, nine, or ten on the dice. The point was four. The shyer players said their prayers silently or fantasized winning, or rubbed good-luck pieces.

"Ten the hard way," the stickman called, and the lucky ones who bet that the ten would be made with two fives rather than six and four collected their odds. The high-rollers knew it was a bet that favored the house, but many bet it anyway. It felt good to see the tap of the stick in front of you. "Pay the gentleman in the corner *three hundred dollars.*" Then, more gently, for it was the stickman who promoted both play and tips, "Your original bet still stands, sir." It would be a hard player who wouldn't toss in a brown (five-dollar) chip: "Ten hard way for the boys."

Now there was a magic at the table, a focus of force and power. And it was felt by Ben Payne, executive vice president of Volta Records, who was walking toward the front entrance where a limousine waited which would take him to the airport to catch United's seven-fifteen flight to Los Angeles.

Ben Payne felt great. In his Gucci briefcase was $186,750 in cash which, deposited in the firm's account by Monday morning, would save him from several charges of embezzlement. His accountant could plaster over the theft, but only before the new people from the conglomerate which had acquired Volta came in. Even that wouldn't be easy, but at least it would save him from going to jail.

Payne looked good, his black face framed against the white raw silk blazer, the blue raw silk slacks, the New Hero shirt. With him was Selma, the sweet little disco dancer who was carrying his baby, who was his good luck. He had confided in her about everything: the cocaine habit, the money, his degenerate gambling. She understood, gave him the optimism of her youth, looked like good luck to him with her wide, large brown eyes, her light hair falling around her shoulders, her body giving, trembling in love.

Ben Payne heard the shrieks, the soul-shouts that rose from the table. He had a moment's tremor in the pit of his stomach, in the solar plexus. It was that feeling—that luck—which hadn't failed him in the three days before. He stopped, hesitated really. The boxman saw him. He knew that Payne was a good customer, had won and lost, was on a streak. "Make room for the players please," the stickman shouted, nodding at Payne. He gently pressed out a space for Payne.

Payne had five hundred in his pocket. He wouldn't go to the money in the Gucci. Selma touched his sleeve. He didn't know whether it was a warning or a gesture of good luck. It didn't seem to matter as the adrenaline went through his body, making him feel pungently alive. The stickman held the red dice in front of him, giving the new player plenty of time to make his wagers. Payne spread five one-hundred-dollar bills on the table. "Change only," the dealer called to alert the floorman. The boxman counted the bills carefully, folded them into the slot in front of him, into the drop, the most important cash point in the casino. The dealer pushed twenty green chips to Payne, who let ten of them sit on the pass line and picked up the other ten.

Impatiently, the blonde called for the dice. The other players, alert to the devices which the house used to cut down a winning streak—slowing the tempo, or forcing it to a faster pace or delaying the roll—were beginning to be impatient. Only the pipesmoker, who was betting "don't pass" against the blonde, didn't seem to mind.

Finally the dice were pushed to the blonde. She grabbed them, held them to her mouth. "E-LEV-EN!" she shouted and sent the cubes rolling. They struck the far end and a scream went up which touched Payne like a snort. "Eleven the winner! Pay the come, pay the field."

Payne knew it was the streak, the moment. He became oblivious to Selma, to the huge concourse of the casino, its colors and lights; he focused into the trough of the dice table. Payne pressed the line bet; that is, he let the two-fifty he won ride with the two-fifty he originally bet. Then, on an irrational belly hunch, he bet the remaining two hundred and fifty dollars on eleven. A fool's bet, he reminded himself. But six and five were like neon lights in his mind. He looked at the blonde shooter with a kind of love. She seemed beautiful. She, in turn, looked at Payne—his open, handsome black face. Eleven, he mouthed to her. She understood. She sent the dice down the table, they spun and rolled and then—six dots and five. The roar broke like a wave on all the tables, blackjack, baccarat, roulette, even over the banks of slot machines like engines keeping the vessel afloat. Payne had won. He looked triumphantly at the boxman. The boxman showed no emotion.

The Boeing 727 banked sharply as the pilot tried to avoid a turbulent desert thermal. Lise Christian gulped as the darkening horizon dipped crazily in the tiny porthole. She had never liked flying. It was better in Europe where she could take trains or drive. Yet, she thought, it was excitement. Part of the quest which had brought her almost six thousand miles. The plane leveled off over the shadowy mountains, still teetering on an ocean of superheated air, and began its descent toward McCarran International Airport in Las Vegas.

Lise tightened her grip around the plastic champagne glass, long since empty but held like a fetish in her hand. She wondered again if she'd made a terrible mistake in leaving her mother's tranquil apartment on Quai Saint Michel, overlooking the Seine. A pang of homesickness touched her in the chest. Yes, she loved the slope-windowed apartment which the painter Archumov had once owned and which he had enlarged by breaking through to the maid's rooms above.

In that two-story studio which had become their living room, her mother lived like a bird in a cage of comfort and isolation. Below were the quai and the river, the book stands, the wandering walkers. Across was the Palais de Justice and the spire of La Chapelle; to the right, if one stood close to the window, there was Notre Dame. On a mezzanine, reached by a spiral ladder, was her mother's Empire bed. That had been Lacy Christian's world. And to a great extent Lise's as well. Why then had she embarked on this journey to Las Vegas?

The answer was obvious. With her mother's death, last spring, Lise had suffered a period of voids, an aimless and solitary time, though there were plenty of men who flocked after her. She was, of course, an heiress. On her twenty-first birthday, three weeks before her mother had died of a stroke —no, she thought, I won't play that game. Lacy had died of an overdose of barbiturates, a mixture with alcohol. No one really knew whether she had intended to die. There were no notes. Lise had always known how sad her mother's life had been; her death was even sadder. At the core was a secret.

And that, in the end, was what brought Lise to this unlikely place.

She had pressed her mother many times to find out about her family, about Lacy's youth. She knew her mother came from New Orleans, of a social and wealthy family, was told that her father was an investor who had been killed in a plane crash in Nevada, while Lise was still an infant. When Helen Whitely, Lacy's best friend, flew to Paris to help with the funeral arrangements, Lise tried to get some clues, something to add to the very little her mother had told her and what she had found out. Helen talked a great deal about Lacy and their life as girls in New Orleans. Yet, when Lise asked for details about her father, Helen was obviously uncomfortable. The answers were general: he had been a handsome man, a good man, very important in his business. Then Helen became vague and urged Lise to join her for dinner at La Perouse.

As Lise thought about it, the idea that Lacy had spent all this time in mourning for her dead husband, an idea which she had long held, was wrong. Lacy had the world come to her. Her Thursday nights were famous for both expatriates and Parisians. She gave intimate luncheons and small musicales. Lacy, Lise began to realize, was not so much an isolate as a frightened woman, hiding from something. Or, perhaps, protecting Lise. Although an American by birth and citizenship, Lise had been laundered and starched in a series of European schools—a convent school near Chichester in England, a finishing school outside Montreux in Switzerland, and finally a course in museum curatorship at the Louvre in Paris.

Although she'd never seen the place called Las Vegas, the words had meaning for her. As long as she could remember, an envelope postmarked Las Vegas would arrive at their Paris apartment early each month. On her twenty-first birthday, their lawyer explained that a second check would now begin coming as interest from another trust set up by her father for her began to be paid. She was a wealthy woman now, the lawyer told her, and would never have to work or worry about money. But he said, in his avuncular French way, that it might be very good for her if she did.

Going through her mother's things, she had found a Paris *Herald Tribune* dated September 15, 1956. She wondered why her mother had saved that particular issue. No item was circled or marked. Lise had studied the paper from front page to last. Only a tiny item was datelined Las Vegas. It told of the disappearance of a man named Augusto Bertinelli.

Now the plane shuddered as the landing gear dropped, and Lise glanced out the porthole for her first glimpse of Las Vegas. But she still could not see the long-awaited destination. The horizon was hidden behind a smoky pall from the brushfires that had been burning around Southern California for the past two weeks; the setting sun threw a lengthening purple shadow over the empty desert stretches below. All Lise could see was a dry, desolate, undulating landscape—a vision of hell, she thought.

And yet, now and then, she imagined that she could spot a tiny light shining in one of the gullies or box canyons. A remote ranch, perhaps, or a grubstake miner at work on an abandoned claim. A tiny circle of warming light in a blasted desert that burned under the daylight sun and then froze under an empty sky at night. A tiny voice crying out—

"Gambler's graveyard," a husky voice whispered in her ear.

Lise spun around. The balding man in the double-knit leisure suit—who'd been snoring in the next seat ever since takeoff—now leaned over. Lise caught the odor of stale cigarettes and raw whiskey on his breath. He seemed friendly enough.

"Gambler's graveyard—that's where they used to put you away if you dropped a bundle at the tables and then didn't pay up," the stranger said. "Must be a thousand bodies, laid out in the sand between the Vegas city limits and the California border."

Lise trembled involuntarily—whether from the man's words or his aura she could not tell.

The plane shuddered again, slipping down at a sharp angle and rocking from side to side. Lise fell back in her seat and clutched the armrests.

"Nice ride, isn't it?" the man said. "Sometimes I think the casinos pay the pilots to shake up the passengers on the way in. If you're scared of crashing, you'll be so grateful to put your two feet on solid ground that losing all your money won't seem so bad. And, in the back of your head, you know that you might not be so lucky on the flight back. So what's the difference if you have a good time and go bust while you're still alive and kicking?"

Lise glued her eyes to the porthole, straining to spot the airport amid the sudden explosion of neon and flashing lights below. She followed the well defined glow of the Strip as it dog-legged through the sprawling city and ended in the burst of color in Glitter Gulch, the incredibly neoned downtown Las Vegas. For a moment, she imagined that the pilot would land the airplane on the wide boulevard and taxi right up to the Mecca Hotel. But then she saw the single runway of McCarran International Airport, a string of muted green lights that mimicked the Strip and an angular glass-and-concrete terminal that echoed the eccentric architecture of the casinos.

"See the crash crew?" the man in the next seat said. On the ground, an ambulance and an emergency truck idled at the side of the main runway. "It's just part of the show."

The wheels screeched against tarmac, the plane bounced once and then settled to the runway, the braking ducts screamed powerfully as the pilot slowed the full craft. And Lise felt the sudden relief, the rush of energy, the magic euphoria, just as the stranger had predicted. She turned to him, almost grateful, and smiled.

"Now the real danger begins. All those hungry men. All those hungry gaming tables. Maybe you'd like me to show you around and keep you out of trouble."

Lise stood up and smoothed her blouse and skirt. "No,

thank you," she said sweetly but sternly. "As I told you before, I'm here on business."

Business, the man thought as Lise eased past his knees and moved down the crowded aisle. Not the kind of business that brings most young women to Vegas. He struggled out of the seat and caught up with Lise on the automated ramp that moved passengers from the terminal to the baggage claim area. Overhead, the public address system carried a series of recorded warnings in familiar voices: "*Volare!*" sang the voice. "This is Jerry Vale, reminding you to keep to the *right—and let others pass on the left.*"

Lise turned to see who was tapping so insistently on her shoulder, and sighed in frustration at the sight of the man in the baggy leisure suit. "I'm really sorry," she said, "but I am not interested—"

"No heat," the man protested. He dipped into his pants pocket and produced a brown five-dollar chip from the Mecca Hotel. "Listen, here's my one-and-only good-luck chip. A chip that makes me a winner at the tables every time. I want you to have it."

"Thank you, anyway," Lise said, shaking her head. "But I can't take it."

"No, no, that's what I want, sweetie." He smiled broadly in what he imagined to be a roguish grin. "You keep it, and maybe it'll bring you some good luck, too. And, of course, if you change your mind later, you can cash it in at the hotel where I'm staying—it's right there on the chip. Just ask for Ray Sarnow. They'll know me."

Lise looked down and studied the chip. She'd expected to see something that imitated a valuable coin, but the casino chip was garish and ugly and slightly comical. "It looks like play money," she said.

"That's the whole point," Sarnow said.

There was little hope here, Sarnow thought. Too bad, for this youngster had class. He shouldn't have slept. Speaking with her on the flight, paying attention to her might have worked. Then he spotted a fortyish woman, trim and tan, struggling with an oversized purse. Nice, he said to himself. Hips, taut and solid, yet inviting. Worth a try. He felt in his pocket for another "lucky" chip. Ray Sarnow smiled at Lise, hastened to catch up with the overburdened woman, took her suitcase, speaking to her as he did. By the time they reached the taxi rank outside, they learned all they needed to know about each other. He didn't even need his lucky chip.

Charley Mellow, the entertainment director of the Sultan's Palace, the Mecca Hotel's main showroom, stood at the door of the dressing room and surveyed the hundred or so young women taking off jeans and tee shirts, changing into their harem costumes for the opening number, the mass strip tease that was still the talk of the tourists in Vegas. The girls stood or sat in an incense of perfume, deodorant, skin creams, makeup. Seeing them this way used to be one of his fantasies. But now his ideals, the tall, full-bosomed nudes, the elegant giraffes of the old days, were used only in background. The girls were more flat-chested. You could tell them from the boy dancers, but only *barely*. They were skinny and small. He remembered the six-foot beauties, the forty busts, the crazy gypsy giving ways of the old show days. Now with these hippies you needed two to make a forty. Scrawny. Still, they were all right. Real people, most of them. In an hour, they'd line up backstage, with the boy dancers, the jugglers and acrobats, elephants and tigers—all part of the Mecca's extravaganza to wow the rubes. Things hadn't changed all that much from vaudeville and the carny days. The routines were smoother; the effects more expensive; the music better. So many good musicians were rooted in Vegas. Not just the few so deep in hock because of their gambling habits, but the rest who just wanted to work at their trade.

So, Mellow thought, it all goes on beyond me and my retirement. He would be out of here one way or another at the end of the weekend. They wanted him to go back to Atlantic City as entertainment consultant for the Mecca

East, a complex Everett was planning. And maybe he would want to do that one day, although he didn't see the need for anything more than lounge shows in Atlantic City. It wasn't the same sort of crowd. People would flock there, didn't have to travel thousands of miles. There would be no crime-free belt provided by the desert, no real escape, no illusion of Sodom and Gomorrah that made the whole Vegas fantasy work.

Well, he'd kept himself whole, and it hadn't been easy. He nodded at Kristina, one of the real showgirls still in the show, to satisfy the older men, even the older women, the generation brought up on Ziegfeld, *his* generation. He wished Kristina were coming with him, away from Vegas, away from the grind. But she was independent. They didn't even live together anymore. Charley walked toward her, marveled at how the dancers were transforming themselves, covering their black and blue marks, the vein here or there, the bad patch of skin, the imperfections, so that when they came on stage they would be as perfect and unreal as Barbie dolls. That was the Man's plan. Charley, who came from burlesque, thought it was the flaws in the bodies which aroused and excited customers, made them see just enough real life beyond the illusion to become involved. But involvement wasn't the name of the game. The name was out there in the casino, in the size of the drop, the amount of the take, the hours the gamblers spent at the table. Everything else was confetti.

He stood in the alcove, close enough to see Kristina, almost to touch her. That body, shared with thousands every night, was dear to him. He couldn't even bring himself to tell her that. Then Rocky came toward Kristina, *touching* his way through the crowd of girls. If only he would have looked like a movie gangster, Charley could have felt some recognizable hate or contempt. But Rocky looked like a high school basketball coach. He came close to Kris, cupped her buttock in his hand. "Kris," he said, "I've got a high-roller from Wichita who wants to get straightened out after the late show tonight."

"Rocky, please," Kristina said. "I'd rather not. It's that time of month."

"That won't bother this dude," Rock said.

Charley's stomach sank. His heart pounded.

"I won't do it. *We* had a date tonight," Kristina said.

Rocky laughed. "You do it, sweetie. Maybe I'll see you afterward." He paused. "You do it," he repeated.

Kristina turned her back on Rocky, who grasped her wrist. Charley could feel the pain and wanted to start toward the pair.

Rocky handed her a key. "Two three-thirty. Here's his room key. Turn him around fast. There's two C notes in it for you. For us, baby."

Kristina turned back toward Rocky. Charley saw her face, knew that she wanted that degradation, that it was what made her function as a woman, knew that he enjoyed it, that it was the whole thing for him, watching. His eyes went dim at the truth. Then, he realized that Kris knew he was there, from her smile, from the glance she gave him. It was a show, he thought, better than most he had ever produced. He had seen through her and Rocky and himself.

Charley heard the call boy passing with the five-minute call. He headed out front for a drink.

The cabin of the Lear Jet was darkened except for a pool of yellow light that illuminated the single passenger in the last row. He worked intently over a legal pad, making quick notations with a gold pencil and occasionally entering a figure on a miniature calculator. These were the tools of his trade, and he used them with an experienced hand.

The other tools were carried in a hand-wrought leather briefcase on the seat next to him. A diplomatic passport issued by a tiny Red Sea sheikdom with a few thousand Bedouins, a few thousand square miles of desert sand, and an incalculable reserve of oil. A letter of credit from a Swiss bank for an amount of money that exceeded the annual incomes of all the Bedouins in the sheikdom. And a chrome-plated Walther PPK pistol with a custom-fitted shoulder holster that did not spoil the cut of his Bond Street suit.

The telephone in the armrest hummed softly.

"We've been cleared for immediate landing at McCarran," the pilot said in a deferential tone. "A limousine from the Mecca Hotel is waiting."

"Very good," he answered in a soft voice with an Oxford accent.

And then he cursed in irritation, a guttural Bedouin curse that called on Allah to inflict a foul disease on the genitals of the infidels who dared to call their house of sin by the name of Islam's holiest city—the *Mecca*.

But the curse would be harmless, he knew. He had long ago forfeited the grace of Allah by indulging himself in every sin and excess that the degenerate infidels offered to a young man from a feudal Islamic sheikdom. He had been sent to Oxford to learn the ways of the infidel; Allah had placed a new weapon—the oil weapon—in the hands of the faithful, and they needed Arab youth to wield the weapon over the infidels.

And he learned well, first at Oxford and then in the quiet clubs and paneled boardrooms where the commerce and politics of the infidel nations were conducted. He soon found himself to be as glib and facile, as poised and well tailored, as diplomatic and worldly, as his tutors. At first, it seemed so harmless to share a snifter of brandy after a meal, to wager a few pounds in the elegant casinos of London, to accept the gracious attentions of young women with blue eyes and blonde hair.

So harmless. So easy. But soon it became too easy. And finally it became impossible to do without the pleasures. When he returned to his native land, he felt like a stranger; when he was forced to leave behind the wagers, the women, the wine, he felt a consuming hunger for them. The crown prince, a distant cousin, recognized his dangerous addictions and decided that the young man would not take his place among the pious of his native land.

Still, a corrupted but graceful Arab gentleman was useful in his own unique way. He would be sent abroad to perform the unsavory tasks that a more faithful man might abhor. Buying and selling armaments. Speculating in the currencies of infidel nations. Securing the secret ownership of land and industry and commerce. Exterminating the misguided souls who fled their own lands to intrigue against the rightful rulers. Wielding the oil weapon, a weapon of money and power, he lived in permanent exile and moved with ease through the world of the hated infidel.

He might share an elegant meal with an African ambassador to the United Nations—and the evening would end with the delivery of a bribe to sway a crucial vote. He might escort a titled lady to the opera—and then use the information gained in an intimate conversation to buy out the stock of her husband's enterprises. He might sip a brew of strong coffee with an expatriate Arab student, talking of revolution and socialism in the sheikdom—and then put an end to the talk with a silenced gunshot.

And if he felt any remorse, if he felt soiled and abused, he knew how to wash away the guilt. Strong liquor would help. An evening with an infidel woman would help. But the wager was the best of all. When he pressed his luck, when he wagered his substance along with his soul, the slightest gamble was like a powerful drug. And it was only a loss—the losing roll of the dice, the losing run of the cards —that purged him of the curse of guilt. If he left his money on the gaming table, he left his regret, too. If he emptied his pockets, he emptied his soul, too.

The guilt would be purged for a few hours, at least until the next act of crime or corruption, but the hatred always remained. Hatred for the temptations of the infidel's world. Hatred for his own weakness and self-indulgence. Hatred for the women who gave him their bodies, the men who gave him their fortunes, the world that had turned him from a pious man of faith into a whore, a sinner, a murderer.

The light over his head blinked once—a signal from the pilot that the craft was on its final approach—and he prepared for his next task. He closed the legal pad and returned it to the briefcase. Then, with practiced movements, he strapped on the shoulder holster, checked the full clip of his Walther, and snapped the loaded gun in place.

Ahmed Ibn Sayd was ready for the mission that would take him to—he muttered another curse—the Mecca Hotel. He'd meet the man who'd brought him halfway around the world to swindle Edward Everett out of his sprawling empire.

The three old men moved from table to table, each one carrying a clipboard and a mechanical pencil, each one counting the stacks of chips with a measuring glance that had been calibrated by years of experience, each one nodding gravely at his fellows when the counts matched up. To the Mecca's vice president of finance and operations, they were the walking accountants who tallied each table's bankroll of chips at the beginning and end of each shift. To the dealers and boxmen, they were the Three Blind Mice.

"Eighty-four five on table two," said Moe, the oldest and most sedate of the three. His colleagues checked their own counts and then confirmed Moe's sum with a flurry of grunts and nods. And then the Three Blind Mice, walking in a solemn single file, headed toward the blackjack pit.

Eighty-four grand on a single craps table, and twenty-four tables working around the clock in the vast casino of the Mecca Hotel. Plus another forty blackjack tables, eight roulette wheels, two baccarat pits, ten draw-poker tables, a 500-seat Keno lounge. And 2,400 slot machines swallowing quarters, halves, and Eisenhower dollars. The Mecca was the first hotel to eliminate nickel and dime slots. Now it was trying some that took only five-dollar tokens.

Moe shook his head. Back in New York, back in the

forties, when he was still running a neighborhood numbers racket in Harlem, a bankroll of a couple thousand bucks would cover a street operation for a week. Nickel bets, dime bets, and the big payoffs were in quarters. Now a big Vegas player could run up a half-million worth of action in a half hour, and the cashiers in the cage would hardly notice.

At the age of sixty-four, Moe found himself reminiscing about the old days in Harlem. He'd wear the flashiest suits, a heavy gold watch chain, a big diamond on his pinky—all to impress the players. He'd slip a few bucks to the comics working the Apollo, and they'd work a few jokes into the act:

"Hey, man, I just hit a number."

"Won't do you no good—them numbers folk don't pay off."

"Wrong-oo! I bet with Moe Black, and Moe Black pays off."

Moe Black. His name was Schwartz, Morris Schwartz, but he figured it wouldn't hurt to flatter the players around Harlem by translating his name. And he did good business, so good that the boys on the white side of town asked Moe to work the numbers in the defense plants over in Connecticut and New Jersey. The action was safer, quieter, and he was cutting out enough to buy Ruth and the kids a nice place in Jersey.

Moe had only one regret. He was still in the rackets, and he never felt comfortable in the synagogue where the kids went to Sunday school. A numbers man just didn't belong in *shul*.

The real money began to roll in after the war, when the boys brought him out to Vegas to work the new casinos. The place was just heating up, and they needed some reliable old friends to run the tables in their glittery new hotels. Old friends who knew their way around the action. Old friends who could spot the high-rollers from back home and keep them happy at the tables and in the sack, too. Moe was one of the best—he could spot a Jersey player in a flash, and remember his favorite action, his favorite booze, and his favorite kind of dame all at once.

And the boys rewarded him: dealer, floorman, pit boss, greeter. But what Moe really wanted, what he always longed for, was a suit-and-tie job. A job in the business end. A job that he could talk about out loud after the Sabbath services at the Vegas synagogue. When the Mecca opened its doors, Moe got what he wanted; he became one of the Three Blind Mice. Sober as a Mormon, dressed up like a Rotarian on Thanksgiving, armed with a clipboard and a pencil.

Keeping the books, Moe liked to say. Just keeping the books.

And the rabbi at Moe's temple—where he was president of the men's club and a big donor to the building fund—always paused after the sermon to shake his hand.

A handshake from the rabbi! Moe shook his head. A handshake every Saturday!

The highway seemed to ripple and shimmer in the pinkish dusk, but John Morrissey knew that it was just a freakish illusion from too many hours behind the wheel. Interstate 15 ran straight and true across the empty Mojave desert, and Morrissey vowed to keep his old Alfa Romeo aimed in the direction of the Las Vegas oasis, even though the indicator lights on the dashboard told him that the oil pressure was dropping and the engine was heating up.

Morrissey gunned it up to eighty, daring the protesting automobile to explode and strand him in the desert darkness. That would be just my luck, he said to himself. At last, when he'd packed up and left behind the suburban junior college where he'd taught introductory statistics for the last seven years, when he'd finally rid himself of the lingering pain of his divorce, when he'd finally embarked on the cross-country odyssey that he'd been promising himself ever since he'd turned thirty—that's when his cranky Alfa threatened to drop dead on him. *Just my luck!*

If I can only make the last fifty miles to Las Vegas,

he thought, I'll put in a couple of quarts of oil and a rebuilt water pump. That ought to hold the clunker as far as Arizona or maybe even New Mexico. He'd always wanted to see the wilds of the Sangre de Cristo Mountains, the adobe pueblo of Taos, the hot-air balloon races outside Santa Fe.

"If my luck holds as far as Vegas," he said out loud to himself, "I'll be okay."

The endless ribbon of superhighway was hypnotic, but Morrissey fought to stay alert by swigging black coffee from his thermos and turning up the volume on the scratchy car radio. The cowboy tenor was crooning an old but durable tune about the death of a lovesick gunfighter in the arms of his sweetheart; Morrissey wondered for a moment if the old wound might begin to hurt again, but he was comforted to find that he felt nothing. No sentiment, no longings, no loss —only a cold numbness that had become his refuge.

His marriage to Joyce had been a mistake from the beginning, but it had taken him too many years to find out. They'd met in college, married too quickly after a too-passionate love affair conducted in odd corners of the men's dormitory and Joyce's sorority house, and settled down in the Los Angeles suburb where Morrissey found a job teaching the mysteries of statistics to junior college students who were only slightly more bored by the subject than he was. He and Joyce were both unhappy with the tedium of life around the bland stucco suburb of West San Carlos and the bland stucco campus of West San Carlos Community College—but for very different reasons.

Morrissey discovered in himself a persistent, almost painful hunger—a craving for some unimaginable risk that would tear him away from the cloying security and sameness of West San Carlos. At first, he was haunted by a restlessness that kept him awake all night and nearly put him to sleep during his classes. And then, as he approached his thirtieth birthday, the restlessness began to turn into recklessness.

He would leave his tract home in the morning—and

drive past the gates of the junior college, heading almost instinctively toward the mountains on the eastern horizon, wondering how far he would drive before the feelings of guilt and obligation drew him back, daring himself to defy his guilty conscience and go through the mountains, beyond the stretches of desert, as far as his uneasy imagination would carry him.

Joyce suffered from an entirely different hunger. "Why don't you sit down and finish your doctoral thesis?" she would urge over and over. "Then you can get a decent teaching appointment at a decent university. Or just forget the thesis and study for the CPA exams. You know, Carla's husband is a CPA and he makes almost thirty thousand dollars a year—and that's more than you'll earn after twenty years as a junior college instructor."

Morrissey treated himself to a used Alfa Romeo on his thirtieth birthday; Joyce threw a party to which she pointedly invited Carla's husband, Max, who delivered an inspirational speech on the joys and profits of a career in accounting. Morrissey listened in polite silence, and disappeared from the party at the first opportunity. He took his faded blue sports car out to the Ridge Route, an old two-lane blacktop that hairpinned its way through the mountains, and pressed his luck against the dangers of a slick road and a fast car.

Intoxicated by three or four champagne toasts—and pushed even higher by the feel of a finely tuned engine under the hood—Morrissey whipped around the curves and thundered down the steep grades, double-clutching expertly and working the gearshift with a sure hand. The old hunger, the longing for a risk and a reckless gamble, encouraged him to ride the accelerator. And only a flash of sobriety—a flash of fear, he later realized—told him to brake the car when the speedometer needle flickered at 120 miles per hour and a carful of cruising teenagers materialized a hundred feet ahead.

The Alfa spun into a shrieking skid, fishtailing wildly and careening past the bright purple Chevy Impala. The headlights swept the shoulder of the road—Morrissey could see down into the brush-covered canyons despite the darkness—and the Alfa's tires rumbled ominously over the edge of the blacktop. For an instant, Morrissey was certain that his restless days—and his young life—were at an end. A moment later, the Alfa was hard against a road barrier, and Morrissey was certain that his days of boredom at West San Carlos Community College were over.

If the boredom is driving me to this, he thought as he listened to the ticking of an overheated engine and the racing of an overstressed heart, it'll kill me in the end.

Morrissey crept back to West San Carlos in the Alfa, never allowing the speedometer to go over thirty-five miles per hour and never pushing the gearshift higher than third. He drove in a stunned slow motion, as if to erase the terror he'd felt a few moments before, and wondered how he would explain his decision to Joyce.

He'd resign his position at West San Carlos College. He'd put up the house for rent. And the two of them would take to the road. A few things in a shoulder bag, a few bucks in their pockets, and a cross-country ramble ahead. Just like in the songs—

The house was dark and seemingly empty when Morrissey pulled up. He glanced at his watch and saw that it was nearly two in the morning; the party must have broken up, and Joyce was already in bed. He opened the front door silently, tiptoed through the darkened living room, and pushed open the bedrom door.

And then he saw them.

Max was still wearing his three-piece pin-striped suit, but the vest was loosened and the zipper was down. Joyce, still in her party dress, hovered over the open zipper. Her head bobbed up and down in rhythm with Max's grunts and groans. Morrissey, silent and breathless and frozen in place, watched for a long moment as his wife indulged in an act of love that she had always refused to perform for her husband.

And to his horror, to his shame and sorrow, John Morrissey felt nothing. No anger, no jealousy, no pain. The numbness that had infected his soul was now spreading to his heart. All he felt was a cold, hard, barren ache. He turned away, still silent and unobserved, and slipped out the front door. The Alfa carried him away on an aimless night of driving.

The divorce came a year later, but only after a polite attempt to reconcile their sharp differences and rekindle the old romance that had blinded them to the differences. Morrissey knew that playing house with Joyce would teach her nothing about the new hungers that haunted him; Joyce soon realized that he was nodding but not listening when she repeated her urgings about the doctoral thesis or the CPA exams. In the end, all that was left for Joyce was a tract house and a bank account; all that was left for John Morrissey was a 1960 Alfa Romeo and a few hundred dollars in cash.

And now, as he approached the range of low mountains that encircle the town of Las Vegas, Morrissey saw the distant glow on the horizon. A half hour later, the mountains were behind him and the explosion of neon materialized like a desert mirage. He spotted the towering hotel signs, one after another along the Strip, and sensed a kind of shimmering energy that added to the ten-thousand-megawatt aura.

A new light caught his eye—the bright red glow of the oil pressure light on the dashboard of the Alfa. He nursed the car along, rolling through the suburbs of scattered cinder-block houses and trailer parks and mobile homes mounted on concrete chocks, and then crawled into the bumper-to-bumper traffic jam that clogged the Strip from the Mecca Hotel all the way to the downtown casinos. He was just turning the Alfa into the driveway of a service station—the first one he'd spotted among the hotels and casinos—when the engine shuddered, backfired twice, and then died.

"It must be the oil pump," he told the attendant, who wrinkled his nose at the stench of scorched oil and baked rubber. "Can you install a rebuilt pump? And maybe a water pump, too?"

The attendant eyed the Alfa skeptically. "Ain't gonna be easy to scare up a pump for an old Italian hot rod like yours," he drawled. "Won't know 'til tomorrow, maybe Monday."

Morrissey frowned and reached for his wallet in the glove compartment. He'd emptied his checking account for the cross-country odyssey—a total of six hundred dollars to pay for an open-ended journey—but he hadn't planned on stopping over in Las Vegas. In fact, he hadn't planned on paying for anything except gas, hot coffee, and a few hamburgers until he reached New Mexico. He'd figured that he could stay at the wheel fourteen, maybe sixteen hours a day, and catch a few hours of sleep at the side of the road with the bucket seat lowered. And now he was facing a weekend in Vegas, where every neon sign screamed out dollar signs.

"Listen," he said to the attendant, "I'm running a little low on traveling money, and I need a place to stay—"

"Hey, buddy, just go back to the casino where you went bust," the attendant interrupted. "If you dropped any kind of real cash at the tables, the pit boss will give you some walking money. Then you can lay over in style and maybe even win some of your money back."

"No, no, I don't gamble," Morrissey said quickly, smiling at the attendant's misunderstanding. "I'm just passing through town."

The clicking of dice, the clatter of the roulette wheel, the clinking of the slot machines—the rhythms of gambling were all around him, and Morrissey could imagine their sounds. Still he was immune to their seductions. After all, he thought, I've taught statistics for too many years to be fooled by a game of chance; I know too well that the odds

—the immutable, irresistable, inevitable odds—are against me. In fact, he had used the dice as a classroom example of statistical prediction.

"No, I don't gamble," Morrissey repeated. "I just need the cheapest bed in town."

"Sure, sure," said the attendant, who had seen enough degenerate gamblers to know when a down-and-out player was trying to preserve the last shred of dignity. "You're going to find 40,000 beds in Vegas. Just start here and keep walking."

Morrissey looked up. The first hotel on the Strip loomed, a giant mosque stabbing into the sky and ending with a stylized star-and-crescent etched against the blackness in glowing red neon. And the arabesque neon lettering spelled out a name: THE MECCA.

"That's the best you'll find in Vegas," the attendant murmured. "But you can always grab an empty bench down at the Greyhound depot if you're really busted."

Soaring twenty-six stories above Las Vegas, and sprawling over 60 acres of prime real estate on the Strip, the Mecca was the grandest, most opulent hotel in a town that measures those qualities in megawatts and millions of dollars. With two huge showrooms, a half-dozen lounges, eight restaurants and coffeeshops, an indoor jai alai *fronton*, two movie theaters, two 90,000-gallon swimming pools, 22 tennis courts, and a subterranean shopping arcade with 80 shops, the Mecca was—all at once—the largest gaming establishment, the largest resort, and one of the largest enclosed retail-and-restaurant complexes in the world.

The competition for superlatives, which had begun in the late forties when the modest clubs and motels started dressing themselves up, came to at least a temporary halt when the Mecca opened for business a year earlier. Of course, the surveyor's flags were already flying over a still larger plot of empty desert where the next hotel—the one that would challenge the Mecca's primacy in Vegas—would begin construction in a year. But even if the big money came in behind the new hotel project, the Mecca would remain unique and unchallenged. And the reason for its uniqueness was invisible to all the thousands who worked and performed and gambled there.

Two hundred feet beneath the floor of the Mecca's subterranean shopping arcade—and an eternity away from the hotel's world of lights and laughter—was its secret soul: A massive concrete-and-steel bunker that was linked to the hotel above only by an umbilical cord of electrical conduits and a pair of high-speed elevators that were equipped with a manual override in case of external power failure.

But there would never be a power failure within the bunker itself. The world contained within the maze of chambers and corridors was like the tomb of a dead pharaoh, equipped with all the necessities for a long journey into the afterlife and hidden from intruders by the distracting monument above. The walls of the bunker were eight feet thick; the ceiling was twelve feet of steel cable and concrete, and the whole structure rested on immense coiled-steel springs that would absorb the shock of an earthquake or a nuclear blast.

Buried in the sands of the Nevada desert, along with the bunker itself, were its own life-support systems. Three high-efficiency generators and three self-sealing fuel reservoirs to power them. Six stainless steel cisterns, each one lined with 24-karat gold, filled with mountain spring water, and linked to a charcoal-filter purification system. Eight sealed storage chambers with a supply of freeze-dried foodstuffs that would sustain the occupants of the bunker for a decade. Twin ventilators that drew air from the surface at a dozen different intake vents as far as six miles from the bunker itself, and a double-filtration mechanism that renderd the air antiseptically pure. This was most important to the old man.

If the Mecca was a monument to the games of chance, the bunker beneath it was a monument to the eradication of chance. A world where risk—of infection and contamination, of drought and famine, of temblor and bomb blast, of betrayal and assassination—had been reduced to an absolute minimum. And the man who had conceived and designed and built the bunker, the man who had buried himself alive within its walls, took far more pride and satisfaction from the burial chamber than from the pyramid above.

Edward Roger Everett had taken many risks in his life. And the Mecca had been the payoff. But he was old now, and the specter of risk had become a demon in his private nightmare.

Taking chances had come naturally to the sixteen-year-old Everett, who quit high school after his father's death and went to work as a fitter in the infant civil aeronautics industry. He soon discovered an aptitude for finding quick, easy, decisive solutions for problems that baffled others; he'd been bolting propellers to biplanes at the Holt Aircraft Company for only four months when he devised a new propeller design that dramatically improved the speed and performance of the plane. Old man Holt rewarded him with the offer of a thousand dollars outright—or 2 percent of the business.

Everett took his first chance by taking the stock instead of the cash. Ten years later, in 1938, the old Holt biplane works had become Everett Enterprises, the largest supplier of aircraft and armaments to the burgeoning defense effort. Business was no longer an adequate challenge.

So he sought another kind of adventure in women. At the heart of it, Everett's relationships were not much different than the fifteen minutes that one of his assembly-line workers might spend with a hooker on Saturday night. But Everett's hungers were more demanding. He longed for more than the brief climax of pleasure. He wanted women who would hang about him like dazzling jewels. Women whose presence at his side would tell others of his power and wealth and influence. Women who excited desires in other men.

Everett felt no greater satisfaction than the look of hunger in other men's eyes. The leading ladies from the studios provided that pleasure, and so did the young starlets who were sent around to him by the front office. He would ride in silence to the dinners, the opening nights, the cocktail parties, and he would stand in silence while his companion of the evening did all the conversational work. And he would scan the room with half-closed eyes, looking for the flash of scheming envy on the faces of the men around him.

Such was the scene in the ballroom of a hotel in New Orleans during the last days of World War II when Edward Roger Everett met a man named Augusto Bertinelli.

The young lady on Everett's arm that night was a petite, dark-eyed, black-haired debutante who had appeared at his hotel room an hour before the grand ball. Everett's Louisiana attorney, the one who negotiated the oil leases for all the Gulf drilling sites, had assured him that the young lady came from one of New Orleans' oldest families—a true aristocrat. the lawyer told him, and a rare beauty. And only eighteen years old, the lawyer whispered breathlessly.

Augusto Bertinello stared at the young lady across the ballroom. And then he moved slowly toward Everett, smiling and nodding at those he passed along the way, until he stood at Everett's side. Everett's lawyer fumbled through an introduction, but it was unnecessary. No one who read the newspapers could fail to recognize the famous aviator and industrialist and film producer, Edward R. Everett. And Everett was far too well informed about the details of his businesses to need an introduction to Bertinelli.

Augusto Bertinelli behaved with the courtly manners of an aristocratic Italian patriarch, but Everett's inquiries had revealed that he was an old streetfighter who'd risen through the ranks of the New Orleans underworld to a position of unchallenged authority over a fiefdom that extended from the brothels of Washington, D.C., to the casinos in the Caribbean. Gambling, prostitution, drugs, black-

33

marketeering—all of these crimes and so many others were concealed behind the soft-spoken voice, the manicured nails, the clean-shaven and powdered face of Augusto Bertinelli.

"It is an honor to meet you, Mr. Everett," he said with a short bow, his eyes never moving from the face of the young woman at Everett's side.

"The pleasure's all mine," Everett drawled, tightening his grip on the young woman's arm as he watched her eyes flash seductively at Bertinelli.

"It's too crowded for a serious conversation," Bertinelli said, taking the young woman's other arm. "Shall we go upstairs to my suite for a glass of brandy?"

"Sure," said Everett calmly. He'd let the man work himself into a frenzy over brandy—and then he'd snatch away the object of his heated fantasies. That was how the game went, and the young woman was playing the game perfectly. He would humble one of the country's most powerful mafiosi just as he had humbled its studio moguls, its politicians, its generals and admirals.

"The war makes it difficult to carry on business, does it not?" Bertinelli said gently, leading Everett to an array of Italian pastas and cajun gumbo and creole roux on a sideboard in his hotel suite, a sure sign that the meeting in the ballroom had been no accident. "But the new circumstances offer new opportunities, too."

Everett squinted at Bertinelli in the subdued light of the elegant suite. The war had put an end to most of Everett's adventures. No more round-the-world flights. No more distant voyages. But Bertinelli seemed to be offering a daring new enterprise that appealed to his predatory instincts. A new adventure. His greatest adventure. And his last adventure.

"Are you trying to peddle your black-market rubber for my aircraft factories?" Everett asked abrasively, cutting through the niceties with the characteristic arrogance and bluntness that made it easier to strike a bargain in serious business negotiations.

"No, Mr. Everett," Bertinelli said slowly, fighting the rage that rose in his throat. "I am offering you an opportunity to join some of my colleagues in a business venture—"

"*Your friends?*" Everett said, grinning to soften the insult and congratulating himself on his audacity. "I never thought I'd end up doing business with people like *your friends.*"

His companion scowled, and Everett saw the sudden flash of light in his heavy-lidded black eyes. "And I never imagined that I'd share a meal with a man of your eccentric reputation."

A moment of tension hung between them—and passed. They had traded insults without coming to blows, and now they could carry on with the business that had brought them together. Bertinelli's colleagues—he called them "the boys," a curiously casual phrase in Bertinelli's otherwise refined vocabulary—were burdened with too much black money, and they were looking for promising investments to launder the cash. Everett stood in an ideal position to launch the legitimate enterprises, to cultivate the politicians, to exploit the secret strengths of an underworld army, to create a vast and entirely legal empire for both himself and his black-money investors. The two men exchanged polite smiles and firm handshakes at the end of a two-hour conversation, and the empire became a reality.

"Well, I can't say that it hasn't been a pleasure doing business with you," Everett said, rising to his feet and gesturing curtly toward the young woman who had waited patiently at the far end of the living room, out of earshot but not out of Bertinelli's sight.

"The pleasure is truly all mine," Bertinelli answered, paying the woman one last compliment with his eyes.

Everett headed for the door, but the woman lingered in the far corner. "Come along now, uh—" He had forgotten her name, and so he simply snapped his fingers.

The young woman's eyes shimmered with anger. Bertinelli's face was frozen. "If Mr. Bertinelli agrees, I'd like to stay here," she said softly, her voice carrying faintly to Everett's ears across the room.

His fingertips burned, his mouth turned downward into a frown, and he fought the hard lump of anger in his belly. No woman had ever played the game like this before. No woman had ever challenged his companionship. And now Everett shook with rage and humiliation. This was not how the game was played!

"You'll come along with me right now—" he managed to whisper between clenched teeth.

"Now, now, if the young lady wishes to remain for another glass of brandy, that's perfectly acceptable to me," Bertinelli said smoothly, opening the door and gesturing toward the empty hallway. "My attorney will contact your lawyer with the appropriate papers—"

A moment later, still shaking with anger but mute with rage, Everett found himself alone in the corridor. The door closed behind him, and he heard the soft laughter of the young woman. The deal with Bertinelli had been sealed, but Everett would never forget the empty corridor, the closed door, the gentle laughter. A lust for revenge would simmer in his soul until the fire consumed itself in the Nevada desert on a moonless night years later.

"I don't get angry," he would say, "I get even."

And the Mecca Hotel, rising over Las Vegas two decades later, stood as a symbol of the hatred, the rivalry, the unforgiven insults. In Everett's eyes, the Mecca was one man's tombstone and another man's victory pylon. But when the sun descended behind the desert mountains on that August weekend, the fires of revenge had been banked, although the identity of the victor was still unknown.

A telephone at Everett's elbow buzzed once. He took his eyes way from the color television monitors and squinted at the receiver; the call was coming in on the single circuit that could be dialed from outside the bunker. That number was known only by a handful of men whom Everett allowed to serve him—the security chief of the Mecca Hotel, the executive vice president of Everett Enterprises, and the tight-lipped Black Muslim bodyguard who supervised his personal staff within the bunker.

Everett blinked painfully as the tiny red light on the telephone console stabbed into his eyes. The ache behind his ear was throbbing steadily, and even the cool glow of the television monitors was a source of agony. Daylight would surely kill him, Everett told himself. But there was no daylight in the bunker.

The pain had set in a year earlier, when he was still in Nicaragua, awaiting the completion of the Mecca and its underground refuge. He'd consented to see a local American doctor in his penthouse suite, but he ignored the doctor's advice to check into a hospital for extended tests. Instead, he sought the tranquillity and safety of his new subterranean home; he ordered the lights dimmed to minimize the pain in his eyes; and he relied on the injections that his bodyguard administered twice a day.

The telephone buzzed again. Why didn't Tate answer it? And then Everett remembered: His bodyguard, Alexander Tate, had gone up to the executive offices of the Mecca to deliver his employer's latest set of business instructions to Lawrence Johnson, the man who managed the affairs of Everett Enterprises from day to day. And the other men who served him in the bunker had strict orders not to answer the private line.

Everett reached for the telephone. He caught a glimpse of himself in one of the television monitors—a sick man, pale, emaciated, hollow eyed. And then he blinked the image away.

"Yes, who is it?" he mumbled hoarsely into the specially amplified telephone.

"They're coming for you, old man."

Everett strained to catch the hissed whisper. He felt

37

suddenly confused, dazed, terrified. "Who is it?" he demanded. "What do you want?"

"They're coming for you, old man," the voice hissed again. "It's over for you now, old man."

And then the line went dead.

two

The fat man ambled down the aisle of the airliner, squeezing his bulk past the crowded seats, calling out like a carnival barker: "Gift money! Gift money! Come on, people, let's show some appreciation for these girls. Gift money!"

"What the hell are you talking about?" groused the passenger in the aisle seat. "I paid for the junket back in Jersey, and now you're talking about gift money—"

"Hey, come on," the fat man gurgled, rolling the ten-dollar bills that he had already collected from the other passengers into a tight roll. "It's a little something for the stews. It ain't easy standing on your feet from Jersey to Vegas and playing nursemaid to a noisy bunch of gamblers."

The passenger glanced toward the front of the plane, where the stewardesses were already strapping themselves into jump seats for the landing at McCarran. The fat man braced himself against the tilt of the descending plane, wedging his flanks between the two aisle seats and using his free hands to snatch ten-dollar bills from each of the junket passengers.

"I've never heard of tipping a stewardess—"

"Then you've never been on one of my junkets before," replied the fat man sweetly. "I take care of my people, don't you see? You get one hell of a good bargain—a round trip to Vegas, a place to stay, and free meals and booze and it only costs you three hundred bucks. So why not cough up a couple of fivers for the stews? Wasn't the creamed chicken good enough for you?"

"The creamed chicken tasted like nothing that ever saw a barnyard, that's for sure," said the passenger. "And three hundred bucks is all you're going to get from me. I'm saving the rest for the tables."

"Well, now, that's mighty tight of you," the fat man said, pushing his face close to the passenger's and breathing hotly into it. "And I don't think tight people are lucky people, don't you see? And only lucky people get to fly my junkets twice, don't you see?"

"All right, all right, here's a ten for the stews," the passenger grunted, digging into his pocket and coming up with two crumpled five-dollar bills. "I just hope I make it back at the tables."

"Sure you will, sure you will," the fat man wheezed, plucking the bills from the passenger's hand and then swinging himself into an empty seat just as the plane touched down on the hot tarmac at McCarran. "You'll have enough to buy a few chances on the raffle on the return flight. We're raffling off a *beautiful* diamond pendant, it's worth a grand easy, and you can buy a chance for a hundred bucks. It's something nice to give the little lady when you get back home."

"Fat chance," the passenger mumbled.

The fat man lingered in his aisle seat until all of the junketeers moved past the flight crew and down the boarding stairs to the runway. His fingers were thick but deft with the roll of greenbacks, and he counted a quick fifteen hundred dollars in ten-dollar tips. Then he stashed the roll in his coat pocket, and brought out a handful of twenty-five-dollar chips from the hotel where his junket would be staying over the weekend.

"Here you go, sweetheart," he said to each stewardess, pushing a single chip into each young woman's hand. "Take this down to the Twenty Four Carat Casino. You're sure to get lucky. All my people are lucky people."

"For cryin' out loud, it's my honeymoon," wailed the young man with the slicked-down blond hair and the newly sprouted mustache. "And I sent you a fifty-buck deposit six weeks ago. Now you're telling me the hotel is full up?"

The lines were six deep along the registration counter of the Mecca at seven o'clock on Friday night, and another three dozen disappointed travelers were lounging around the upholstered benches and planter boxes nearby. The Mecca had overbooked its 4,000 rooms by the customary 14 percent; and thanks to the crowded summer junkets—and a request from the casino manager to hold open twenty-four extra suites—the front desk was turning away the low-rollers, the tourists, and the honeymooners.

"I'm very sorry, sir," said the clerk, a suntanned blonde woman with a stunningly bored smile. "It must be an error on the part of your travel agent—"

"But I made the reservations myself," the young man objected. "I called the hotel myself, and then I sent the check. Here's the confirmation."

The desk clerk ignored a slip of paper being waved in front of his nose. "Sir, the Mecca will find other accommodations in Las Vegas for you and your wife. The Wee Kirk of the Pines still has a few vacancies. It's a very popular motel and wedding chapel right next door to the Exxon station out on Interstate 15."

"But I promised Linda we'd stay at the Mecca," he muttered, shooting a nervous glance at his newly acquired wife and suffering a new wave of anxiety about the impending rigors of his wedding night obligation.

Linda was the foxiest secretary in the typing pool back in Dayton, John Warner told himself—a strawberry blonde with a body that could put an ache where it really counts— and he'd been damned lucky to keep her out of the clutches of the other salesmen. He'd seen their lecherous smiles; he'd heard their filthy speculations. And while he was out hustling new policies and running up the best sales record in the office, the older salesmen were buzzing around her desk.

But young Warner needn't have worried. Linda typed up the monthly sales reports, and she knew that the shy young man with the sparse mustache was outgrossing everyone else in the office. And after she encouraged a proposal and accepted it, she sweet-talked the office manager into giving the young couple a Las Vegas honeymoon as a bonus. The appreciative manager figured that marrying her off to his star salesman would put at least three more salesmen back in the field.

John waved across the lobby and caught Linda's attention. "They're full up, honey," he shouted, gesturing at the registration desk and then shrugging. "We'll have to stay somewhere else."

Linda frowned, then pouted, and finally broke into tears. She plopped down on the suitcase and sobbed demonstratively into her clenched fist.

"Oh hell," he moaned. He felt like pulling up a suitcase and joining her. "Go ahead and get us a room at the—"

"—Wee Kirk of the Pines," the clerk offered helpfully. "It's really very nice, Mr. Warner. They've got waterbeds and slots in the lobby and free breakfast on Sunday."

"Yeah, great, really great," he muttered. "At least we

won't have to spend our wedding night on a bus back to Dayton."

He turned around and tried to catch his bride's eye once more, but he saw with a sinking heart that she had already attracted someone else's attention. The guys back in Dayton had warned him about the dangers of bringing his virginal bride—they winked and guffawed at that line—to a town like Vegas, and now their warnings had come true. Like a shark with the scent of blood, the stranger circled Linda and then struck.

The shark was dressed appropriately enough—a tight-fitting pin-striped tuxedo, a frilly purple shirt open at the neck, and at least a dozen gold chains and pendants glittering amid the wolfish hair on his bared chest. The stranger smiled a smile that John knew so well—a predatory grin, an expression that spoke of boundless experience and a mastery of the erotic arts—and Linda smiled back through her tears. John's heart leaped into his throat as the stranger eased up to his wife, taking her elbow in his firm grip and whispering into her ear. Then the stranger slipped something into Linda's hand and cruised away.

John could restrain himself no longer. "Forget the damned motel," he hissed at the desk clerk, and then he fought his way through the crowd around the registration counter toward his wife. She was still smiling when he reached her.

"Who was that man?" he demanded in a voice that threatened to crack. "What did he give you? What the hell did he want?"

Linda giggled, the tears suddenly gone, and opened her palm to reveal an outsized brass key with a numbered tag in the shape of a star and crescent.

"Oh, he was so sweet," Linda squealed. "He said it was a shame to see a pretty girl ruining her makeup with tears, and he asked me what was wrong, and when I told him I didn't have a place to stay, he gave me his room key—"

"Are you kidding, Linda?" John squeaked in response, impulsively stroking the bristly mustache on his upper lip. He'd grown it to make himself look older, but he felt like hardly more than a pimply teenager at the moment. "It's our honeymoon, for cryin' out loud, and you're taking another man's room?"

"Don't be silly! I told him I wasn't alone, and he said it's okay, he's a high-roller and they'll give him another room. And then he winked."

John shuddered at the meanings of the stranger's wink. "It's out of the question," he said as sternly as he could manage. "I'm not sleeping in a stranger's hotel room."

"Aw, Johnny," Linda said in her little-girl pout, bending her shoulders forward to show the breathtaking cleavage barely contained in her lacy white gown. "It's our wedding night. And we've been so good about, you know, *saving ourselves* for each other. But tonight's the night. And—" Linda giggled again, licking her lips with a darting tongue and allowing her hips to slide seductively toward him "—the room has a mirror over the bed!"

"A mirror?" John moaned. The whole task of the wedding night would have been hard enough in the dark, he worried, but now he would have to watch himself every step of the way. "A mirror, for cryin' out loud."

The old man sat in silence, the dead receiver still in his shaking hand, and he wondered if he'd only imagined the hoarse whisper over the line.

"*They're coming for you,*" the voice echoed painfully in his skull. "*It's over for you now.*"

No, the voice had been real. He dropped the receiver as if it carried some hideous contagion, and he pressed his long fingers against his eyeballs in a desperate effort to stop the pain, to hold back the panic, to control the fear. But it was a useless gesture. The threat had penetrated the perfect security of his subterranean world; the man who delivered the threat had violated the perfect safety of his secret bunker. And if the bunker could not protect him, if the perfect safety and secrecy and security had been violated, then what would prevent the threat from being carried out?

For a moment he teetered on the edge of madness—the threatening hand was at his throat, the tons of concrete and steel were about to crush him, the contagion that had seeped through the airlocks and filtration systems was about to poison him. He pressed harder and harder against his eyes; he waited for the pain to explode within his skull and put the fear to an end. And then the moment of madness passed.

What replaced the glimmer of madness was a spark of anger. *How dare they?* he asked himself. How dare they insult me with a whispered threat? How dare they flout the life-and-death authority that he wielded over the world of the Mecca? How dare they trifle with a man whose power was perfect, absolute, unchallenged? *How dare they?*

The spark of anger ignited a fire-storm of emotions that the old man had almost forgotten in his tranquilized refuge—the emotions of the hunter, the warrior, the gambler. He'd been threatened before, by men who were jealous of his ambition, of his talent, of his wealth; he'd been threatened by assassins who used silenced pistols, by assassins who used cartels and boardroom conspiracies, by assassins who used writs and grand juries. But they'd never succeeded in taking a dime of money or a minute of life away from him.

And they will not succeed now, the old man vowed. The pain behind his eyes subsided, and the panic that clenched his heart eased. He reached with a steadier hand for the telephone, and one long finger hung over the dial. A threat had been made, and he must act now to turn away the danger before it struck.

He would summon his bodyguard, Alexander Tate, and order a room-by-room search of the bunker, including an electronic sweep to pick up any bugs or taps.

He'd call Louis Bianco, the Mecca's security chief, and direct him to set up an around-the-clock surveillance of the hotel lobby.

And he'd reach Lawrence Johnson, the executive vice president of Everett Enterprises, and ask him to start making the discreet inquiries among the black-money boys to see if a hit had been ordered. Some of those boys have long memories, he thought, and they never forget a betrayal—

A new current of terror buzzed through the old mans spine at the thought: *Betrayal!* Slowly, almost painfully, he pulled his finger away from the telephone dial and replaced the receiver. His eyes nervously skimmed the bank of television monitors in front of him—the elevator was not in use, the corridor outside his private chamber was empty, the plainclothes guard was on duty in the control room where the life-support systems were constantly monitored—but Everett knew that the elaborate precautions were worthless if the threat came from within. And the thought struck him again: *Betrayal!*

No, he dared not call Tate or Bianco or Johnson. Not yet, not until he'd learned more about the shadowy presence that had infiltrated his secret world and reached into his underground bunker. The threatening call might have come from any one of them. If he had been betrayed by those he had dared to trust, then Everett was alone. Alone for the first time since he'd ventured into the world after his father's death. Alone in the face of a danger that loomed up in nightmarish proportions simply because Everett faced it on his own.

But he was not helpless, the old man told himself, despite the curse of age and failing vision and unrelenting pain. No, he was not helpless. He still had the advantage of one more weapon, the weapon that was now arrayed in front of him, the weapon that had been his greatest inspiration and most expensive eccentricity during the building of the Mecca Hotel and the secret bunker.

From his seat at the control console, Everett faced a solid wall of television monitors—twelve rows of twelve color screens, each linked by a web of electrical cable to the tiny video cameras and microphones that had been hidden in the walls of the Mecca Hotel as it was built. The glow of 144 monitors bathed the bare-walled concrete chamber in soft light; the touch of a button on the control board in front of him would snatch an image from one of a thousand camera eyes and snap the image into place on the selected screen.

These were the old man's eyes and ears. These were his only reliable weapon. And he would use them as he had once used his own powers—his quickness, his cold intelligence, his ruthless insight into other men's motives and hungers and passions—to seek out the betrayer, to unmask him, and to eliminate him. Only then would the old man rest again. Only then would he sleep again. Only then would the secret world beneath the Mecca be safe and secure once again.

But now he was the hunter, the warrior, the gambler once again. And he would take the deadly risk once again.

The old man's finger floated over the control board, paused for an instant over a button that controlled one of a thousand distant camera eyes, and then punched down.

Lucille Sheaffer smiled faintly as she scratched out a name and address—Lucy Star, a plain phony—on the registration card at the Mecca's front desk. If all those little darlings in the third grade at South Platte Elementary School in Denver could only see their prim Miss Scheaffer now, she thought. If all those self-righteous bastards on the school board could only see her now!

The desk clerk hardly glanced at the registration card. "Back again, Lucy?" he asked with a sarcastic leer.

Lucy's heart raced for a moment—she'd been tossed out of a couple of Vegas hotels before she finally convinced one of the blackjack pit bosses at the Mecca to put her in the book—but then she calmed herself.

"Always nice to see old friends," she said sweetly. And stop acting like a lousy amateur, she warned herself. Once a pit boss puts your name in the book, you don't have to worry about getting turned away at the front desk. Or getting busted by security when you work the lounges. Or getting beaten up by the hardboiled pros in the restroom.

"Sorry, Lucy," the clerk said with an extravagant lisp, tossing a room key on the counter. "But the third floor is the best I can do. We're full up tonight. But at least you'll get some exercise."

Third floor—it wasn't as good for business as a first-or second-floor room, where the turnaround was a lot faster and the elevator ride from the casino was too short to worry about making small talk. But the third-floor room would do. And a full house at the Mecca would mean a lot of action on the floor tonight.

"Thanks a lot, sweetheart," Lucy said with a grin. "And I hope you're off the monthlies next time around."

She didn't wait long enough for the clerk to reply. Lucy was already at the elevators, swinging her big suitcase easily and eyeing the crowd with an experienced eye. The suitcase was empty except for a toothbrush, a douche kit, and three changes of lingerie. And the crowd was promising: a lot of junketeers, a lot of boozed-up men wearing convention nametags, and the usual assortment of middle-aged couples who would split up after the dinner show— the wife to the slots, the husband to the craps tables and maybe a third-floor room.

The guard who was stationed in the lounge area on the third floor—a precaution against burglars, street hustlers, and guests who thought the room television sets were souvenirs— just nodded at Lucy. She hurried to her room, stashed her suitcase in the closet, and picked up the phone to dial the casino.

"Blackjack pit," a voice answered her call. "Jack—"

"It's Lucy," she said too quickly, fighting the breathlessness that seemed to choke off her words. "I'm in 310, Jack, and I'm ready to go. Same split as last time, right? Eighty-twenty?"

There was a long moment of silence as the pit boss

made her suffer for her indiscretion. "Lucy?" he asked in a flat mumble. "I don't know anyone named Lucy—"

"Lucy Star?" she pleaded. "From Denver? You put me in the book on my last trip—eighty-twenty split, re-member?—and you told me to check in next time around."

"Sorry, lady," he said in a voice that turned loud and clear. "But it's against the rules to split with the women who work here. And I don't know anyone named Lucy Star."

"Oh, I'm sorry—" she mumbled, and then she hung up in a blind panic. Now I've screwed up nicely, she lectured herself. Now I'm going to find myself out on the street and flat broke. And I went ahead with the down payment on the new Mercedes because I was so sure about the weekend.

Her misery was interrupted by the ring of the telephone.

"Hello?" she said brightly, praying that it wasn't hotel security or the Vegas cops. "Hello?"

A crackling silence preceded the soft voice. "Listen, you dumb cunt," the pit boss whispered. "You're gonna get both our asses bounced right out of here. And if you call me in the pit again and start spouting off about splits, I'm going to bounce your ass all by myself."

"Sorry, Jack," she said miserably. "I'm really sorry. But I'm still new at all this."

"Okay, okay, just shut up for a minute," he said. "We're carrying a lot of action at the tables tonight, and I'm gonna need you for two, maybe three tricks. And I mean quickies—I don't want these guys slam-banging all night when they could be back at the table." He paused. "You got any specialties?"

Lucy shivered. "Anything," she whispered. "Anything you want to send me, Jack."

"Right," he said crisply. "Now I won't be needing you till maybe eleven or midnight. So go ahead and work the lounges if you want—that's all yours, no split—but I want you clean and clear by the end of the dinner show."

"Okay, Jack," she said, still whispering, still shivering. "Anything you say, Jack."

If the third grade could only see me now, Lucy thought, staring out the open window at the scattered neon jewels, in the black desert night. It wasn't the money, she told herself. Just the risk, the excitement. Something like life, better than television or bowling or groping at drive-ins with a married principal. But she knew better. She wanted the power it gave her.

Ahmed Ibn Sayd followed the assistant manager through the lobby of the Mecca Hotel. A procession of three bellboys in stylized red fezzes had been left behind at the front desk; despite the lavish attentions of the hotel management, Sayd insisted on a quiet and inconspicuous reception. His business at the Mecca required discretion, diplomacy—and secrecy.

But even if Sayd had been wearing robes and a kaffiyeh headdress instead of a tailored suit, he still would have been ignored by the hungry-looking men and women who crowded around the noisy slot machines and the oversized gaming tables. None of the gamblers looked underfed, but Sayd noticed the gleam of starvation in their eyes. A starvation of the soul, he remarked to himself, a starvation that he knew so well.

And Sayd marked each new insult with cold fury— the red fez worn jauntily on the bellboy's head, the star-and-crescent that hung from the crystal chandeliers, the ersatz Arabic script that defaced every uniform and sign. He would not forget these offenses against the dignity of his faith; he would not forget how the infidels played so casually with the sacred symbols of Islam.

The assistant manager, an attentive young man who had sized up the guest as a wealthy Arab from the moment of his arrival, noticed as Sayd's close attention to the casino. "If you'd like to use our private gaming facilities in the Penthouse," he said obsequiously, bowing two or three times out of a vague impulse of courtesy and deference, "it's only a short distance from your suite. And it's very discreet."

Sayd dismissed the young man's bobbing head and transparent efforts at gentlemanly manners. So the infidels have been warned that a man of Islam would not gamble—at least not in public—and so they seek to corrupt him by offering him a secret place to sin. But Allah's eyes are everywhere, and He sees every poor sinner.

"The Penthouse?" Sayd repeated. His Oxford accent and soft voice concealed his scorn.

"Yes, sir," the young man said enthusiastically. "The top floor of the hotel has been reserved for private gaming parties, private banquets, and VIP guests." He beamed triumphantly. "Your suite is a VIP room, of course."

"Of course," Sayd said.

The two men reached the bank of elevators, but the manager escorted Sayd to an unmarked door that led to a locked elevator. He inserted a key, and gestured toward the opening doors.

"A private elevator to the Penthouse floor," the young man explained. "Your room key will operate it, or you may ask any of the front desk personnel to escort you."

"How considerate," Sayd murmured. But it was his intention to remain unescorted until his mission at the Mecca Hotel was accomplished.

The elevator whooshed powerfully and silently to the twenty-sixth floor, and the doors opened with a whisper. Two guards stood outside the elevator, and the assistant manager presented Sayd's room key.

"For your own security," he said apologetically, "you will be required to show your key each time you return to the Penthouse. And the security guards will have a physical description of you to make sure that no one else uses the key." The young man looked down. "Of course, if you wish to have any, uh, *guests*, just call the front desk and they'll have security make the proper arrangements. It will all be handled, uh—"

"Discreetly?" Sayd offered, finishing the manager's halting sentence.

"Exactly," he said happily, charging ahead toward the suite and busily working the key in the lock.

Sayd watched as the young man puttered around the living room of the suite, opening the drapes and checking the thermostat on the humming air conditioner. At last, he pointed toward an immense basket of fruit on a low table near the picture window.

"Compliments of the Mecca," he said smartly. "And your luggage will be here in a few moments."

Sayd debated whether to hand the young man a tip. But he decided that it would be a cheap insult, inappropriate for a man of his refinement and experience. And he was preparing to deliver a much more devastating insult to all those who built the Mecca and boasted of it as the jewel of Las Vegas.

"That will be all, thank you," Sayd said softly, waiting at the door until the assistant manager—bowing and smiling —had backed out.

As soon as the receding footsteps of the young man faded away, Sayd carried his briefcase to the writing desk and opened the case delicately. Reaching beneath the sheaf of yellow legal pads and folders, he brought out two electronic instruments—a U-shaped wire wand with a flashlight-shaped handle, and an elongated rectangular case with a fine-wire mesh at one end and an electrical meter at the other. And then, working slowly and meticulously, Sayd swept the VIP suite to see exactly how much attention the Mecca Hotel paid to its very important guests.

He waved the wand over the obvious hiding places for a listening device—the telephones, the television set, the built-in clock radio, and the other appliances around the suite. As expected, he found a permanent telephone bug in each of the suite's four receivers, and an old but now in-operative spike-mike in the wall adjoining the next suite.

But it was the bedroom that yielded the most elaborate

surveillance equipment. From the high readings on the wand, Sayd guessed that the bedroom must be fitted out with a full video-and-sound system, including servomechanisms to control a zoom lens and closeup focus, and separate microphone pickups at a half-dozen locations around the sleeping quarters and bathroom.

"Voyeurs," he spat. A blackmail setup, or perhaps just a form of degenerate sexual amusement for some of the hotel's top management. But in Sayd's world, in Sayd's life, nothing of importance could be overhead in the bedroom. "We will put a blade in the eye on the other end."

Satisfied that he could secure the living room for confidential conversation simply by disconnecting the phone bugs, Sayd picked up the rectangular black instrument and repeated his painstaking search. The mesh-covered vent would pick up the faintest traces of explosives and indicate their presence on the meter at the other end. But the voyeurs who had bugged the VIP suite failed to plant anything more dangerous than a video camera and a microphone.

Sayd made one pass over the fruit basket, but the needle on the explosive detector did not waver. So he reached for an orange—the infidels might corrupt him with the flesh of a pig in their dining rooms, they might intoxicate him with strong spirits in their bars, but he did not sin when he bit into the sweet, juicy fruit.

But when his eye caught the purple lettering on the discarded peel, he spat out the half-eaten orange pulp and cursed aloud. "HAIFA," the orange peel was marked. "PRODUCE OF ISRAEL."

"Dogs!" Sayd said to himself, reaching into his shoulder holster and removing the loaded pistol. "Heathen dogs!"

And he fired one silencer-muffled shot into the basket of fruit, neatly exploding a Hawaiian pineapple.

Ben Payne couldn't believe it. And the fish-eyed boxman, as well as the floorman, in charge of the section of tables, had trouble believing it. Payne's run of luck was phenomenal. In a short time, he was up eighty-five thousand, had paid off his markers in the amount of fifty thousand, his credit limit. Selma stood by with the Gucci bag, a step or two behind Payne. The table was crowded now, too crowded even for the companions of high-rollers to take up a space. The floorman was a *sweater*, an executive who fretted visibly when players won, relaxed noticeably when they lost. Sometimes they call them *bleeders*. The floorman was one of those, tending to take it out on the dealers and stickman as though they were personally hoping for the players to win.

The word was out that Payne was a big winner and paying off his markers clinched it. The important thing was to keep him at the table. The black man had already missed his Los Angeles flight. His limousine still waited.

The roller was an elderly man with the face of a New England banker. He had made three passes, and it looked like the table was ready for another streak. The roller had fifty dollars on the pass line but he was tiring visibly. The blonde had long since left, informed perhaps by instinct of what was about to come. Payoffs and betting were taking much longer between rolls, always a damper. Selma plucked at Ben's sleeve, whispered in his ear. He didn't like the interruption—it impaired his concentration. "Let me take the money to Los Angeles," she said. "I'll have it put into the safe for Monday morning. I'll wait for you at the apartment," she pleaded. He shook his head.

"Be patient. Wait." Ben watched the roller. He felt an ominous pang. The floorman sensed Payne wasn't going anyplace. The roller sent the dice down the table and there was a groan of disappointment as one die jumped the wall. The stickman intoned, "Over the end. No dice." The white-haired man picked out another two red cubes from the six shoved toward him. He held them between forefinger and thumb, tapped them gently on the table—a four and three showing—and rolled them. They bounced up seven. A wave of relief around the table. But something had happened.

Some change. The tide of numbers the house counted had changed as imperceptibly as the sea's. Instead of a long series of numbers which would pay off the odds the high-rollers really wanted, he rolled two—craps, then twelve, another craps, clearing off the pass-line bets twice.

Payne suppressed an instinct to call off his back-line bets, collect his winnings, and leave. They could drive to Los Angeles in the air-conditoned limousine, make love, talk about his narrow escape, get out of the old life. It sounded good. The words to withdraw his bets were trapped in his throat. The roller sent the dice along the table and they came up six. Everybody relaxed. If he could roll those numbers now. More bets went on the back line, on the propositions, the hard ways, the horns; other bettors took the don't side.

With all the preparation, disappointment. Just as he was about to call off his bets, the twelve thousand he had riding on the numbers, white-hair rolled out with a seven. He looked embarrassed, the kindly old financier who disappointed everybody by embezzling from widows and orphans. With a glare of resentment, he took his leave and the dice passed to a new roller, someone who could have been an oil rigger or even the cowboy he was dressed up to look like. The floorman and boxman both relaxed. They knew him as a loser. He was a bartender at an Italian joint in South Vegas. Ben put a thousand on the pass line. It was stupid; he should leave now. He knew it. Selma knew it. Selma. She had broken his streak of luck; it never failed. Never mind. In the Gucci was his life and freedom. Now he was playing with the house's money. He felt safe, if not lucky. The dice would turn his way again.

"What's your handle, stranger?" the red-faced Texan in the Stetson and Hawaiian shirt asked.

"My name is Tuthill," said the man on the next stool in the Mecca's bar. He gestured at the nametag on his shirt. "Ira Tuthill. I'm here for the morticians' convention."

"Undertakers, you mean?" Sam laughed again. "In Vegas? Well, that's about right--maybe you'll pick up some extra business when they start putting away the poor slobs who can't pay their gambling tabs."

Tuthill nodded. He'd heard the same joke at least three times since he and his wife checked into the Mecca with the other four hundred morticians. But he still didn't think it was funny.

"Say, Ira, what's your action?" Sam asked good-naturedly, slapping the slender man on the back, nearly knocking him off the barstool.

"Well, I'm drinking a wine spritzer right now—"

"No, no," Sam guffawed. "I mean, what's your *game?* I'll bet you're just another blackjack grind, right? No, I keep to the poker tables in the back, where you can work up a little Texas-style action for seven-card stud."

"I'm not really a gambling man," Tuthill objected in the mildest tone he possessed. "Oh, I'll put a nickel in the slots on the way to the airport, but I keep a tight watch on my money while I'm here."

Sam leaned back and sized up the little undertaker with watery, bloodshot eyes. "Yeah, I guess you're the type to pump the nickels down the slots and then fly home feeling all righteous and pure. But it sure seems a shame to come all the way to Vegas and go home with nothing to tell the folks about. By the way, Sam is the name."

Tuthill looked down at his wine spritzer. "The wife and I are going to the Wayne Newton show tomorrow," he offered. "Tonight we're going to see *Salaam, Sultan!* here at the Mecca. They say it's the best show in Vegas."

"Tits 'n' ass," Sam said. "Just tits 'n' ass. If you're a real man, Ira, you'll get straightened out by a pro between deals and then get on with the game."

"I don't know what you mean," Tuthill said.

But Tuthill knew.

Even since the convention announcement had arrived at the funeral home a few months before, ever since he'd sent in a deposit for his room at the Mecca, Ira Tuthill had been thinking about Las Vegas. And the thoughts put a dangerous ache in his gut—a strange ache that he felt every time he looked at the bare-breasted showgirls in the travel brochure or the big roulette wheel with the playing surface covered in one-hundred-dollar and five-hundred-dollar bills.

His wife had sensed the hunger almost immediately. "You're not going to that place alone," she announced. "And you're not throwing away a dime on gambling, d'ya hear me?"

Tuthill tried to convince himself he was grateful for his wife's words, his wife's commandments—and his wife's presence.

"The wife and I don't gamble," Tuthill said to Sam, tipping the last of the wine spritzer down his throat, which had suddenly gone very dry. "We'll just catch a couple of shows, and the convention sessions, of course. Tomorrow's main speaker is some young fellow who wrote a book. He's going to talk about 'Winning Through Intimidation in Undertaking.' Senator Harwell's going to give the keynote speech."

"Sounds like a thrill," Sam said, dismounting from the stool as if it were a stallion and throwing a twenty-five-dollar chip on the bar. "The spritzer is on me, buddy. Looks like you need it."

"Thanks, Sam," Ira called as the Texan strode away. He remembered the stranger's name without half trying; that was one of the essential skills of a good undertaker, and he was going to polish them up at a seminar on "Memory Tricks and Techniques for the Funeral Director" on Sunday morning. "See you around, Sam."

But Ira Tuthill's eyes did not leave the bartop, where the twenty-five-dollar chip now sat in a pool of beer and pretzel crumbs. He and his wife had been in Vegas since noon, but they still didn't have any chips; Gertrude refused to allow Ira to buy any at the cashier's cage.

"You remember what we decided, Ira," she had admonished him when they entered the dazzling Mecca lobby at noon. "Ten dollars each for the slot machines, and not a penny more."

Wouldn't Gertie be scandalized if she knew that I was tempted to steal another man's twenty-five-dollar chip off the bar, just like a common thief? Ira thought. And wouldn't she be surprised if she knew what I would do with it?

Ira slid down off the barstool, gave the chip one final glance, and walked uneasily toward the casino.

Lise Christian stood next to the window of her darkened suite on the twenty-sixth floor of the Mecca Hotel, dressed only in a half bra and panties, gazing beyond the rainbow of sparkling electrical color toward the encircling mountains where she'd imagined a solitary light in a lost canyon. The lonely light that she'd seen from the airplane—and it must have been an optical illusion, she reminded herself—was outshone by the thousands of neon tubes and incandescent bulbs that marked the sprawl of Las Vegas across the desert floor.

She still felt slightly breathless, and placed one hand over her breast as if to soothe her own heartbeat. The breathlessness had started as soon as the taxicab pulled up in front of the Mecca. Instantly, she was hypnotized by the unrelenting spectacle of the Strip—one spangled billboard after another, one towering hotel after another, all stitched together by the solid rush of headlights from on the Strip. By the time the cabbie had delivered her and her luggage to the grand entrance of the Mecca, Lise was dazed and dizzy and out of breath.

"This is quite a place!" she'd exclaimed to the cabdriver. After all, Lise had asked her mother's attorney to arrange a visit to a bank, not a casino; she was traveling to Vegas for business, not pleasure. And the Mecca seemed too explosive, too energetic, for the solemn purposes of her journey.

"There's only one Mecca, sister," the cabbie had said.

And her reception at the front desk had done nothing to calm her. The desk clerk asked for identification: "We don't allow minors to register without their parents," the clerk said, eyeing Lise's slender figure and pale skin. But when she offered a passport to prove her age, the clerk's manner changed dramatically. He ran a pencil down a typed list of names behind the counter, and then came to attention with a slight click of the heels.

"I'm sorry for the delay, Miss Christian," he said in a new tone of deference. "The bell captain will see you to your suite in the Penthouse. And a maid is waiting to unpack your bags."

"The Penthouse?" Lise asked, mentally calculating the dollar amount of the traveler's checks in her purse and the likely cost of a suite in the glittering hotel. "I booked an ordinary room—"

"Oh, you've been comped," the clerk said quickly. "An RFB comp, Miss Christian."

"Comped?" she asked. "RFB?"

"Complimentary accommodations," he explained with a slight smile. "Complimentary room, food, and beverage. Courtesy of the management."

"Are you quite sure?" Lise asked. "I don't know anyone here at the Mecca—"

"Well, they certainly know you," he replied, glancing once more at the list of names. "The comp has been authorized by Mr. Johnson, the president of the Mecca."

"Johnson. I don't know anyone named Johnson—"

But it was too late. The bell caption had swept up her flight bag, and a bellboy was loading her luggage onto a cart. A few moments later, still breathless and bewildered, Lise stood in the enormous living room of her Penthouse suite, watching mutely as the bell captain drew open the drapes to reveal the spectacular view and the maid unpacked her clothing.

"I've taken the liberty of drawing a bath for you, Miss Christian," the maid said, sounding unlike any maid that

Lise had ever encountered. "And I'm on duty for the Penthouse suite until six o'clock tomorrow morning. Please feel free to call on me if I can help in any way. Just dial 'I' on the room phone."

Flustered and fatigued, Lise dipped into her purse for a tip.

"Oh no, Miss Christian," the maid said, backing toward the door, "it's been taken care of. Everything has been taken care of."

And now Lise Christian stood alone in the suite, trying to catch her breath before easing into the perfumed bath. Her gaze returned from the mountains on the horizon to the better defined sprawl of the Mecca Hotel—the brilliant blue of the twin swimming pools, the massive Tiffany glass dome over the casino, and the hotel tower on which her suite perched.

She looked at the two lower towers, the round ones which glistened in the violet light of the evening, wondered what went on behind those opaque windows. Were there children here? What did *they* do? A few people walked along the Strip. She saw them as dots from that height. Who would want to walk in that unremitting heat? The short distance from the cab to the air-conditioned lobby had hit her like a wall of fever. One little scene had caught her eye while she waited for the sweating bellboy to take her bags. She had seen three people walking toward the giant doors —a thin windburned man, wearing a white robe, wrinkled and dried out, but with eyes as blue as the desert sky, an old Indian woman, and a young boy in jeans and a tank top —holding signs which proclaimed: YOU ARE A CREATURE OF GOD, STAY OUT OF THE DEVIL'S TEMPLE. Two security guards quickly appeared, hustled them into the parking lot. "They come back every day," the bellboy had said. "Like clockwork."

There were people like that on the streets of Paris. In fact, everywhere, she thought, except Switzerland. So neat there that the police practically organized the demonstrations and scheduled them to end at six p.m. She had the feeling that for all the excitement and the seeming absence of care, things were organized here in the same way. It was just less apparent.

Suddenly, she thought about her own life, and felt a stranger to herself. Being alone in the world hardly frightened her. In fact, she felt that her mother's death had released her. Lacy had tried hard to make the control she exercised as benevolent as possible. She had found Phillippe for Lise, heir of an insurance dynasty, well past the stage of his youthful rebellion and lust, ready to settle down and have a family. The odd thing is that Lise liked Phillippe, enjoyed watching him play polo, or going to the theater with him, or even spending an occasional weekend at the family's country house near Amboise along the Loire. The trouble was that she saw her future as certain as a railroad track. Married as a virgin, providing children for the line, then, later, almost certainly, when Phillippe went to his mistress, she could, if discreet, have her lover.

Some women might think her lucky, ungrateful for the protection and the money that the world had bestowed on her. But there were feelings within her that had nothing to do with a solid future. She wanted to love someone, to have that marvelous viral pleasure-pain she dreamed love was, sweet sadness, a sense of falling, a poignancy. She had wondered about sex, had had a few experiences at school, groping with a girl on whom she had had a crush, a few kisses and hugs with the son of the Mexican ambassador who adored her from afar when she came home on school holidays, and managed to take her to the Bois on one of the few times she had lied to her mother about where she was going.

Now she was in Las Vegas, where anything went, alone, on the edge of a quest which, not so strangely, began to feel physical, sexual. Her father and mother must have been in love, must have known, if only briefly, the kind of mad wild affection which brought two such desperate people together. It was the risk which brought her here, the need to know which part of her was connected to this place, what it meant.

The thoughts excited her. She stretched out on the bed as though floating. She began to cry—not out of unhappiness, but out of yearning for contact with a person for whom she would have that feeling she dreamed was love. She wanted to be held, touched, spoken to. Lise felt that she could fall in love, could experience what she had never felt. In this place. It seemed like the beginning of luck.

Then Lise heard a strange sound—a faint whirring, as though the air conditioner had been electronically adjusted. She looked up at the mirrored ceiling, laughed, stuck her tongue out, and saw the reflection of the face she made. That, she thought, was the first time the mirror had been used that way. The whirring stopped. It must have come from the air conditioner. I'm too tense. Too tired from the long trip. She rose from the bed, stripped off her lingerie, walked to the bathroom where the steaming, perfumed bath awaited. She had forgotten the strange whirring sound.

Somewhere within the depths of the Mecca Hotel, buried beneath many hundred tons of desert sand and steel-reinforced concrete, the old man peered at a television monitor. The eerie glow of an image from an infrared camera bathed him in soft light; the screen was filled with the closeup image of a now empty bed in a now empty bedroom.

And somewhere within the depths of the old man, buried beneath twenty years of pain and fear and remorse, something stirred.

Clink-clink-clang! The slot machine swallowed another Eisenhower dollar, and with a nylon-dampened tap, the polyethylene arm was levered downward. But no wheels spun: The face of the slot machine was a video monitor, and a color cathode-ray tube played out the images of cherries and bells and oranges.

Click. The computer circuitry activated a simulator that imitated the familiar clockwork sound of the old-fashioned slots. And the video screen showed an angular approximation of three purple plums. A winning hand.

The woman who stood in front of the slot machines didn't scream. Her heart didn't race. Something about the cool light of the video screen hypnotized her, and the ghost-like flutter of images didn't burn themselves into her consciousness. She hardly heard the solid clatter as fifty Eisenhower dollars dropped into the plastic cup of the slot machine and then overflowed to the floor. As she bent down to gather the coins in a cardboard bucket, she thought of ice cubes and the icemaker down the hall at the motel where she and her husband were staying.

"Another payoff on another lucky Mecca slot." The amplified voice of a young woman in scarlet hot pants and cleavage-squeezing vest boomed out over the slot-machine gallery. The barker strolled back and forth on an elevated platform, speaking into a hand-held microphone and surveying the hundreds of slot machines for another winner. "The lucky lady hit a fifty-dollar jackpot!"

The other players paused for a moment and stared reverentially toward the lucky lady. A few of them grabbed their coffee cups full of coins and edged over to the lucky lady's machine, praying that she would abandon the charmed slot to them. And the lucky lady's husband materialized behind her.

"Well, I guess you were right all along," the man exulted, seizing his wife's elbow and pulling her away from the video slot machine. "I've lost two hundred at blackjack and you pick up fifty on a lousy dollar slot."

She numbly extended the bucket full of silver dollars with both hands, and then abruptly turned back to the slot machine that had been so lucky. The insistent machine had not yielded the lucky lady yet; its video screen played out a series of enticing love songs in flickering, light-formed letters. And the lucky lady absorbed each endearment without reading the words.

"TODAY IS YOUR LUCKY DAY," the slot machine's video screen cooed.

"Edna," her husband said. "It's after seven o'clock, and they're already lining up for the dinner show."

"Edna, you've been talking about seeing *Salaam, Sultan* ever since we got here."

"Edna, they've got a live tiger in the show. And a magician. And a pair of jugglers."

Edna said nothing. Her hand dipped into the cardboard bucket and her fingers closed around a dollar. She fed the coin to the machine and then moved her hand slowly to the lever, fondling the blunt end in a trance of expectation.

"Edna!"

She closed her eyes and stroked the machine in a single downward motion.

The weather seemed to be cooling off but John Morrissey wasn't. He stood in the forecourt of the Mecca with its fountains which gave the illusion of coolness but no relief from the furnace heat. He was depressed. In fact, he felt as though he had entered the first circle of hell. The entry was crowded with people and he felt almost invisible. He couldn't get the doorman's attention. The man was elaborately costumed in billowing scarlet pantaloons, a bangled vest, and a turban. Horn-rimmed glasses and digital wristwatch, John Morrissey thought, didn't quite spoil the effect. Las Vegas never took its masquerades too seriously.

The doorman stood in the curving driveway of the Mecca's main entrance, directing cabs and cars and limousines with a voice like a klaxon. If he noticed Morrissey at his side, he gave no sign of it.

"Excuse me," Morrissey said. "My car is being serviced at the gas station across the street, and I need someplace to stay—"

The doorman glanced at the man in the rumpled suède coat and faded blue Levi's. Then he turned away from Morrissey, neatly slipping a gowned-and-tuxedoed couple into the back seat of a waiting cab. His beefy hand hovered insistently near the open door like a bird of prey; the man in the tuxedo dug into his pocket and handed him a dollar bill.

The doorman turned back to find Morrissey still by his side. "How much does a room cost here?" John asked, clutching a fistful of greenbacks. "I'm on a tight budget, you see."

The doorman scowled. "Then you probably can't afford the Mecca, Mister."

Morrissey felt a moment of anger that quickly dissolved into sadness. What the hell, he thought, this man, sweating in his foolish outfit, was making a living. Morrissey had been a college teacher for so long, he had lost touch with the way people had to hustle in this other world. "Sorry to bother you," he said. The doorman appeared not to notice but John felt a quick pat on the shoulder. In this madness of slamming doors, of taxis pulling in and out, of limousines waiting for the potentates and company presidents, the doorman managed to call, without turning around, "Try the Hops Motel on Paradise Road. It's clean and reasonable. Tell 'em Monty sent you."

John walked into the lobby, into the rush of frigid air. He felt miraculously transported from the desert into an icebox palace. He saw the public phones behind a lattice-work screen. He sat in a divan that could have come from Topkapi in Istanbul, too tired to move for a moment, grateful for the respite. His life was a disaster area, a minefield. Nothing had gone right for years; no feeling of belonging to another person, of loving and being loved. Sex was facile and all of its permutations a momentary release. The need came in cycles. And all those coeds he had taken to bed meant little to him. Of course, they were people, warm, some of them, and giving, perhaps interesting as well. It was he who had lost touch with himself; he was a hollow man, a man of numbers. Christ, he thought, I want to know what it is to be in love again.

A few moments later they met. Morrissey could have calculated the odds against it. Lise might never have thought about it in those terms. Perhaps it was destiny or karma. John got up to make his phone calls for a room. He didn't have a dime. Well, he reflected, with all these cashiers I shouldn't have any trouble. He bumped into a young girl wearing a white dress of such a light fabric that it seemed more an aura than a garment. She saw a stranger in a worn suède jacket and faded jeans, looking harassed. He looked like one of those American graduate students Lise knew from Paris. She looked like a vision.

But it happened too quickly. He asked her if she had change for a quarter—telephone change. She felt confused, thought he meant a *jeton*, those coin-like slugs one used in Paris pay phones and bought from the *patron*. Drawn to her black eyes, he was experiencing that dizziness he knew was the first symptom. She felt her heart go out to this man. She almost laughed. That cliché. Yet, that's what it did feel like, as though some ghost of her heart came out of her chest and went toward him.

"I need some dimes for the phone," he said. The words came out gruffly through his constricted throat. She looked in her purse. There was no change. Only a folder of traveler's checks and the chip, the "lucky" chip she had been given. "Here," she said. "Take this. It's supposed to be lucky —and you look like you could use some luck." It came out sounding condescending. She knew it and immediately regretted it.

Neither really heard the other's tone. The words floated. She had to get to a limousine which waited to take her on a drive around Las Vegas. That, she had no way of knowing or even caring, was the same car which Ben Payne had canceled. She put the chip in John's hand. "Just for luck." His back ached; he thought about his wounded car. He wanted something of hers. "Yes," he said, smiling, "that's nice." They touched fingers and parted.

In the cool limousine, Lise wondered why she hadn't invited him along for the ride. Such a missed chance, she reflected. Well, I'll never see him again.

In the lobby, he knew he had missed his chance. But how could he have detained her? They came from opposite sides of the mountain. He should have asked her for a drink. Or, at least, asked her name. Oh well, he mused, the pattern of my fucked-over life again. At least it's consistent. He thought of writing that Orwell book, brought up to date and set in this town, "Down and Out in Las Vegas." He drifted into the Minaret Coffee Shop. There, slowly, it came to him that this was where *she* was staying. He hadn't anything better to do. He'd *wait* for her.

Ben Payne knew he was in trouble. So did Selma. His luck was turning and he didn't have the sense to leave the table. The cast was changing. It always did at the table. Changing, one floorman reflected, but the types remained the same. He thought it was funny, strange—the customers sometimes worked longer shifts than the crew. He stared at Payne. The crisp clothes were wilting, the gold miniature record given him by his most successful group, The When, seemed pasted to his chest by a thin film of perspiration. His eyes were tired. The good-looking mulatto-bronze skin was paling.

"Order another limousine," Payne said to Selma. She turned to go toward the lobby. He caught her. "Leave the bag," he said gruffly.

"Sucker!"

John Morrissey nodded at the stranger in the slot gallery, and repeated his original question. "Can you break a

67

dollar into dimes? I've got to use the phone." Morrissey had to line up a place to stay.

"Sucker!" the stranger repeated, gesturing in disgust as another jackpot discharged a tankful of Eisenhower dollars. "Of all the sucker games in Vegas, the slots are the worst. No gambler with any self-respect is going to stand up like a jackoff artist with a paper cup full of dimes." He was glassy eyed and exuded stale beer.

"Yeah, sure," Morrissey mumbled, looking around the casino for one of the busty young women in hot pants and change aprons.

The stranger pulled at his string tie and ran one hand over an ill-fitting toupee. "Dimes?" he said with a sneer. "A grown man—and you're going to feed dimes to a one-armed bandit?"

"No, it's not for the slots," Morrissey tried to explain. "I need to make a few phone calls—"

"Dime slots. That's pussy action," the man in the toupee sputtered. "Anyway, they don't have dime slots at the Mecca. Now, pal, if you really want to gamble like a man, you try some craps. Or blackjack. But not the dime slots, for Christ's sake."

Morrissey shrugged and turned away. But the stranger had linked arms with him and was dragging him toward the closest craps table. The stranger's drunken grip and two-hundred-pound bulk kept Morrissey in tow.

"The phone," he shouted in the stranger's ear. "I have to get dimes for the phone."

"Here," the stranger said triumphantly, careening against the craps table and easing Morrissey alongside him. He reached into his coat pocket and drew out two green chips which he placed on the pass line. "Make a bet, son, and we'll show 'em how a couple of real men gamble."

"Listen," Morrissey said, protesting as the other man's grip on his arm became so strong as to become painful. "I just want to change one of these dollars for dimes—"

He was holding out two dollar bills; the man grabbed

them and plunked them on the pass line. Immediately, the dealer exchanged the bills for dollar tokens.

"Roll the dice," the stickman called. "New shooter coming out."

Morrissey frowned. He was trapped. He'd seen the same kind of drunk before—a generous, exuberant drunk who could turn ugly in a moment. And so he reached for the dice.

"Let me show you how, buddy," the stranger said, elbowing Morrissey aside. He picked delicately at the half-dozen dice on the table, prodding and poking until he found a pair that seemed to suit him. Then he spent another few seconds tormenting the two cubes until a five and a two showed on the facing sides. At last, he picked them up, blew on them, raised his eyes toward heaven, and thrust the dice under Morrissey's nose.

"Say 'fifty-two,'" he ordered. "For luck."

"Luck won't do you any good," Morrissey mumbled.

"For luck," he repeated.

"What the hell," Morrissey mumbled, taking the dice and rolling them in his palm. "Fifty-two. Fifty-two."

"Gentlemen," the dealer said, politely, "let's go. You're holding up the game."

"Now roll the little bastards," the stranger ordered, running his hand over his toupee once again. "And roll 'em right, like I told you."

Morrissey threw the dice with a slight shrug—the odds were preordained, he knew, and etched into the precise surfaces of the dice—and the stranger seemed to throw himself halfway over the bumper to watch the roll. Morrissey leaned back from the table, trying to spot the pay telephones or the strolling cashiers, wondering if he would end up sleeping on an empty bench at the Greyhound depot, as the service station attendant had suggested.

"Natural seven," the dealer barked. "Pay the line."

Morrissey glanced back at the craps table to see that the stranger's two chips had doubled, and his own two dollar coins had become four. The stranger hooted and pounded on Morrissey's back, and he could not help but grin like a schoolboy.

"You did it," the stranger whooped. "You see now, buddy? You better leave those dime slots alone and play with the big boys.

"Hey, buddy, you're going to press the bet, ain't you?" the stranger boomed. "I've got a hundred bucks on the table, and I'm pressing."

"These are mine?" Morrissey asked. The dealer nodded and he grabbed the four dollar tokens. "I'm sorry," he mumbled. "I've got to get to a phone." He backed away and hurried into the crowd.

"Hell, you're not going to drop me just when you're starting to purr, are you?"

But Morrissey was gone, lost in the rush of the crowd, working his way toward the bank of pay telephones on the far side of the bustling casino. He passed the cashier's cages, decided to cash in his chips, laughed as he realized what the words had come to mean.

The man in the string tie and the toupee cursed aloud as he lost sight of Morrissey, and then he turned back to the table. Four twenty-five-dollar chips remained on the pass line, and the dice awaited him. But the young man with the fistful of dollar bills and the lucky purr was gone.

"New shooter," the dealer monotoned, pushing the dice toward him with the long stick.

"Damn," the stranger muttered. "I just pray that some of the dumb bastard's luck rubbed off on me."

Ben Payne had dropped ten thousand dollars betting the don't side. He was glad to see the back of the guy in the suède jacket. Something about him, Payne thought, the aura. The man had luck and didn't know it. He shrugged. There was no time for thinking. What he needed now was the guts to leave this table.

His hand hesitated over the pass line. He dropped five

hundred on the don't pass. A slender girl wearing a Harvard University sweatshirt and little else rolled the dice with lots of giggles. Payne felt relieved, knew before the dealer called "two, craps" that it would happen. He signaled the floorman for a drink with a turn of his hand. The adrenalin was flowing again. In a few minutes when Selma returned to say that another limousine was waiting, he had won the ten thousand back and a little more to boot. The crew was happy. He had bet all the hard ways for them and they were six hundred and twenty dollars ahead. They were rooting for him now; even the floorman was happy. He knew that a winning streak was the best insurance for the house.

three

The stack of chips was eroding with each throw of the dice, and so were the spirits of the fellow in the crew cut and the new hound's-tooth sports coat. He had started with twenty hundred-dollar chips only four hours earlier, fresh off the Greyhound bus and fairly bursting with excitement at the prospect of celebrating his first day of civilian life after four years in the Marine Corps. That two-thousand-dollar stake was every penny he'd been able to save in the last four years, every dollar he'd won in the barracks card games, in the back-alley craps games on liberty in San Diego, and in the shipboard poker during the last voyage aboard a missile frigate.

Four years' worth of smart gambling, the street-smart

gambling that he'd learned in the service, and it was gone in four hours. Christ, how he'd planned this day in Vegas—all the bets, all the odds, all the stakes, all of it lovingly dreamed about a thousand times on a thousand different nights over the years of enlistment. But the street smarts didn't do him a damned bit of good. He was losing the stake as surely and swiftly as the dumbest rube who ever walked into a Vegas casino and plunked down his dough on a fool's bet.

He ran one hand over his close-cut Marine Corps haircut. He'd been hoping to win big in Vegas so he could afford one of those fancy new Camaros, the ones with the decals and the pinstriping and the racing scoops. He wanted to drive into Sumner Wells, Tennessee, in a car so grand and gaudy that everyone in his home town would know that he'd come back from the Marines. But that dream, just like the dream of winning big in Vegas, was disappearing before his eyes. He'd have to go home by Greyhound instead, and the only thing he'd have to show for this hitch would be a crew cut and a tattoo on his right arm.

"New shooter," the dealer called, pushing the dice in front of him. "Place your bet, shooter."

The young man glanced mournfully at the five chips that remained in front of him. Out of luck, he thought, and out of dough, too.

"Can I bet, too?" a shrill voice giggled.

He turned to his right and saw the girl for the first time. A gawky kid with stringy red hair, and too many freckles, and the soft twang that was so familiar to him. "Sure you can," he drawled, warmed by the sound of another Tennessee accent after too many years of Brooklyn and Georgia and Massachusetts dialects. "Here, bet one of mine."

"I couldn't do that, Mister—"

He beamed at her. "Ah, go ahead, I'm not doing too well for myself. Maybe another Tennessee hand will bring us both some luck here."

"Tennessee? Is that right? I'm from Poston."

"Poston? Are you kidding? Hey, I'm from Sumner Wells, just across the Patawattie Valley. We're practically neighbors."

"Place your bets," the dealer said wearily. "All bets on the table, please."

"Here's fifty for me and fifty for my friend," the young man said, dropping four chips on the pass line and pushing the dice into her hand. "Now roll those dice, sweetheart. Roll them for a couple of Tennessee kids too far from home."

"But I don't know anything about the game," she protested with a squeal. "I don't know what I'm supposed to do."

"Just roll 'em, roll 'em," he urged, "and let lady luck take care of the rest."

She grinned, shrugged, and carefully threw the dice toward the far end of the table, hunching over to watch them roll and waiting breathlessly to see whether she'd succeeded.

"Seven," the dealer called. "Pay the pass line."

"Shoot, that's what I call luck," the young man hooted, grabbing her around the waist and planting an impulsive kiss on her cheek. "You're doing better with beginner's luck than I've been doing with four years of practice."

"But I did terrible," she said shyly. "Look how far apart those dice are. And I thought you were supposed to roll the dice so they'd end up as close together as possible. Like horseshoes, sort of."

"Like horseshoes?" the young man laughed. "That's right, sweetheart, just like horseshoes."

The blond kid seemed too big for his uniform. His beardless face was painted with a sheepish grin, and his eyes sparkled with playfulness; he looked like a little boy kept after class for playing a prank. But his hands—meaty hands with long fingers and calloused knuckles—belonged to someone far more dangerous than the class prankster.

"Gee, Mr. Bianco," the kid said to his boss, the security

74

chief of the Mecca Hotel, "I was just trying to calm the guy down. I didn't meant to hurt him."

Louis Bianco leaned back in his chair and waved at the open file folder on his desk. "Mike, you busted the guy's jaw in two places," he said in a lazy, good-natured tone. "And he's got a concussion, too."

"Christ, I just hit him once," the young security guard protested. "And I did everything according to the book— when he started hassling the other players at the blackjack table, I just slipped up behind him and asked him to come with me. Very polite, Mr. Bianco, I swear! And then I took him to the restroom to sober him up under the faucet. But the old queer tried to grab me. I mean, he had me by the balls."

"And so you laid him out?" Bianco asked. "A paying customer with a good credit line?"

"I'm really sorry, Mr. Bianco," he said miserably. "Are you going to can me?"

Bianco smiled. The kid couldn't be more than eighteen or nineteen, fresh out of the local high school and moon-lighting as a security guard while waiting for a football scholarship at the University of Nevada. He looked so damned clean cut—and that's exactly how the hotel management wanted the guards to look—but he could break a jaw with one punch.

In the old days, Bianco thought, they didn't care how you looked as long as you could handle the rough stuff. That's why Louie Bianco—a young streetfighter from Hell's Kitchen with a broken nose and a few missing teeth—managed to land a job with the boys when they headed out to Vegas to work the casinos. And Bianco had done well enough as a strongarm, busting up burglars and cheats and freeloaders, bouncing drunks and deadbeats and hookers with the clap, laying out skimmers and snitches and unfriendly lawmen in the desert.

And then Louie Bianco made the hit that took him out of the strongarm crowd and made him one of the boys.

Bianco glanced toward the ceiling, where a camera lens linked his office to Edward Everett's bunker beneath the hotel. Bianco had supervised the construction of the bunker and the installation of the bugging equipment, working with a crew of carpenters, masons, and technicians who had been individually recruited from a dozen different countries throughout Central and South America to do the secret and sensitive tasks. When the job was done, they were paid off and flown back to their homes.

Only Bianco remained. Only Bianco knew the old man's secrets. And that was Bianco's lock on a lifetime contract as security chief of the Mecca Hotel.

Bianco glanced down at a control panel mounted under the desktop. One more secret that even the old man didn't know about—a mechanism that warned Bianco when the old man was monitoring his office in the bunker's control room. Whenever the cameras or microphones were turned on from the bunker, a tiny red light on Bianco's control panel woud start to flash.

But now the lights on the control panel were dark, and Bianco knew he was unobserved.

"Gee, Mr. Bianco," the young guard spoke up. "If you give me another chance, I swear it won't happen again. I swear."

"Mike, you know the hotel policy about dealing with customers—no rough stuff, not even if the customer has a meat cleaver at your throat," Bianco said quietly. "It's a different game in Vegas nowadays. When I got started, you had a free hand with drunks and deadbeats. And if you caught a chiseler at the tables, you could bury him upside-down in the desert—and you'd get a fat bonus for it. But those days are over, Mike, and the front office is going to want your ass."

"I really need this job, Mr. Bianco," the young guard said, staring at the floor. "Until the scholarship comes through, it's all I've got."

Bianco studied the young man's hands again. And then

he smiled. "I think we can handle the whole thing between ourselves, Mike," he said gently. "We'll send a couple of affectionate male nurses over to the guy whose jaw you broke. And we'll see about jacking up his credit limit and his comps for his next trip. And then maybe I'll just lose the report."

The guard's eyes widened. "Gee, Mr. Bianco, that would be awfully nice of you—"

"Don't worry about it, Mike," Bianco said, leaning forward in his chair and fixing his eyes on the young guard, who involuntarily straightened up under the stern gaze. "But don't forget about it, either. I may be needing some help, Mike, and I think you're the man for the job."

"What job, Mr. Bianco?" the guard asked.

"You'll stay on the casino detail, but I may ask you for a little overtime tomorrow night. Just to take care of a customer who may cause a little trouble."

"Whatever you say, Mr. Bianco," the guard stammered. "And thanks a lot, Mr. Bianco."

The telephone on the desk buzzed softly. Bianco stood up, shook the guard's hand firmly, and waited until the young man closed the door behind him. "Bianco," he said into the telephone, leaning back in his chair.

"This is Jones at the front desk," a timid male voice said. "I've got a guest here who's demanding to see Mr. Everett."

Bianco sighed. A half-dozen cranks and curiosity seekers called for Everett every day; the front desk personnel were briefed on how to turn away the inquiries with a few polite phrases. And there was no reason for an assistant manager at the front desk to bother him with yet another annoying request.

"Jones," Bianco asked in an acid whisper, "how long have you been working here?"

"I'm sorry, Mr. Bianco, I know the routine," the young man said, flustered and faltering. "But the guy's a doctor. And he says it's a life-or-death matter."

As the assistant manager spoke, the tiny red light on the control panel started blinking. Hell, Bianco thought, the old man is playing with his toys again.

"A doctor?" Bianco asked the assistant manager. "What's his name?"

"Hagen. He's an American, but his place of residence is Nicaragua. Says he treated Mr. Everett there, and he's got urgent medical information for him. A matter of life or death, he says."

Bianco pressed his fingertips against his temple. So Carl Hagen was suffering an attack of conscience, he thought. Or maybe he'd spent all the money—a chunk of cash that the doctor had called a fee, but which Bianco called a payoff —and now he was back for more. If only he'd handled the bastard like they did in the old days, Bianco scolded himself.

"Uh, Mr. Bianco," the assistant said after a long silence. "Do you want me to give him the standard brushoff about Mr. Everett, and tell him the hotel is full?"

"No, let him check in," Bianco said quickly. "Put him anywhere except in the Penthouse, do you understand? But tell him that Mr. Everett is not in residence at the Mecca. And tell me what room you're giving him."

"Yes, sir," the assistant snapped. "I'll put him in room 818, if that's okay."

"Good," Bianco said. He paused and then spoke again in a gentle voice. "And I want to commend you for bringing this matter directly to me, Jones. Of course, you'll let me know if Dr. Hagen checks out—"

"Yes, sir," he replied. The young assistant manager knew he'd taken a risk in calling Bianco directly, but now he was flushed with pleasure at the compliment. "I'll keep my eyes open, Mr. Bianco."

"And one more thing, Jones," Bianco said, reaching into a desk drawer and taking out a heavy, cream-colored envelope with a name written across the front in ornate calligraphy. "Will you send a bell captain up to my office—

I've got a personal invitation to be delivered to a guest in the Penthouse."

"Right away, Mr. Bianco," the assistant manager said, barely finishing the sentence before Bianco hung up.

Bianco ran his finger gently over the envelope to make sure that it was sealed. And then he turned it over, reading once again the name that a secretary in the guest relations department had so painstakingly lettered on the elegant stationery: *Ahmed Ibn Sayd.*

"Four hundred dollars?" John Morrissey asked again, his voice climbing to a new octave. "Are you kidding me? All I need is a new water pump—"

"Four hundred and seventy-nine dollars," the mechanic corrected him, shaking his head. "And up front, buddy."

Morrissey stared at the sand-chipped hood of his faded blue Alfa, and felt something close to bereavement at the loss of a loved one. He silently counted up the cash in his wallet. He'd called a dozen hotels and motels from the lobby of the Mecca before he found a vacant bed at eight bucks for the night.

"Listen, buddy," the mechanic said in a fatherly voice, wiping his hands solemnly with a greasy rag. "When you push an overheated engine on the desert road, you're just begging for a blown head gasket. And when you blow the gasket, you're just asking for a burnt-out transmission. And when you're driving a fancy Italian job, and you have to order parts from L.A., you're looking at four hundred and seventy-nine bucks."

Well, Morrissey thought, I'm not going to let a burnt-out transmission put an end to an odyssey that I've waited years to make. And I'm not going to abandon my Alfa in the middle of a godforsaken desert. Even if it takes my last dollar—and I have to limp back to West San Carlos and bum a couple hundred off Max, the CPA in the three-piece suit—I'm staying on the road.

"Okay," he said to the mechanic. "But how long will it take you to get her running again?"

The mechanic yawned, allowing his false teeth to click like tumbling dice. "Parts won't get here 'til Monday morning. If I can figure out how to put 'em in a twelve-year-old pasta jalopy, you should be able to hit the road by sundown. But I'm not going to let your hunk of junk litter up my garage unless you pay up front."

"All of it?" Morrissey asked. "Right now?"

"This is Vegas, buddy," the mechanic said. "If I don't take your dough now, by Monday morning it'll belong to the casinos. And I'll have an old heap with nobody to ransom it. You understand, buddy?"

"But I don't gamble—" Morrissey began.

The mechanic shrugged and yawned again. "Four hundred and seventy-nine bucks, right now, my friend."

Morrissey reached for his wallet and counted out the money, glancing dolefully at what remained—a five-dollar bill, some loose change, and the five-dollar chip that the young woman had stuffed into his pocket in front of the Mecca. That was a bit of good luck, Morrissey thought. Every buck counts now. "Well, that blows my hotel room," Morrissey said.

"Lots of folk breeze through a Vegas weekend without a place to stay—you just float through the casinos, watch a few lounge shows, and maybe some hot-'n'-bothered broad will let you share her bed."

"Great," Morrissey muttered. "But I can't even afford a cup of coffee to stay awake."

The mechanic rolled his eyes. "Christ, buddy, a cup of coffee at the Mecca can cost you two bucks—but you can drink all the booze you want just by hanging around the tables with a few chips in your hand. Watch for a table where there's a lot of action, a high-roller or two, and the casino waitresses will be pushing drinks by the trayfuls."

Morrissey reached into his coat pocket and fingered the

chip that the young woman had given him. Then he walked back toward the glittering outline of the Mecca Hotel.

Dr. Carl Hagen sat on the edge of the bed in his room at the Mecca, staring at the flickering images on the television set without focusing on them. An unlikely couple— a silver-haired male model in a tuxedo, and an overaged blonde with a fake English accent—carefully explained how to play all the games in the casino downstairs: blackjack, craps, roulette, baccarat, keno.

"And now," the blonde on the television set said, her English accent disappearing and her right eye closing in a lewd wink, "why don't you hurry down to the casino before some else picks up on *your* action?"

The television set fell silent for a moment, and then the same couple reappeared for yet another showing of the film on how to gamble. Hagen rose and walked to the writing desk, where he'd spread out the documents that had brought him from Managua to Las Vegas—a medical laboratory report, a letter marked "Addressee Unknown, Return to Sender," and a frayed newspaper clipping.

Hagen thought back to the night, a year and a half before, when he'd received the telephone call at his home on the outskirts of Managua. A cool whisper over the phone told him that an American tourist staying at the Oso de la Plata Hotel had taken ill and needed to see a doctor; the American embassy had recommended Hagen as an American doctor of great skill, sophistication, and discretion. The voice over the phone repeated the word twice: *Discretion.*

A few minutes later, a Cadillac limousine with darkened windows appeared at Hagen's home—and Hagen was escorted to the top floor of the hotel, where he was presented to a curious assortment of men: two or three tall, black, somber-looking bodyguards in moderately priced black suits with close-cropped haircuts; a short, wiry man with a broken nose and a pale, pockmarked complexion; and, in an elaborate hospital bed, an old man with long white hair and the yellowish pallor that comes from the prolonged absence of sunlight.

"Dr. Hagen," said the short man with the broken nose, "your patient's name is Edward Rogers. If you'll proceed with the examination, please—"

Hagen approached the bed and spoke softly to the old man. "Can you tell me what's troubling you, Mr. Rogers?"

"Aspirin," the old man barked, waving a Kleenex at the congregation that stood at the foot of his bed. "My head hurts like it's going to explode, and all they give me is aspirin."

The doctor glanced back at the short man, whose eyes shrieked with authority though his voice was silent. And Hagen knew instantly that he was receiving an instruction from the dangerous-looking man at the foot of the bed: Treat the old man, make him comfortable, but don't ask questions.

"How long have you been suffering from headaches, Mr. Rogers?" he asked brusquely, raising the old man's wrist and taking his pulse.

"Seems like forever. Seems like my head's busting open."

The short man spoke up. "He started complaining of the headaches six weeks ago. But they've become more severe in the last few days—or so he says."

Hagen proceeded with a thorough physical examination, drawing a blood sample, examining the old man's eyes and ears and throat, measuring his blood pressure, even sending him into the bathroom with one of the silent black bodyguards to produce a urine sample. He was troubled from the beginning by the old man's complaints—sensitivity to light and noise, a solid throbbing pain behind his ear, a loss of equilibrium, and a tremor in his left hand.

"It could be a stroke," he whispered to the short man, who pulled him away from the hospital bed. "Or something as simple as an inner ear infection. But it could also be a tumor in the brain. I'd like to hospitalize him for some diagnostic tests."

"For how long?" the short man asked.

"A week," Hagen said. "The tests will take only two or three days, but I'll have to send the samples to the States for a really competent analysis. And that'll take time."

The short man walked over to one of the black bodyguards for a whispered conversation, and then both of them bent over the old man for several minutes.

"Christ, Louie, you're not going to stick me in some banana-town morgue for a week," the old man stormed. "Just get the bastard to give me something for the pain. Something strong—none of this piss-shit aspirin! And then get rid of him!"

The man called Louie returned to Hagen's side. "You heard him, doctor," he said with a shrug. "What can you give him to kill the pain?"

Hagen frowned. "We can deal with the pain," he said slowly. "Morphine, if necessary. But if he's carrying a tumor inside his skull, he's in acute danger. He should be hospitalized tonight just in case he goes critical."

"Just write a prescription for the morphine, doctor," Louie said coolly. "And maybe something to tranquilize him, too. Of course, we'll need an open prescription—unlimited refills."

"But if it's a tumor," Hagen protested, "he shouldn't be tranquilized at all."

Louie led Hagen to a battered red-plaid suitcase that had been casually left on a chair near the door. He unzipped the flap, and the doctor saw that the suitcase was filled with neat stacks of worn U.S. currency.

"We're sorry to inconvenience you so late at night," Louie said, pulling out a thick stack of one-hundred-dollar bills. "And we appreciate your discretion, Dr. Hagen."

"I really must insist—" Hagen began to say. But his

eyes stayed on the money—it must be five thousand, or maybe more, he thought—and his voice fell silent even as his fingers closed around the bills.

"The prescriptions?" Louie reminded him. "Morphine and a strong tranquilizer? Unlimited refills?"

"Yes, of course, I'll telephone the dispensary at the Central Hospital," Hagen said, unable to meet Louie's chilly stare and unable to glance back at the old man. "They're open around the clock."

And Hagen backed out of the room with his eyes on the floor. One of the black bodyguards drove him back home; he counted the hundred-dollar bills in the darkness of the limousine, his guilt mounting as the number of bills rose past fifty and seventy-five, to an even one hundred—ten thousand dollars. A fee that paid for more than a house call after midnight; a fee that paid for *discretion*.

Out of discretion, Hagen put a false name on the blood and urine and cell tissue samples that he sent to the medical laboratory; as well as the X-ray negatives. Out of discretion, he did not try to call the mysterious Mr. Rogers to tell him that the lab reports confirmed the presence of a possible life-threatening tumor of the brain. But as the months passed, a sense of ravaging guilt drove Hagen back to the hotel where he had seen the old man. Out of discretion, the front desk told him that no one named Mr. Rogers had ever stayed at the Oso de la Plata Hotel.

Months passed, and the soiled money remained in a strongbox in Hagen's home. By now, he expected, the old man was dead and gone—a tumor is like a ticking time bomb, and it can bring an instant death at any moment. And so the doctor was doubly shocked when he saw the headlines in an American newspaper that he received by mail from the United States.

"MYSTERY MILLIONAIRE LAUNCHES VEGAS CASINO," the headline said. And the photograph—a much younger version of the man whom Hagen had seen in the

Managua hotel room—was captioned: EDWARD ROGER EVERETT.

Hagen's reservoir of guilt and remorse could not be held back by the ten thousand dollars in the strongbox. He wrote a letter to the old man—out of discretion, he marked it "Personal and Confidential"—and mailed the letter to the newly opened Mecca Hotel in Las Vegas. When the letter was returned—"Addressee Unknown"—Hagen packed the lab report, the letter, the newspaper clipping, and the ten thousand dollars in a suitcase for a flight to Vegas.

And now he was in the heart of the Mecca Hotel, but no closer to the old man named Edward Roger Everett. The young man at the front desk had insisted that Everett did not maintain a residence in Las Vegas, but the newspaper story about the hotel opening had reported that Everett himself moved out of his Nicaragua hotel penthouse and into specially designed quarters in the Mecca.

Hagen glanced out the window of his room, and he saw the distant lights of the Penthouse on the twenty-sixth floor of the Mecca. That's where the old man must be, Hagen thought, and that's where I must go to find him.

Two hours after sunset, the desert heat still hung over Vegas like a blanket. Yet, Lise Christian remained cool and comfortable inside the limousine. The chauffeur was taciturn; he knew this girl with the faint French accent was an important passenger, didn't know why. He didn't want to know why. So he drove her on the standard tour through the Strip, downtown, avoided the tackier sections of north Las Vegas, took her over to the Dam, and then toward Mount Charleston.

She had asked to be driven around—"just around"—and had said little. He knew enough not to speak unless spoken to.

"Do you like living in Las Vegas?" she asked.

"Not much," he said. "It tries to be a town. It is a

town. Little league, girl scouts, the university. But it doesn't quite make it. Too much heartache."

They talked for awhile. She was dying to get some things out. The driver sensed that. And he gradually eased up. This was not one of Bianco's chippies, or the daughter of a high-roller, or some Arab's girlfriend. This girl had class. He knew enough about people to be certain of that.

"Why did you come to Las Vegas?" the driver asked, surprised at his own boldness.

"On personal business," she said. "I've got an appointment tomorrow morning with the president of the First Mercantile Bank of Nevada."

"Jim Beilenson?" the driver asked. "On a Saturday. Vegas is a town where nothing much stops on weekends, but they still close the banks. Beilenson hasn't spent a weekend in Vegas since they put the railroad through." Vegas was a small town. Everybody knew everybody—or thought they did.

"But no, he's coming to my hotel," Lise persisted, wondering why she was trying so hard to convince a stranger of her sincerity. "My father set up a trust fund for me at the bank before he died, and I want to ask Mr. Beilenson some questions about him . . ."

"About your father?"

"That's right," Lise said, closing her eyes wearily, suddenly thinking of the faint light in the desert that she'd seen from the airplane. "I never knew him, and my mother wouldn't tell me much about him. So I came here to find out."

The driver began to get a feeling that he did not want to know this story. "Maybe you knew about him—Augusto Bertinelli." The driver felt a sharp almost physical press of fear. "That is the road to Mount Charleston," he said. "It's getting dark now so there's no point in going up there. The sunsets are spectacular."

Lise caught the man's tone. He was frightened. She sat back on the comfortable seat, watched the sherbet-colored buildings, the neon glows, the sunburned people as they rolled smoothly back into Las Vegas. This, she thought, was what colonies on the moon will look like when they are settled. In the war of light, the glitter of signs, the desert's night must always win. She was aware of that darkness behind the glow of the Strip's hotels and casinos. Perhaps people came here to gamble and watch the shows because that mystery always waited.

She felt a tremor, a sense of a presence in the car. It was uncanny. Her father. Out there somewhere. She couldn't shake the feeling.

Lise spoke to the driver again. "Take me back to the hotel." He nodded. He was relieved.

"Just once?" Linda asked in her little-girl's voice, pressing breasts against her husband's arm. "Just one little chip —and then we'll go upstairs, okay?"

John Warner picked at his new mustache and frowned at his new bride. She was begging for a chance to play the roulette wheel that they'd passed on their way to the elevator, and he could only think of the dollar-by-dollar budget he'd drawn up for their Vegas honeymoon. But now he had a new thought—a minute at the roulette wheel was a minute's postponement of his obligation in bed.

"Here," he said expansively, tossing a ten-dollar bill on the playing surface. "Have a ball."

The croupier turned the bill into two stacks of blank blue roulette chips. Linda perched on one of the stools and cupped the two stacks in her hands.

"Where should I put it, Johnny?" she squealed. "On thirteen? That's my lucky number, you know. Or maybe on our wedding date?"

"Anything you want, dear," John mumbled. "But you'll have a better chance by playing a color—red or black—or the odd-and-even bet."

"That's no fun, Johnny. It's good luck to bet on our wedding date." She carefully centered two chips on the playing surface over the number nineteen. The croupier set the big wheel in motion and then started the ball along the rim in the opposite direction. Linda held her breath as the wheel slowed down and the ball started popping in and out of the numbered slots.

"Double-o," the croupier called as the ball settled into one of the two green slots on the roulette wheel. And Linda watched mournfully as he swept away all the chips on the playing surface.

Linda bit her lower lip and then broke into a grin. She held up the brass room key that the stranger had given them when the front desk had turned them away. "Room 2001. I'm going to bet on two, and double-o, and one."

The roulette wheel spun again, and John held his bride's shoulders as they watched the tiny ball dance over the numbered slots. Linda squealed as the ball came to rest on number two, and the croupier stacked two more piles of blue chips on the sides of her bet.

"Now that's good luck, Johnny," she said, dangling the room key in front of his eyes. "And that room is going to be good luck when we get upstairs, too." Her voice dropped to a husky whisper. "Mirrors, Johnny! Mirrors over the bed!"

John Warner sighed. At least the lucky room number had paid off thirty-five to one, and the newly enriched stack of chips would keep his bride busy at the roulette table a little longer. He glanced impulsively at the ceiling and saw the one-way mirror panels of the eye-in-the-sky that kept a constant watch on the play below.

"Mirrors in the ceiling," John moaned to himself, rolling his eyes and pulling at his bristly mustache. "Mirrors in the ceiling."

Lawrence Johnson pivoted in his oversized desk chair and hit the button on the desk intercom. "Miss Percy?" he barked. "Did you hear anything from Mr. Sayd about my invitation?"

"No, sir," a woman's voice crackled over the speaker.

"You delivered it over an hour ago, didn't you?" he said irritably.

"Yes, sir," the woman answered, not bothering to explain why she delivered the invitation to Louis Bianco, the chief of security, rather than to the Arab gentleman in the Penthouse.

"Well, shit," Johnson said, "you let me know the moment he calls, okay?"

"Yes, sir," the woman replied, not bothering to explain why she would alert Bianco first.

Johnson pivoted back to the expanse of plate glass that opened his office to a view of the Mecca Hotel complex—the tower, the dome of the casino, the distant swimming pools and tennis courts. A damn fine piece of real estate development, Johnson thought. Too bad it still belongs to that antiquated, senile, paranoid bastard Edward Everett.

Oh, the old bastard had been decent enough at the beginning, when he recruited Lawrence Johnson from one of the hottest go-go mutual funds on the New York Stock Exchange and made him president of the Mecca Hotel and executive vice president of Everett Enterprises. Of course, Johnson had heard all the rumors about Everett—the exotic flights and voyages that were said to be cover stories for intelligence operations on behalf of the government; the shadowy connections with the underworld, including the New Orleans mafioso who made the big move to Vegas and took Everett with him; the strange fears and obsessions that drove the old man from one hideaway to another and finally to the tomblike security of his bunker underneath the Mecca.

But Johnson didn't care about the old man's eccentricities. All he cared about was the opportunity to run one of the world's largest and wealthiest privately held companies. He had some suitably ambitious—and suitably modern—plans for Everett Enterprises. Private ownership, he told Everett, was wasteful and old-fashioned; Everett Enterprises should go public, offer stock, and raise vast amounts of new

capital to finance expansion, diversification, unlimited international growth.

And the old man said no.

Johnson coaxed and cajoled and cooed; he brought in
consultants and financial analysts and stockbrokers to convince the old man; he produced elaborate twin-projection
slide shows to illustrate the untapped wealth that was available to Everett Enterprises if it went public. And all the
while he thought of his own shares—two points in the Mecca
Hotel, and 5 percent equity in Everett Enterprises—that
would skyrocket in value if the old man okayed the plan.

But the old man still said no.

Johnson was banished to his office at the Mecca Hotel;
the old man left him with the day-to-day operations of the
companies, but he refused to listen to any more appeals. He
sent messages through Louie Bianco—another dinosaur, Johnson thought, a throwback to the gangster days—and Alexander Tate, the tight-lipped Black Muslim who ran the
bunker like Martin Bormann ran the Fuehrerbunker. And
Lawrence Johnson had not seen the old man in the flesh
since the day he descended into his crypt below the Mecca
Hotel.

And good riddance! Johnson told himself. He still had
plans, brilliant plans, and he could carry them out even if
the old man refused.

He scanned his spacious office. The old man disap-
proved of opulence and self-indulgence among his paid em-
ployees, but Johnson was a man who sought wealth because
of the pleasures it afforded him. His corner office in the
Mecca Hotel was furnished with rare antiques and handmade
furniture; the carpet was mink, and the walls were covered
with the hides of specially raised Belgian cattle that allowed
each wall section to be hung with a seamless covering of fine
leather; the desk at which Johnson now sat was a massive
half circle of polished rosewood and teak, with ivory-and-
gold fittings and a bank of electronic toys.

At the far end of the office, in a sunken pit with a

wood-burning fireplace, was a living room arrangement whose centerpiece was an antique, satin-covered couch on which Napoleon had once made love to Josephine. Or so the antique dealer said, and his word was enough to stimulate Johnson's voracious appetite for women. With the lights turned down and the air conditioning turned up to compensate for the added heat of a roaring wood fire, he would personally interview a steady procession of young women whose applications for jobs as cocktail waitresses or slot-machine cashiers were routinely sent to his private office.

Of course, the old man had never seen the office. A separate suite of offices—small, sparsely furnished, staffed by a prim receptionist and a matronly secretary—was maintained just in case the old man decided to pay a visit. The decoy office was carefully decorated with business papers and open files, but it was an unneeded precaution. The old man never ventured from the bunker nowadays, and Johnson knew it.

He also knew about the cameras mounted in his bogus office, but he managed to find an unused suite of offices where no bugging equipment had been installed—and there Johnson built his own palatial hideway. He complimented himself on his cleverness and caution. The old man would not find out about his grand scheme until it was too late.

The intercom buzzed. "Yes, Miss Percy," Johnson snapped. "Did you hear from that Arab?"

"Yes, sir," the secretary said. "Mr. Sayd said he would be pleased to join you for a late dinner tomorrow night."

"Good, good," Johnson bubbled, rubbing his fingertips lightly over the star-and-crescent symbol that was inlaid in gold and ivory on the desktop. "Now call the boathouse at Lake Mead and make sure the yacht is ready for a dinner cruise at midnight—and tell the chef that he's got an Arab coming. Make sure he finds out what the hell it is that Arabs like to eat."

"Yes, sir," the secretary said, making careful notes on an open steno pad at her desk.

"And listen, Miss Percy, don't put any of this down in my engagement calendar or the office diary," Johnson added. "It's a private affair, and there's no need to clutter the records with it."

"Yes, sir," she answered. Miss Percy understood perfectly. And as soon as the intercom fell silent, she dialed the private office number of Louis Bianco.

Lucille Sheaffer paraded in front of the long mirror over the dresser, patting a stray hair into place and smoothing out her black silk pants. An hour before, she still looked like a schoolteacher from Denver; now, with her hair up and her cleavage carefully elevated by a pushup bra, she was ready to venture out into the casino of the Mecca Hotel. She had another three or four hours before Jack, the pit boss, would call on her to service his high-rollers. And she wanted to clear at least five hundred dollars before she started splitting with him.

Lucille avoided the stare of the guard who was stationed near the elevator on her floor, and she rode in silence with a middle-aged couple to the casino. And then she slipped into the chilly waters where she would glide like a barracuda for the next two days. When it was over, Lucille thought, she could be carrying a couple of thousand dollars back to Denver in her overnight bag.

She headed for one of the half-dozen lounges on the main floor of the Mecca. That's where she'd met the hard-eyed hooker who took her to task for putting out for free, the experienced pro who taught her all the techniques—how to douche after each trick, where to find the discreet clinics that would run Wassermann tests and perform quick abortions if necessary without asking names, how to get a slow trick to reach an orgasm by pulling up her knees and whispering those deliciously obscene words in his ear. And now Lucille was one of the pros.

None of the regulars were out yet, and so Lucille took an empty stool at the far end of the bar. The bartender brought her a club soda on the rocks without bothering to ask, and then left her alone. It was his job to recognize the hookers whose names were in the book of approved prostitutes in the front office, and it was her job to sit alone—and look alluring—until a trick came along.

The first one was a disheveled young man in a worn suède coat and faded blue jeans; he was distinctly out of place in the glittering elegance of the Mecca, but Lucille found herself attracted by his slim hips and piercing blue eyes. The best-paying tricks, she knew, would be older and better-dressed than the man at the bar—but they would also be fatter, clumsier, uglier. Lucille wet her lips quickly and slipped over to the stool next to him.

"My name is Lucy," she said huskily. "You're all alone tonight, I see."

"Huh?" he asked distractedly, glancing at her for the first time. "Oh, hello—Lucy."

She allowed the soft, silky blouse to brush against his arm. "I wouldn't call a cop if you tried to buy me a drink," she said. "And I didn't catch your name—"

"Morrissey," he said. "John Morrissey."

Lucy smiled. "Nice to meet you, John."

"Listen, uh, Lucy, I'd love to buy you a drink, but I'm close to flat broke—and I can't even afford to buy one for myself." He returned her smile, and Lucy felt a sentimental lump in her throat at his boyish expression. "I just needed someplace to sit down and kill some time."

"Oh," she said. A real pro wouldn't waste another word or another moment on a broke gambler, she reminded herself, but she didn't move.

Morrissey kept his eyes on her for a long moment. "Listen, Lucy," he said slowly, "I don't know much about Vegas, but someone told me that I could cadge a drink at one of the tables just by hanging around. Is that true?"

"Yeah, sure," Lucy said, smiling and then scolding herself for smiling. Christ, the bum was trying to freeload a few drinks—and she was wasting her precious minutes on him. "Just be sure you've got a few chips in your hand, or the pit boss will nix your order after the cocktail waitress leaves the table."

"Chips?" Morrissey repeated. He patted the pocket where he carried a five-dollar bill and a few dimes—and then he remembered the chip that the young woman had pushed into his pocket. "Chips," he said again.

Lucy looked up as another man strolled into the bar and pointedly took a seat next to her. The badge on his lapel identified him as one of the undertaking conventioneers; the nervous smile on his face identified him as a horny but guilt-ridden trick. She sighed, smiled once more at John Morrissey, and turned to the man on the other side.

"My name is Lucy," she said. "I wouldn't call a cop if you tried to buy me a drink."

Lucy was a pro, and now she was acting like one. She didn't notice the young man slip off the stool and wander into the casino, a single chip in his hand.

The old man watched attentively as Alexander Tate prepared the syringe for his next injection of morphine. The pain was much worse now, throbbing angrily behind his ear and stabbing into his eyes, but he could not leave the bank of television monitors that were now his only weapon. The hours of observation had stoked the pain to a new intensity, but at least he had learned the truth—his wealth, his power, his concrete-and-steel cocoon, his electronic umbilical cord all counted for nothing now. He had been betrayed, and he was all alone.

"*They're coming for you, old man,*" the voice over the telephone had said. "*It's over for you now, old man.*"

He watched Tate's smooth black hands as the bodyguard filled the glass syringe with morphine and then cleaned a patch of skin with an alcohol swab. His movements were quick and sure; he had been attending the old man—feeding him, washing and dressing him, medicating him—for nearly three years. And how easy it would be to inject a fatal bubble of air in a vein, or slip a fatal dose of poison into a hot bowl of soup. If it had been Tate's voice over the telephone, then the old man knew that he was already dead and buried inside the bunker.

But surely, the old man debated with himself, if Tate wished to betray him, to kill him, he would have done it sooner. Back in Managua, when he could have walked away with a million dollars in cash in a plaid suitcase. Or in Geneva, when he could have walked away with the gold bullion that Everett was withdrawing from the Swiss banks for redeposit in his own vault beneath the Nevada desert. Surely Tate would have acted before the entourage moved into the bunker, where every movement was monitored, where every act of treachery would reveal itself immediately.

No, the old man corrected himself, it was impossible to predict when a man would turn into a betrayer. He had spent a lifetime and a vast fortune in an attempt to reduce every risk to a minimum—earthquake and flood, drought and famine—but there was one risk that could not be avoided: the risk of betrayal. He knew that every man carried within himself a hunger for treachery; in fact, Everett had built his power on the weakness of others who could be manipulated to betray on command.

Tate eased the needle into the old man's flesh, and Everett grimaced as if in terrible pain—but he was thinking not of the injection, but of a man named Augusto Bertinelli, a greasy gangster who fancied himself a Renaissance prince, the only man who had ever succeeded in humiliating Everett by taking away one of his playthings. Not that Everett had felt any need of the young woman in New Orleans on that night, not that he had felt any love or even any carnal desire for her youthful beauty. No, he had been insulted and degraded by the simple fact that another man had taken something away from him. And he vowed then and there that Bertinelli would pay for the insult.

How he had loathed Bertinelli from that first moment in New Orleans! How he had raged in silent fury when he heard that the gangster had gone so far as to marry the young woman. How he had ached with rage when Bertinelli had the nerve to bring his new wife to Las Vegas for the grand opening of their first joint venture in the Nevada desert. And all the while the dirty wop gangster would piously sentimentalize about loyalty, and fidelity, and the sanctity of a man's word of honor.

"When I have given my word, and a man has given me his hand," Bertinelli had said pompously as they shook hands, "we are bound unto the grave."

The old man sneered as his bodyguard removed the needle and dabbed the skin again with a swab. Bertinelli had been wrong all along about loyalty and fidelity and honor. Oh, the collaboration had been successful enough: Everett had fronted for Bertinelli and his black-money boys, buying new companies, creating new industries, doubling and then redoubling his own empire while laundering the soiled cash of his silent partners; and Bertinelli, in exchange, had taught Everett about a new era and a new enterprise: Las Vegas.

And then, when he had learned everything that Bertinelli could teach him, Everett put an end to the collaboration. "Unto the grave," the wop had said. And that's where it ended. The Vegas enterprise slipped from Bertinelli's dead fingers into Everett's grasping hands. And the blade that loosed Bertinelli's grip on the Vegas empire was wielded not by Everett himself, nor by Everett's loyal retainers, but by a man whom Bertinelli had trusted with his life. That was Everett's final insult to the man he loathed; that was his way of showing Bertinelli what a fool he had been. A fool, the old man repeated to himself, a fool who died because he believed his own foolishness.

"Are you ready to dine?" Tate asked quietly as he cleaned the syringe and packed it away.

The old man returned his gaze. Could it be Tate? Had through his blood and eased the pain. And Tate stood by

96

in silence, watching the old man's face, waiting for the old man's words.

The old man returned his gaze. Could it be Tate? Had it been Tate's voice over the telephone? Was Tate ready to betray him just as another man had once betrayed Augusto Bertinelli?

"Alexander," the old man said slowly, "what is it you call yourself on the outside? Your Muslim name?"

"Ali Akhbar," the bodyguard said softly, his eyes still on the old man. It was an old game, but the old man never tired of it.

"Ali Akhbar," Everett repeated, trying to glimpse any sign of anger or resentment in the black man's face. "And you don't mind that I call you by your old name, Alexander?"

"No, sir," Tate answered. "That was our understanding, sir."

The old man nodded. In an effort to reduce the risk of betrayal, he'd decided to assemble a personal staff of Black Muslims to serve as his bodyguards, attendants, nurses. Their faith was an added measure of security for the old man; since they did not drink or gamble or stray from their wives, the Muslim bodyguards would be immune to the temptations that Everett himself had often used to lead other men away from their vows of loyalty and fidelity and honor. He paid them well, and he asked little more of them than their own faith demanded—sobriety, orderliness, discipline.

And yet the old man had put them to yet another test of discipline by asking them whether he could call them not by their Muslim names but by their old heathen names. They did not object. They did not bargain for more money as a compensation for this eccentricity. They merely nodded— cool, dispassionate, almost chilly—and went about their tasks in the bunker, deferential but dignified.

"Alexander, I wonder if you sometimes hate me for calling you by that name," the old man probed. "I mean,

97

Alexander Tate is a white man's name, isn't it? A Christian name? A slave name?"

"Yes, sir," Tate said. "But these things mean little in the eyes of Allah. And if it is your preference, Mr. Everett—"

"Yes, Alexander, that is my preference," the old man said. A fire of resentment might be burning behind those cool black eyes, but he revealed nothing. And the old man knew that he had to gamble on what he saw. He was the hunter again, he was the warrior again, and he needed eyes and ears outside the bunker. Betrayal was stalking him, and he needed an obedient dog to raise a cry when it came close.

"Alexander," he said. "I have something for you to do."

"On the outside, Mr. Everett?"

"That's right," the old man said. "Tomorrow night, Lawrence Johnson will be taking out the hotel yacht for a dinner cruise on Lake Mead. He will be taking along a guest, an Arab named Sayd. And I need to know what the two of them talk about. I need to know why they are talking at all. Do you understand, Alexander?"

"Yes, sir," the bodyguard said. "And now, Mr. Everett, are you ready to dine?"

The old man nodded vacantly, but his thoughts were elsewhere. Alexander would take care of Johnson and the Arab, but there were so many other threats, so many other impulses, so many other images that appeared on the old man's bank of television monitors and burned themselves into his imagination. Johnson, Bianco, the doctor from Managua, the Arab—and the young woman in the Penthouse.

The old man felt a new stirring in his loins, a long-forgotten hunger, a demanding curiosity about the black-haired, black-eyed woman who had aroused something dangerous inside him. Yes, he was the hunter again; yes, he was the warrior again. And now he would be the conqueror again. The old man's finger crawled to a button on the console, and the image of an empty bed in an empty Penthouse room filled one of the television screens.

Gone, the old man thought in a sudden panic. But then the panic subsided and a new confidence filled him. She will be back, he said to himself. She will be back, and I will be waiting for her.

four

Outside, beyond the heavy blackout curtains that hang in every hotel room in Las Vegas, the sun was burning relentlessly. But the hotel room was dark, cool, and comfortable. A bottle of champagne in an ice bucket was close at hand on the nighttable, and the room-service waiter had delivered his second steak sandwich promptly. And the four local channels on the television set were all showing movies that he remembered from the Saturday matinees of his childhood: *Sahara*, with Humphrey Bogart, *It's a Wonderful Life*, with Jimmy Stewart, *Sunset Boulevard*, with Bill Holden, and—

The telephone rang. The man who sat on the king-sized bed amid an array of magazines and packs of cigarettes was struck with a stab of apprehension. Who knew that he was in Vegas besides the junket organizer who had taken his three hundred dollars back in Jersey? And what the hell did the pleasant fat man want in the middle of the day?

"Yes?" he said into the telephone. "Who is it? What do you want?"

"Oh, it's just me," gurgled the fat man who had organized the junket. "I've been wondering why we haven't seen you down in the casino yet? I mean, we've been here for a full day, and I'll bet your money is burning a hole in your pocket."

The man on the bed glanced around the darkened room. He had everything he wanted in Las Vegas: Three bottles of expensive Scotch ordered from room service—on the junket's tab. An empty suitcase waiting to be filled with hotel towels and washcloths and ashtrays. A television set and a bottle of champagne and a steak sandwich.

But that's not why the hotel sold junket tours. They want the junketeers in the casino, where the hotel has a good chance to earn back the cost of the room and the booze and the stolen towels. A junketeer who hides in his room is no better than a thief in the eyes of the hotel, and the junket organizer, and—

"So why don't you get on down here and make a bet, okay?" the fat man wheezed over the telephone.

"Sure, sure, I'll be down," he mumbled in response. "I'm just freshening up after the flight."

"Yeah, well, it don't take eight hours to freshen up, don't you see? And believe me, the pit bosses know a junketeer on sight, and they keep real good records about how much you bet and how much you lose, don't you see?"

"Sure, sure," he answered. "I'll be right down." He hung up the phone and then picked it up quickly. "Housekeeping? Listen, somebody forgot to put towels in my room —that's right, no towels at all. Why don't you send up a half-dozen sets, okay? I like to stay clean, okay? I take a lot of baths, okay? And, listen, there'll be a buck or two in it for making a special trip."

He lifted himself out of the bed, but his eye was caught by the opening credits of the new movie that was starting on the television set. *The Fighting Seabees*, with John Wayne —one of his favorites. He settled back against the pillows on the bed and reached for the telephone once more. "Room service? Could you send up another steak sandwich, please? And maybe another fifth of Cutty Sark while you're at it. No, I don't need ice—just the booze, thank you."

Moe Black bent forward while the Three Blind Mice compared their tallies for the blackjack pit. The action at the tables had been heavy in the four hours since their last inspection tour of the casino, but the house's win at the blackjack tables was running low. Odds might bring the percentages up or down by a few points, but Moe's experienced eye and seasoned intuition had been alerted by the dip in the casino's take.

"Might just be a bad run," one of the other Three Blind Mice suggested, running his mechanical pencil down a column of figures on his clipboard. "Maybe it'll even out by the next round."

Moe shook his head. "I checked with the pit bosses," he said, squinting slightly as he surveyed the blackjack pit. "No big runs. No big stakes. Just steady action all evening."

The others nodded. A run of good luck and a player betting the limit could bring the casino's win down, but the immutable house advantage should prevail over a few hours of steady play. Unless, of course, someone wasn't playing by the rules.

"Call upstairs and tell them to watch the blackjack pit carefully," Moe said quietly to the others. "And I'm going to stay on the floor for awhile."

Moe moved away, floating through the bustling casino, watching the action with eyes that never settled on a single table or a single gambler, picking out the telling details without pausing for a moment. The dealers and pit bosses, alive to the presence of one of the Three Blind Mice, stiffened slightly as he swept past them. But the players hardly noticed the elderly man with the clipboard under his arm.

He noticed them. He saw the hookers sitting in with two-dollar bets at tables where the big spenders were playing. He saw the counters whose moving lips and fingers betrayed their attempts to beat the house advantage by keeping track of the cards. He saw the dealers whose sloppy handling of the cards allowed the players occasionally to spot the hole card. But he didn't see the kind of cheat—dealer or player—who could be running down the win.

Moe shrugged and slipped into the blackjack pit. The pit bosses floated toward him as if they were being drawn by an invisible cord, and the dealers nearby inclined their heads in an effort to catch his whispered words.

"Keep an eye on the action," he said without moving his lips. "We may have a counter at work. Maybe a team. Keep the shoe on the shuffle after one deck is dealt. Pass the word to all the dealers."

The bosses nodded silently, and Moe returned the gesture. He glanced at his watch—it was nearly ten-thirty, and the dinner show would be emptying soon—and then drifted through the blackjack pit to the nearest lounge. He'd treat himself to a cup of coffee with a shot of whiskey, and then he'd go upstairs for a look through the one-way mirrors and the eye-in-the-sky cameras.

Moe took a seat by the low hedge of plastic greenery that separated the lounge from the casino, and he let his eyes wander over the crowds around the tables. The faces told him a lot, and Moe prided himself on his ability to read the eyes of a total stranger. The young man in the suède coat, for instance—Moe knew instantly that he was edging up to the blackjack table with no intention of dropping a buck in the action; the guy was just looking to pick up a free drink, and then maybe he'd drift down the Strip to the little clubs or the downtown casinos where the nickel-and-dime tables could make a tenspot last all evening.

Moe smiled. A tough-assed pit boss would probably

ignore the guy; a sadistic one would let him stay but cancel every drink order after he'd given it to a cocktail waitress. But Moe was feeling charitable. After all, it was Friday night—and tomorrow he'd be in the front row of the synagogue for the rabbi's sermon. And he'd be in front of the receiving line for the rabbi's handshake.

Moe's eyes swept over the crowd in search of the telltale signs of a counter—one hand in a coat pocket manipulating a blackjack computer, or one ear cocked in the direction of an accomplice who would count the cards and whisper the information to the player. But what stopped Moe's eyes was not a counter or an accomplice but a young woman with midnight black hair, intense black eyes, and a silky white gown.

Moe stared across the casino at the woman as she entered from the taxi entrance and stood hesitantly near the private elevator for the Penthouse. Even from a distance, his intuitive eye was sparked by the sight of the woman's face; he studied her features and scanned his memory for the recollection that would place her in context. Was she the wife of a high-roller? The girlfriend of an old acquaintance? A hooker, a chip hustler, an aspiring chorus girl—Moe struggled to identify the stunningly familiar face.

The elevator doors opened, and the young woman stepped inside. A moment later, she was gone—and all that remained in Moe's eyes was the shadow of a dimly remembered dream. He felt bewildered, bewitched, bedazzled; for an instant, he was unsure and unsteady, wondering if the vision had not been an illusion of an aging mind.

But then Moe remembered.

He rose from the table and took two steps to the bar, calling sharply for the house phone. He dialed the guard's station on the Penthouse floor, and waited impatiently as the guard moved from his chair by the elevator to the telephone.

"Penthouse," the voice snapped.

"Moe Black calling," he said brusquely. "Did a girl in a white dress just get off on your floor?"

"Yes, sir, Mr. Black," the guard answered. "But don't worry, sir, she's a registered guest. She's staying in 2630."

"Name?"

The guard fell silent as he double-checked the guest list and wondered at the pronunciation of the guest's unusual first name.

"Christian," he said slowly. "Lise Christian."

"God in heaven," Moe said out loud, lowering the receiver gently to the bar. "The little girl has come back to us after all."

The final curtain fell on the dinner show performance of *Salaam, Sultan,* and the house lights in the main showroom slowly came up. Visions of bare breasts, bare bellies, bare buttocks filled Ira Tuthill's head and blinded him to the stout, serious woman with the bun who sat next to him at the long, narrow table.

"My goodness, Ira," his wife bleated for the fiftieth time. "Those men were half naked."

"And the women, too," he mumbled, still seeing their flawless fiigures, their twitching breasts and fluid hips, their hardened smiles.

"It's disgusting," his wife announced firmly. "I'm going to complain to the management. And to the Funeral Directors Association, too. They should have better sense than to bring God-fearing people to a Sodom and Gomorrah like this."

"The magician and his disappearing tiger were awfully nice," Ira offered mildly, still thinking of the 120 pairs of young breasts on which he had just feasted.

"Sodom and Gomorrah," his wife stormed.

"But Sally Martin sang awfully well," Ira suggested hesitantly, still thinking of the intimate view of her spangled crotch that he had caught when the two boy dancers in jockstrap-tuxedos threw her into the air.

"And just look what Las Vegas did to that poor woman," his wife railed. "I've seen every one of her movies, right back to 1944, and now she's doing those *despicable* dances and singing those *dirty* songs with a bunch of naked boys. And a woman of her years—she must be fifty if she's a day."

"She looks awfully good for fifty," Ira said, sneaking a quick disappointed glance at his forty-eight-year-old wife. "Did you see her legs?"

Gertie Tuthill poked one finger into her husband's stomach. "Ira, we're marching right back to our room, packing our things, and going home right now."

"But Gertie, what about the Wayne Newton show tomorrow night?" he said soothingly. "And the Funeral Directors Auxiliary is having a thanksgiving breakfast on Sunday morning at the Baptist church. You know you were looking forward to that, Gertie."

"But the naked men," she insisted in a somewhat softer voice. "The lewd dances."

"And don't forget, Gertie, that we paid for everything in advance. We'll lose all that money if we go home now."

Ira noted with some relief that his wife's face had returned to its customary paleness after flushing red with anger. "And you wanted to see the Sally Martin Film Festival in the theater on the shopping arcade," he urged. "They're showing every one of her movies, one right after the other. Now that's a real treat, isn't it?"

"All right, all right, we'll stay," Gertie conceded. She waved a finger in her husband's face: "But you've got to promise me that neither of us will have to see another naked body for the rest of the weekend."

Ira gulped and felt pinpricks of cold sweat beneath his clothing. "I promise, Gertie," he said hoarsely, still thinking of the promise in the eyes of 120 half-naked chorus girls. "I promise."

Sally Martin's flesh-colored body stocking hung limply

over a chair in her dressing room. Her flesh-colored skin was considerably paler, and more flaccid, than the covering that the audience had just seen during her six-minute appearance as the star of *Salaam, Sultan*. But the young man who now prepared to lower himself between her pale, flaccid thighs didn't care. He was a trouper, and he acted like one.

"Ride me, ride me, ride me," she grunted into the young dancer's ear, thrusting her hips upward to meet his narrower, leaner, more compact body. "Oh, yeah, fuck me! Fuck me! Fuck me good, Bobby!"

"It's so good," he lied, simulating a breathless grunt on each downward stroke. "It's so good, Sally, so hot and wet and tight—"

"Oooh!" she shrieked, digging her fingernails into his taut buttocks. "Oooh, Bobby, I'm coming, I'm coming, oh Bobby, are you coming too?"

"Yes, yes, yes," he lied again, ramming harder and harder on each word. "Oh, yes, Sally! Oh, it's so good."

The dancer held her for a few more moments—he was a trouper, Bobby reminded himself, and he had to act like one—and then rolled off. He reached for a cigarette a bit too desperately, nearly knocking over Sally Martin's third brandy since the dinner show ended eleven minutes before.

"Bobby, I've been laid by all the greats—Gable, Cooper, Grant," Sally lied. And then, with more sincerity, she continued: "I've never been laid right until I met you."

Bobby Reed smiled affectionately at the woman who was six years older than his own mother. He'd come to Vegas to dance, and he was convinced of his own considerable talent as a dancer. But he wasn't a fool. When the casting director picked him out of two hundred boy dancers at an open audition and sent him to an executive office in the Mecca Hotel, he understood that it didn't have much to do with dancing. And when the man in the executive office explained what his duties would be, Bobby nodded confidently. Although he was only nineteen, Bobby knew exactly what was expected of him, and he delivered. He was a trouper, and he acted like one.

And Bobby had seen enough of Sally Martin's musty old movies of the late forties and early fifties to know that she had never been laid by Clark or Gary or Cary. She'd been a busty ingenue, a girlfriend of the mysterious and powerful Edward R. Everett, and a carefully manufactured leading lady for Everett's independent film studio. And her former lover had been kind enough to find her work in Las Vegas when he sold everything but Sally Martin's contract to a larger studio. They wanted Everett's cameras and sound-stages and backlots, but they didn't want Sally Martin.

Now Sally was installed as the top-billed performer in *Salaam, Sultan*—but her six-minute, twenty-two-second pre-recorded song-and-dance number was almost an afterthought in the spectacle of chorus lines and magic acts and ex-travagant stage fantasies. Bobby Reed was one of two boy dancers who sang live backup while she moved her lips to the prerecorded song over the loud-speakers; he was one of two boy dancers who leaped in the air, and pranced across the stage, and manhandled the leading lady, who wasn't spry enough to do much more than smile during all the exertion.

"You make me a real woman, Bobby," she whispered into his ear between swigs of brandy and puffs of a mari-juana cigarette. "You remind me that I'm still a real woman, Bobby."

"And you make me feel like a real man, Sally," Bobby said, thinking about the handsome blond animal trainer in the disappearing tiger act.

Sally sighed deeply, and then pushed him playfully from the king-sized bed in her suite on the Penthouse floor of the Mecca Hotel. "Now leave me alone," she said girl-ishly, pulling her silk dressing gown around her shoulders. "We've only got a couple of hours until the late show, and you know that I'm no good on stage unless I've had my little beauty rest."

Bobby slipped out of the bed, bent over to kiss her,

and dressed quickly. "I'll come back at eleven-thirty so we can do warmups together," he said. "And don't forget, love —no more brandy until after the show."

He was a trouper, and he was doing his job.

"Oh, you're so good to me, Bobby," Sally said, and then she started to sob. "An old woman like me, a drunken old woman, and you're so good to me."

"Don't cry now," he scolded, kissing her once more. "Just sleep, love, and you'll be looking like a flower for the late show."

The sobbing subsided as he stroked her shoulder. "Oh, Bobby," she said in a slurred, sleepy voice. "I love you so, Bobby. And I've got a plan, Bobby. A plan for the both of us. A plan that will keep us together always. I've got a plan, Bobby—"

"Shhh," Bobby purred. "Sleep now, love, and we'll talk later."

Bobby turned off the bedside lamp, finished dressing in the dark, and then backed out of the room. He knew about the plan, of course, but he needed to find out more. The man in the executive office wanted the details, the destination, the departure date. And it was up to Bobby to deliver the information.

He was a trouper, Bobby told himself, and he would act like one.

He did not know the origin of the impulse which came over him as he stood watching the white-shirted, green-aproned dealer who turned the wheel of fortune. The man had the face of a country tractor driver, friendly, dependable. John Morrissey was not aware that the soft, snapping purr of the wheel of fortune with its memories of county fairs, and carnivals, its evocation of fortune tellers and spun sugar, was always put at the entrance of the casinos, always manned by a decent-looking chap who stood for confidence and sincerity in this hall of illusion.

The five-dollar chip was in his hand. Without quite

realizing it, John placed it on the spread. On the five-to-one space. The dealer gave him a warm smile—and was it a wink? Morrissey felt an odd sensation is the pit of his stomach. The root chakra, one of his students who was into yoga had called it, the primitive sensor at the base of being which drew its energy from the earth and brought luck. He had always sneered at the easy way the kids went in for the occult, a sign of twilight times, times of desperation. But that was the way of his life at this moment.

He hardly looked as the dealer reached up and swung the big wheel, its lights and numbers blurring as it sped around, the leather tab snapping as it struck the two brass pins between which the winning odds would appear. The wheel slowed down, then with heart-chilling slowness snapped until it reached the end of its swing. "Five to one. A winner on the big wheel," the dealer intoned, in a Kansas voice flat with the vastness of wheatfields.

Reaching into the rack of chips, the dealer put five of them next to John's lucky chip. He reached down and picked it up, put it in his shirt pocket. There was something to it. That girl. She was his luck. He had to see her again.

He felt a sense of exhilaration as he walked over to the nearest blackjack table. It was being dealt by a slight and slender girl with the look of a failed country singer. He had twenty-five dollars of *their* money and felt rich, richer than he had with the hundreds he had had before the car died on him. He stood about two feet from the table and watched the action. Morrissey knew something about the game; it was the chess of the odds players, full of strategies on betting and pulling cards to beat the dealer, a test of memory as the cards came out of the shoe and the odds on getting low or picture cards changed.

I ought to get a chair in the lobby, where I can see the entrance, John thought, so I can intercept the girl. What he didn't know was that she had returned while he was at the wheel of fortune. Morrissey figured that he could see her on the way to the room elevators if he sat at the black-jack table.

The blackjack girl dealt with all the animation of a robot but Morrissey was fascinated by the players. There was a man in a golf cap and plaid shirt, toothless as Popeye, who bet fifty dollars each in two separate betting boxes on the table. Alongside him was a woman wearing slacks and a top which looked as though they were made from flocked purple bedspreads. She bet the minimum and kept talking about her vacation in Hawaii. The third player was a heavy smoker and the blue haze around him kept Morrissey hanging back.

Popeye was winning steadily. He played a cautious game, locked in his private counting house. For that was what he was doing. Counting the face cards which were dealt. Morrissey knew enough about blackjack and winning theory to see that. Like most mathematicians and statisticians he had his fascination with odds, probabilities, and systems. It was no accident that the great mathematicians of the past often became interested, as the great and tragic scholar Cardano, or, after him, Pascal, had, in gambling, in games of chance.

Blackjack was deceptively simple: the player needed to get a higher score than the dealer. But if he drew cards that totaled more than twenty-one he lost. Picture cards counted for ten. The ace was either one or eleven. Number cards counted their face value. The dealer gave two cards to each player face down—to herself the first down, the second up. The player could hit, take another card or even more and try to improve his hand. The dealer must stand at 17, hit at 16. If he went over 21, he had to pay any player with under 21. If the dealer had under 17, 18, 19, 20, or 21, he collected from those who had less than he and paid those who had more. A standoff or "push" meant dealer and player had the same total—in which case neither won.

Except for the burbling lady, there wasn't much talk

at the table. The pit boss kept watching Popeye; Morrissey watched the scene. Once the pit boss signaled the dealer to shuffle long before the shoeful of cards ran out.

Finally, the cigar smoker left and John eased into his seat. He took the five five-dollar chips from his pocket. He bet two five-dollar chips. The cards came. He looked at the first, a jack of spades; the second, an ace. *"Blackjack,"* he called. Adrenalin raced through his blood. He felt alive, excited. The girl put three five-dollar chips down. Blackjack paid off at one and a half to one. The pit boss signaled the cocktail waitress. "Would you care for a drink—compliments of the Mecca?" she asked. John nodded. "Early Times and water," he said. He smiled, thinking, a high-roller's drink. He didn't really know how high.

Two tables away, another young man glanced anxiously from the playing surface to the dealer to the pit boss. The young man checked his watch for the hundredth time since he sat down at the blackjack table with a stake of one hundred dollars. In his coat pocket, he calculated quickly, was close to a thousand dollars in chips. At eleven o'clock sharp, he was due to leave the tables and return to the room on the seventh floor where the others were waiting.

"Bets, please," the dealer said.

The young man paused a moment, as if waiting for inspiration, and then pushed five twenty-five-dollar chips in front of him. And, for the hundredth time since he sat down at the table, he prayed that the inspiration would be proven right.

The dealer pulled the cards crisply from the shoe, dealing first to the blonde at the end of the table, then to the man in the hound's-tooth sports jacket, and finally to the nervous young Oriental whose stack of chips never seemed to grow in spite of his run of good luck. The dealer's card was a six, and he nodded at the blonde: "Card?"

The blonde shook her head. The man in the hound's-tooth took two cards and then went bust with a third. The dealer glanced at the young Oriental, who once again seemed to wait for inspiration and then brushed his hand toward the dealer—no cards.

The dealer turned up his hole card, and—with a six and a three showing—dealt himself another six, and put himself over twenty-one with an eight of diamonds.

The blonde's cards added up to seventeen, and the dealer paid off two dollars against her two-dollar bet. And then the nervous Oriental at the other end of the table showed a seven of clubs, and a six of hearts—a total of only thirteen. He grinned nervously while the dealer paid out a hundred twenty-five dollars against his bet.

The young Oriental nodded, checked his watch again—it was eleven o'clock sharp—and left the table. He half expected to feel a guard's hands on his shoulder, half expected to see a pit boss looming up ahead of him, but reached the elevator bank without being stopped.

And then he was gone.

The security guard and the pit boss who might have stopped him were too busy with the old man in the golf cap to notice the nervous gambler who started with a hundred bucks and dragged a thousand in an hour. And they hardly noticed when, an hour later, the same young Oriental reappeared at another blackjack table and repeated his lucky run.

Lucille Sheaffer stared dubiously at the glass coffee table and shook her head, signifying disbelief rather than unwillingness, but the old man in the old-fashioned tuxedo misunderstood.

"All right, chickie," he said gruffly, "I'll make it three hundred. Three hundred dollars, okay?"

She looked up and nodded slowly. "Three hundred's okay," she said. "Up front, please."

"Yeah, yeah, chickie," he said irritably, counting out

two hundred in fifty-dollar bills and then dropping a one-hundred-dollar chip on top. "You'd think I was some down-and-dirty sailor for God's sake. Up front, she says."

The old man pointed at the coffee table. "Okay, okay, let's get going so I can win some of this back at the tables," he said, already untying the purple cummerbund. "Take it off, chickie, and crawl under the table."

Lucy slipped easily out of her loose-fitting pants and blouse, then peeled off her bra and panties, and took one tentative step toward the coffee table. The pro who'd turned her out taught her a great deal—including how to dress in clothing that was easy to take off—but she'd never mentioned the kind of john that this old man turned out to be.

"Under the table, chickie," he commanded. He produced a bright red lollipop from the top drawer of the dresser, and handed it to her. "Take this. Suck on it! Suck on it good, chickie. That's what I want."

Lucy crawled carefully under the glass coffee table and then reclined on her back, knees up, the lollipop in her mouth. The old man was already undressed, wearing only stockings and calf-high garters, and a moment later he was squatting on the table. When Lucy looked up, she saw that he had positioned himself squarely over her face.

"Craps," the old man said conversationally. "Chickie, did you ever wonder why they call it craps? Because people love their own shit, that's why. They love it, they want to rub it all over themselves, but mommy and daddy say it's dirty, no, no, it's *dirty*. So they come here, they play *craps* —do you hear me, chickie? *Craps*." And then, in a whispered aside he ordered: "Suck on it! That's what I want, chickie. Suck on it good."

Lucy noticed that one of the old man's hands was between his legs, the other was resting casually on one bended knee, and he continued to banter as he squatted over her face on the coffee table.

"*Craps*, chickie! They love to handle those dice, *rub* them, *blow* on them, *tease* them." Lucy sucked frantically on the lollipop; the old man's hand was moving faster now, and he was grunting and straining as he talked. "Craps, that's my game. Craps! Craps! Craps!"

Lucy noticed the watch on the old man's wrist, and she tried to read the time despite the violent up-and-down jerking motion. Almost eleven-thirty, she said to herself. Christ, I hope the old guy gets off soon. Jack's high-rollers will be off the tables at midnight and looking for some high-priced action. Lucy closed her eyes and sighed.

The old man peered down at her from his perch on the table. "Open your eyes, chickie. Open your eyes, and *suck* on it, *suck on it*." He was grunting harder now, and Lucy's mouth worked desperately on the lollipop as she tried to keep from retching. "Here it comes, chickie. *Craps*, that's my game. Here it comes, here it comes, oh god, here I come!"

The elevator shot to the twenty-sixth floor and opened silently. Instantly, a tooth-filled smile materialized on the previously dour face of Alan Simpson Harwell, and his hand flexed in anticipation of a hearty handshake. The only person awaiting him on the other side of the elevator doors was a lone security guard, but the instincts of a four-term U.S. Senator run deep.

"Hello there," Harwell boomed, seizing the guard's hand and pumping it vigorously while he scanned the man's uniform for a badge that would reveal his name. "Officer *Adams*, a real pleasure, a real pleasure to meet you, officer."

"Uh, thanks, Senator Harwell," the guard stammered, glancing at the two unsmiling men behind the exuberant guest—a member of the Senator's staff named Carne, and the executive vice president of Everett Enterprises, Lawrence Johnson. "The Senator's room is ready, and so is the private casino—"

"Yes, yes, well, that's fine," Harwell bubbled, stepping past the guard and patting him stoutly on the shoulder. "But I've got a speech to give tomorrow morning—" he shot a poisonous glance at the two men beside him "—and I think I'll just order a late dinner and hit the hay. Anyway, Officer Adams, I never gamble."

The guard nodded mutely as the Senator and his escort moved down the corridor and disappeared into a suite.

"Well, what kind of a royal asshole do you think I am?" Harwell shouted as soon as the door closed behind James Carne. "Nobody is supposed to know that I'm gambling here. Not one fucking soul! And now I find out that everybody in the hotel knows."

Lawrence Johnson stepped forward, smiling broadly and chuckling to himself. "Well, now, Alan, only the security guard on the Penthouse floor knows that you're using the private casino," he said cheerfully. "And that's unavoidable, Alan. We've got to bring a dealer up here, and a couple of girls, and the guard has to know why. It's for your own protection."

Harwell frowned, but he no longer shouted. "Well, is the goddamn casino ready for me?" he asked with a pout. "Can we get the goddamn show on the road?"

"Of course, Alan," Johnson said. "Everyone's waiting—"

"Excuse me," Jim Carne interrupted in a soft voice, fixing a stern gaze on the Senator, "but you've got an important speech tomorrow morning. Don't you think we should go over it once or twice more?"

Johnson caught Carne's stern gaze, looking back and forth between the Senator and his aide, and knew instantly that something more was being said between them. Something that he should know about.

"Hey, Jim," he said cheerfully, "a silver-throated songbird like Senator Harwell doesn't need to practice a speech that he's given a hundred and fifty times. And the baccarat table is waiting. So are Melinda and Belinda, the twins from the line in *Salaam, Sultan*. We had to send in a couple of understudies so they could join the party—"

Jim Carne shook his head again, and both Johnson and

the Senator caught the full impact of the gesture. "Uh, listen, Larry," the Senator mumbled, looking down. "Just keep the table hot for a couple of hours, will you? And maybe my schoolmaster here will let me out of class for a little while. But he's right about working on the speech."

"Sure, sure," said Johnson, fighting the catch in his throat. Something was damn wrong, he thought, and he'd better find out what it was. "I'll be in my office or out on the floor. Just page me when you're ready, Senator."

Jim Carne's disapproving stare and Al Harwell's sudden change of heart haunted Lawrence Johnson as he retreated from the Senator's suite and walked slowly down the corridor toward the private casino. He'd never seen Alan Simpson Harwell—known among Washington lobbyists and his fellow congressmen as "the Senator from Everett Enteprises" —refuse an opportunity to run up a big debt at the baccarat table at the expense of his host.

In fact, that was the whole point of his bimonthly visits to the Mecca Hotel, where he routinely served as keynote speaker for whatever convention happened to be meeting at the time. Harwell's constituency back home— sober, hard-working, unsmiling Calvinists who labored on the land or in the factories—would hardly approve of his taste for games of chance and ladies of the evening. Nor would they be pleased to know that their Senator's largest campaign contributor was a reclusive old man who lived underneath a casino in faroff Las Vegas. So the frequent trips were always announced as "speaking obligations," and the campaign contributions from Everett Enterprises were always filtered through local fund-raising committees back home.

The old man had picked Harwell out of the freshman class of the House of Representatives back in 1948, one of a dozen promising young politicians who suddenly found themselves with fat war chests and open invitations to visit Edward Everett himself in Las Vegas. Some of these young men declined the contributions and the invitations; some accepted but lost at the polls anyway; and a few—Harwell among them—prospered under the old man's generous attention.

And Harwell, who ran successfully for the Senate and then secured the influential chairmanship of the Intelligence Operations Committee, repaid his mentor. Encouraged by Senator Alan Simpson Harwell, the various intelligence services turned to Everett Enterprises for unusual services and convenient cover stories. And thanks to Harwell's presence on the committee, cost overruns and accounting irregularities in Everett Enterprise contracts would be overlooked.

When Everett sent a newly designed jet airliner on a good-will flight around the world, the crew included intelligence technicians who monitored the Soviet nuclear testing program as the aircraft skirted the Soviet Far East. When Everett sent ships and divers on an underwater expedition in search of rare minerals, the real objective was the recovery of a Chinese spy satellite that had crashed into the South Pacific.

But the arrangement had grown too complicated for everyone, Johnson thought. Harwell's compulsive hunger for the baccarat table drove him to Vegas too frequently, and the gambling debts that were routinely written off by the Mecca had grown to six figures on each trip. And Harwell's inevitable appearance as keynote speaker at any convention that happened to be meeting at the Mecca was beginning to attract attention. Johnson had sent urgent messages to the old man—the Senator must be written off once and for all—but the messages were ignored.

And now something was brewing within the Senator's suite.

Johnson reached the unmarked door to the private casino. He nodded at the security guard who stood at attention in the corridor and held open the door while he surveyed the casino. Everything was ready for the Senator: the tables were uncovered and stocked with chips, the bar was open, the musicians were tuning up, the twin redheads and the dealer and the bartender were waiting expectantly.

"Just stand by," Johnson called. "Our guest won't be up for another hour or so."

Then Johnson turned away. An hour from now, he promised himself, he would know what was keeping the Senator from his favorite pastime. The twin redheads—who were Harwell's second-favorite pastime—would take care of it.

"Oh Johnny, I'm sorry," Linda Warner squealed, following close behind her new husband as they stood by the elevator. "I mean, I just meant to bet a dollar or two. And my luck was so bad, Johnny—"

"A hundred and thirty dollars' worth of bad luck," he mumbled under his breath. And ahead was another bit of bad luck: the honeymoon night in a room with a mirror *over* the bed and a long-legged blonde *in* the bed. "That's roulette for you, honey. You just can't win."

"Oooh" she purred, allowing her hand to dart between his legs. "I think my luck is changing, Johnny."

"Linda," he snapped, pushing her hand away and flushing embarrassment. "Not in public!"

He rolled his eyes as the elevator opened and Linda dragged him inside. For the last two hours, he'd watched patiently as his bride lost consistently on every impulse bet she could think of: *her* birthdate, *his* birthdate, *her* mother's birthdate, the number of times they'd *kissed* on their first date, and even the number of times she'd allowed her fiancé to touch her *there*. And then, as Linda grew more reckless, her choice of numbers at the roulette table grew more ribald.

"I'm betting on twelve," she whispered into John's ear. "That's how many times we're going to—*oooh!*—tonight."

John, who'd been watching disconsolately as Linda gambled away his carefully budgeted honeymoon money, stopped counting the losses. He just wanted to keep her at the table, keep her distracted with the roulette wheel and the free drinks, keep her away from the suite with the mirror on the ceiling where he'd have to—*oooh!*—a dozen times.

But the drinks and the gambling seemed to stoke Linda's passion as the minutes passed, higher and higher, until she was openly panting and leering as she pushed chips to ever more suggestive numbers on the playing surface.

"Sixty-nine," she whispered with a giggle. "That's for *after* the first four times, Johnny."

And finally she pushed herself away from the table, lurched unsteadily toward the elevator, and towed John along with her. Now, as they stood at the threshold of the Penthouse suite that a stranger had given them out of a generosity that John mistrusted, the bridegroom felt his heart rise abruptly to his throat. The room was decorated in scarlet and black, with flocked walls and old-fashioned brass lamps with red-tinted bulbs and a covered bed with a mink spread. John cocked his head and spotted the telltale reflection of the mirror—the unforgiving mirror—that hovered over the bed underneath the frilly canopy.

"Carry me over the threshold, Johnny," Linda demanded.

"Sure, sure," he said, struggling to balance her long legs and full hips without stumbling. "Here we go."

"Our wedding night at last," Linda sighed. "We've saved ourselves for each other, and now everything is right, Johnny."

"Yeah," he said between gasps, staggering toward the bed. Christ, but her thighs are solid, he thought. And her hips—so round and full and heavy. A pair of legs that could cut you in half, that's what one of the salesmen back in Dayton had said. A pair of hips that could roll you like a rubber ball.

John almost made it to the bed, but the deep-pile carpeting swirled around his feet and caused him to trip. Both of them hurtled forward onto the bed, which bounced under their combined weights and sent them sprawling over each other. Linda giggled wildly, and John could not help but laugh at his own boyish clumsiness and his bride's high spirits. Linda snuggled into his arms and began whispering into his ear; John kept his eyes closed, realizing with an enormous sense of relief that her words were rousing the organ that he so had to depend on tonight.

"It's so funny, Johnny," she purred into his ear, running her long fingers over his lips and then over the promising bulge in his trousers. "All the time I was playing roulette, I felt so hungry. So awfully hungry."

"Do you want to order a sandwich from room service?" he asked, eyes still closed, hopes still rising.

"Oooh, no," Linda whispered. "I'm hungry for *you,* Johnny."

John opened his eyes, and what he saw instantly froze his heart. Overhead, only a few feet away, was a perfect reflection of two entwined bodies—one a long-legged, full-breasted blonde, the other a skinny, straw-haired kid with a scrawny mustache on his upper lip. And his hopes fell abruptly.

"Say, Linda, don't you want to get ready for bed?" he asked brightly, struggling to extricate himself from the scissor-lock of his bride's legs. "I mean, don't you want to freshen up and everything?"

Linda squealed and bounced out of bed. She pranced across the room to rummage through her luggage, mumbling and giggling to herself, and then triumphantly raised a flimsy piece of red lace, waving it in the air like a flag.

"I'm going to take a nice warm bath, Johnny," she said, parading across the room toward the bathroom. "And I'm going to put on a very special nightgown that I ordered from Hollywood. By mail. Very special, Johnny."

"Uh, yeah, right, good idea," he called as she disappeared into the bathroom. To himself he muttered, "Take a nice *long* bath, dear. No rush. No rush at all."

He listened to the faint sound of her voice as she sang to herself in the bathroom; he listened to the faint rumble of hot water as it poured into the tub. And he looked again at the mirror over the bed. A little boy's face, a nervous and hesitant face, looked back down at him.

Christ, he said to himself, I need a drink. He reached for the phone to call room service, but he paused before his hand touched the phone—no, that would take too long, it would be too late. No, he said to himself, I'd better just dash downstairs and treat myself to a stiff shot at the bar. Yeah, yeah, that's the best idea: a quick drink at the bar while Linda takes a long bath. A quick drink and a long, long, bath.

"Hey, Linda, how long you gonna be in there?" he shouted, pounding on the bathroom door.

The singing stopped and then the rush of water. "What, Johnny? What did you say?"

"How long you gonna be in there?" he repeated hoarsely.

"Oooh, you're so impatient," she queaked. "Now you just cool off for awhile, Johnny, and let me pretty myself up for you. I want everything to be just right."

"Okay, no rush," he shouted at the door. "I'm just going to run downstairs and buy myself a quick drink. Just to give you some time to pretty yourself up. I'll be right back."

"But Johnny—" Linda called from inside the bathroom.

The door slammed behind him, and his bride sighed. "He's so impatient," she said to herself, wiggling her toes in the perfumed bathwater. "We've waited so long for each other, and now he can't even wait while I take a bath."

Ahmed Ibn Sayd pushed at the morsels of lamb and rice with a heavy silver fork, but he didn't lift a bite to his mouth. The chef had been trained in the preparation of Middle Eastern dishes—a nod to the wealthy Arab guests of the Mecca Hotel—but he was more familiar with American cuisine, great slabs of raw steak and baked potatoes the size of footballs and those great bushel baskets of cold greens.

And Sayd didn't hunger for the food of his native land. His other appetites had been aroused—the infidel appetites for spirits and the flesh of women and the gaming tables. It was all around him, it rose like an overflowing sewer and reached him even in the cool sanctum of his room on the twenty-sixth floor of the Mecca Hotel. Words from the Koran flashed in his mind. "And how canst thou have patience about things about which thy understanding is not complete?"

But he wouldn't give any satisfaction to his hosts at the Mecca Hotel, the clumsy heathens who tried to cultivate his tastes while flaunting their blasphemous disrespect for the symbols of his faith. Sayd lifted the silver fork and turned it slowly; even the silverware was stamped with the stolen star-and-crescent symbol. He allowed it to clatter to the plate and then pushed himself away from the elegant tray with the single flower in the crystal vase. No, if tonight he indulged the tempations of the flesh that the heathens teased him with he would do so where they could not watch and gloat and laugh.

Sayd crossed the room to the telephone table and lifted the directory, flipping quickly to the yellow section where he knew he would find the services that he required. Escort service, that's what they usually call it, although some establishments persisted in using the more vulgar euphemisms: outcall massage, nude modeling, dating service. He glanced at one page after another of listings, each one more breathless and suggestive than the one before. At last, he chose— "Discreet Introductions by Elizabeth," the escort service ad read. He dialed the number.

Arrangements took only a moment, and the woman at the other end of the line seemed perfectly agreeable to Sayd's meticulous requirements: the escort must be young, tall, blonde, blue-eyed, clean. And she must not come to his hotel room; he would meet her at a downtown hotel at midnight.

Sayd hung up the telephone and reached for the cream-colored envelope that had been delivered to his room a few hours before. An invitation from Lawrence Johnson, the executive vice president of Everett Enterprises and president of the Mecca Hotel, for a dinner aboard the hotel's private yacht at midnight on Saturday.

Reaching quickly into his pocket, Sayd produced a slim gold lighter and ignited the invitation. The thick paper burned sluggishly, but he turned it carefully in his hands until the flames devoured the message and only ashes remained in the ashtray with the inevitable star-and-crescent symbol.

Twenty-four hours from now, Sayd thought, I will find out why the man named Johnson wants so badly to see me. I will find out which of my services—the dark services—are in demand in Las Vegas. I will find out what profit is offered to me to solve the problems of these offensive infidels who slander Allah with every breath and every gesture.

Twenty-four hours from now, Sayd thought, we will do our black business. But now there is time for the guilty pleasures—the spirits, the women, the games.

Sayd removed his gun from its shoulder holster and reloaded the empty magazine. Then he counted out one hundred crisp thousand-dollar bills, and slipped them into a slender leather wallet. And finally he crossed the room, darkened the lights, and stepped into the corridor.

The telephone rang in Lise Christian's suite, but she slept too soundly to hear it. She'd returned to the hotel and gone directly to her room, feeling only the fatigue of jet lag that fogged her mind and softened the memory of what had happened at the club and in the desert. Lise sprawled on the couch of the living room, fully dressed. She slept.

But the caller was persistent and the ringing finally caused her to stir and reach for the phone. For a dizzy moment, she thought the call was from her mother—a call summoning her home, telling her to abandon her mission, urging her to return to the tranquil life. And for that dizzy moment, Lise wanted nothing more than to say yes, yes, and rush back to the airport for any flight that would take her away from Las Vegas. But, wakening, she realized that her mother was dead. The voice over the telephone was a man's, and she knew instantly that her stay in Vegas was not over.

"Miss Christian?" the voice asked, a gruff and gravelly man's voice. "I hope I haven't disturbed your sleep, Miss Christian."

"Who is this?" she asked in bewilderment, fighting the haze that still clouded her mind. "What do you want?"

"I'm sorry, Miss Christian," the voice said softly. "I've waked you up, I'm terribly sorry. Please, please, just go back to sleep and I'll call again tomorrow."

"Who is this?" she said again, shrilly, half panicked.

"My name is Black," the man said apologetically. "Moe Black."

She struggled to identify the name—was he connected with the bank? The hotel? "I'm sorry, but I don't know anyone named Black," she said, puzzled. "What do you want?"

"Uh, you might say that I'm a friend of the family, Miss Christian," he stammered. "A friend of the family, and I just wanted to see if there's anything I could do for you while you're in Las Vegas."

"A friend of *my* family?" Lise said. Her mind was clear now, alert and awake, but she was still troubled by the stranger's words. "Do you mean you knew my mother?"

"Yes, I knew your mother," he answered slowly, "but I was also a friend of your father." He paused. "Your late father, Miss Christian."

A moment of breathlessness, of silence, of profound panic and deep dread. And then, speaking slowly and softly, Lise whispered into the telephone: "Where are you right now, Mr. Black? I must see you right now."

"It's late, Miss Christian," he answered, "and I'm afraid that I've been thoughtless in waking you up. Maybe we can have breakfast together tomorrow morning and just talk about how the family is getting on—"

"Where are you right now?" she repeated, a bit louder, a bit more commanding. "I must see you right now!"

"I'm here in the Mecca, Miss Christian."

"Here? Then you must come to my room. Can you come immediately, Mr. Black?"

"I don't think that would be wise," the man said. "If it's not too much trouble, why don't you come downstairs and join me for a late dinner in the Harem?"

"I beg your pardon?" Lise asked.

"I'm sorry. The Harem is the hotel's gourmet restaurant. However, if you'd rather wait till tomorow—"

"The Harem," Lise repeated. "I'll be there in ten minutes, Mr. Black." A note of desperation, a child's shrillness, crept into her voice. "Please wait for me, Mr. Black."

"Don't worry, Lise," he said, speaking her first name out loud for the first time. "We've waited many years to see you, and I can wait ten minutes longer."

Lester Masaoka rapped loudly on the door. "Hurry up, hurry up," he urged in a loud whisper. "It's me, it's Lester."

The door opened as far as the chain lock would allow, and another pair of Oriental eyes met Lester's. A moment later the door closed, the chain was removed from its lock, and Lester was welcomed into the room.

"Let's see," demanded Homer Sato, the man whose eyes had inspected Lester a moment before. "I figure it must be close to a thousand dollars—let's see!"

Lester could not help grinning despite the pain in his lower back and the raw nerves that had afflicted him ever since he'd flown into Las Vegas a few hours earlier. He reached into his coat pockets and began pulling out one-hundred-dollar chips, one after another, eleven in all.

"Eleven hundred dollars," he said triumphantly. "On a hundred-dollar stake."

"And that's just the beginning," said another voice from

the bedroom of the suite. A third man appeared in the door-way. "We're going to walk out of here with a quarter-million apiece, I promise you."

The ache in his lower back wiped the smile from Lester Masaoka's face. "Yeah, great, but what about me?" he complained, rubbing his back and frowning. "The thing began to ache like the devil an hour ago, and it's hurting a lot worse now."

Homer Sato frowned, too. "What's going wrong, Pierce?" he asked the third man, the only Caucasian among them. "You said he wouldn't feel it."

Pierce waved Lester over to the bed. "Don't worry, gentlemen, nothing is going wrong," he said, lifting Lester's shirt and peering closely at the neat rectangular scar near the small of the back. He prodded and probed the freshly healed surgical scar, then grunted with satisfaction. "It's nothing—just nerves, Lester, just nerves and stiff muscles from spending four hours on an uncomfortable stool. Take a nap, have something to eat, and then we'll send you back downstairs."

"How about something for the pain, Pierce?" Lester demanded.

"Take a couple of aspirin—but nothing more," Pierce replied. "You've got to keep a clear head, and you've got a long night ahead."

Lester followed Pierce into the bedroom and watched as he cleared the bed of the wires, alligator clips, and as-sorted electronic odds and ends. On the dresser, in a clearing amid still more random bits of electronic hardware, stood the open suitcase that carried the key to their quarter-million apiece.

"Is it working?" Lester asked, still rubbing his back.

"Like a dream," Pierce replied. "Homer is a genius, a real genius."

Lester nodded. "But it's all for shit without me," he complained. "And I'm the one who has to sit in that damned casino, half scared to death that somebody's going to tap me on the shoulder and run me into the slammer. I'm the one who has to case the deck and punch up the numbers and figure the bets."

"You're a genius, too," Pierce said. "And Homer and I both know that the whole operation depends on you."

"Well, I hope to hell you remember that," Lester snapped.

"Sure, Lester," Pierce said soothingly. "Now why don't you grab a few winks before the action heats up down in the casino. You know, midnight to four a.m. is when we'll make our big move. You'll start doubling up and then hitting the limit. Christ, if you keep tapping up the numbers quick enough, and they don't go to more than four decks in the shoe, you're going to clear a hundred, maybe a hundred fifty grand tonight."

"Yeah, a hundred fifty grand," Lester said, reclining on the bed and closing his eyes. "Unless some smart pit boss catches on. And then we're all going to fry."

"Don't worry, Lester," Pierce said. "There isn't a pit boss alive who's smart enough to catch on to this scam. And that's a promise, Lester."

Morrissey wasn't fooled for a moment. The busty blond on his right—the one who'd been running through five-dollar bets steadily for the last forty-five minutes, the one who'd been leaning into his shoulder at every chance—was a house-approved hooker. And the greasy bastard on his left was probably a shill, too—a professional sidekick with a maroon jumpsuit and a lot of gold jewelry around his neck and nothing much to bet but a lot to say.

They'd sent in the shills only as a last resort. Morrissey played the first hour on the money that he'd won just to earn the right to that free drink at the blackjack table. He started playing small bets, five or ten dollars after the black-jack, going up and down by twenty bucks for an hour.

Then Morrissey began to sense the way the cards were running. At first, it had been just a game that he played in his head—an idle mathematical exercise in the brain of a college statistics teacher turned roadrunner—but then he found that he could know when the pictures were going to show, when the dealer would go over by hitting on sixteen, when a big bet would pay off. At last, he realized that he'd been casing the deck almost unconsciously, counting the cards that were dealt and calculating the changing odds as the deck was depleted. When the luck went his way, Pop-eye left, just vanished.

Morrissey began to play the hunches, doubling down and pressing his bets when the run of the cards told him that he had the odds with him. And he began winning big. By the end of the second hour, he'd parlayed his original win into slightly more than twenty-one hundred dollars—and he'd attracted the attention of the pit boss again. He was sending over drinks as soon as Morrissey's glass was half empty, and the drinks were doubles.

Another hour went by, and Morrissey—still not drunk despite the best efforts of the pit boss, the bartender, and the cocktail waitress—was pressing his luck and his intuition to the limit. The game seemed to take on an oceanic rhythm of its own, and Morrissey was carried along despite his own admonitions: The odds are immutable, the house starts with a 5.9 percent advantage, which in time will drown the player as inevitably as a tidal wave. The admonitions were those of a college statistics teacher; the play was that of an intuitive gambler. His stake rose by another thousand dollars.

And before each bet, Morrissey's hand went instinctively to his breast pocket where he'd stashed the lucky chip. The gesture was unconscious at first; he feared what he was risking by pressing each bet, he feared what he might lose once the cards turned against him, and he feared most of all the loss of the lucky chip. And as good fortune ran with him, he began touching the chip consciously, intentionally, prayerfully: it was his talisman. His stake redoubled, and when he'd won more than five thousand dollars, they sent in the girl.

"Ooooh, baby, you've got the luck," the blonde had whispered in between hands, her fingers tugging at his sleeve. "God, I'd like to take a long pull at what's making you so lucky."

His hand shook a little as he put ten black chips in the betting box. The dealer dealt him an ace and a jack of spades. He watched intently as the dealer paid him fifteen hundred dollars.

"Hey, buddy, you're really purring," the guy in the jumpsuit had whispered when the hooker had given up. "I'd like to see you take your winnings and run them up into something really big at the roulette table. I'm telling you, buddy, it's roulette where you can really make a big killing."

Morrissey had ignored them both. And now, at midnight, he'd dragged slightly more than seven thousand dollars from the blackjack table. The dealer, who'd been sending him the secret encouragement of a natural gambler who likes to watch anybody's lucky run, offered him yet another deal. But Morrissey shook his head and slipped off the high stool. He threw a hundred-dollar tip to the dealer. The gesture made him feel strangely good.

His legs nearly gave out. The booze, the run of the cards, the stack of hundred-dollar chips where there had once been only a lucky five-dollar chip—all this rushed into Morrissey's consciousness, and his head swirled. Now he'd be able to gas up the Alfa on Monday and push on toward New Mexico; he'd be able to take to the road with a glow of good luck around him. But first he'd buy himself the fanciest dinner the Mecca Hotel had to offer, and then he'd check into the fanciest room in the hotel.

"A table has been reserved for you at the Harem for dinner," the pit boss said, still at his shoulder and looking morosely at the chips on the table. "If you'd like some company, we'd be happy to arrange for a young lady to join you. And Mr. M, you mentioned that you weren't staying with us so we've reserved a special suite for you." The pit boss painted a quick smile on his face. "And, of course, it's all with the compliments of the Mecca, Mr. M."

Morrissey grinned at the pit boss. "When I was flat out and busted, I couldn't even bum a free drink around here," he said. "Now that I've got your money, you won't let me pay for anything."

"That's Vegas," the pit boss said with a nod and a thin smile. The smile turned into a toothy, almost wolfish grin. "You're going to find that it gets into the blood, Mr. M. Flat out or flush, it gets into the blood. And that's Vegas, too."

A moment later, with more than seven thousand dollars in one pocket and a lucky five-dollar chip in another pocket, John Morrissey strolled rapidly across the crowded casino toward the cavelike entrance of the Harem restaurant. And deep within its darkened interior, almost hidden by the shadowy figures who moved back and forth inside the restaurant, Morrissey saw a faint but beckoning light.

five

"Quarters, please," said the housewifely woman in the too-tight sequinned gown, waving a single dollar bill in the air.

Tina's hand moved automatically to the change machine on her belt, working the lever four times and then slipping the quarters deftly into the woman's hand. At forty-nine, with six grown children who were growing their own families, she was grateful to be working as a change girl in the casino. And after a year in the Mecca, she had learned the survival skills that are required for a human being who works surrounded by the chaos of clanging bells, clacking wheels, and flashing lights.

She was an island of serenity in the sea of slots, a witness to the endless rhythms of the slot machine, a mechanism that dispensed change as quickly and mindlessly as a robot. But she was not a robot. Her mind was alive, and she saw everything around her: The runs of good luck and bad luck, the payoffs big and little, the minor dramas that were played out every moment in the casino. And she knew within her soul that if she were not dispensing change to the middle-aged women with coffee cups full of quarters, she would be one of them.

And she would be damned good at the slots, too, she told herself. She knew the history of every machine in her section. She knew their quirks, their timing, their preferences. The dollar slot machine at the far end of the first row, for instance, had never paid a five-way jackpot of ten thousand dollars in its eleven-year life and it probably never would; she had watched too many hundred-dollar payoffs to believe that it would ever hit the big combination.

"More quarters, please," a voice asked. Tina smiled; it was the same woman in the sequinned gown, but she was waving a fiver instead of a single.

That's how it always worked in the slots, Tina knew. First a harmless dollar, then five, then they'd be asking for change for a twenty, and before long they'd be scratching out a new traveler's check at the cage. Now the ritual was reenacted as the woman with a cupful of quarters headed back to the machine that she'd been working—and with a single bell, the machine paid off on three cherries. The woman shoveled quarters into her handbag.

A moment later, the woman was back. "Dollars, please," she said, presenting a twenty. And then she headed for the tight-fisted dollar slot machine at the far end of the first row.

Good lucky, honey, Tina thought. You're going to blow your fifty-dollar payoff from the quarter slot, and then the souvenir money to buy pennants for the grand-children, and then maybe your plane fare. And that big shiny bastard in the first row won't spit back anything but bad luck. That's how it had been for a year, and Tina was hardened enough to the inevitabilities of Las Vegas to know that it wouldn't change now.

Her thoughts were interrupted by a clanging worthy of a five-alarm fire and an eruption of flashing red lights. She was startled to see that the lady at the dollar slot was shrieking "Jackpot! Jackpot!" at the top of her lungs, and the machine was answering in its own way: "Yes! Yes!" A pit boss materialized at the woman's side, verified the five Mecca symbols on the face of the machine, and then signaled to to the security guard.

"Ladies and gentlemen," a voice announced over the p.a. system, "we've got a very lucky winner at the Mecca slots—a ten-thousand-dollar jackpot."

For a long moment, the clamor and chaos seemed to freeze the attention of a thousand gamblers, and everyone in the casino experienced a communion of prayerful silence. Winner and loser alike shared the moment of bliss that had touched the life of a housewife in a sequinned gown. And then, a fraction of a second and an eternity later, the play resumed at its full volume and velocity. The woman in the sequinned gown was forgotten, but not her ten-thousand-dollar jackpot.

"Congratulations, honey," Tina muttered as the woman passed, escorted by the pit boss and the security guard toward the cage. "I always knew I should've stuck a buck into that bastard."

The woman looked at Tina in bewilderment. Then, with a grin and a sparkle in her eyes, she dug into her handbag and pulled out a coin. "That's for you," she gushed. "That's for bringing me luck."

Tina opened her hand and stared at the single quarter that the woman had given her.

Twenty-four hours ago, the lobster on John Morrissey's dinner plate had been scuttling along the ocean floor off the coast of Maine—only to be caught in a lobsterman's trap and unceremoniously dumped into a seawater-filled container with thirty dozen other lobsters for the flight to Las Vegas. The charbroiled steak next to the lobster had been attached to a 380-pound side of Kansas City beef that arrived at the Southern Pacific depot in a refrigerated boxcar. The butter on his Idaho potato had been churned from a Wisconsin cow's milk and then shipped with two tons of other dairy products in an eighteen-wheel refrigerated rig. And the Sebastiani cabernet in Morrissey's crystal wineglass had been loaded aboard a cargo flight from San Francisco on a pallet with nearly eight hundred bottles of wine and brandy.

But Morrissey's dinner, which he now ate hungrily, lovingly, in a dimly lit booth of the Harem restaurant in the Mecca Hotel, was just a tiny fraction of the foodstuffs that were shipped into Las Vegas every day of the year. The Mecca alone needed more than seventy tons of fresh food, canned goods, and bottled beverages every week to supply its eight restaurants and coffeeshops around the clock. And not so much as a cocktail onion was homegrown, even though the settlers who gave the town its name—"The meadows," in Spanish—were Mormon farmers who tried to scratch out a living by irrigating the land with water from the local artesian wells. In fact, the only part of John Morrissey's dinner that was raised locally was the thirty-nine-year-old waitress, whose father had come to Vegas in 1928 to pour concrete for Hoover Dam and then stayed on to pour the foundations for Benjamin "Bugsy" Siegel's Flamingo Hotel in 1945.

"Would you care for some company, Mr. Morrissey?" the waitress asked quietly, as if she were offering another refill for his wineglass. "The young lady at the bar would be delighted to join you for—" her voice faltered for a fraction of a second, and then dropped by a fraction of a decibel as she finished the sentence, "—dessert."

Morrisey glanced across the darkened dining room and spotted the woman in the silky black pants and the revealing silk blouse. She turned on a momentary neon smile, and then smiled with more enthusiasm as she recognized the trick that the pit boss had picked out for her. He was the same disheveled young man in the worn suède coat and the faded blue jeans, the same down-and-out grind whom she'd met in the lounge only a few hours before. Of course, she wasn't surprised that his fortune had changed so suddenly. At eight o'clock, he seemed to have been a down-and-out mooch who asked her if he could cadge a drink at a blackjack table without placing a bet; now he was being comped to a fancy dinner at the Harem—and an hour with a house-approved hooker.

"Her name is Lucy," the waitress whispered to Morrissey, who gazed at the woman without remembering their earlier encounter. "And she's very friendly."

"Yeah, I'm sure she is," John said. But he wasn't going to need any company in bed. Or at the tables. Thanks to the wild run of luck that turned a five-dollar chip into more than seven thousand dollars, he was going to catch some sleep, see the mechanic who was holding his Alfa, and hit the road for New Mexico. Alone. "Thanks, but I'm not going to need any company," he said.

He returned the hooker's smile with a boyish grin and turned back to his half-eaten steak, raising a chunk of the rare meat in lazy anticipation of the next mouthful. As he chewed, his eyes wandered around the Harem—a roomful of potbellied men and big-busted women attended by waitresses in mock Arabic costumes and a tuxedoed captain wearing a frozen smile. And then Morrissey's gaze reached the entrance of the Harem, where a slender young woman with black hair and a rumpled white gown stood by herself and surveyed the tables and booths and bar.

The food in his mouth seemed suddenly dry and tasteless. He reached clumsily for his wineglass, half spilling its contents, and then choked down the mouthful of food with a hard gulp of wine. But Morrissey knew why the woman on the far side of the restaurant turned his mouth dry and filled his belly with a new sense of hunger and excitement.

He recognized her flashing dark eyes and short-cropped hair. It was a moment in a dream. He realized with a sudden certainty that he owed the young woman an enormous debt, as he remembered the five-dollar chip in his coat pocket. The lucky chip that he had wagered only once at the wheel of fortune and then touched on each blackjack deal for its gift of good fortune. His hand again reached for the chip, and as his fingers closed around the grooved plastic disc, he remembered. The crowd at the entrance of the Mecca Hotel, and the young woman who'd given him a smile and a chip. "Just for luck," she'd said before moving away.

Morrissey pushed himself to his feet and raised the chip in a salute—but he saw that the young woman had turned to the maître d' and whispered into his ear. The maître d' nodded briskly, took her gently by the elbow, and escorted her to a booth at the back of the Harem. John strained to see and felt a profound disappointment when he saw that she was joining an aging man in a black suit. A man with a clipboard under his arm and a strained smile on his face.

A waitress materialized at Morrissey's table. "May I help you, sir?" she asked in a puzzled voice.

He was half standing. He sat down slowly, without removing his eyes from the distant table where the young woman now sat in huddled conversation with the old man. "Who is that man?" he asked hoarsely. "The one sitting with the young lady over there?"

The waitress followed his gaze to the table where one of the Three Blind Mice was seated. "That's Mr. Black," she said quickly. "He's one of the bosses."

"And the young lady?" Morrissey feared the answer: A hooker? A chip hustler? Another one of the hard women who seemed to fill Las Vegas?

"I don't know, sir," the waitress said. "I've never seen her before."

Morrissey nodded. "Good," he said out loud, without knowing quite why.

The waitress gestured at his dinner plate. "Would you like coffee or some dessert?"

"What?" John glanced down, then waved one hand over the dishes. "Yes, please, bring me some coffee."

Morrissey settled back against the soft upholstery of the booth without removing his eyes from the distant booth in which the young woman sat. He clutched the lucky five-dollar chip. He had done well at the tables, but felt terribly poor; he had been offered the companionship of a smiling woman, but felt terribly alone; he had eaten a fine dinner, but felt terribly hungry.

And he knew what would satisfy his strange sensation of poverty and loneliness and hunger. So John Morrissey glued his eyes to the young woman and tightened his fingers around the chip she had given him.

"Star," she said in response to the gentleman's question. "My name is Star."

The swarthy man with the shiny black hair refused to look at her. They sat side by side in the bar of the Mother Lode Casino on Fremont Street in the noisy downtown district of Las Vegas, and he asked her one question after another—but he spoke only in a muted whisper and he refused to look at her.

"Where do you come from, Star?" he asked without moving his lips.

"St. Louis," she said, stirring her watered-down drink with a plastic swizzle stick. "I dropped out of high school two years ago to study dancing, and everyone told me that I was a good dancer—a really good dancer, you know— and so I came out here to audition for the chorus line in one of the big shows. I was in the showboat number at the Frontier—well, I was an understudy but I got to dance twice —and I'm still trying for a spot in the big show at the Mecca. The trouble is Vegas is lousy with good dancers."

She took a long sip of her drink and scolded herself silently. The man she'd been sent to meet by the escort service didn't want to hear her troubles; he just wanted to get laid like all the others. But he was so quiet—too quiet—and it made her nervous. And when she was nervous, she started to chatter. She just couldn't help it.

"Are you a real-blonde?" the man asked in a soft whisper.

Star laughed and threw back her head, allowing her long blonde hair to sweep across the gentleman's shoulder. "Of course I'm a real blonde," she said. And then she threw back her shoulders. "All of me is real, everything you see is real."

The gentleman remained silent, two hands wrapped around the double bourbon that he'd ordered but hadn't touched yet. Star studied his profile. He was dark, very dark, but he wasn't black. He spoke with an accent, a funny sort of an accent that sounded English, but he was too dark to be English. No, he looked like an Arab or maybe someone from India. And the name that he'd given to the escort service was probably a phony. She was dying to ask him where he was from, but all the girls who worked for Discreet Introductions by Elizabeth were sternly warned not to ask a customer any personal questions.

"Woman, I want you to go to the front desk and check into a room," the gentleman said abruptly. Then he raised the shotglass and threw the drink down his throat in a single gulp. "Check into a room, and then come back and tell me which one."

The gentleman did not look up when Star stepped down from the barstool. He did not look up as she pushed her way through the crowds in the lounge to reach the front desk of the Mother Lode Casino and Hotel. And he did not look up when she returned with a room key clutched in her hand.

"Room number?" the gentleman asked.

"Five fifty-one," she said.

"Now," he said slowly, "go directly to the room. You must wait for me."

"If you're going to gamble first, I could come with you and bring you luck—" Star said quickly, thinking of the bills in his wallet, but she stopped herself. That was another rule of Discreet Introductions by Elizabeth: No chip hustling.

The gentleman expressed his displeasure by slowly closing his eyes and opening them again a moment later. He still did not look at her. Star shrugged, repeated the room number—"It's 551, and I'll be waiting for you!"—and then slipped away.

Ahmed Ibn Sayd—who was known to the young woman from Discreet Introductions by Elizabeth only as Mr. White —waited ten minutes and then headed for the baccarat table in the Mother Lode Casino.

Sally Martin beamed as the audience for the late show of *Salaam, Sultan* applauded the closing extravaganza, which featured 120 nearly nude chorus girls, 60 nearly nude boys, and the two boy dancers bearing the aging matinee star in a gilt-and-feather-bedecked throne down a boy-and-girl-be-decked staircase. She leaned over slightly and whispered to Bobby Reed, who wore a toothy smile and a red-leather bikini and nothing else.

"Don't strain yourself, darling, 'cause I'm going to need every inch of you when we get back to the room."

Bobby Reed struggled to keep up his side of the throne, and he shuddered inside at the thought of yet another session in Sally Martin's suite, but he kept smiling.

The act continued between Sally Martin's legs until her final protesting shriek—"Oh, God, don't take it out!"— and then Bobby consoled himself with a snifter of Sally's brandy. She was too drunk, too tired, and too nearsighted to see the weary expression that he wore behind his smile.

"And now for the big surprise, Bobby," she said with a giggle. "I want you to go to the closet and take down the gray suitcase. The one that I always take to the chalet in Interlaken."

Bobby rolled off the bed and walked to the closet, preparing for the next scene of his performance—a scene of feigned surprise when he opened the suitcase and removed the false bottom and discovered the thick bundles of well worn American currency. Of course, Bianco had briefed him about the suitcase and the money and the regular trips to Interlaken when he hired the young dancer to be Sally Martin's companion. And Bobby knew that Sally Martin's long-term contract with the Mecca Hotel included some unwritten but well understood duties for Louis Bianco—a monthly flight to Geneva, where a certain sum of American currency would be deposited in a private bank account before Sally continued on to her Interlaken chalet for a weekend of rest with Bobby Reed.

"Jesus Christ," Bobby said with as much conviction as he could muster. "There must be a hundred thousand dollars here."

Sally giggled. "Wrong, Bobby. Three hundred thousand!" She blinked back her tears of sheer exhilaration. "And do you know what that three hundred thousand is going to buy us, Bobby?"

He looked up from the suitcase. "What is it going to buy, lover?"

"Freedom," she exulted, sitting up in bed. "When we catch the Sunday morning flight, it's going to be for the very last time. That three hundred big ones are going with us, Bobby, and we're never coming back here again. Tomorrow night will be the last time we ever dance on a stage together."

"What are you talking about, Sally?" he said, wondering if she would believe his act now that it counted for so much. "How can you leave the Mecca? How can you leave the stage? You've always told me it's your whole life."

Sally's eyes glistened with a new wave of tears. "Oh, God, don't you think I hear them?"

"I don't understand, Sally."

"Bobby, don't you think I hear those dreadful people

in the audience? All those horrid people who come to see the Sally Martin they remember from the matinees—and then see *me?*" She started sobbing violently. "I hear them, Bobby: 'Oh, she's so *old!* Oh, she's so *fat!* Oh, she's so *wrinkled!*' I hear them, Bobby, but I won't have to listen to them ever again. Not after tomorrow night."

He stared at the packages of money in the suitcase. "Sally, I don't understand what you're talking about. I don't understand where all this cash comes from—"

She choked back the next sob and laughed instead. "It's that greasy bastard's money. Bianco! It's his goddamn money. It's his skim, and I've been carrying it to Geneva for the last five years. I'm his bag woman. I carry his money to his Swiss bank every month. I must have carried millions! That's why the hotel bought me the place in Interlaken. That's why they send me to Europe every month."

And that's why they bought you a boy dancer to go along, Bobby thought. For a moment, her eyes caught his; for a moment, she stared into his face, Then he smiled the trouper's smile, and he knew that she had not seen behind the mask of deception.

"Where will we go with the money?" Bobby asked in a carefully staged whisper. He must find out now; he must find out before she changed her mind about him. "Interlaken?"

Sally paused for a moment. And then she laughed. "No, Bobby, we can't go to Interlaken," she explained patiently, like a mother to a child. "Never again to Interlaken. Bianco's people will be looking for us when he finds out that I haven't deposited his money. He's a hood, Bobby, and he's used to the old ways of doing things. Like putting people under three feet of hot sand when they steal your skim."

"So where will we go, Sally?" Bobby asked again.

"Just pack your bag like you always do," she said with a motherly smile. "And when we land in New York on

Sunday night, I'll tell you. And if you've packed the wrong clothes, I'll buy you some new ones."

Bobby bit his lower lip but fought back a frown. He must find out before they boarded the New York flight; Bianco would insist on knowing before she left Las Vegas with the money. And Bobby knew that it would take every bit of his trouper's skill to find out.

"Finish your brandy," he said softly, taking a step toward the bed. "Finish your brandy, lover—"

"Oh Bobby!" she said with a groan, easing back against the pillows and opening her legs on the satin sheet. "Oh Bobby!"

The elevator door opened on the twenty-fifth floor of the Mecca, and Dr. Carl Hagen found himself face to face with a security guard wearing a sidearm, a walkie-talkie, and a nametag that identified him as Mike Adams.

"Yes, sir, can I help you?" the young man said with studied courtesy. Ever since his conversation with Louis Bianco about breaking the jaw of the high-roller who'd groped him in the hotel restroom, Mike Adams was on his very best behavior. And it was a sign of his boss's confidence in him that the young man was given the swing shift just below the twenty-sixth floor.

"Uh, yes, I'm looking for someone," Hagen muttered. "I want to get upstairs to the Penthouse floor."

Mike studied him carefully. He'd been briefed on the guests who were staying in the Penthouse, but the man with the frantic gleam in his eyes just didn't belong here. "Your name, sir?" Mike asked, taking a half step to block the man's movement down the corridor.

"Hagen," he said, glancing anxiously down the empty hall. "Dr. Carl Hagen."

"I'm sorry, Dr. Hagen," Mike said, "but the Penthouse is only open to guests who are staying on that floor."

Hagen nodded. The extra security, the close questioning, the empty corridor—it all added up to mean that the old man must be in the Penthouse. Edward Roger Everett, the old man who'd left his Managua hotel room a year before with a potentially dangerous tumor in his skull. And now Hagen felt a new stab of guilt, a new sense of urgency, an aching impulse to erase the act of cowardice and avarice that he'd committed by taking the old man's money and leaving him to die of the tumor.

"I must see Mr. Everett immediately," the doctor said, leaning toward the security guard and clutching his forearm. "It's literally a matter of life and death."

Mike backed away, but the man's hand remained on his arm. He didn't like being touched so casually by a stranger; he didn't like the intensity of the stranger's stare and tone of voice. His free arm dropped to his side, ready to grab the lead-filled sap that he carried in his back pocket, but he warned himself against breaking another jaw tonight.

"I am very sorry, Dr. Hagen," he said, trying to sound stern but succeeding only in sounding squeaky. "The Penthouse is only open to guests who are staying on this floor—"

"But I must see Mr. Everett. His life is involved."

"—and Mr. Everett is not in residence at the Mecca," Mike continued, reciting the phrase automatically.

Hagen's hand fell away from Mike's arm and his eyes darted toward the long corridor. Before Mike could assimilate those two subtle gestures, Hagen broke away and started to run.

"Everett!" he shouted up at the ceiling as he ran down the corridor. "Everett, I must see you."

Mike bounded after him, and his mind raced even faster than his legs: What the hell am I going to do when I catch him? If I bring him down, Mike thought, I might really hurt the crazy bastard—and then Bianco is sure to fire my ass out of here. But if I don't stop him, he's going to raise the goddamn roof. And then Mike thought of the guest who'd arrived only a few hours before—the Senator, an honored

144

guest of Lawrence Johnson, a keynote speaker at the convention of the Funeral Directors Association.

If I let this crazy bastard get to the Senator, Mike thought, it'll be my funeral.

Mike decided. He reached Hagen at a full run and threw himself at the man's legs. Mike hit the floor with a lineman's grunt, and Hagen's head hit the floor with a muffled crack. He was dazed by the blow, but he still kicked at Mike's arms, trying desperately to break free, screaming desperately to the empty corridor: "Everett! I must see you, Everett."

Mike was close to tears when he decided that he couldn't allow the wild man to scream anymore. He held the man's legs with one powerful arm and reached for the blackjack in his back pocket with the other arm. All it took was a single stinging blow against Hagen's skull, and the man's body went suddenly limp in Mike's arms. And he could feel the warm ooze of blood from the sapped skull.

"Oh Jesus," Mike muttered to himself as he carried Hagen to the couch near the elevator. "Oh Jesus H. Christ!"

He lifted the walkie-talkie from his belt to call the security desk—the crazy bastard was going to need a doctor—but then he paused. Bianco was going to hear about the guest with the broken skull soon enough. And Mike didn't want him to hear it from the swing-shift sergeant at the security desk. So he reached for the house phone and dialed the hotel operator.

"Adams, security," he said gruffly. "Emergency page for Mr. Bianco, please."

"One moment," the operator murmured. And a moment later, he heard a click and then the soft voice of Louis Bianco: "Yes, this is Bianco."

"Mr. Bianco, sir, this is Mike Adams," the young man squeaked, fighting back the tears again. "I'm awfully sorry, Mr. Bianco, but there's a crazy bastard up here trying to get to the Penthouse, and he kept asking for Mr. Everett, and then he started to run, and I had to hit him."

"Mike," Bianco said, silencing the young man abruptly. "Slowly, now—who was asking for Mr. Everett?"

"Oh, Christ, his name is, uh, Hagen. Carl Hagen. Said he was a doctor, Mr. Bianco and it was a matter of life and death, and then he started running toward the Senator's suite, and—Christ, Mr. Bianco!—I had to stop him, didn't I?"

"Is he dead, Mike?" Bianco asked.

"Shit, I sure hope not, Mr. Bianco," he said, looking down at the senseless body on the couch. "He's bleeding from where I sapped him, but he's not dead."

There was a long moment of silence over the line, and Mike waited to hear the angry words of dismissal from his boss. Instead, when Bianco spoke again, his voice was gentle, reassuring, almost fatherly. "It's okay, Mike. Just put him in one of the empty rooms. Put him in 2550, Mike—and I'll be right up." He was silent for another moment, and then spoke again: "Have you called the security desk about this, Mike? Or the infirmary?"

"No, sir, I called you first thing, Mr. Bianco. I thought I'd better tell you myself."

"You did right, Mike," Bianco said in a stern whisper that reminded Mike of a snake's hiss. "You did just right."

"John Warner." A woman's voice echoed above the din of the Mecca casino. "Paging Mr. John Warner, please."

The bartender poured another shot into John Warner's glass, and the stout lady with the blue wig on the next stool shot another amorous glance in his direction. But John only heard the voice over the public address system. That was the third page in the last fifteen minutes, and he knew what it meant—Linda had finished her bath, slipped into her flimsy red-lace negligee, and was waiting for him to return to their room.

Waiting. Waiting in the bed. Waiting in the bed with the mirror over it.

John Warner lifted the glass to his lips, gulped down the fiery liquor, and fought the wave of panic that rose in his belly. Now or never, he told himself. Act like a man, he told himself. Go back to the room and give her what she wants, he told himself. Or else she'll tell the girls back in the typing pool that you're a sissy, and they'll tell the other salesmen, and you'll never live it down. Act like a man, he told himself—and he kept telling himself the same thing as he left the lounge and crossed the crowded casino floor.

The late show of *Salaam, Sultan* had ended, and new waves of players flooded into the casino and filled the tables. John picked and pushed his way through the crowd, pausing here and there to watch the action at blackjack or roulette or craps. No big rush, he told himself. It's still early, and you've got the whole night ahead of you.

"John Warner," the p.a. repeated for the fourth time. "Paging Mr. John Warner."

He came to the last craps table in the casino, where the crowds began to thin out and the movement toward the elevator lobby was unimpeded. And he realized that the craps table seemed like such a friendly scene—a dozen men, shoulder to shoulder around the table, leaning forward over the action, shouting encouragement to each other, sharing the excitement of the game. A comradely crowd. And at this moment, the crowd was watching a black man who stood at the far side of the table.

"Gimme a natural," he hooted, shaking the dice. "Show me a seven."

"I'll take some of that good luck," said another man, tossing a chip on the pass line.

The black man hooted again and threw the dice. "Natural! What'd I say?"

John smiled along with the others. He recalled what one of the other salesmen had told him—always bet with a black man if you're playing craps. "A black man's got a natural feel for throwing the ivories," the salesman had told him in perfect seriousness. "He's going to throw you a winner every time."

And John found himself reaching into his pocket for a

bill. Linda had run down their honeymoon budget at the roulette table, but John reassured himself that a couple of two-dollar bets couldn't hurt. He tossed a wrinkled twenty-dollar bill on the felt—there were only a dozen more of them in their honeymoon budget—and carefully collected the four five-dollar chips, leaving one on the pass line and palming the other three.

"Hey, watch out, I'm coming again," the black said, rattling the dice and throwing them hard against the far wall of the table. "And it's a—ten! Big ten! My point's a ten, boys."

Always bet with a black man, John told himself. And he dropped another five-dollar chip just outside the pass line to back it up. The players on either side pushed against him, and he felt strong, supported, sturdy.

So sturdy, in fact, that he ignored the fifth page from his bride—"Paging Mr. John Warner!"—and leaned over the table to watch the black man's roll. A six, then an eight, then another six—and then the winning point.

"Fifty-five," the black man said.

John felt a shiver at the man's words—slang for a hard ways ten on the dice—but he was quickly reassured by the dealer's payoff: even money on the pass-line bet, and two to one on the backup bet. He could drag the five chips now and go back to his bride with a fifteen-dollar profit on a single roll of the dice.

"John Warner," the p.a. system boomed.

"I'm going to make ten passes," the black man laughed.

John closed his eyes. "Press the bet," he muttered, and opened his eyes to watch the black man's roll.

The injection of morphine dulled the pain behind his eyes, but the old man still could not sleep. It wasn't the lingering ache that kept him awake, or the fear of the plots he'd discovered on the television monitors. No, it was the young woman with those haunting black eyes whose face lingered in the old man's imagination like a ghost.

A ghost seeking vengeance from the grave.

The old man felt a new stab of pain behind his eyes, and he felt a new stab of fear in his heart. The young woman's face swam in front of him in the darkness of the subterranean bunker, and he suddenly remembered where he'd seen those black eyes before. And he suddenly realized whose ghost was seeking vengeance from beyond the grave.

He struggled to sit up in the narrow bed and pressed the callbutton on the table next to him with desperate fingers. A few moments later, the figure of Alexander Tate glided quietly into the room. The tall black man stood silently beside the bed, and it took several long moments before the old man realized that he was not alone in the small room.

"Holy Jesus," the old man wheezed, feeling the fingers of panic closing around his heart. "Is that you, Alexander?"

"Yes, Mr. Everett," Tate whispered.

"For Christ's sake, you nearly scared me to death, you nigger bastard." The old man fumbled for the light switch beside his bed, and he felt a second jolt of pain. The bodyguard was standing only inches away from him. "And I could have choked on my own puke by the time you shuffled in here."

"Do you wish something, Mr. Everett?"

"Yes. Yes, for Christ's sake! Help me into the control room."

"Yes, Mr. Everett," the bodyguard murmured, offering a strong arm to lift the weak old man to his feet.

"And get me another shot of morphine, for Christ's sake."

"Yes, Mr. Everett."

The old man grunted in satisfaction. At least the injection would ease the panic and the pain. But he knew that it wouldn't erase the vision of the young woman that now seemed to float within his consciousness—a ghost, an assassin, an accuser. No, the woman's face would remain there until one of them destroyed the other. Only one would survive, and Edward Roger Everett had always been one thing above all—a survivor.

He switched on the power to the array of television monitors and then punched up the camera in the young woman's room. The lights were still off and the room was still empty, but he could survey the room just as well through the hidden camera's infrared lens. And he could wait all night for her to return. He had waited twenty-one years for the avenging ghost to return from the grave, and he could certainly wait one more night.

"Hell's bells, Jim, it's the last time around for me," said the Senator from Everett Enterprises, pacing back and forth in front of his administrative assistant. "What's wrong with leaving the old man with just one more bad marker and a couple of girls who know they've been properly laid?"

Jim Carne shook his head. "We're here for just one thing, Senator—to cut loose from the old man once and for all. And it'll be a lot tougher later on if we don't do it clean and now." Carne picked up his drink from the fully stocked bar and walked into the living room of the Penthouse suite. "Anyway, Senator, they've got lots of casinos and lots of women where we're going."

The Senator stalked over to the living room window and gazed out over the sprawling Mecca Hotel. "Yeah, maybe you're right, but the fanciest casino in the Caribbean looks like sawdust joints compared to the Mecca. And I've never known two women who can do to me what Melinda and Belinda do when they climb aboard this old cocker."

Carne recognized the pouting, little-boy frown on the silver-haired Senator. And he knew that the mournful expression in those milky-blue eyes meant that the Senator was desperate to sack out with the chorus line twins. But Carne wasn't going to let him bury himself any deeper in the swamp of Edward Roger Everett's Vegas empire. No, his job was to extricate Senator Alan Simpson Harwell from the old man's grip once and for all.

Carne lowered himself into one of the plush armchairs and put his feet up on the coffee table. "Senator, you've been sucking up to that scumbag for too damn long already," he said sternly. "And you'd better thank your goddamn lucky stars that I came along to save your ass. Otherwise you'd be heading for a federal penitentiary instead of a fat Senate pension and a fat salary as an ambassador."

Harwell turned away from the window and stared at the hard-eyed young man. On the floor of the Senate—or out among the home state voters—Harwell was loved, respected, revered. But Jim Carne was too brash and too arrogant to respect or revere a saint, much less a man who'd allowed himself to be bought and sold by Edward Everett for the last twenty-five years.

"Look, Jim, I'm not arguing with you," the Senator pleaded. "And I really appreciate how you managed to bail me out with the President and the Majority Leader. On Sunday, when I get up to give my speech at the convention, I'm going to keep every one of my promises—I'll announce my resignation from the Senate, and I'll announce that the Intelligence Operations Committee is launching a full-scale investigation into cost overruns and bribes in government contracts held by Everett Enterprises."

Jim Carne swirled the ice around his glass. "And you're going to *deplore* the misconduct of Edward Roger Everett, Senator. You're going to *deeply regret* your misplaced trust in him. You're going to *condemn* the apparent involvement of Edward Everett and his corporate holdings with organized crime—"

"Yeah, yeah, I know the goddamn speech by heart," Harwell complained. "I just hope to God the FBI and the Justice Department remember their part of the bargain."

Carne smiled. "Sure they do, Senator. Immunity from prosecution for all past conduct. Sealing of all investigative records. And the President will submit your nomination as ambassador to that little island paradise in the Caribbean.

You can bet that your esteemed colleagues in the Senate will confirm the nomination promptly."

"Christ, won't Larry Johnson shit a brick when he hears my speech Sunday morning," Harwell said with a grin. "And I'll bet the old man—wherever the hell he's hiding nowadays—will turn over and die of apoplexy on the spot."

And don't you wish he would, Carne thought. That's the part of the bargain that the Senator doesn't want to think about. But the old man is a lot less forgiving than the FBI or the Justice Department or the Senate. And, Carne smiled to himself, your fat carcass won't be worth its weight in lard when the old man starts sending out the word. What was old Everett's favorite dictum? Oh, sure. I don't get angry, I get even.

The triumphant gleam in the Senator's eyes turned quickly to mournful pouting. "Hell's bells, Jim," he repeated. "What's wrong with leaving the old man with one more bad marker, anyway?"

"Bad faith, Senator," Carne said crisply. "You go and make a deal, you promise to cut the shit—and then you take the old man's money and the old man's tail on the night before you make the big speech? That's bad faith, Senator, and it'll piss everybody off."

"Thanks for the lecture in ethics, Jim," Harwell said with a sarcastic smile. "I guess I'm awfully damned lucky that the Majority Leader insisted I hire you as my administrative assistant."

That's awfully damned right, Carne said to himself. The party leadership had known that Everett was crooked for years, but it took a smart in-fighter like Jim Carne to move in and set up the deal and then move him out. And when Harwell was safely deposited in the Caribbean, Carne would move on.

"Yes, Jim, I'm really grateful for the lecture on ethics," Harwell continued, his voice growing sharper with irritation. "But I don't think I'm going to sit down for a lecture on morality, too. So if I want to go down the hall and shoot some craps and get laid, I don't think it's any of your goddamn business."

Jim Carne shrugged. "You're over twenty-one, Senator," he said. "And if you want to get down in the shit once more before you leave town, I'm not going to stop you."

Harwell stared at the young man—half surprised, half triumphant—and then moved toward the room phone. He asked the operator to page Lawrence Johnson, and then he boomed out a greeting: "Hey, Larry, I've memorized my lesson and school's out and I'd love to come to your party. No, no, I don't think Jim will be joining us tonight. But I'm sure Melinda and Belinda won't mind, will they?" And then he laughed.

Carne watched as Harwell disappeared into one of the bedrooms and reappeared a few moments later with a cloud of shaving lotion around his slicked-down hair. "Don't wait up, Jim," Harwell said briskly. "And don't worry about me —I've been fighting down-and-dirty with the best of them when you were still picking your nose and beating off under the sheets."

Carne waited until the Senator's hand was on the doorknob. "I'm not worried about you, Senator," he said cooly. "I'm worried about your heart. A man your age might roll over and die of pure joy when the twins both go round the world on you at the same time. And that might be a little hard to explain to the folks back home, Senator."

"You'll find a way, Jim," Harwell said as he slipped into the corridor. "A fancy devil like you always finds a way." He winked.

Ira Tuthill scanned the Oasis coffeeshop for a wall clock, but the walls were too crowded with garish murals of buxom harem girls and palm trees and camels to accommodate something as humble as a clock. It didn't occur to him that there wasn't a single clock in any casino in Vegas. He'd left his watch back in the room, and he had only the vaguest notion of the time. But time didn't matter in Las Vegas. The lights always sparkled, the roulette wheel always clicked, the liquor always flowed—and time took on a circular rhythm that made hours and minutes disappear. Some people called it "the city without clocks."

He and Gertie had returned to the Mecca after catching the Wayne Newton show—"He puts on such a good show," Gertie kept saying—and then she had gone straight to bed. But Ira couldn't sleep. Despite the rubbery steak and the dry baked potato and the two bottles of Rocky Mountain Spring Water that they'd been served before the dinner show, Ira felt ravenously hungry and desperately thirsty. He tried to lull himself to sleep by watching one of the old black-and-white western movies that seem to run continuously on the local Vegas television stations, but Gertie made him turn down the sound. And the movie couldn't hold Ira's attention or take his mind off the strange hunger in his belly and the thirst in his throat. At last, when he heard the steady rumble of Gertie's snoring, he slipped into his clothes and left the room.

Ira figured that it must be past two o'clock in the morning, but the casino of the Mecca Hotel was as busy and boisterous as it had been at eight o'clock. The lights and the crowds cheering and the spinning roulette wheels made Ira feel a little dizzy, and so he headed for the relative calm of the Oasis coffeeshop. There were two empty seats at the counter—one next to a pleasant-looking matron wearing a nametag for the Funeral Directors Association convention, and the other next to a lithe young woman in a dress that seemed to squeeze flesh into her well rounded buttocks and pump flesh into her cleavage.

Ira felt a sense of comradeship for the lady conventioneer, but he sat down next to the lady with the tight dress. She was deep in thought over the menu; he was deep in thought over her. And he nearly jumped with fright when the young lady addressed him.

"Well, what's good to eat around here?"

Ira licked his lips. His mouth was dry, too dry to speak, and he coughed twice. "Don't know, Miss," he mumbled at last. "Never been here before."

She turned and looked him up and down brazenly. "Doesn't surprise me, John."

"Uh, my name is Ira," he corrected her meekly. She was young, as young as his daughter back in Denver, but he found himself instantly uncomfortable with the comparison. After all, he told himself, the young lady on his left was not a prim high school senior. The young lady on his left was a pro.

The waitress appeared in front of them. "Are you ready to order, sir?"

Ira glanced at the young lady, licked his lips again, and then turned to the waitress. "Take her order first," he said huskily, "and put it on my tab."

"Oh, yeah?" she said. And then she turned to the menu with renewed interest. "In that case, I'll take the crab louie. And a chocolate malt."

"Good, good," Ira mumbled, scanning the menu and discovering that she'd ordered the most expensive item—a late-night snack that would show up on his room bill as a fourteen-fifty charge. He wondered how he'd explain that to Gertie. "Uh, I'll have a cup of tea. And, uh, a piece of apple pie with vanilla ice cream, please."

"You shouldn't have the pie," the young lady said bluntly. "It's going to make you fat."

Ira gulped. If she was a pro, why was she talking like his mother? If she was a hooker looking for a man to spend the night, why was she reminding him of his growing paunch? Suddenly, he was no longer hungry. Instead, he suffered a sick feeling that he'd already sinned by buying the young lady a crab louie.

"Hey, my name is Dawn," she said, touching him first on the shoulder and then allowing her hand to cover his on the counter. "Where's your wife tonight?"

Ira gulped again. The slight nausea turned into a hard ache in his belly. "She's upstairs."

Dawn laughed and then traced a dollar sign with one long red fingernail on the back of his hand. "Looking for a party tonight?"

"Huh?" Ira said.

She leaned into his shoulder, allowing her breasts to brush against his arm and pressing them against him, and whispered in his ear: "Two hundred, sweetie, and we'll party for the rest of the night. Straight or special, any way you like it."

He shivered. He dared not allow himself to think of how he liked it. In twenty-seven years of marriage, Gertie had never really liked it at all—and he'd never hinted at the way he wanted it. "I don't have two hundred dollars," he said out loud, but he was really arguing with himself.

She increased the pressure of breast against shoulder. "Hey, it's late, and I'm not going to haggle with you, sweetie," she said softly. Then she whispered again: "Make it a hundred and a half."

Ira thought of Gertie, asleep and snoring in the bed upstairs. He thought of her silent, somnolent body. And then he thought of the funeral home. The solemn Sunday services on the cemetery lawn. The consoling arm on the widow's hand. The nodding and murmuring of the grieving family. The long line of black Cadillac hearses.

Those long black cars symbolized something special to Ira Tuthill—a somber responsibility, a sense of social position, a genuine authority in the community. After all, he told himself, a pillar of the community can't go whoring after a woman as young as his own daughter. You're a funeral director. You're an elder of the church. You're a member of the school board. And what kind of example are you setting for all the fine young men and women back home?

Ira stood up abruptly. "Oh my, it's late, very late," he stammered. "And the convention gets under way at ten o'clock in the morning. It's a seminar on embalming fluid and I'm one of the panelists."

Dawn glanced up at him and tried one last winking leer. "All right, a hundred for one pop," she purred. "Any way you like it, sweetie."

Ira panicked. He put some money on the counter and got up. His head swam as he stumbled away from the young woman, as far away from those bewitching words—"Any way you like it!"—as he could go. You're a funeral director, he reminded himself. You're an elder of the church. You're a member of the school board.

But her words still lingered in his ears when he returned to the room and found Gertie—still sleeping, still snoring—in one of the twin beds. He listened to make sure that she was soundly asleep, then locked the bathroom door, turned on the water, and hand-wrestled with his guilty conscience until the sudden spasm put an end to his fantasies: "Any way you like it."

Mike Adams flinched each time the wet towel struck the man's face, back and forth, slopping and slurping with each blow. But Louis Bianco displayed no emotion at all as he worked the doctor from Nicaragua back to consciousness. When, at last, Carl Hagen stirred and groaned and then grunted in protest, Bianco threw the wet towel into his face with a final slap.

"Everett," the man mumbled, reaching for the wound at the back of his skull and then moaning at his own touch.

"You've made a terrible mistake, Dr. Hagen," Bianco said.

"Everett, I've got to see him—"

"Mr. Everett is not in residence at the Mecca Hotel," Bianco interrupted.

Hagen blinked and shook his head gingerly, looking back and forth between Louis Bianco and Mike Adams. And then his gaze settled on Bianco's unmoving features.

"I know you," Hagen said slowly. "I know you from the hotel back in Managua."

Bianco said nothing, but motioned Mike Adams to the door. The young man, now doubly grateful for Bianco's second dispensation for drawing a patron's blood in the line of duty, moved quickly across the suite and stationed himself outside the door. Just in case he was needed.

"You were there, weren't you?" Hagen asked Bianco. He recalled the pockmarks, the pale skin, the flattened nose, the dangerously tense stance of the short man. "You're the one who paid me off and sent me away, aren't you?"

Bianco shook his head. "You're making a terrible mistake, Dr. Hagen," he repeated. "I've never seen you before. All I know is that an unruly guest of the Mecca Hotel tried to break into the Penthouse. All I know is that a security guard had to use force to subdue him. And in cases like that we usually call in the Clark County sheriff."

"Go call the sheriff," Hagen shouted. "I'll tell him exactly why I came here. I'll tell him that the man who owns this hotel is dying of a tumor but his own people won't let him see a doctor. I'll tell him how you're trying to murder Edward Roger Everett by letting the tumor eat away his brain—"

Bianco silenced Hagen with a blow across the face. But instead of a wet towel, he used a leathery fist that tore ligament and muscle in a single punch. And then he glanced nervously around the room; if the old man was staying up late over the television monitor, he might have heard the whole thing. He might be listening and watching at this very moment. And then Louis Bianco would be forced to end the old man's paranoid fantasies once and for all, instead of allowing the malignancy to do the work for him.

"Dr. Hagen, I'm afraid you're just not making much

sense," Bianco said softly. "You're not talking like a sane man."

Hagen's jaw did not allow him to speak, but he glared back at Bianco with fierce, frustrated anger.

"I'm going to give you a couple of choices, Dr. Hagen," he continued. "I'll put you aboard the next flight back to Managua, first class, courtesy of the Mecca, and you'll start thinking twice about what you say about people you've never met before." Bianco paused. "Or else I'll have to make sure you don't get much of a chance to say anything at all."

Hagen tried to speak, stammering in pain as he moved the sore muscles and bruised bones of his jaw, and then sighed in deep frustration.

"There's a flight to Mexico City tomorrow at noon, and a connecting flight to Managua from there," Bianco said. "Shall I book a seat for you?"

Hagen nodded slowly, but his eyes still showed anger. And Bianco, who'd seen so many men die with the same expression in their eyes, just smiled. Hagen might not intend to honor his promise, but Bianco wouldn't give him a chance to change his mind.

"Mike," he called out. The door to the suite opened, and Mike Adams peered inside with a panicked expression on his face. "Come on in, Mike. Dr. Hagen's going to need company for the next few hours until he leaves Las Vegas. Isn't that right, Doc?"

Mike looked down at the man who now glared and rubbed his jaw. "Isn't that right, Doc?" Bianco repeated, but the man just continued to glare.

His lower back still ached, but Lester Masaoka was too intensely involved by cards at the blackjack table to pay much attention to the pain. Two hours ago, Homer Sato had wakened him from his nap and Pierce had sent him back to the tables. "Back to work," he'd said brightly. And now Lester was working hard, watching the cards as they were dealt out, softly and silently touching his thumb to his fingertips, then waiting for the answering impulses that seemed to hum deep within his body.

His thumb-to-finger tapping beneath the table was superbly accurate. And so were the answering signals. He followed their instructions carefully, standing or hitting on each hand according to the wordless voice, doubling or tripling his bet whenever the voice said so. Together, Lester Masaoka and his inner voice ran up his winnings steadily and silently, first at one table and then another, first at an empty table and then at a crowded one.

The pit boss was baffled. The quiet Oriental man would bet five dollars and lose, five dollars and lose, then bet the house limit and draw a twenty or blackjack. The dealer rubbed his fingertips nervously, unconsciously mimicking the invisible gestures of the player's hand beneath the table, and he glanced up at the eye-in-the-sky. He hoped to hell they were watching, because he certainly couldn't figure out how the Oriental bastard was dragging down as much as a thousand bucks a minute.

The pit boss went into action. He tried every trick he knew to break the player's lucky run. He told the dealer to use two decks in the shoe, then four, and finally six decks —all the shoe could hold—but it made no difference. He put a couple of watchers around the table where the Oriental played, looking for a counter who might be feeding signals to the player. And he kept a suspicious eye on the dealer himself, wondering if he wasn't tipping the cards or hitting on seventeen or somehow playing to the Oriental's advantage.

Finally, the pit boss called upstairs on the house phone to complain. "You guys catching anything funny up there?" he asked irritably. "Because I can't see anything but a winner down here."

"He's a counter, Jack," the voice responded.

"No shit?" the pit boss answered sarcastically. "A

counter? With a six-deck shoe? And a shuffle every five hands?"

"He's playing like a counter," insisted the man who watched each hand from the television camera overhead. "He bets as though he was a goddamned computer rather than a human being."

"He's no machine. He's human. And I want to know what he's doing. I can't see any backup. I've cased the other players when he sits down and they seem kosher. His hands don't go into his pockets, so where's the computer? How is he doin' it?"

"However he's doing it, Jack, you'd better send in an undertaker."

Jack had a different idea. He retreated to the blackjack pit and called for Fisheye. His bulging walleye gave Fisheye the appearance of a dimwit, but he was one of the best pickpockets ever to work the Atlantic City boardwalk and then the Vegas casinos. Louie Bianco would have put him under six feet of sand in the old days, but now the casino had a special use for Fisheye. Thanks to microcircuitry and miniature electronics, a blackjack computer—which kept track of the cards and calculated the changing odds on each hand and instructed the player on which and how much to bet—could be concealed in a coat pocket or strapped to a knee under a pair of trousers.

But Fisheye's soft touch and knowing fingers would seek out even the most cleverly hidden blackjack computer. And so Jack relaxed a bit when he spotted the old man in the hound's-tooth sports coat and the bad toupee as he eased through the crowd around the table where the Oriental was playing. Fisheye pressed up to the table twice, but if he put a finger on the Oriental player, Jack couldn't spot it. Only when the player dragged his last thousand dollar payoff and headed for the elevator bank did Jack spot Fisheye at work —an accidental collision, a flurry of apology, and a fast body search by Fisheye's invisible hands.

The Oriental broke away angrily and headed for the elevator, patting his full pockets as he went, and Fisheye floated back to the blackjack pit. Jack moved to a nearby table, and the two old hands spoke without facing each other.

"So?" Jack demanded. "What's he carrying?"

"Nothing," Fisheye shrugged. "A pocketful of thousand-dollar chips, and a wallet in his breast pocket, and a watch on his left wrist, but nothing that you can bust him for."

"Shit," Jack said to no one in particular. "I've never seen a counter run up a bundle like that without a computer."

"Yeah," Fisheye shrugged again. "But if he's carrying one, it's got to be five inches up his ass, 'cause I didn't feel it anywhere else."

Three floors away, Lester Masaoka was greeted triumphantly by Homer Sato and then examined lovingly by Pierce. They counted Lester's winnings with equal attention and affection—well over seventy thousand now and climbing. And even though the inner voice had kept a meticulous count of each bet and each win throughout the night, no one missed the yellow thousand-dollar chip that had remained in Fisheye's well trained fingers.

If the old man in the bunker had cocked his head and listened carefully, he might have noticed the lingering presence of Alexander Tate in the doorway of the master control room. If he had punched up Sally Martin's suite or the room where Louis Bianco was talking with Carl Hagen, he might have fueled himself with new energy to stoke the fires that burned inside him. And if he had begun to play with the sophisticated electronic equipment that automatically swept the Mecca Hotel in search of bugging devices other than his own, he might have noticed the unusual microwave transmissions that centered on the room where Lester

Masaoka and Homer Sato and a man named Pierce were piling up ten-thousand-dollar stacks of Mecca chips.

But the old man was too intent on the single image on the television monitor to notice anything else. The image had not changed for an hour—an empty bed in an empty suite, a few pieces of clothing and underwear tossed casually on an empty chair—but he stared continuously, without blinking, without closing his eyes against the mounting pain, without allowing his mind to wander from the single thought.

"*They're coming for you, old man,*" the voice over the telephone had said—and now he knew who was coming.

"*It's over for you now, old man,*" the voice had said—but now he was ready to strike out before the ghost could reach him.

"Unto the grave," the old man said aloud. "But it did not end with the grave."

Ahmed Ibn Sayd smiled to himself as the baccarat shoe was passed once again to the portly cowboy in the Stetson hat and the string tie. Sayd had played the aristocrat's card game in the casinos of London and Monte Carlo, where the croupier's tuxedo was always immaculately pressed and the shills were often truly beautiful women in exquisite gowns, but he preferred to play amid the down-at-the-heels gamblers and soiled young women in the casinos of Glitter Gulch, the sawdust joints of gaudy downtown Las Vegas.

He preferred to play here—and he preferred to lose.

The fat man took the shoe, and the croupier called for bets around the table. Once again, Sayd placed two bills on the kidney-shaped table—a two-thousand-dollar wager on the player's hand. And that was the limit of skill and intelligence in the aristocrat's card game; the dealing of the cards to the cowboy, who held the shoe, and to Sayd, who would receive the player's hand because his bet was once again the largest around the table, would proceed according to the rigid rules of the game.

As the fat man in the Stetson began slapping out the cards, the croupier deftly handled them across the table with his long wooden palette. The shill sitting next to Sayd—a tired-looking young woman with red hair piled high on her head and a sequinned gown that was beginning to split along the seam over her generous hips—feigned interest in the banker's hand, but Sayd knew that her eyes were on him. Not only because she was playing with the house's money and would walk away from the table with nothing more than her hourly wage and whatever the men around the table offered for her after-hours company. No, the shill was watching him because a man who is suicidally determined to lose a fortune is an irresistible sight, even in Las Vegas where so many players suffer from the same obsession.

The man in the Stetson dealt himself a two and a queen —a total of two, since the picture card has a zero value in baccarat—and then he dealt a five and a two to the player's hand. Sayd leaned back in his chair and silently calculated the course of the evening's play—a run of winning hands that brought his hundred-thousand-dollar stake up by some ten thousand dollars; then a huddled conversation with the casino manager, who approved a two-thousand-dollar limit for the player who called himself White; and finally a relentless streak of losing hands that brought his stakes down to a few thousand dollars by the early hours of the morning.

And now Sayd was facing the last hand—the player's seven, which meant that he would have to stand pat, and the banker's two, which meant that one more card to the banker would decide the game. The fat cowboy slapped down one more card, the croupier turned it quickly with the palette and announced the banker's winning hand—the card was a seven, the banker's hand totaled nine, and the player's two thousand dollars once again disappeared into the cash slot.

The shill—although she had been trained to maintain a fixed smile and empty eyes throughout the game—involuntarily shook her head in disapproval. Sayd flushed with pleasure at the murmur that arose from the other players and the small crowd that had formed outside the baccarat pit. It was not often that a player wagered and lost a hundred thousand dollars amid all the dollar blackjack tables and two-dollar crap tables of the Mother Lode Casino. And Sayd felt cleansed and lightened and somehow redeemed by the fact that so many of the crisp green bills had slipped out of his grasp; he knew that the losses at the gaming table would buy him a certain freedom from the disgust he felt at being in the infidel's hell and taking the infidel's money to do the dirty work—the black jobs—that they couldn't do for themselves. And he knew that the woman who was waiting for him in room 551 of the Mother Lode Hotel, would also ease his discontent.

He could hear the babble of a television set as he approached the room and knocked softly. Then the voices were cut off and the young woman's footsteps approached the door.

"Who's there?" she demanded.

"It's Mister—" He hesitated for a moment. "Mister White."

"It's about time," she mumbled as she opened the door. And then she giggled nervously. "I've been waiting for three hours, you know, and I began to wonder if you were coming back at all, but I took your money and I just couldn't leave without—"

Sayd stepped past her and shut the door. His hand moved to her hair, and she was silenced instantly by his touch. She sighed softly and waited for an instruction or an embrace. But he pulled his hand away and said nothing.

"You don't have to be afraid," she ventured. "Everyone who works for Discreet Introductions by Elizabeth gets a checkup every week by a doctor."

"Are you a real blonde?" the man interrupted.

"I told you yes before," she said hesitantly. His question and the strange glimmer in his eyes frightened her. "Look here, didn't they tell you? No funny stuff, Mr.

White. That's a rule at Discreet Inroductions. No weirdo stuff, no shaves, and no golden showers. We're willing to show a gentleman a nice time, but no kinky stuff."

"Will you undress for me now, Star?" he asked in a monotone whisper.

"Sure," she said as she began to unbutton her pants suit. She turned away to hang her clothing on a chair so they wouldn't get wrinkled and when she turned around, Sayd could see that she was indeed a real blonde. And she could see that the stranger was about to break one of the rules of Discreet Introductions by Elizabeth.

"Do you know what this is, Star?" he asked, flexing the thin, leather-covered rod in his hands.

"Oh, God, please," she stammered, glancing desperately toward the locked door but frozen in place by her fear and her nakedness.

"Do you know what this is?" he repeated.

"A whip?" she asked in a voice that verged on tears.

"It's an officer's swagger stick," he explained. "I saw quite a few of them when I was growing up. All of the British officers carried them."

"Oh, please," she cried.

He laughed, and Star shuddered at the sound. "I think you misunderstand," he said, extending the swagger stick and pushing it into her hand. "I'm not going to hurt you, Star. I'm not going to hurt you at all."

"You said that you were a friend of my father."

The young woman did not offer a greeting. She sat opposite Moe Black, her dark eyes shining with light, and she repeated the statement.

"You said that you were a friend of my father."

"Yes, that's right, Miss Christian," Moe said. In so many ways, the girl looked like her mother—the same delicate features, the same delicate figure, the same sensuous lips. But those flashing black eyes—those chillingly familiar eyes—

belonged to no one but her father. "You call yourself Lise, Miss Christian?"

She nodded.

"Your father always called you Lisetta," Moe said.

Tears seemed to well up in her eyes, muting the fire and the depth that Moe found so familiar, and she seemed to shrink into her chair. "Then you really knew him, Mr. Black?" she asked, suddenly sounding vulnerable. "You really knew my father?"

"It was so many years ago, and I can feel every one of those years in these old bones," Moe said, with a weary groan. "But one doesn't ever forget a man like your father—"

He stopped abruptly and stared at the young woman. "What do you know about him, Miss Christian?" he asked cautiously. "I mean, what has your mother told you about him?"

"Nothing," she answered. "That's why I'm here. I know that he was a financier, and I know that he died when I was very young, and I know that he established a trust fund for mother and me with a bank here in Las Vegas. But that's all."

"Oh," Moe said in a small voice. He wondered how he could tell her. He wondered what he could tell her. After so many years, what's the point of tearing open the old wounds? "Well, then, I'm not sure that I understand why you've come all the way out here. I mean, if the trust fund is taking care of you—"

"That's not enough, Mr. Black," she said. "A check in the mail once a month is simply not enough. And my mother refused to tell me anything more. But I flew six thousand miles to ask questions, and I'll keep asking them until I find out about the man who gave me my name."

"Christian?" Moe asked.

"That's right," she said crisply. "I want to find out everything I can about the man named Christian."

Moe Black sighed. It was already close to four o'clock,

and in another few hours he'd have to change into his best suit and pick up the wife and head for the morning service at the synagogue. How could he begin to tell her the story when there was so little time and so much to recall? But Moe knew that he could not allow her to ask the questions on her own—especially in the Mecca Hotel—and he knew, too, that he would be unable to convince her to return to Paris with the questions unanswered.

"Christian is your mother's maiden name," Moe said wearily. "And your father's name was Bertinelli. Augusto Bertinelli."

"Give me another marker, you tight bastards!" shouted the Senator. "I'll sign away my soul, but I'm going to stay on this crooked wheel until I win back every dime I've lost to you greedy sons-of-bitches."

Lawrence Johnson smiled expansively at Senator Alan Simpson Harwell and signaled the tuxedo-clad pit boss who stood politely by the door of the private casino. The markers were strictly a charade—every dime that Harwell lost during the gambling sessions in the Mecca were written off by the hotel—but the Senator enjoyed the pretense. He scrawled his signature across the marker and then reached for a new stack of roulette chips.

"Save that signature, my man," he called to the pit boss. "After they pull my franking privilege, that's going to be a pretty rare bird of an autograph."

Johnson continued to smile good-naturedly, but he was instantly attuned to the Senator's casual remark. Something was brewing inside the Senator's suite—he had sensed it from the moment of Harwell's arrival—and it was his mission to discover the Senator's secret before his Saturday night dinner cruise with Sayd. The Arab down the hall was the agent of Johnson's grand ambitions for the Mecca, but the Senator could queer the whole deal with an indiscreet remark or an attack of conscience.

And so Johnson stayed by his side throughout the evening, feeding him liquor and women and rim credit. He hoped that the artful tongues of the twin chorus girls, Melinda and Belinda, might loosen the Senator's tongue—but Harwell had taken the girls into the adjoining bedroom twice already without loosening up. He hoped that the double shots of straight bourbon might put the Senator in a talking mood—but the bartender had poured one after another without any visible effect. And the markers, which now amounted to more than forty-five thousand dollars, were nothing more than play money.

But the Senator's last remark—"After they pull my franking privilege . . ."—sparked Johnson's attention. If Harwell lost his influence and authority in the Senate, the federal government might be all over Everett Enterpises before Johnson carried out the plan that would sanitize the company and make it his own. And Johnson would not let the remark go by until he satisfied himself that the Senator was not going to queer the elaborate preparations.

"Hey, Alan, have you been writing home to the folks too much these days?"

"Huh?" The Senator looked up from the spinning roulette wheel.

"You said something about losing your franking privilege," Johnson said, forcing a chuckle from his anxiety-constricted throat. "I guess the only way you could lose the frank is to lose the seat, isn't that right?"

The Senator stared at Johnson for a long moment, then turned away and hunched toward the roulette wheel. Johnson knew instantly that he had stumbled across the secret that had made the Senator and his assistant so irritable earlier in the evening—the secret that now prompted the Senator to choke back his drunken tears.

"Hey, Alan, I didn't mean to spoil the party," Johnson said, throwing one arm around the Senator and forcing a fresh drink into his hand. "Christ, you've been holding onto that seat for four terms running, haven't you? Who the hell can they put up against you that's going to unseat a four-term Senator, anyway?"

Harwell gulped convulsively, fighting the sobs, and then fell into fitful coughing. At last, he raised the glass to his lips and drank down the straight bourbon in two hard swallows. "Larry, I'm down on my knees in a shitload of trouble," he said, his voice cracking. "And I don't think there's a goddamn thing I can do about it. I'm being diddled by the dirty digit of destiny."

"Hey, let's talk about it, Alan," Johnson reassured him, although his own misgivings were quickly filling him with gloom, too. "Maybe I could help. Maybe the old man could help. A few bucks, a few words with the right people—"

Harwell pulled away from Johnson and lurched to his feet, pacing to the far side of the private casino while the others—the pit boss, the twin chorus girls, the dealers—watched with silent but unabashed interest. Johnson was on his feet a moment later, motioning the others out of the room and easing up behind the Senator.

"Alan, maybe if I had a word with Jim Carne—" Johnson said.

Harwell spun around and extended a shaking finger at Johnson. "It's Jim Carne I've got to thank for the whole mess," he shouted. "It's that traitorous little bastard who is maneuvering me right out of the Senate and into some foul backwater in the Caribbean. And there's not a single goddamn thing you or I or anyone else can do about it. Not your filthy mob money, not the crazy old man downstairs, not your thugs and hit men—not a soul can do a godddamn thing about it."

Johnson allowed the venom to splash over him, nodding and encouraging the Senator to purge himself, but he was planning: *I have to cut him loose before he does any damage.* And he had to know exactly how badly he had been damaged already. There were ways of coping—and

Johnson knew them all—but he had to know what deals the Senator had already made.

"Alan," he said quietly, "what are you going to say on Sunday at the convention?"

Harwell seemed to go limp, and Johnson moved closer to brace him and ease him into one of the armchairs. "I can't tell you, Larry," he said miserably. "That bastard will cut off my goddamn balls if I tell you."

"You're not really going to let some self-righteous creep tell you what to do, are you?" Johnson said sternly. "Remember, you're Senator Alan Simpson Harwell. A four-term United States Senator." He allowed his voice to soften slightly. "And don't forget who pushed you into the Senate when Jim Carne was bullying second-graders instead of senators."

Harwell nodded hypnotically. "I'm going to announce my resignation from the Senate," he said tonelessly. "I'm going to announce that the Intelligence Operations Committee is starting an investigation of all Everett Enterprises contracts." He looked up with an injured desperation in his eyes. "And then the President is going to nominate me for an ambassadorship."

"Alan," Johnson said, "you are not going to give that speech. I won't let you."

Harwell shrugged. "How are you going to stop me, Larry?" he asked without anger or bitterness. "Break both my legs? Send out press releases about my markers? Or send out eight-by-ten glossies of me and the twins in the sack?"

Any or all of those things, Johnson reminded himself— whatever is necessary to keep the lid on Everett Enterprises until the Arab has done his work.

"None of those things, Alan," he said softly, putting his arm around the Senator's shoulder. "Hey, we've been buddies for a long time now, haven't we? And you know we're not musclemen around here." Johnson forced another laugh. And then his voice took on a deadly and perfectly authentic seriousness: "But Senator, you just can't make that speech."

Linda Warner studied herself in the overhead mirror, and she met with her own approval. Good legs, good hips, good breasts, good hair—and good in bed. A cunt you could eat with a spoon. That wasn't just her opinion; she'd been told the same thing by everyone who had ever been there with her. Everyone except her new husband, who'd never ventured farther than a lingering kiss and a clumsy caress during their short engagement. But tonight she'd show him what she expected from any man who called himself her husband.

She sat up in bed and reached for the watch that he'd left on the nightstand. For Christ's sake, she said to herself, he's been gone for more than an hour and he hasn't answered a single one of the pages. Linda giggled; she'd heard of nervous brides, but never a nervous bridegroom. Oh, the silly thing was probably skulking around the slot machines, putting off the moment of ecstasy that she had carefully advertised for the last three months.

Sighing deeply, she swung her long legs over the side of the bed. If he was too nervous to come to bed on his own, she'd have to give him one or two good reasons to do it for her. And she knew considerably more than two good reasons. She allowed herself a last look at herself in the red negligee, then a last look at herself in the nude, and finally she slipped on her dress and shoes—and headed for the casino in search of her stray bridegroom.

The maître d' glided up to Moe Black's table and stood obsequiously in the shadows until he looked up. "Telephone for you, Mr. Black," he said, holding up the telephone that he'd brought to the table. "Do you wish to take it here or in the office?"

"I'll take it here."

The maître d' plugged the telephone into the tableside jack, and then nodded at Moe and Lise Christian.

"Black speaking," Moe said. Then he muttered, "What the hell do you want?"

"The Jap is back at the tables," said the voice over the telephone. "He took us for more than seventy grand before he went upstairs the first time, and now he's worked us for another forty. We thought you ought to know."

"Is he a counter?" Moe asked.

"We've been watching him good and close. No computer. Nobody feeding him the dope. We've been switching to a six-deck shoe whenever he sits down but it hasn't seemed to stop him. He's taking us good. Should we eighty-six him?"

"Well, there's no law against luck," Moe said, thoughtfully. "Keep shuffling and changing dealers."

"Just thought you'd want to know that we may go down as much as two hundred big ones on the shift."

"Yeah, yeah, you were right to call me," Moe said. He'd heard of lucky runs—and lucky runs where a crooked dealer or a crooked player provided most of the good luck. "I'll be there shortly."

Moe hung up and returned his attention to Lise Christian, who sat stiffly in the chair across from him. Over the past hour or so, he'd recounted the story that she'd come to Las Vegas to hear—the story of a rebellious New Orleans debutante from a good family who met and married Augusto Bertinelli; the story of a short, stormy marriage that produced a daughter and a disillusioned debutante who fled to Europe rather than risk her life at the side of a violent man among violent men; the story of Bertinelli's early years in Las Vegas, the good years when Moe Black escaped from the numbers racket and earned the right to shake the rabbi's hand on Saturday mornings.

But Moe didn't tell the young woman the whole story. He was interrupted by the telephone call before he reached the end of the tale. Not a fairytale, he knew, but a nightmare that ended in a dark canyon in the mountains outside Las Vegas. A nightmare of treachery and betrayal. And Moe realized that he could not bring himself to raise the ghost of the man who died on that night of treachery.

"How did he die?" Lise Christian asked. "You've told me everything except how he died. And that's what I came here to find out, Mr. Black."

Moe shook his head. "I've got to go back to the casino, Miss Christian," he said. "And I swear to you—it wouldn't help you to know how your father died. It would only upset you." He raised his arms in a half shrug and rolled his eyes around the restaurant. "And believe me, there are many people in this city who've spent a lot of time and money making sure that nobody talks about how he died."

"If you won't tell me, Mr. Black, I'll just keep asking until I find out," she said. She caught his eyes and stared into them. "You know that I will, don't you?"

"Yes, I suppose I do," Moe said. "That's a gift from your father, too. Or maybe it's a curse, I don't know. But it would kill me good and dead if you got hurt asking questions. And yet there's nothing I could do to protect you if you ask the wrong questions of the wrong people."

"That doesn't matter to me, Mr. Black," she said. "I've got to know."

Moe reached across the table and took her hand—a sweet, soft hand—and the thought of what might happen to her stabbed through his heart again. "Listen, I'll tell you what we'll do," he said. "You go upstairs and lock the door and go to bed. Then tomorrow, instead of asking a lot of questions of strangers, I'll pick you up and drive you to the airport, and I'll tell you everything you want to know if you promise to leave town immediately."

"I'll consider your offer, Mr. Black," she said as he rose from the table.

"Ali Akhbar," the black man said with a deferential nod

that was almost a bow. "All is prepared for the trip, if you will sign the ledger and the receipt."

"Not Ali Akhbar," Alexander Tate complained mildly to his friend. "Not in here, at least. You must call me by my infidel name. You understand that."

The young black man nodded seriously. It was all understood—the Muslims who were recruited by Alexander Tate knew him as Muhammed Ali Akhbar, but they agreed to the minor indignities of service because they understood the larger benefits. "As you wish, Mr. Tate."

Tate pulled the old-fashioned ledger across the desk of his cubicle in the bunker and ran a careful eye over the figures. Every penny that was spent on supplies—food, medicine, machinery—was accounted for in the pages of the ledger, and every penny that was issued to a member of Tate's bunker staff bore the signature of Everett's trusted bodyguard. And each week, a single member of the staff would venture to the surface and journey to a different city to buy new supplies for the bunker.

With short strokes of the pen, Tate initialed the orders that would be filled in Salt Lake City—antibiotics, morphine, organically grown fruits and vegetables, purified sea salt, and the other foodstuffs that Everett insisted on. Then he examined the receipt that he and the courier would cosign before withdrawing money from Everett's vault to pay for the latest monthly expedition. As always, what would be withdrawn from the vault in the innermost portion of the bunker was gold Krugerrands, each one a mint-condition coin stored in airproof stainless steel canisters.

Before descending into the bunker, the old man had converted all of his cash accounts and most of his stocks and bands into the simplest and most enduring form of wealth—gold. More than half of it was stored in the form of heavy bullion, but a substantial amount was converted into the currency of the apartheid regime of South Africa. Of all the indignities, of all the insults, Tate found this one the most difficult to endure—the purchase and storage and spending of the Krugerrands that represented to him the most cruel section of the white man's world.

But even this indignity had its benefits. As he initialed the receipt for 100 gold Krugerrands—about twenty-five thousand dollars' worth of American currency—he knew that the courier would be carrying 250 gold coins. The excess would go unnoticed in the ledger, thanks to Tate's careful planning during the original inventory of Krugerrands, but the money would be very much noticed when it was delivered to the brethren who were buying more acreage for the vast farm holdings in Georgia and South Carolina and Virginia.

"Many of our brothers and sisters will eat tonight because of what we must endure here," Tate said solemnly to the courier, pushing the receipt into his hand and closing the ledger book. "And never forget the pledge that we have taken."

"I won't forget—Mr. Tate," the young black man responded, halting at the Christian name of the man he knew as Ali Akhbar. "And I won't forget what the old man has done to gather his gold into this hole in the ground."

Tate brought one finger to his lips in silent admonition, but he said nothing more. It would do no good to be harsh on the young man, he told himself. And Tate understood as well as any of them the deep hatred that a faithful man must endure in the service of a man like Edward Roger Everett. A hatred that had its uses, he reminded himself. A hatred that would put bread on the table for the children.

John Morrissey poured the last of the brandy into the last of the coffee, and swigged down the warming mixture as he stared into the darkness at the far end of the Harem restaurant. And then he nearly choked when he saw the couple at the far table rise—first the old man, then the young woman in the white gown—and head for the casino. He scrambled to his feet and trailed them into the casino. When he saw the old man turn toward the blackjack pit while the young woman continued toward the elevator lobby, his heart danced into his throat.

"Uh, Miss, excuse me," he stammered as he came up behind her. "Uh, you probably don't remember me, but I ran into you in front of the hotel, and you gave me a chip, and I just needed change, but the chip did me a hell of a lot of good tonight and—"

He silenced himself and scolded himself for his schoolboy giddiness. The young woman was no older than his students back at West San Carlos Community College, and *he* was acting like a stupid teenager with two left feet. He saw the mixture of anger and exasperation and confusion in her eyes, and he felt suddenly ashamed.

"Christ, I'm sorry," he mumbled. "I must sound like I'm a sappy sixteen-year-old."

She glanced at the man holding a five-dollar chip in his hand and faintly recalled his tousled hair, his piebald suède jacket, his patched and faded jeans—and she smiled despite the mournful weariness that Moe Black's story had brought to her.

"Yes, you do sound like a sappy sixteen-year-old," she said.

And then they both laughed.

"Well, it's been a hectic night," Morrissey said. "I managed to do incredibly well at the backjack table, and it all started with the chip you gave me, and I just wanted to thank you."

"You're perfectly welcome," she said. The man exuded a curious, comfortable warmth, and she began to forget the cutting pain of Moe Black's reminiscences. "I'm glad that someone in this godforsaken place is having a little luck tonight."

"Maybe you should take this back," Morrissey said gently, offering the chip in an open palm.

"No, no, you keep it," Lise answered, reaching out and closing his fingers around the chip. "Nothing will change my luck tonight."

Morrissey felt a new giddiness at the sensation of her fingers around his, and he thrilled at her pause before taking her hand away. "Well, maybe I can buy you a drink," he said hoarsely, fighting the urge to take her hand back again. "I mean, it's the least I can do—"

She smiled wearily but playfully. "If they'll serve a giddy sixteen-year-old a drink," she said, "then I'll let you buy me two of them."

six

Out of luck, Harvey mumbled to himself as the last five-dollar chip disappeared into the croupier's rake. Dead out of luck!

He pushed himself away from the craps table and wandered numbly through the noisy crowd on the casino floor. I should have known all along that I was dead out of luck, he told himself. I should have known that a trip to Vegas was just going to put a lid on it. And when a man's dead out of luck, what's the point in going on?

Harvey allowed himself to be carried through the revolving doors of the Mecca and stood motionless in the dead heat outside. He'd known his luck was going bad when the foreman walked down the line, passing one man after another, and stopping only when he reached Harvey's welding station: You've been laid off, Harvey. Sorry, Harvey. No hard feelings, Harvey. Bad luck, Harvey.

Then he'd tempted his bad luck by drawing every penny out of his credit union account and heading for Vegas to soothe himself with a little gambling under the glittering lights. No point sitting home and feeling out of luck—why not go to Vegas and *prove* that I'm out of luck? It had all been easy enough: Bad luck at roulette, bad luck at blackjack, and then bad luck at craps. Cold wheel, cold cards, cold dice. Cold as the dead.

Hell, what's the point? Harvey fumbled in his pocket for his car keys and pushed himself through the parking lot toward his car. Nothing more to bet, nothing to go home for, nothing to live for—and so why not end it all, neat and clean? Do it right for once, Harvey. Take the old Chrysler out on the Interstate, crank it up to eighty-five miles per hour, and then point it at one of those big concrete columns at the first overpass. That's right, Harvey—turn out the lights, all very quick and easy, and nobody'll know the difference.

The engine coughed into life. Harvey rolled up the windows despite the intense heat—he wanted to seal himself up in the automobile that would be his coffin, and he didn't want the world to penetrate at all. Blindly, automatically, he worked his way through the dense traffic along the Strip and then rolled onto the ramp for the freeway. Slowly, deliberately, he pushed down on the accelerator, urging the old car to new speeds, feeling the momentum build around him, losing himself in the numbing roar of the tortured engine. Faster and faster, hurtling along the broad freeway on a collision course with destiny, holding his breath against the moment when steel would meet concrete in a glorious explosion—

Pop!

Harvey gasped.

Pop! Pop! Pop!

Harvey groaned.

And then: *Nothing*. Harvey stared in amazement at the

dashboard as the engine fell silent and the car slowed to an uneventful halt on the shoulder of the road. The fuel gauge pointed at "E" like some obscene wheel of fortune. Harvey began to weep, but he wasn't sure whether he was crying out of regret or relief. He knew only one thing: He was out of luck. Out of gas and out of luck.

The ghosts materialized and then disappeared in a fluid fantasy as the old man stared hypnotically at the television monitor. It was nearly dawn on the desert two hundred feet above, and the young woman had not yet returned to her room. Still, the old man did not see an empty penthouse suite bathed in the deep red shadows of the infrared camera. No, he saw the faces and heard the words and exulted over the act of betrayal as if it were all happening in front of his eyes at that very moment, instead of twenty-one years before.

Bertinelli's face. Bertinelli's words. And the flash of fire from the muzzle of the betrayer's gun.

Of course, Bertinelli had made it all so easy. The greasy wop gangster relied on a curious code of honor among his "boys," and he took terrible risks because he believed that a man's world—and a man's fear of solemn and inevitable reprisal—were the strongest bonds against betrayal. For the same reason, he disdained the formalities of a man's signature on a piece of paper to establish title over the empire that he and Edward Roger Everett had built in the Nevada desert in the years after the war.

"My name must never appear on the papers," he had insisted, lecturing Everett as if he were a schoolboy. "You will own the land. You will own the hotels and casino. And I will own *you*."

And then Bertinelli laughed—a cruel, cutting laugh that injured Everett even more deeply than his patronizing words. Everett smiled thinly as he took Bertinelli's hand for the shake that would bind them together. But he had already marked the latter as a fool, and he knew that fools die.

"Done," said Bertinelli as he pumped Everett's hand. "Now I own you."

"Done," said Everett softly, thinking only of the dark-eyed woman that Bertinelli had taken away from him so casually, so many years before.

And he repeated the same words aloud on that night when the three of them—Everett, Bertinelli, and Bertinelli's trusted bodyguard—rolled out the desert highway in a somber black Cadillac limousine for an urgent talk. That's how the gangster preferred to discuss the business matters of their secret enterprise—and Everett was delighted. He wanted Bertinelli alone.

"I hear that we are buying more land on the Strip," Bertinelli had said in a good-natured but probing voice.

"That's right," Everett mumbled, staring out the smoke-tinted window of the limousine at the empty desert around them and the deep folds of the mountain canyons ahead.

"It's a sound investment," Bertinelli nodded. "But I wonder why I must always hear of such things from other people and never from my partner."

"I'm not your partner," Everett grunted. Then he picked up the telephone that connected the passenger compartment to the driver in the front seat. "Turn up the air conditioning? It's like a stinking steambath back here."

Bertinelli's eyes flinched in anger. "You do me a dishonor when you speak so disrespectfully to me," Bertinelli said solemnly, a mannered style of speech that he used only to discipline his subordinates and frighten his enemies. "We are partners by your word of honor and your handshake."

"Tell that to my lawyers, and they'll laugh in your face," Everett said. "Look at the deeds, look at the contracts, look at the bank accounts—I don't see any spaghetti-smackers on the books. And the books are what count in America, not a greasy handshake from a wop gangster."

"*I own you,*" Bertinelli hissed. His face was flushed and iron-red; his hands were held open as if in a benediction. "I own you, and I urge you not to forget it."

"Whatever you say," Everett said, turning slowly and meeting the gaze of his companion's angry black eyes. "Anything you say."

It was then that Bertinelli's eyes flashed from Everett's face to the back of his driver's head, and he sensed that in some way he was being set up. But how?

The driver was his man. His muscle. They drove in silence for another ten minutes. The limousine turned off the highway and probed into the canyons of the low desert foothills on a one-lane dirt road. At last, the driver turned sharply into a blind canyon and brought the car to an abrupt stop. Everett, staring out the window, did not look up.

"You own nothing, Bertinelli," he said softly. "It's all of it mine."

A moment later, the driver had walked around the limousine and opened the door on Bertinelli's side. Slowly, solemnly, Bertinelli pulled the cuffs of his starched and monogrammed shirt, touched his silk tie to assure himself that it was still properly tied, and paused for a moment with fingertips pressed together in a gesture of prayer or thoughtfulness. He looked around through the car window. "This is where you get off, Everett," he said. He nodded to the chauffeur.

"You're a dead man, Everett," Bertinelli said. He stepped lightly from the car, brushing aside the hand of his chauffeur-bodyguard.

Bertinelli looked about him. The sun was already descending on the horizon; the high walls of the box canyon cut off its last rays and turned the landscape a deep purple. But the heat was still like a smothering blanket, and Bertinelli found himself sweating under his silk suit and silk shirt.

"Come out, Everett," he said. "This is showdown time." Then he turned to the chauffeur-bodyguard. "Mr. Everett is an unhappy man. He doesn't like Italians and he doesn't like life." Bertinelli lowered his voice. "Mr. Everett may wish to die. Fulfill his wish, Luigi."

"Yes, boss," the chauffeur said. He reached inside his

jacket and brought out a polished Luger. It flashed in the fading sunlight.

Slowly, Everett pulled himself out of the car.

"For many years, my dear Everett, I have endured your insults as I would endure them of no other man. But we have both gotten very rich and that's good. Now, however, the time has come to dissolve the partnership. You sign over all rights in the Mecca to a company in Luxemburg and Luigi will drive us both back to the hotel. Otherwise, Luigi will have only one passenger."

Everett leaned against the car. "Just like that?"

Something in his voice caused Bertinelli to whirl about. Luigi was pointing the Luger directly at his head from six feet away.

"But why, Luigi? Why, *paisano?*"

"I'm sorry, boss. Mr. Everett is giving me a lot of money to do this thing. A lot of money."

"Perhaps I can match it?"

"Don't move toward me, boss!" The bodyguard backed away, still holding the gun steady.

"Perhaps I can match the money?" Bertinelli said, but even as he said it he knew his situation was hopeless. "I have never been able to tolerate the heat of this place," he said. "If it were not for the air conditioning, I would never have come to Las Vegas at all."

There was no answer.

"How did you get him to do it?" Bertinelli asked, staring directly into Everett's eyes.

"One hundred and fifty big ones and a job at the Mecca. An executive job."

"At least it's not humid here," Bertinelli remarked. "Back in New Orelans, it was always so humid. I had to change undershirts three times a day."

"You're a cool cookie," Everett said grudgingly. "I got to hand it to you guappos. You don't know how to live but you sure know how to die."

"I have a wife and daughter whom I love. Is there nothing we can work out?"

The first shot rang out even before he spoke the last word. It went into his skull, blowing out chunks of brain matter. A stream of blood squirted up and fell on the car fender. Drops of it splashed on Everett.

The second, third, and fourth shots, all unnecessary, went into the abdomen of the dead man.

The bodyguard shook his head and breathed deeply.

"Good job," Everett said.

"I feel like a rat bastard."

"You are a rat bastard, Luigi. A spaghetti-eating rat bastard."

Luigi didn't seem to hear him. And then, as if he heard him suddenly, he whirled and pointed the gun at Everett. "You mother fucker, I think I'm gonna kill you too!"

Everett seemed unperturbed. "No, Luigi, you don't kill me. For if you do, who will pay you the money that will make you rich?"

The logic was overwhelming. Luigi holstered his gun. "You know this guy has friends—"

"—had friends. Now bury him and let's get cracking. I have an appointment at the Mecca in two hours."

"Yes, Mr. Everett."

And now, years later, the scene replayed itself in front of the old man's eyes. But the face no longer belonged to Bertinelli; it was the young woman's face.

"Alexander," Everett called. "Alexander, come when I call you, goddamn your black hide."

"Yes, Mr. Everett," said a gentle voice at his shoulder.

The old man pressed his long fingers into his eye sockets; he was tired, he was hurting, he was bewildered—and yet he knew what he had to do.

"There's a girl staying in that penthouse suite," he said, nodding at the image on the television monitor. "I don't know where she is, I don't know her name, but I must see her, do you understand?"

"Yes, Mr. Everett," Tate said. "Shall I bring her here, Mr. Everett?"

The old man's head began to ache. No, no, he couldn't bring her right into his bunker; he couldn't allow a ghost to penetrate his only refuge. "The Mecca," he groaned. "I will see her in the Mecca."

Alexander Tate allowed a moment of silence to pass, and then he spoke softly. "You have never left here before," he murmured; it was a statement that asked a question.

"The Mecca, goddamn you!" the old man stormed. "And when I tell you to bring me out of here, I don't want to hear a lot of nigger backtalk. Don't forget who you work for, Alexander."

"Yes, Mr. Everett," he answered. "Shall I dress you now and take you outside?"

The pain stabbed deeply into his eyes. "No, no, not now," the old man said. "Not yet. But I don't want her to leave Las Vegas until I say so. Do you understand, Alexander? Do you understand—the girl is not to leave here until I say so."

"Yes, Mr. Everett," Tate said. But he did not understand the palsied shaking that suddenly gripped the old man's hands as he clenched them into pale white fists, and he did not understand the silent tears that formed in the old man's eyes and ran down his corpse-like cheeks.

"Do you have *any idea* of how long I've been waiting for you?" Linda demanded shrilly. "And on my wedding night?"

John Warner shuddered at the sound of the voice behind him. One or two other players around the crap table stared, and the dealer smirked to the stickman. But John could not bring himself to turn around and face his bride. The shooter was coming out, he had twenty bucks on the pass line, and he was trying to catch up on the last two hours of losing play. He didn't need a wife; he needed a natural.

"Seven," the dealer intoned. "A winner!"

John felt a new charge of energy as the stick man pushed his winnings across the table, and so he finally found the will to confront his wife. She glared at her wedded-but-unconsummated husband—his eyes were red-rimmed and feverish, his skin was pale and drawn, and the armpits of his new sports coat were soaked with perspiration.

"What the hell is going on here?" she said, slipping into the tone of voice that she usually reserved for tougher men than her new husband. "I mean, really, I'm all hot and bothered upstairs, and you're down here playing games."

The dealer and the stickman exchanged another smirk, and the player on the right guffawed out loud. "Gee, Linda, I'm awfully sorry," John mumbled. "I guess I lost track of the time, and there aren't any clocks—"

"Okay, okay," she said crisply. "No excuses. Just cash in and come upstairs." She allowed him one girlish giggle. "Let's learn some new games together."

"Yeah, yeah," he stammered, looking back at the small row of chips on the table. "But I'm a little behind right now, honey, and I want to win some of it back."

"How much have you lost?" she asked, no longer giggling and not a bit girlish.

"Oh, not much, not much at all," he said. "A few bucks, that's all."

"How much?" she asked again.

"Four hundred dollars," he said miserably, not able to look up at her when he said it.

"Are you kidding me? You blew every dime of our honeymoon on a lousy dice game while I sat alone in an empty room?"

"Well, I've been up and down all night, sweetheart."

"Don't sweetheart me," she hissed. "You've got a lot of nerve to pull a stunt like this on me."

John stared at his bride—not so sweet, not so fresh and innocent anymore—and the thought of returning with her to the mirrored bedroom seemed all the more forbidding. "You know, honey, you win some and you lose some," he said halfheartedly. He was embarrassed because he felt all eyes were on him. "I'm on a run now, and a few more good passes will put me right again."

Linda's face stiffened with fury as she looked back and forth between her husband and the crap table and the pitiful stack of chips. She leaned forward until her lips were an inch from his ear. "Listen, Angelface, you've got five minutes to join me in the room," she hissed, "or else I'm going to pack my bags and return to Ohio."

She wheeled about and strode toward the elevators. John stared after her in abject misery—he didn't know how he was going to tell her that he'd lost more than eight hundred bucks, thanks to a pit boss who was generous with rim credit and a black player who was unlucky on the pass line —but he didn't hear the gambler at the far end of the table call out to Linda as she passed.

"Hey gorgeous," he purred, "I'll take your action if your little hubby don't want it."

Exactly one hour later, after signing a counter check to cover his rim credit and extend another thousand dollars in the cage, John Warner appeared at the suite—exhausted and yet resigned to begging for Linda's forgiveness and yielding to her demands. And so he was vastly relieved to discover that she had fallen asleep on the bed with the mirrored canopy. As he crawled under the covers, he was too tired and too grateful to wonder why she was naked, why she was lying spread-eagled on the bedspread, or why her right hand was resting delicately on her blonde mound.

Pierce hovered over Lester Masaoka's prone, naked body, probing here and there around his lower back with a stethoscope and a rubber mallet and an electronic instrument with a looped coil. Now and then he grunted with apparent satisfaction. Lester, on the other hand, only groaned each time a finger of flesh or rubber or stainless steel touched the newly healed surgical scars that outlined a neat rectangle on his back.

"Hmmm," Pierce said. "Hmmmmmmm."

"Ooooh," Lester answered. "Ohhhhhhhh."

"Does that hurt?" Pierce asked with genuine concern. "That shouldn't be hurting you, Lester."

"Well, it's been hurting me for the last two hours," Lester complained. "As if you'd give a damn about it as long as your money keeps coming across those tables."

"*Our* money. It's your money, too, Lester," Homer Sato pointed out. "Yours and mine and Dr. Pierce's, an even split three ways around."

"Yeah, an even split," Lester moaned, "but all you've got to do is twiddle the dials in a comfortable hotel room while I'm out there suffering."

Pierce walked to the table where a black medical bag lay between a small black radio set with a six-foot whip antenna and a larger electronic unit with flashing lights and glowing panels. He took a syringe and a phial of clear fluid from the bag, prepared an injection, and returned to Masaoka with the syringe in one hand and an alcohol swab in the other.

"Okay, Lester," he said. "I'm going to give you something to relax those sore back muscles and let you sleep for two or three hours. Then we'll feed you and freshen you up and send you back downstairs for another session."

"How much more can we get away with? I mean, shouldn't we start working the other casinos?" Homer asked. "We're already very high profile here."

"Yeah, what if they do a microwave sweep?" Lester demanded, already a bit groggy from the injection. "Or a triangulation on the transmitter? They'll backtrack right to our setup."

"Not to worry. They can frisk you up and down, and they're never going to find the transmitter. Lester, it's implanted between your kidneys. Even if they see you tapping your thumb to your fingers, they have no way of knowing that you're transmitting information over the sensor implants."

"And the rig is so nicely calibrated," added Homer, gesturing toward the electronic equipment on the table, "that they'd have to be awfully lucky to find the microwave transmissions even if they were sweeping."

"Listen, Lester," Pierce added sternly. "Don't worry about being found out—they haven't even begun to dream of the stuff we're pulling. I'm more concerned about the pain in your back."

"Me, too," Lester murmured.

"Maybe it's the receiver implant," Homer suggested. "Lester, are you having any trouble reading the coded instructions from the computer?"

"No, I'm getting the code loud and clear—a fast tick over the sensor implants in my fingertips," he said. "It's just the ache in my back, the ache—"

Lester's eyes fluttered, and he sighed deeply as the sedative eased him into a deep sleep.

"Is something going wrong, Dr. Pierce?" Sato asked, when he was certain Lester was in a deep sleep. "You said that he wouldn't feel a thing except the coded pulses in his fingertips."

Pierce frowned. Yes, something *was* going wrong. And their grand technological scam was suddenly in terrible danger of collapsing under its own weight.

The scheme had been conceived two years before during an all-night conference in the research and development laboratory where all three of them were employed. Homer Sato was a designer of microcircuitry systems for the airborne computers that linked military aircraft with master computers on the ground; he knew that a unit no larger than a pack of cigarettes could relay sophisticated navigation and target instructions from the ground to a fighter plane in the midst of battle.

Dr. Arnold Pierce was a surgeon and biomedical researcher who had devised surgical techniques for implanting pacemakers, prosthetic limbs, and artificial joints with absolute precision and a minimum of trauma to the patient's body;

he knew that the latest technology made it possible to implant a computer signal deep within a man's body.

And Lester Masaoka, a theoretical mathematician, was an expert code-breaker who programmed computers to intercept and analyze the coded transmissions of enemy aircraft and ships; he knew that the skill required to encode and decode a series of blackjack hands was absurdly small, and yet he also knew that his obsessive need to win at blackjack was driving him deeply into debt.

So the three of them designed a theoretical research project that consumed their nights and weekends for two years. Sato designed and fabricated a microminiature transmitter that would be implanted in the small of a man's back, with threadlike circuitry that connected the transmitter to a series of pulse sensors in the man's thumb and fingtertips. By touching thumb to finger, he could transmit coded information to a distant transmitter and computer unit; a few seconds later, the computer would respond in a code that took the form of faint ticks within his fingertips.

Pierce trained Sato to act as a surgical nurse, and proceeded to implant the devices in Lester Masaoka's body in a series of eight clandestine operations in the borrowed operating room of a fellow doctor. And then Masaoka spent three months drilling himself to send and receive a simple code that could record the cards dealt in a running blackjack game and analyze the changing probabilities of a winning hand. Once the base computer was programmed to respond with betting strategies, the three men were ready to make their fortune at the blackjack tables of Las Vegas.

But now something was wrong.

"I think his body is rejecting the implant," Pierce said out loud, glancing at Sato and then back at Masaoka. "There was always the chance that the muscle tissue would become too irritated by the presence of the transmitter."

"But it's so small," Sato said, "As small as I could make it, Dr. Pierce. As small as anyone could have made it."

He nodded. "It's just bad luck, Homer," he said. "Nine

hundred and ninety-nine times out of a thousand, a stainless steel plate or a nylon hip joint or a pacemaker is completely acceptable to the body. And once in a thousand patients, you find a traumatic rejection. That's what is happening to us."

"What about Lester?" Sato asked, nodding toward the sleeping figure on the bed. "We'd better get him to a hospital and cut that damn thing out—"

"No," Pierce said sharply. And then he repeated the word in a conciliatory tone. "No, Homer. At least not yet. The tissue around the transmitter is inflamed, but let's wait to see if it becomes serious. In the meantime, we'll control the pain with drugs and keep him at making it. Homer, this is our fortune—the one we all dreamed about."

"But if his body is rejecting the implant," Sato asked, "won't that cause the transmitter to malfunction?"

Pierce shook his head. "No, the system is working fine. And it would continue to work fine even if Lester was hit on the head. So we've still got our chance to take home some real money. Maybe not the million we talked about but more than we've got now."

"And you're willing to risk Lester's health to do that?"

"Yes, I am," Pierce said coldly. "We'll let him sleep. Then we'll send him downstairs for another go. We'll play the house limit all the way. Then we'll put him out for a couple of hours, and when he goes back, we'll ask for a special table limit."

Sato shook his head. "The Mecca won't do it," he said. "They're not going to lift the limit after he's walked with that much of their money."

"Well, he can ask. Keep in mind they haven't thrown him out yet. That's because they still think he's just playing his luck. And they know that they can always beat a man's luck by letting him play long enough." He paused. "What they'll never know, Homer, is that we've got our little black box. We'll go for one hundred thousand each. Tax-free, Homer. We've got it made."

"If Lester lasts that long," Homer muttered.

Three sharp raps brought Lucille Sheaffer to the door of her hotel room, and she broke into a grin when she saw the pit boss standing silently outside the door.

"Jack," she said, pulling him into the room and snuggling against his arm. "Oh Jack, it was just like you said—I've scored nearly fourteen hundred dollars in the last five hours. Fourteen hundred! I'd have to spend weeks and weeks on my feet in front of thirty third-graders to take home that much money."

Jack gave her a thin smile and then crossed to the wet bar, where he reached for the bourbon and a shotglass. "How many tricks, lover?"

"Three," Lucy said. Then she paused, wrinkling her brow and counting quickly on the fingers of one hand. "No, it was four. Or maybe five." She giggled. "I sort of lost count after the guy who wanted me to pee all over him while he, *uh*, masturbated."

"Lot of kinky action, eh?" Jack said, lowering himself into an easy chair by the window. "You remember to ask for three bills for the kinky stuff?"

"Sure, Jack, sure," Lucy said. She dipped one hand into her bra and pulled out a thick roll of bills. Here's the money —fourteen hundred dollars."

"Are you sure, lover?" Jack said coolly. Lucy noticed a dangerous edge to his voice, a narrowing of his eyes, an intimidating strength in his outstretched legs. "You couldn't count up your tricks too well. Maybe you can't count up your dough either."

"No, Jack, that's the truth—five tricks, fourteen hundred dollars," she said uncomfortably. "And that includes the tips, too, every dollar."

"And how much did you make on your own?" he persisted. "Before I started sending them around?"

"Oh, just one trick out of the lounge, that's all," she said. "Straight stuff, two hundred, that's all."

Jack sipped twice from his glass then placed it carefully on the coffee table, and raised his arms behind his head. "Come on over, lover," he said sweetly. "Let's cuddle up and talk business, okay?"

Lucy approached the pit boss slowly. Her head was full of other men's faces and other men's bodies; her body was drained by the demands of other bodies. And yet she had felt nothing but exhilaration throughout the evening—a sense of triumphant release from the strict regulations and inevitable *niceness* that were her obligations back in the classroom. Even at the moments of fear and shame and disgust—when the last trick asked her to urinate on him, or when the one before insisted on thrusting himself into her body from behind while she fingered herself—the prevailing emotion was one of conquest, the ultimate conquest. *She* was controlling *them*, she was using them, she was making a mockery of their expectations that a third-grade teacher is something pure and pristine.

But now, as Jack's eyes played over her body, Lucy felt panic. So many strange men, so many strange appetites, so many moments of utter surprise—and now the pit boss who had sent her the tricks was beckoning with a threatening glint in his eyes. She'd heard of pimps who took all of their hookers' money, beat them, killed them. What kind of hunger, she thought, was shining in Jack's eyes?

"Here, lover," he said, patting his knee. "Sit down and get close."

"Sure, Jack," she said in a small voice, riding his bony knee like a third-grader on Santa's lap. "You want to make the split now? Eighty-twenty, right?"

"Yeah, yeah, eighty-twenty," he murmured, gazing at her with a cold expression and unmoving lips. "But there's something else I want, lover."

Lucy nodded slowly. If she'd learned one thing in the last five hours, it was that they always wanted something else. Something that she'd never guessed one human being would want to do to another. Something that seemed so distant from a sexual impulse that she wondered if she was really a prostitute after all. "What do you want, Jack?"

"You got any specialties, lover?" he asked. "Got any tricks up your sleeve?"

"Anything you want, Jack," she said wearily. "Any way you want it."

"Good," he sighed. " 'Cause I want it straight. I want it straight and clean, lover."

Lucy laughed out loud. "Come on, Jack," she said, pulling him out of the chair and leading him toward the oversized bed in the center of the room. "I've been waiting for someone to take it straight and clean all night—lover!"

Moe ran his eye up and down the columns of figures for the third time, but there was no way around it. The action at the tables had been unusually heavy—but the shift sheet was badly off balance. He remembered the Oriental who was upstairs and probably asleep on a chunk of it. But they seemed to be losing at too many tables.

"Maybe it's not our night, Moe," said the blackjack pit boss. "Sometimes it happens, Moe."

"Sometimes," Moe Black muttered, studying the count for the run of numbers that might give him an intuitive sense of what had gone wrong with the house odds. A counter, a cheat, an inside job were all more likely than an honest win; he had seen enough action over the years to know. "Okay, this blackjack whiz—let's call him honest and let's keep him in the house so he can give us a shot at our own money. You've given him a full comp? See if he wants a broad."

"He's got a couple of buddies in the same suite," the pit boss reported. "Maybe he's gay."

"Maybe. If so, see if he wants a boy instead of a broad. Get him a goat if he wants one. But keep him happy, and keep him playing." Moe gave the ledger one last look and then dropped it back on the table. "And when he shows again in the casino, give him his own table. And watch him carefully."

Moe turned away from the pit boss and glanced at the clock on the security loft wall. The wall clock—the only one in the casino—told him that it was a few minutes past six on Saturday morning. If he was to make the Sabbath service with Ruth, he'd have to hurry. Because he had one more stop to make before going home.

It was as much a Saturday morning ritual as the synagogue services and the handshake with the rabbi. It was as much a part of Moe Black—Moe Schwartz—as his faith in the God of the Hebrews and the rebirth of Zion. It was, indeed, much more a part of his soul than even the rounds of the Three Blind Mice through the casino of the Mecca Hotel.

He signaled the valet parking attendant for his convertible Cadillac Coupe de Ville—white on white, he always boasted to the other members of the synagogue's men's club —and eased into the traffic on the Strip. The time-and-temperature sign on the corner showed that it was already eighty-two degrees at six in the morning, but the blast of chill air from the Caddie's powerful air conditioner kept him cool and comfortable. Only the thought of his rendezvous with Lise Christian, and the inevitable question that she would expect him to answer, made him uneasy.

But his next stop would allow him to forget the rendezvous for an hour or so. To forget what he owed Augusto Bertinelli, and Bertinelli's daughter, to forget the world of hard men who had built Las Vegas and invited Moe Black to become one of its quiet functionaries. Instead, Moe would return for a few minutes to a world that he'd known as a boy in Brooklyn, long before he began to run numbers for the black-money boys, a world of simple risks and modest stakes and trustworthy bookies.

Moe spotted the low stucco-and-glass building between

a laundromat and an all-night liquor store on a side street—
SPORTS BOOK, read the oversized plastic letters with a
covering of bright metal reflectors that glittered not at all
in the windless air of the desert morning. He pulled the
Caddie around the back, and when he entered the room, a
half-dozen old men greeted him with grunts and vague nods
and pursed lips. He could collect backslaps and kisses and
sweaty handshakes at any casino up and down the Strip, but
none would be as straightforward and sincere as a sharp nod
from one of the old men who made the Sports Book their
home and hangout.

Moe scanned the room. No slot machines, no blackjack
tables, no craps—only a room full of cheap folding tables, a
raised platform at the far end, and butcher paper posted
along all four walls. The action was almost invisible: the
bets would be decided two thousand miles away when the
Cubs finished their doubleheader against the Dodgers, when
the fifth race at Belmont Park or the daily double at Hollywood Park was decided, when the Celtics ended their season.

And the old men—many of them, like Moe, veterans of
the hard-scrabble bookie rackets of the east coast—stood in
small clusters around the room, like so many Talmudic
scholars, watching the odds and debating the strengths of
the athletes and racing animals whose performances would
reveal the winning bet. They were old men whose notion of
heaven on earth was a place where summer never ended,
where the dry air was kind to their asthma and emphysema,
and where a man could wager on any horserace or baseball
game in the country—and never worry about going to jail
for it.

"So how are things at the Mecca?" called one old man
in a treadbare hound's-tooth jacket and pair of shiny-bottom
slacks. "You had to call it the Mecca? The Mecca, Moe?
You know how many Arabs are gambling at your fancy
hotel?"

"Not many, Ezra," Moe bantered in a familiar litany.

"That's right, Moe, not many. But how many good Jews are throwing their money away on showgirls and roulette wheels? How many, Moe?"

"A lot, Ezra."

"That's right, Moe, a lot," the old man said with a grin and a click of his ill-fitting false teeth. "So you should call it the Wailing Wall instead." He grinned and tapped his forehead with one bony finger. "Smart idea, isn't it, Moe?"

"That's a smart idea, Ezra," he answered. And, the preliminary ritual over, Moe turned to the dark mysteries that had brought him to the Sports Book on that Saturday and every other Saturday before *shul*. "I've got a twenty to put on the Cubs over the Dodgers—what kind of odds are you going to give me on the Cubs?"

"Cubs, shmubs," said Ezra, glancing at the butcher-paper posters where the changing odds were displayed in bold strokes of grease pencil. "Eleven to one, that's what the thief who runs this place is giving. Eleven to one, can you imagine? On the Cubs?"

A small group began to gather around Moe and Ezra. "The Cubs are showing early foot," said one of the old gamblers with a sagelike nod. "Last week they only lost to New York by two runs."

"Foot, shmoot," Ezra retorted. He reached for Moe's elbow and held it insistently. "A thief gives eleven to one. An honest man—if, God willing, you could find one in this Sodom and Gomorrah—would give a *hundred* and eleven to one."

Mike Adams kept glancing at the man in the passenger seat, even at the risk of drifting occasionally into the oncoming lane of traffic. Despite the groggy expression and the bandage over his head wound, Dr. Carl Hagen seemed too quirky to be trusted on the drive from the Mecca to McCarran Airport, where Mike—according to his strict instructions from Louis Bianco—was to put the doctor on the morning flight to Mexico City, with connections to Managua.

Mike had wanted to cuff him and be done with it, but Bianco had shaken his head. "Mike, I don't want you to explain why you've got a guest of the Mecca Hotel in handcuffs if you're stopped by the cops on the way to the airport," he'd said patiently. "I guess we'd both agree that you're not too good at talking your way out of things, are you?"

Mike had nodded in silence. He owed Bianco a lot—twice he'd sapped a guest, and twice Bianco had intervened to protect him from being sacked—and so he could take a lecture or two from the boss. But he still didn't trust the doctor with the mad gleam in his eye, and so he kept an eye on Hagen and his left hand on his sidearm.

"Young man, do you know what a tumor can do to the human brain?" Hagen prattled on. He hadn't stopped talking since Bianco deposited him in a Mecca Hotel station wagon and sent the two of them on their way to the airport. "The tumor grows—sometimes fast, sometimes slow, but it always grows—and when it reaches a major nerve or artery, it simply chokes the brain to death."

"Uh-huh," Mike said, trying to ignore him. "Sure."

"And do you know that there's a tumor growing inside Edward Everett's brain?" Hagen persisted. "A tumor that could snuff out his life at any moment? A time bomb that could be defused if only I get to him in time?"

"Edward Everett isn't in residence at the Mecca Hotel," Mike repeated for the hundredth time, although he was beginning to tire of the obvious lie. Everyone in the hotel knew about the bunker, the locked doors that led to an elevator shaft, the air intake ducts scattered around the Mecca's grounds. "And Mr. Bianco already told you that Mr. Everett is under the best medical care in the world."

"Bianco is a liar," Hagen said. "He lied to me in Managua, and he paid me to keep my mouth shut about Everett, and now he's going to let Everett die. Bianco is a murderer!"

Mike took a long look at the doctor, allowing the station wagon to drift back and forth over the center line, and debated whether he ought to sap him once more just to shut him up. But he was afraid to hit him twice—if he killed the talkative little bastard, then *he'd* be the murderer.

"Listen, Dr. Hagen, why don't you give it a rest, okay? In another two hours, you're going to be safe and sound on an airplane, and we can all just forget about it, okay?"

Hagen's eyes darted from the young security guard's face to the speedometer—it read just under forty miles per hour—and then to the road ahead. Mike noticed the eye movements, but too late he saw Hagen seize the door handle and shove it open.

"Hey, are you nuts!" Mike shouted, reaching for the open door with one hand and struggling to control the car with the other, unconsciously pressing the accelerator to the floor as he tried to brace himself. "For Christ's sake, you're going to get us both killed!"

"Let me out!" Hagen screamed, struggling to break Mike's grip on the door. "I'm going back to the Mecca—"

Mike's hand slipped from the door handle, and he flailed desperately until he found a grip on Hagen's coat. But the door was swinging wildly and Hagen was pushing toward the opening. And so Mike cranked the steering wheel to the left, sending the car in a shrieking curve across the road in an attempt to force the door closed.

But Hagen's resolve was stronger than Mike's grip. The doctor leaned with all his weight against the door, and he tumbled out of the car as it crossed the lane of oncoming traffic, spilling both the doctor and his suitcase into the roadway. And a moment later, as the Mecca's station wagon careened off the road into an empty patch of scrub and sand, an oncoming trailer truck slammed into the body that was already unconscious from the fall to the street.

Mike Adams did not see the impact, which pulverized Hagen's chest and nearly decapitated him, nor did he see the double wheels of the trailer truck roll over the suitcase and scatter its contents across the road. All he saw, as he raised his head and stared in horror, was ten thousand dollars in American currency caught in the draft of the speeding truck like a thousand green snowflakes in a desert snowstorm that was only a mirage.

Ahmed Ibn Sayd walked stiffly across the lobby of the Mecca Hotel, glancing with half-closed eyes at the gamblers who still lingered at the slots and the roulette wheels at seven o'clock on a Saturday morning. He prayed that they would not notice the faint traces of blood that had soaked through the rumpled fabric of his clothing; he prayed that they would not see the glow of contentment that burned in his dark eyes. That would be a deadly embarrassment, he told himself—for these overfed American infidels to see his weakness would be a shame too great to endure.

He reached the elevator without attracting more than a passing glance. The guard on the Penthouse floor nodded a greeting with the bland expression that had been washed clean of any disapproval in the hotel's careful training program. As he reached his suite, Ahmed Ibn Sayd reminded himself of the complex of electronic eavesdropping equipment that he'd detected earlier—and he forced himself to remain upright and unsmiling until he reached the sanctum of the shower.

There, beneath a cascade of ice-cold water from twin showerheads over the sunken bathtub, Sayd permitted himself the full enjoyment of his night's pleasure. The splash of water against broken skin reminded him of each blow of the officer's swagger stick, delivered at first with fear and hesitance by the young girl from the escort service, then with the sting of anger and resentment, and finally with the punishing strength that told him of the girl's own need for pleasure. And then a new climax reminded him of the exquisite moment when the pain that filled every fiber of his body was translated into the purest rush of ecstasy.

"And what about me?" she had pleaded when Sayd's pleasure was over. "I want it, too."

He had laughed at her. At her sudden hunger, her sudden loss of innocence, her sudden need to be paid for her time with more than money. He'd laughed aloud and thrown a few more dollars in her face, taking back the swagger stick and leaving behind a sobbing woman who had just discovered an appetite that she'd never dreamt of before.

Now, alone in his suite, Sayd laughed again. The night's events at the baccarat table and then in the hotel room had prepared him for the work ahead by filling him with the bittersweet taste of pleasure and then the foul aftertaste of shame. Yes, shame, Sayd reminded himself, and that would make the next night's work so much easier. He would do their black work with a sense of purity that comes from punishment. He had been punished well, and now he would punish them. He reminded himself to read his Koran as words from the Holy Book echoed in his mind: "What is with you will vanish and what is with God will endure."

Sayd dried himself roughly with the oversized towels, hissing in silent agony as the terrycloth rubbed against the thin welts on his back and his legs, and slipped into a white silk robe with embroidery of gold and silver thread. At last, he sat at the table in the living room and opened his briefcase. Adjusting the lid of the briefcase to block the eye of the camera that might be watching him, he carefully examined each of the documents that had been prepared in advance by the man who had asked him to come to Las Vegas.

He nodded in cool admiration—it was a very fine job of forgery, a very elegant and sophisticated piece of work. "Praise Allah," he said aloud. The business stationery and the watermark and the typewriter impressions were perfectly authentic, of course; Lawrence Johnson had taken them from his own desk at the Mecca Hotel. But the words that were written on them and the signatures that gave them the force of law were as fraudulent as the Islamic decor that tainted the Mecca.

Of course, Johnson did not suspect that Sayd knew of

their fraudulence. As far as the greedy American knew, Sayd was an unsuspecting dupe who would be easily fooled with forged words and forged signatures. But Johnson underestimated Ahmed Ibn Sayd's exeprienced eye and exacting professional standards. If he'd been as gullible as Johnson thought, he would have been a dead man long ago.

The Arab returned the papers to his briefcase. Dinner aboard the hotel's private yacht on Lake Mead at midnight —that's when the infidel would learn the measure of the man he'd tried to deceive.

Sayd decided to sleep. Why venture into the glaring sunlight and the 109-degree heat when the blackout curtains kept his suite in darkness and the air conditioner kept the temperature at a comfortable 70 degrees? No, he would wait until sundown before leaving the suite again—he no longer tolerated daylight and desert heat as well as his countrymen. He'd been away from home too long, Sayd scolded himself as he slipped into a deep sleep. He'd been away from the desert too long.

Lawrence Johnson watched impatiently as the twins, Melinda and Belinda, shoveled forkfuls of scrambled eggs and hashed brown potatoes and sugar-cured ham down their slender throats in the crowded Oasis coffeeshop. The tables around them were filled with potbellied men in leisure suits and their bleached-blonde wives in halter tops, and the kitchen had already served nearly a hundred pounds of hand-sliced belly lox along with a crate of air-freighted eggs, bagels, and a dozen tubs of whipped cream cheese.

"How the hell do you stay so skinny when you eat like that?" Johnson asked the twins, glancing pitifully at the cup of black coffee that he allowed himself for breakfast. "If I ate half as much, I'd outweigh you by two hundred pounds instead of just a hundred."

Melinda forced down another gulp. "It's the dancing, Mr. Johnson," she said between sips of orange juice. "If you rehearsed four hours a day, and then stripped three shows a night in the lounge, you'd burn up a lot of calories too, Mr. Johnson."

"Yeah, and working out for that horny old bird upstairs helps, too," Belinda added, fighting a yawn. "By the time I've gone down on Melinda, and she's gone down on me, and we both go down on the Senator, we've probably burned off another two pounds each."

"Sure, sure," Johnson said, glancing nervously at the tables around him. "Not so damn loud, okay? I just want you to keep the old bastard interested and happy for another twenty-four hours, and then you'll never have to service him again."

"You want us to go upstairs now?" Belinda asked. "I mean, don't we get a few hours' sleep before we have to eat that senatorial cock?"

Johnson said, "No sleep for now. Keep him happy." He added, "Keep the details to yourself, okay?"

"Right, Mr. Johnson. Just let me finish my danish, and we'll hurry back. Okay, Belinda?"

Belinda frowned. "Yeah, sure—but I've been wondering, Mr. Johnson, about our take—"

"You'll get two bills each for every hour you spend with him. You're losing money sitting here."

"The money isn't what I'm referring to, Mr. Johnson," Belinda said. "I'm talking about a spot in the main showroom. A job in the line is what you promised."

Melinda blushed, but Belinda's defiant scowl remained on her freckled face. Johnson looked back and forth between the two women, and recalled the hour he'd spent interviewing them in his private office before the hotel's entertainment director booked them as a twin-sister strip act.

"We'll see, ladies," he said sternly. "Tomorrow morning, when the Senator gives his keynote address at the undertakers' convention, we'll see if you've done your job. And then we'll talk about a spot in the main room."

"If we've done our job?" Belinda asked sarcastically.

"You mean gettin' him up and then gettin' him off? We've done that pretty goddamn well, you know."

Johnson shook his head. "I want you to keep him in the suite next to the private casino. I want you to keep him away from his own room. And I want you to keep him away from Jim Carne." He paused. "I don't want Jim Carne to get near him under any circumstances, is that clear?"

Melinda gulped, and her eyes brimmed with tears of bewilderment. But Belinda nodded slowly, coolly. She'd been paying careful attention to the ramblings of the old Senator, and she understood.

Two tables away in the Oasis coffeeshop, John Morrissey sat across from Lise Christian. He'd faced dozens of women as young as Lise over coffee and flirtatious conversation in the student lounge of West San Carlos Community College, but they were different from this tensely graceful creature.

Lise's elegant white gown contrasted with their blue jeans and peasant blouses; her coiffure had nothing in common with their long, loose hair; her bearing—so regal, so self-possessed—had nothing in common with their slouching intimacy. As he gathered bits of random conversation that painted a portrait of her upbringing—an English convent school, a Swiss finishing school, a sojourn at the Louvre, an adolescence of summers on the Riviera and winters in the Alps—Morrissey realized that she had nothing in common with a thirty-year-old statistics instructor from a suburban junior college.

As Lise nursed a glass of orange juice, Morrissey's successive cups of black coffee began to sharpen his awareness of the young woman. He noticed the glimmer of raw emotion beneath her poised and polished manner. Something in her flashing black eyes—a dangerous anger softened by a hint of childlike vulnerability—pleaded for his attention and yet warned him to keep his distance. Her youthfulness made him feel very old indeed; her mask of cold beauty made him feel shabby and burned out. At the same time, he was aware of an urgent question in her eyes. She was asking for something, and he burned with the desire to understand what she needed.

"How much longer will you stay in Las Vegas?" she asked idly. "Now that your luck has changed, I mean."

"My car will be ready on Monday sometime, and I guess I'll get an early start on the road," he said slowly, trying to recapture the old excitement over the prospect of an open road to New Mexico. But the adventure seemed flat and pointless now, and the open road seemed like a lonely place. "I guess I'll be leaving on Monday," he repeated listlessly.

"Are you going to do something unusual with your lucky winnings?" she asked, smiling faintly, her eyes fixed on the half-empty glass of juice in front of her.

Morrissey rolled the five-dollar chip between thumb and forefinger. He felt an ache, an emptiness, that he'd almost forgotten over the last few hours of play at the tables. The rhythm of slapping cards and sliding chips at the blackjack table had erased the pain, the loneliness, the uncertainty of his crazy escape from West San Carlos. But now the pain was back, and it choked into a whisper.

"I'm not a man who believes in good luck, Lise," he said softly. "And the only good luck I've had in this town is meeting you."

She stiffened slightly at his words, and avoided his gaze. "Surely it takes some luck to get a five-dollar chip from a perfect stranger and then win thousands of dollars?"

He studied her face for a fraction of a second and saw the uncertainty beneath the mask of composure—he was pushing too hard, he was asking too much of the young woman, and he warned himself to lighten up. "I know enough about the law of averages—too goddamn much—to believe in luck," he said with a shrug. "It's all a matter of probabilities, and the probabilities never change. A certain number of hands are going to win, and the law of averages dropped those winning hands in the cards that I was dealt. But a lot of other players around the casino took a lot of bad hands so that I could win. And if you look at all the action in the Mecca Hotel tonight, you'd find that the casino won about as much money as it did last Friday night, or as it will win next Friday night."

"That doesn't answer my question," she insisted, raising her eyes and catching his gaze. Then she looked away. "Why did the winning cards end up in your hands and not the next player's? Isn't that good luck?"

Morrissey flipped the chip into the air and caught it deftly. "Maybe it's luck, if that's what you want to call it. A set of random circumstances, completely unpredictable, completely uncontrollable." He sipped again at the black coffee, trying to fight down the giddiness that possessed him each time he looked at Lise. "Who could have predicted that my water pump would conk out in the middle of the desert? But the probabilities are still there. Somewhere there's an automotive engineer who could have told me that the water pump on an Alfa Romeo is likely to fail after ten thousand hours of use—and I was in the desert when the ten thousandth hour came. But that was a random circumstance, not bad luck."

"And what are the probabilities that I'd be standing outside the Mecca when you started asking for a handout?" Lise said in a low voice, allowing the innocence to sparkle in her eyes.

Morrissey nodded solemnly. "Competely random, Lise," he said. "Completely unpredictable. But it was the best damn luck I could've asked for."

For a moment, he thought that she was flushing with a new embarrassment. Her eyes shone, her mouth tightened, and her pale skin was painted with a veil of color. And then she laughed—a hard, cold laugh that filled Morrissey with a despair that he could not understand. It was as if he had ventured too near again, and she had turned him away again.

"Maybe those probabilities are just an illusion," she said in a flat tone. "Maybe it's not so random and unpredictable. Maybe we are predestined to follow our fate whether we know it or not. Maybe there is a karma for each of us."

"And what's yours, Lise?" Morrissey asked, fighting the imploring tone in his voice—and failing.

"I don't know," she said, sounding at once like a little girl and an old woman. "I don't know yet, but I've come here to find out."

"To find out what?" he persisted.

She shook her head. "About my father. About the things that happened here. I haven't gotten the answers yet." Lise paused, and then frowned. "I haven't gotten the answers yet—and I won't leave Las Vegas until I do."

And neither will I, Morrissey promised himself. *Neither will I, Lise.*

"Not yet," the young man repeated, unflustered by the repeated questioning. "She hasn't told me where she's taking the money yet. But she will. Don't get so hot about it— she'll tell me."

Bianco shifted slightly in his office chair and squinted at the dancer. He was accustomed to deference and even dread among those who took his orders, and failed to understand why Bobby Reed was speaking so casually about his all-important task—to discover where Sally Martin intended to take the three hundred thousand dollars when she boarded a flight out of Las Vegas on Sunday morning.

"You been servicing the old lady?" he asked bluntly.

Bobby fought the urge to wince. "Yes, Mr. Bianco. Three times a night, sometimes more."

"And she hasn't spilled yet? Are you sure you know how to do it with a woman?"

"Yes, Mr. Bianco," he said with a smile, leaning back in his chair and wrapping his hands behind his head. "Sally's in pig's heaven, believe me. And last night she even showed me the dough, just where you said it would be. But she's playing a little game with me about where we're going. All I know is that it's not Interlaken this time."

"I'm glad you're so damned relaxed about it," Bianco muttered, "but I've got to know where she's going before the broad gets on the plane. And I've only got you to tell me."

"And then what are you going to do?" Bobby Reed asked.

Bianco sighed. The faggot dancer had been a cool one from the start—always smiling, always nodding, always saying what he thought you wanted to hear and never meaning it for a moment. But now the young man's self-confidence was beginning to make Bianco nervous. And when Bianco got nervous, he got angry, too.

"D'you really want to know the answer to that question?" Bianco demanded. "D'you really want to know more than you do already?"

Bobby laughed. "Hey, no pressure, Mr. Bianco," he said good-naturedly. "I just wondered why you don't take the money back, tell Sally you're on to her, and let it go at that."

"Because that's not the way I work," Bianco said aloud. To himself, he thought as he studied the insolent young man: If you knew how I work, you wouldn't laugh in my face.

Bianco understood how to use fear and terror, and he understood very little else. He knew no other way to inspire loyalty and obedience than to frighten those who were not already frightened. Mike Adams, for instance, could be handled like a scared little boy because he was already frightened of Bianco. But Sally Martin wasn't so easy—she needed a lesson in loyalty that only Louis Bianco could administer: a weekend without booze in a padded room somewhere in the desert, a working over of her already ravaged face with something that wouldn't leave a scar, or maybe just a ride into one of those box canyons where so many others had gone without returning.

Yes, Sally Martin would respond nicely to a little lean-ing, but the boy dancer was a problem.

"You know," Bobby remarked pleasantly, "I was think-ing. Why not let her take the money and blow? After all, it must be only a fraction of what she's already carried for you."

Bianco hunched forward, and the dangerous tension in his body silenced Bobby Reed. His snakelike eyes played over the young dancer's face for a full minute, and then he stood up like a judge delivering judgment over a condemned man. "Listen, my simpering little faggot," Bianco hissed. "You'd better stop thinking, and you'd better start moving your tight little ass before the old lady gets on an airplane with my money. Or else you'll find something rammed up your asshole—and it won't be a boyfriend's cock."

Bianco watched the boy's face carefully for the inevit-able signs of terror—the widening eyes, the flared nostrils, the quiver of a cheek or a chin—but he saw nothing but com-posure. "Hey, no pressure, Mr. Bianco," Bobby prattled, rising from his chair and prancing toward the door. "I'll get back to you, Mr. Bianco—but no pressure, okay?"

Bianco stared at the office door long after Bobby Reed had slipped into the outer office and then into the corridor. Something had to be done about the faggot, Bianco re-minded himself. Something had to be done to put the fear of God in him. Because he knew all too well—he knew from firsthand experience—how dangerous a man became when he stopped fearing the man he worked for.

The blonde lifeguard in the bright yellow bikini smeared a new coating of zinc oxide over her freckled nose to ward off the occupational hazard of sitting in a tower under the desert sun for six hours at a stretch. Then she raised her sunglasses with one delicate finger and surveyed the swimming pool of the Mecca Hotel—twin rectangles of dazzling aquamarine water shimmering amid palms and patches of Astroturf, separated only by a flagstone bar nearly as long as the twin pools and cooled by an artificial water-fall.

The pool boasted two high dives, two dozen Olympic-sized racing lanes, and three highly trained lifeguards. But the young woman in the yellow bikini was rarely called upon to save the life of a swimmer. Thanks to the solid carpeting of air rafts that covered the surface of the pools and supported the weary bodies of all-night gamblers and all-day gambolers, no one was in much danger of drowning.

No, the far greater risk was stroke and heart attack—and the lifeguard was an expert in cardiopulmonary resuscitation, with an oxygen tank next to the lifeguard tower and an open line to the ambulance dispatcher. As she glanced over the crowded pool area, she saw dozens of potential victims—men with bulging bellies who'd spent the night at the tables and would now spend the day beneath the pounding desert sun, consuming too much alcohol along with too much heat and too much stimulation from the barely covered bottoms of the women around the pool.

One such potential victim was also surveying the crowd with as much diligence, and a good deal more interest. Ira Tuthill, still dressed in the slacks and sports coat that he had donned for the panel on embalming fluids, sat on a lounge chair next to the prone body of his wife Gertie. And while she slept like an oil-slathered lizard in the undulating heat of the morning, Ira gorged himself on the sight of too much feminine flesh in too little clothing.

"Oh my God," he mumbled to himself as yet another lithe body in a string bikini sauntered by. He sipped again on the watery club soda that he'd ordered from the roving cocktail waitresses who worked the poolside. "Oh, my God."

He thought again of the words of the woman who'd offered herself to him the night before: "Straight or special, any way you like it."

The words had haunted him through a few hours of fitful sleep next to Gertie, and over a quick breakfast of dry toast and skim milk and Postum—the doctor's orders, enforced dutifully by Gertie Tuthill—and then during the panel on emblaming fluids. In fact, as his fellow panelists answered questions from other conventioneers about fluid storage in hot weather, and seepage from badly injured corpses, and the revolutionary new Seedman X-440 embalming needle, Ira Tuthill's mind was fixed on the dangerous promise of those words: "Straight or special, any way you like it."

Ira knew full well how he would like it. Warmed to a feverish temperature by the desert heat and Vegas fantasy, he realized that he'd played with the idea in a dreamlike way a dozen times before. During the meeting of the school board. During meetings of the disciplinary committee. And during the panel on embalming fluids. He'd thought of the young women who came before the school board to seek jobs as teachers of the young and innocent; he'd thought of the young women who came before the disciplinary committee to answer for their too-tight clothing or their too-loose morals. And he'd thought of the young women again while the others talked of the Seedman X-440 or the double-seal method of fluid refrigeration.

If they only knew, Ira warned himself. If they only knew what daydreams possessed him.

If his fellow members of the school board knew, they would throw him out of the elementary school auditorium and into the city jail. If his fellow members of the Funeral Directors Association knew, they would drum him out of the profession in disgrace and dishonor. And if Gertie knew, she would kill him.

"Ira!" The voice was muffled but unmistakable. "Ira, would you spread more cocoa butter on my back?"

"Yes, dear," he mumbled, pulling back the sleeves of his seersucker sports coat and lathering up some of the thick brown butter. "Is this enough, dear?"

"Hmmm," she said, drifting back into sleep.

He worked the cocoa butter into her warm, flaccid

flesh with long fingers that were more accustomed to the cold touch of dead skin and muscle and bone. He thought of the cool, damp darkness of his embalming room back at the funeral home; he thought of the deep quiet and profound soliude of the hours spent with men and women who did not speak with their own voices. And then he thought again of the daydream that came to him so often.

If they only knew, he thought. If they only knew.

A soft buzzing from the console signaled that the door to the suite had been opened; a faint whirring sound indicated that the infrared camera was now scanning the room. And the old man's eyes opened slowly to catch a glimpse of Lise Christian as she crossed her suite to the bedroom.

He listened carefully to the speaker, which played out only the vague sounds of footsteps, opening and closing closet doors, and running water—she did not speak. He longed to hear her voice, the sound of her words, to confirm his revelation that the ghost had returned from the grave. But he did not really need to hear the young girl's voice. The eyes were enough to tell him that the ghost had returned.

"Her name is Christian," murmured Alexander Tate from the doorway of the control room. "Lise Christian."

"Yes," the old man said, nodding, weeping silently, clutching the armrests of his chair. "I know that now, Alexander."

"Do you still wish to see her, Mr. Everett?" Tate asked.

"Yes," he answered with an impulse of strength and resolve. "I must see her. And I must show her that she was wrong."

"Wrong, Mr. Everett?" Tate repeated, hanging back in the doorway and watching the old man.

"*They're coming for you,*" he mumbled, repeating the words that he'd heard over the private telephone line. "*It's over for you now.*"

"I'm sorry, Mr. Everett, but I don't understand—"

"Alexander," he interrupted, "I will see the girl upstairs. In the private casino. The Penthouse."

Tate waited for a moment—the old man had never ventured outside the bunker in the years since he'd first descended into his private world. He'd watched the outside for hours at a time on the master console, but until a few hours ago there had never been talk of leaving the bunker. Tate waited.

"Arrange it, Alexander," Everett commanded. "An invitation. Delivered to her room. Very proper, do you understand? Very proper, Alexander."

"Yes, indeed, Mr. Everett," Tate replied. "When would you like to see her?"

"This very evening," the old man said firmly. "I will see her tonight."

Tate hesitated. Then: "Tonight is Mr. Johnson's dinner cruise on the lake with Mr. Sayd," he said. "Remember? You asked me to find out why they're meeting, Mr. Everett."

"Of course I remember."

The old man's long fingers went to his eyes; the pain returned in a sudden spasm, his head spinning with pulsing pain and confusion. "Yes, of course, that's important," he mumbled. "Johnson. He's a dangerous man, Johnson. Yes, you must find out why—but I will see the girl anyway. I'll have one of the others take me upstairs."

"If you wish, Mr. Everett," Tate said. "But it seems unwise, if you'll allow me. To see her alone, without my protection. After all, Mr. Everett, she is a stranger."

"She is no stranger, Alexander," the old man said. "She's no stranger."

Tate wondered at the old man's sudden interest in one young woman. If he wanted a girl, the hotel was full of them—and he could find a clean one, bring her down to the bunker for whatever amusement the old man relished, pay her off, and send her upstairs again. That would be the soundest plan if the old man merely wanted a young girl.

"I will instruct one of the staff to assist you tonight while I am away," Tate said. "Would you prefer Henry or Edward or Theodore?"

The old man's hands began to shake again. The others—black faces, black hands, a knot of nameless men who changed his linen and took him to the toilet and fed him the meals that only Tate prepared—were unknown to him. It was only Alexander who had been tested with insulting questions and demeaning ordeals. It was only Tate who showed him allegiance, loyalty, fidelity. It was only Tate who could be trusted—not the others.

"Alexander, it must be you. So I will see the girl to-morrow morning. Take care of it, Alexander."

"Of course, Mr. Everet," Tate said crisply. "Consider it done."

The old man's eyes returned to the television monitor, and he noticed that the girl had slipped beneath the covers of the big bed, and in the dark appeared to be asleep. Something close to tenderness, something not unlike the indulgent affection of a father for a daughter, crept into his voice.

"Wait, Alexander," he said quietly. "She's been out all night. She needs to sleep now. Let her sleep. Later on you can tell her that I must see her."

Why is she here and how much does she know? he asked himself. Then he shuddered.

It's too damn big, Morrissey complained to himself as he paced back and forth in the suite they'd given him. A spacious bedroom, a living room bigger than the bachelor apartment he'd rented after the divorce, and a bathroom with baffling devices, most of which he could not understand how to use.

He'd left Lise Christian at the elevator an hour earlier, after extorting a promise from her to meet for dinner, and then returned to the front desk to pick up the key to his complimentary room. Twelve hours of sleep, that's what he'd planned for Saturday, but the thought that Lise Christian was occupying a bed somewhere on the same floor kept him from sleeping. His imagination flashed with vaguely impure thoughts about her childlike hands, her thoroughly grownup body, and her sternly beautiful face.

If Lise Christian appealed to him in a carnal way, she also appeared to him as a kind of magical vision—a creature of mists and vapors, an alien in the harsh light of Vegas—and Morrissey suspected that the vision might evaporate if he tried to go to bed with it. Lise might appear to be older and more worldly-wise than her years, but John had seen the innocence and the vulnerability in her eyes. She did not need him as a lover, and he'd be damned lucky if she wanted him as a friend.

Lucky—the word rang false and leaden in his mind. It was a notion that John Morrissey had trained himself to doubt and disbelieve, paying attention and allegiance only to the iron law of probabilities. A failed marriage had soured him on the romantic myths of marital bliss; a failed teaching career had taught him the futility of study and scholarship; but the numbers had never failed him. Numbers, random numbers, were the only law of the universe. And nowhere was the law more rigidly enforced than here, in Las Vegas, at the gaming tables, where men and women hoped for good luck and saw their dreams ground up by the probabilities.

Still, Morrissey knew he now felt the irrational lure of the game—the intuition that grew like a cancer on the intellect, a longing so deep and so demanding that a single turn of the card or a single roll of the dice only made the longing more profound. Others fell under a blind spell, a madness, that kept them at the tables until they were broken; he had taken pleasure in playing his intuition against his intellect, calculating the unbeatable odds and then going with the wild hunch that allowed him to beat the odds.

Now, twenty-four hours and seven thousand dollars later, the game had changed him. He recalled the peculiar satisfaction—not a thrill, but a serene pleasure—of *knowing* that he would lose a hand and yet *feeling* that he would win.

Each deal of the cards had eroded his conviction that random numbers ruled the universe and all the anonymous men and women within it. Each deal had nutured a tiny seed of wildness and daring in his soul. Now, as he paced back and forth in his empty suite at the Mecca Hotel, a new word began to haunt him.

Fate. Maybe the Arabs believed that everything about a man's life "is written" in advance. *Fate.* The word represented a notion that Morrissey had ridiculed over the years, a silly and useless idea that he ignored during the lock-step progress of his life. School, marriage, a teaching career, a series of unthinking, unfeeling choices that did not allow him to speculate on another fate or another future. It had seemed so solid, so permanent, and yet it had all crumbled as his thirtieth year approached. Now the marriage was over, the teaching job abandoned, the lock-step broken, and Morrissey had neither goal nor direction. The road toward New Mexico had lost its appeal. A new enchantment had captivated him—the enchantment of risk, of daring, of chances taken. The law of probability was losing its power over him, and a woman named Lise Christian was taking its place.

"Maybe those probabilities are just an illusion," she'd said. "Maybe we are predestined to follow our fate whether we know it or not. Kismet. Karma."

Morrissey reached into his coat pocket and pulled out the lucky five-dollar chip. Standing in the glaring desert sunlight that filtered through the suite's picture window, he studied the little disc—the garish star-and-crescent motif, the lettering that spelled out the dollar value and the name of the hotel, and the random bits of color-coded plastic that were blended through the design to make forgery difficult. And he realized that the cheap plastic chip had become something fateful in his life.

Fateful—the breakdown of his Alfa in the desert, the chance encounter with Lise Christian in the lobby of the Mecca Hotel, his luck at the wheel of fortune, and the seven-thousand-dollar run of winning hands at the blackjack table? *Fateful*—or just the hand of random numbers in an insignificant little man's life?

A tiny door in John Morrissey's soul—barred and barricaded for so many years—had cracked open ever so slightly, and a bedazzling light shone forth through the narrow slit. He was drawn toward that light now, he was under its spell, and he vowed to follow it. Would it lead him to still more good fortune at the gaming tables? Morrissey was less concerned with that prospect than with a more intriguing one: Would it lead him to Lise Christian?

The massive, double-decked bus vented its exhaust in a great cloud of dirty smoke that washed over Moe Black's white Cadillac, and chugged away from the entrance of the Mecca Hotel with a full complement of passengers headed for Lake Mead and Boulder Dam. Moe choked back a deep cough as the foul smoke filtered into his car through the air-conditioning ducts.

"Are you all right, Mr. Black?"

Moe glanced at the young woman in the seat next to him—so erect she sat, so fine and ladylike—and he couldn't help but smile. And he couldn't help but think that Augusto Bertinelli would have been proud of the woman his daughter had become even without him.

"Yes, Lisetta, I'm just fine," Moe muttered. And then he remembered the man who'd given her the nickname, and flushed with awkwardness. "I'm sorry, Lise—I didn't mean to get too personal."

"If my father called me Lisetta," she said, "then I want you to call me Lisetta, too. You were a friend of his."

"Not a friend," Moe interrupted. "A man deeply in his debt. Your father was a man who commanded a lot of respect and a lot of loyalty, but there aren't many men he would have called friends. But even his enemies respected him, and that's something pretty unusual in this place."

Lise spent a long moment contemplating Moe's words and turned away abruptly, staring out the window as he pulled away from the Mecca and onto one of the side streets that radiated from the Strip into the outlying desert. Moe drove unthinkingly, without purpose or destination, just pushing the big car as far away from the Mecca as he could.

"Where are you taking me, Mr. Black?" Lise asked, still looking away.

"Just a drive, Lisetta," he mumbled. "Just a nice drive and some pretty scenery. So we can talk."

"Why couldn't we talk back at the hotel, Mr. Black? Why were you so anxious to escape the Mecca?"

"It's the old man," Moe said absentmindedly. "Edward Everett. It was the old man who built the Mecca Hotel, and when he did, he made sure there were listening bugs in every corner of the place. You can't say a word inside that hotel and be certain you aren't sharing it with the old man."

"So what?" Lise snapped. "I don't care about Mr. Everett. I've read all about him in the French magazines. He's a hermit, isn't he? Nobody sees him. So why should I care if he overhears what you've got to say to me?"

"Everett knew your father," Moe said in a slow, cautious voice that barely rose above the whine of the tires on the road and the purr of the air conditioner. "You might say that they were partners, Lisetta."

"My father and Edward Everett were partners?" Lise asked.

"Listen carefully. You want the truth and I'm telling it to you. Your father was in a dirty business. He wanted to get out of it. Las Vegas was his big chance." Moe was remembering. "It was a chance for all of us, Lisetta. For years and years we were the illegals—running business on the other side of the law. It was profitable but it was dangerous and we were all tired of it. Too much heat, too much violence, too much trouble. Then Las Vegas happened and we saw the answers it held."

"What answers?"

Moe turned the Cadillac onto Paradise Road. "The gambling was legal here, and there was a lot of money to be made if you knew how to run a gambling joint. And who the hell knew how to run a joint except the boys who'd been doing it all their lives? Like me and your father and a lot of others—we came out here after the war, and we put our lives into the place, and Lord knows we made it work."

Lise glanced up at the rear-view mirror and saw the skyline of Las Vegas receding into the hazy horizon. "What about Edward Everett?"

Moe shrugged. "Your father had the money but it was all submarine money. He needed a way for it to surface. He also had the organization, and he had an idea of what Las Vegas could be. He was on the dark side of the law, if you know what I mean, the dark side. And he needed someone to front for him, to sign papers and pose in front of the gambling commission and the tax boys and the Feds. Everett's name was clean. He'd been holding hands with Uncle Sam since before the war, and he pulled the strings on a lot of the right people. So Everett's name went on the paper—but the whole thing belonged to your father, Lisetta. It was his dream, and he made it come true—not the old man."

"But Everett owns the Mecca now," Lise said slowly, and Moe realized that she was beginning to understand the terrible truth. "Not my father."

Moe drove a few miles without speaking, but her question hung over him with a power that forced him to answer. "Listen, I'm not going to tell you that your father was an angel, Lisetta, if you know what I mean. He was a strong man, and a lot of big men were scared of him. When you fear a man, you also hate him. Your father was feared and hated by many."

"You're saying my father was a gangster?"

Moe paused. "Let me put it this way. You knew where you stood with him. If you didn't cross him, you didn't have anything to worry about. And only one man managed to cross your father without paying a price for it."

Lise said, "Edward Everett?"

"That's right, Lisetta," Moe said in a pleading tone. "But that was twenty-one years ago. A lifetime ago. And it's all over now, Lisetta. Your father is gone, and there's no one left to settle the score."

"How did he cross my father?" Lise asked.

Moe paused again, but before he could devise an answer to satisfy the girl's curiosity without endangering her life, he was distracted by the sudden rumbling of the Cadillac's fat tires. The desert highway had given out to unpaved road, and the car bounced up and down on the rutted surface. A few hundred feet away was the first of a succession of bare hills enfolding box canyons and lost mineheads and a hundred forgotten graves.

"Why have you brought me here?" Lise asked, her eyes darting over the shadowy canyon ahead of them.

Moe eased the Cadillac to a stop only yards from the mouth of the box canyon. "A lot of high school kids come out here on Saturday nights to drink beer and, uh, play around a little, if you know what I mean."

He did not mention the uses to which the pretty scenery had been put in the early years, long before there was a bustling high school and crowded churches and not one but two synagogues in Las Vegas. He did not mention the casual phrase that had attached itself to the bleak desert landscape—"Gambler's Graveyard"—and he scolded himself bitterly for having brought the girl to the place where her past might haunt her.

"What happened to my father, Mr. Black?" Lise said. "You promised to tell me and I want to know." Her voice softened into a little girl's whisper: "I need to know."

"God help me, Lisetta, right ahead of us is where your father died," Moe said, reaching for her hand. His eyes were moist. "They killed him right there."

Lise stared off into the purple, shadowy folds of the

desert mountains—and once again saw the distant, flickering light. "Are you saying it was Mr. Everett who killed my father?"

"Maybe it was another man who used the gun," Moe said in a solemn whisper, almost muted by the pain and sorrow that played over her face and made her seem a thousand years old. "Maybe it was another man who pulled the trigger. But it was for the old man that Augusto Bertinelli was executed."

"Who pulled the trigger, Mr. Black?" Lise asked.

"Lisetta, I may have made a terrible mistake by bringing you here." Moe squeezed her hand again. "Please don't ask me to compound it by telling you who shot your father. It was done on Everett's orders. That's enough to know."

"It's not enough, Mr. Black," Lise warned.

Moe shook his head. "You can't bring your father back to life, Lise."

"I am my father's life—I'm his flesh and blood. I'm all that's left of him. You *must* tell me. You *promised* to tell me."

"It was your father's bodyguard. He was just a tool. He who your father trusted to keep him alive. He took Everett's money and betrayed your father."

Moe seemed to age in front of Lise's eyes. Suddenly, the pleasant old man in the expensively tailored suit and the carefully groomed toupee dissolved into a primitive kind of grief, a deep sort of mourning that touched her heart. But she didn't join him in weeping.

"The bodyguard's name, Mr. Black?" she insisted. "You have to tell me that, at least."

Moe shook his head to regain his composure and choke back his tears. "Your father is dead," he said. "Let him be dead, Lisetta. I'm the one who brought you here. You look like your father and I'm sure Everett recognized that. I'm sure he is fearful. Your father would have enjoyed that. Through you—your father has had the last laugh on a mean dying old man."

Lise was silent. Moe stared at her—so young, so beautiful, so gentle.

"Please take me back to the Mecca, Mr. Black," Lise said. "And I hope you don't have problems because of what you've told me."

Twice Moe Black started to say something, but a glance at her face caused him to change his mind. They drove back in total silence.

Ben Payne knew he wasn't in the limousine when he began to stir awake. No, he was in a bed at the Mecca, with Selma at his side, still exhausted from the hours at the craps table. Had he passed out? he wondered. Then, like a stab in the side, the panic started. The money. Had he won or lost? Ben gently tugged at Selma. She opened her eyes and he knew the answer. Deep sadness there.

The Gucci bag lay on the couch. He padded over to it, picked it up. He didn't have to count the few fifties to know that he was down. Selma told him, her voice low and hollow: "You signed markers for twenty-eight thousand." Then, a sob. "Oh, Ben," she said.

He felt strangely tranquil despite their trouble. What was it? he asked himself. What was wrong with him? Why did he seem to need to lose at the crap table? Now he would go to jail and that would kill his parents in Cleveland. They were both doctors, had won their degrees when it was tough for blacks. His mother, particularly, had struggled. It had all come so easily to Ben, the chances, the groups, the tempo of deals. Only this, the gambling disease to remind him of his deep sense of unworthiness.

"What are we going to do?" Selma asked. Ben noted that she had used *we*. She was the good thing in his life and he had brought her little but trouble. "I am going to win it back," he said. "Before Monday." He picked up the phone and called room service. "First, we'll have breakfast," he said, feigning an enthusiasm he didn't feel.

seven

Skip walked slowly down the catwalk, pausing here and there to peer over the railing through the one-way mirrors that lined the ceiling of the Mecca casino. These carefully designed panels allowed the supervisors to study the play at every table in the casino. And Skip was proud of the fact that he didn't need bifocals to read the markings on the cards held by dealer and player alike.

"Hey, Skippy, I've spotted a pair that will knock your eyes out," called one of the men sitting around a bank of television consoles at the far end of the mezzanine. The screens displayed the precise images relayed from the cameras mounted in the eye-in-the-sky that hung over the casino floor like a revolving mirrored ball in a speakeasy.

"Nothing knocks my eye out anymore," Skip called back. He'd seen it all from his perch above the casino—the cheats, the dips, the skimmers, the crooked dealers, and the crooked pit bosses—and more than once he'd given the word that broke a scam or put a cheater in Gambler's Graveyard. Of course, nowadays they relied more and more on the cameras instead of the cool eye, and they would blackball a man from Vegas rather than put him under.

"Why don't you just amble over to table five in the blackjack pit and see what's hanging around there?"

Skip sauntered along the catwalk to the peephole over table five. He leaned over the railing—and then he whistled out loud. Three players crowed around the table, and the play was fast and heavy, but that's not what caught his eye. The blonde on the right was leaning over the table, and her ample bosom was spilling out like a jackpot from a slot machine.

"Now is that a pair, Skippy?" the man at the console asked.

"Forty-twos in a D cup," Skip replied expertly. He'd seen it all, and he could read the spots on a pair of dice from twenty feet.

"Shit," replied the man at the console. "I say those are forty-fours, or else I never sucked my old mamma's teats."

Mike Adams stood in the harsh glare of the fluorescent lights with a deputy sheriff in the morgue, where the remains of an American doctor from Nicaragua were neatly laid out on a marble slab. The deputy, who had seen far worse sights while scraping suicides off the sidewalk under hotel balconies and automobile accident victims off the interstate highway, was unmoved by the sight of a crushed torso and a severed head—but Mike fought the urge to retch or run from the room.

"Now tell me again how this bird managed to get in the way of that truck," the deputy asked in his best imitation of the hard-boiled dicks from the detective bureau. "And tell me why he was carrying all that cash around with him, okay?"

"I told you, goddamnit, I already told you—he was nuts, he tried to jump out of the car, and when I tried to stop him, I lost control of the car. That's it, for Christ's sake!"

"And the money?" The deputy was not much older than the young security guard, but he carried his badge and uniform with far more assurance. "What about all that dough?"

"Hell, I don't know," Mike whined. "It's just like I told you—I work for Mr. Louis Bianco. And he told me to escort this guy to the airport. That's all. As for the money, maybe he was a lucky gambler."

The deputy smirked. "It's old, dirty money. It's not casino dough. Anyway I've heard all the stories about your Louie Bianco and the rough stuff he used to pull in the old days. Well, let me clue you in, buddy—Vegas is a different town nowadays. If you spill somebody's guts in the middle of town, you've gotta answer to the law for it."

"And you're the law?" A new voice rolled over them, and the deputy snapped to attention as a stout man eased up behind him. "Is that what you're saying, young man?"

"N-n-no, sir, Lieutenant," the deputy stammered, his smirk gone and his jaw noticeably stiffened. "I was investigating a death under suspicious circumstances—"

"I've read the kid's statement, and it looks like accidental death to me," the stout man said coolly, scanning the security guard with eyes that reflected sympathy and weariness at the same time. "Let's put the stiff in the cooler and send this kid back to work, okay?"

"Yes, sir," the deputy said, snapping to attention and watching the lieutenant lead the security guard out of the morgue.

"So you work for Bianco, eh?" the lieutenant said, walking Mike toward the rear door of the sheriff's substation.

"Yes, sir, I do," Mike said. "He'll tell you that I was just driving the guy to the airport."

"We've already talked. You know, I used to work for Louie, too, when I wasn't too damn much older than you appear to be. He can be a hard man, Louie can."

"I'm not complaining," Mike said. "He's helped me out of a lot of jams."

"Like this one?" The lieutenant laughed. "That's the way the boys work, you know. They help you into a jam, and then they help you out, and then you belong to them. That's the old way of doing things, kid. And Louie Bianco has never embraced the new ways."

"I don't understand," Mike said.

"You a local boy?" the lieutenant interrupted.

"Yes, sir. Graduated high school last year. Played on the varsity team two years in a row. And if I get a football scholarship, I'll be starting college next fall. But in the meantime I gotta put in the hours at the Mecca."

The older cop smiled. "What does your old man do?"

"Worked construction for a long time, but nothing since they put up the Mecca. My uncle's a dealer, and he's trying to get my dad into dealing school, but he's too old to learn new tricks. At least that's what he says. And so I work at the hotel to help out at home."

"You know, the Mecca may look spiffy clean, but there is still the feel of the mustaches around there."

"What do you mean?" Mike asked uneasily. "Listen, am I in some kind of trouble?"

"No, no trouble," the lieutenant sighed. "Your boss took care of everything. After all, like I told you, I used to work for him, too. But I don't know how much longer Louie Bianco will have any juice in this town. He's an antique— one of the old boys who still depends too much on muscle —and that's out today. The men in the business suits with their Lear Jets have taken over, son, and the 'boys' are long gone. Vegas is big business now, not a Meyer Lansky concession. A nice young man like you ought to remember that. You ought to think about your future."

"Yeah, my future," Mike repeated, getting slightly sick to the stomach again at the sight of Carl Hagen's dismembered corpse. "I'm doing my time at the Mecca until the scholarship comes through, and then I'll return to school."

"Do that, son," the lieutenant said, patting Mike on the shoulder. "For your own sake, I certainly hope you do that."

The putting green shimmered in the undulating heat of the summer afternoon as Senator Alan Simpson Harwell, Larry Johnson, and Jim Carne rolled across the Mecca's golf course in the hotel's enclosed and air-conditioned golf cart. The water that was required to keep six acres of imported topsoil covered with a luxuriant growth of Bermuda grass would have been enough to plant a hundred acres in rice, but a golf course was as much a staple of life in Las Vegas as any crop.

"You're three under par," Larry Johnson said, elbowing the Senator good-naturedly. "I'll bet you've been spending more time on the putting green than on the Senate floor back in Washington."

"You're damned right," the Senator chuckled. "I knew that I could take a couple grand off you here even if I lose it back there," nodding at the Mecca.

Jim Carne scowled. He'd waited up most of the night in the Senator's suite, but the Senator hadn't returned from the private casino—with its conveniently placed bedrooms and its conveniently available girls—until after lunch. And then Larry Johnson had whisked them all out to the golf course, not allowing Carne even a moment to drill the Senator on tomorrow morning's speech.

Carne was sickened by the display of camaraderie and intimacy between these two corrupted men. How could Harwell keep up the appearance of good will and good spirits when he knew what he had to do in his convention speech? In another twenty-four hours, Larry Johnson would be heading for a penitentiary, the old man in the bunker would be heading for a congressional hearing, and Senator Alan Simpson Harwell would be heading for an honorable refuge on a Caribbean island—and yet the Senator acted as though he would go on screwing Larry Johnson's women and spending Edward Everett's money forever. Well, Carne told himself, that's just a measure of how thoroughly degraded the Senator had become in recent years.

"What's on the agenda tonight, Larry?" the Senator asked with a wink and a leer. "Can I sweet-talk you out of another set of markers, and maybe have another play in the private casino?"

"Don't forget tomorrow morning," Carne said sharply. "I think you should turn in early tonight so your head will be clear for your speech."

Johnson's eyes met the Senator's, and the Senator smirked. "Yes, why don't you hit the sack early, Jimmy boy," he said with extravagant sarcasm. "But I think I'll stay up with the grownups. And don't wait up for me."

Carne squinted at the Senator and Larry Johnson. Had the corrupt politician broken down and spilled his guts? Carne swallowed a sudden bitter bubble of indigestion and reminded himself that it was his job to make certain everything went according to plan. And that meant keeping a short leash on the Senator.

"Well, maybe you're right, Senator," Carne said smoothly. "After all, Saturday night in Las Vegas—that's the time for a little fun, isn't it? And maybe I'll join you and the twins in the casino tonight. If you can spare one of them for me."

Larry Johnson smiled. "Melinda or Belinda?" he asked, laughing in what was almost a giggle.

"Either one," Carne said, realizing he was expected to reply. "Whichever one the Senator doesn't want."

"Why, Jim, I'm surprised at you," the Senator boomed. "Don't you know that I like 'em both at the same time? Hell, I thought you paid more attention to detail, Jimmy boy."

Larry Johnson joined the Senator in a burst of raucous laughter, and Jim Carne joined in with as much enthusiasm as he could muster. But deep inside he wasn't laughing at all.

His back hurt. His head hurt. Even his fingers were cramped and painful. But Lester Masaoka persisted at his tedious work with one eye on the cards and one hand in his pocket, tapping out the run of the cards and then receiving the computer's pulsed instructions a few seconds later, making the bets and pulling the bets at its instigation, losing a few hands and winning a lot more. Hour by hour, as the afternoon passed, his stacks of chips grew higher and higher.

A crowd surrounded his table as he played alone. Now he fingered the five-hundred-dollar whites and the thousand-dollar yellows as the dealer shuffled the six decks under the watchful eye of the pit boss.

Without being asked, they'd given him the whole table. He could play one hand or all six. And they agreed to double the limit so he could play as much as two thousand dollars on each hand: twelve thousand dollars a deal. He thought about it and began to sweat. His back was hurting something awful so that sometimes even when he won he winced.

The house was trying everything. They were mixing cards after a single deal. They were playing out all the cards. They were changing decks every ten minutes. All of this industrious work had taken its toll. He was losing big hands as well as winning them. But, on balance, his stake had climbed—and was climbing.

And yet Lester was depressed, not pleased. His back hurt, his head hurt, his fingertips hurt.

The cards hit the table with a muted snap, the dealer scanned his hand, and nodded toward Lester: "Cards?"

Lester tapped thumb against forefingers in a message that told the computer upstairs about the cards on the table; the dealer was showing a nine, and on his first hand Lester held a nine and a two. It was a decision that even the greenest blackjack amateur could make, but Lester dutifully called upon the computer to confirm his decision: "Hit."

The dealer dragged another card from the shoe and passed it across the table to Lester: Seven, a total of eighteen in Lester's hand, and Lester felt the quiet satisfaction of a cardplayer with a hard eighteen to the dealer's none showing.

But Lester's instincts and experience and intuition counted for nothing. He tapped out the new cards to the computer, which cogitated and computed and counted, and then whispered back to Lester: "Hit."

He shook his head, but gestured for another card with a short brush of the cards on the table. The dealer's face showed a glimmer of surprise, and the pit boss on his left was frowning. How could the lucky Jap hit on eighteen? But the computer knew better, and the next card out of the shoe was a deuce. The dealer turned his hole card, showing a five, and then hit for an eight—total of twenty-two. He was over, and he paid off Lester's three bets.

The crowd around Lester sighed. The security guards studied him still more closely. A hooker leaned ever more intimately into his shoulder. But Lester was aware of only one message, a pitter-patter in his fingertips that told him to bet the table limit again. The deck was picture rich. The computer was predicting another blackjack, and Lester simply followed the order. The crowd sighed again as he pushed two thousand dollars back into each of four betting boxes.

The dealer slapped down the cards crisply, automatically, but watched with uncharacteristic interest as Lester turned up his cards for a quick glance. But Lester was not interested, nor was he surprised when he saw an ace and a jack. Almost embarrassed, he flipped over the cards of his first hand: "Blackjack."

The crowd oohed and aahed as the dealer pushed the three-to-two payoff across the table, and Lester sighed in deep fatigue as the stack of chips grew three thousand dollars higher. For the hundreth time since he'd returned to the tables at noon, he checked his wristwatch—a cheap plastic watch with a clockwork movement that would not interfere with the transmissions of his implants and sensors—and saw with immense relief that it was nearly four o'clock in the afternoon. According to Pierce's plan, he could quit the blackjack table for another rest break.

As soon as he got upstairs Lester would ask Pierce for another injection; the pain in his lower back was getting worse. He had long ago forgotten about his fear of discovery by the casino officials or detection by a microwave sweep. He was dimly aware of the run of the cards, but he was vividly aware of the hot, throbbing pain in his body. Groggy from both the pain and the pain relievers, almost blind from both headache and backache, Lester intended to ask Pierce for another injection—and an explanation. Something was going wrong, Lester knew, and he wanted to know why. Pierce had promised that the whole thing would be painless.

The crowd behind him parted slightly as he slipped down from the stool and wobbled toward the elevator, a security guard trailing him with his winnings in a canvas bag to be deposited in the cage for a casino receipt. As Lester passed, he felt a dozen fingers touching and caressing him, and a dozen voices whispered in his eyes. For a moment of flashing panic, he thought that he'd gone delirious from the hours of tedium and fever and pain—then he realized that the voices were whispering "For Luck!" and the fingers were reaching for a talismanic touch. And for just a moment he felt the flashing pride of a winning gambler.

And then a somewhat firmer grip on his elbow and a less adoring voice in his ear stopped him halfway across the casino floor. Lester turned and faced the somber, unsmiling face of the blackjack pit boss.

"Mr. M," the pit boss said in a tone of icy deference, "may I buy you a drink before you go upstairs? I'd like to have a chat with you."

Lester felt a prickle of cold sweat on his feverish brow

as he pulled his arm away. "Later," he said. "Thank you very much, but I'm very tired and I have to lie down now."

"Of course, Mr. M," the pit boss persisted, "I just wanted you to know that I'll be happy to arrange anything you need—a little entertainment, maybe a little companionship."

Lester stared. They weren't going to arrest him after all. They wanted to keep him in the hotel so he could lose back the two hundred thousand dollars.

"Yes, yes, that's fine," Lester said. "But now I'd like to get some sleep."

"Of course," the pit boss murmured, reaching into his coat pocket and flashing a business card. "My name is Jack Davis, Mr. M, and be sure to call me if there's anything you need."

Lester pushed on toward the elevators, suddenly lightened by the knowledge that they'd managed to pull it off again. Wouldn't the others be pleased! Then another stab of pain erased the exultation and replaced it with new despair. Pierce said the goddamn thing would be painless, he thought angrily as he rode toward their room, but it was hurting like bloody goddamn hell. And he intended to tell Pierce exactly that.

The old man watched, unaware that he was breathing heavily and shaking with a subtle palsy that gripped his hands. He was too intent on the images that played across the television monitor in the master control room of his bunker—the opening door of the Penthouse suite, the slender young woman crossing the room, the discovery of an envelope propped up against a basket of flowers on the coffee table. And the old man stared at the girl's face as she discovered the gift, picked up the envelope, tore it open, and read the words.

"Dear Miss Christian," the letter said in the plain, sturdy handwriting of Alexander Tate. "Mr. Edward Roger Everett, proprietor of the Mecca Hotel, invites you to join him for supper in the Penthouse Casino at midnight tonight."

Would she pale and tremble? Would she panic and weep? Would she flee the hotel? The old man had waited for hours in aching anticipation to see how the invitation would effect the young woman who'd come to haunt him. Would she call his bluff and appear in the casino on the twenty-sixth floor at midnight to face him?

Alexander had taken care of it all with his customary efficiency. A note prepared and delivered. A basket of flowers as a gentlemanly touch. A call to Larry Johnson's office—he was gone, as usual, but an obsequious secretary took the message—to arrange for the use of the private casino at midnight. And finally an order to the black men on the bunker staff who would prepare a meal of the required sanitary and nutritional qualities that the old man always demanded.

None of the preparations mattered now. The old man saw only her face, her eyes, as they materialized on the television screen in a pattern of blue-gray lines. And she did not pale. She did not panic. She did not flee. No, the young woman named Lise Christian smiled with a quiet strength and a cool satisfaction that the old man had seen before on another face, in another pair of eyes. And it was the old man who felt fear.

Somebody had to do it, Bianco told himself. Or else the little faggot was going to let Sally Martin get away with Louie Bianco's skim.

Bianco drew a finger idly over his lips in a gester of contemplation, a mannerism that he'd acquired during the years when silence was the essence of loyalty. But those times were gone, he reminded himself as he sat alone in his empty office, and he could not count on silence anymore. He could not count on loyalty. He could not count on anyone but himself.

Of course, there were always a few hard-fisted flunkies who were dumb enough or scared enough to follow Bianco's orders and shut up about it. The young security guard, for instance, was stupid *and* scared at the same time. And he had managed to get the troublesome doctor from Nicaragua killed without being asked. That was the best kind of loyalty, Bianco knew, but it was a dead song in Las Vegas. Everybody wanted to work thirty-five hours, pay union dues, and go home to the wife and the kids and the backyard barbecue. People wanted to act like goddamned solid citizens, and even the cops were beginning to take their badges too seriously.

Yes, Mike Adams was a rare bird in Vegas nowadays, but Bianco had other plans for him tonight. The young security guard was already aboard the hotel's private yacht on Lake Mead, detailed to the crew on Bianco's orders and waiting for the dinner cruise at midnight. Mike would be his eyes and ears aboard the yacht; he would discover why Larry Johnson was taking the Arab on a pleasure cruise in the middle of the night; and he would report back to Bianco.

That didn't solve the problem of Bobby Reed. Someone had to wipe the smirk off the pretty boy dancer's face and convince him to deliver the goods on Sally Martin before the old bag tiptoed out of town with Bianco's money. And Bianco knew exactly what had to be done. Every detail, every moment of terror, every word of intimidation. If only he could do it himself, he thought, just like the old days.

If only he could do it himself. Bianco licked his lips with a darting tongue, and then he ran a finger over his lips in the old gesture. If only he could.

He reached for the telephone on his desk and buzzed his secretary. "Call the main showroom and get Bobby Reed on the phone," he ordered in a whisper that could barely contain his excitement and anticipation. "Tell him that I want to see him in my office after the second show."

Bianco licked his lips. Every detail. Every moment. Just like the old days.

Two dozen carnation corsages perched on two dozen

ample but well camouflaged breasts. Two dozen white patent-leather belts encircled two dozen ample waists. And two dozen bottoms settled comfortably into the reclining seats of a chartered bus for a tour that was cheerfully called "Las Vegas by Starlight."

"See, we get to see a lounge show—a magician, Ira—and then a dinner show. Liberace, Ira, he's such a decent and clean-thinking man. And then a visit to Circus Circus." Gertie poked one finger at a photograph in the brochure that the tour operator had circulated among the delegates to the Funeral Directors convention. "Acrobats, Ira. Trapeze artists. No naked women, Ira. Just a nice evening for decent folks, and we'll be in our rooms again before midnight."

"That's nice, Gertie," Ira agreed, glancing out the bus window at the bustling crowd in the casino entrance of the Mecca Hotel.

The driver started the engine of the bus, and Ira felt the vibration under his feet. And a moment later, he was struggling out of his seat, and over his wife, and into the aisle.

"Ira," Gertie barked. "The bus is leaving. Where do you think you're going? Didn't I tell you to use the bathrom before we came downstairs?"

"Uh, listen, I'm sorry," Ira said in a nervous stammer, "but I'm very tired tonight. Very tired, Gertie, it must have been all that sun today. I think I'll just go back to the room and lie down for awhile."

Gertie studied her husband's face and then looked around the bus. "But we're about to leave, Ira, and I was looking forward to the tour."

"Gertie, go ahead and have a wonderful evening," Ira called, bolting down the aisle, stepping high over the legs of his fellow funeral directors, leaping toward the front of the bus before the driver sealed the doors and doomed him to a nice night on the town for decent folks.

"Ira!" He heard Gertie's voice as he clattered down

the steps and headed for the crowded casino. "Ira, you come back here right now."

But it was too late. The driver closed the doors, released the airbrakes, and eased the bus out of the Mecca's driveway and into the dense Saturday night traffic along the Strip. And Ira disappeared into the surge of flesh pressing toward the Mecca's casino for an evening that would be something less than wholesome but something more than nice.

"Careful," John Warner groaned as his bride's fingers brushed over his flesh. "Oh God, please be careful."

"I'm sorry," she purred, rubbing another scoop of the greasy ointment over his body. "But it's so nice and slippery and I *like* it nice and slippery. Just like a Wesson Oil party."

"Huh?" John gritted his teeth against the pain.

"Oh never mind," she giggled. "We've got plenty of time to learn about that. Right now I want to make up for last night. Ooooh!"

He rolled over on the bed and pulled the spread over his exposed groin—the only part of his body that wasn't thoroughly and painfully sunburned from a long afternoon at the Mecca pool under a blazing desert sun. Back in Dayton, a suntan was a sure sign of a newly returned vacationer, and he wanted to have something to show for his Vegas honeymoon besides a virgin bride and a big debt. His insistence on lounging by the pool had been enough to postpone the moment of truth in the bed with the mirrored canopy, and it had been enough to keep him from running himself deeper into debt at the craps tables. The only drawbacks had been the unending stares and open propositions that Linda's string bikini seemed to attract—and the lobster-red sunburn that now made every touch a painful ordeal.

"Please, honey, can't you see how badly I'm burned?" John protested, twisting away from her groping hands. "We can't do anything until the pain goes away."

Linda rolled one shoulder seductively. "It's my *honey-moon*," she sighed. "And I *want* it. I really *need* it. Ooooh!"

"Later, honey," he pleaded. "A little bit later, okay?"

"Well, I'll be damned if I'm going to spend my honeymoon in a hotel room unles we're using the bed for something other than sleeping." The anger returned to her voice with a vengeance. "You'd better figure out something to do besides sitting around here moaning and groaning."

"Sure, sure," he said, sensing a threat. "Listen, why don't we both get dressed, and we'll go downstairs for some dinner, and maybe we'll fool around at the craps table."

"I'd like to fool around right here."

"Please, honey," he said. "We'll go downstairs for a little while, and then we'll do whatever you want. I promise you."

"What I came here for is to get laid," she said sweetly, rising from the bed and heading for the bathroom. And as she moved away from her husband, she said to herself: *And I'm going to get laid tonight one way or another, I promise you* that.

"Power to the people," the young black man said, raising his left hand in a closed-fist salute and showing off his star-sapphire pinky ring.

Morrissey paused for a few more moments as the host of a local television talk show waded into an interview with the leader of the Las Vegas Black Panther Party, a well mannered fellow in a purple double-knit sports coat, a black silk shirt with a string tie, and a pair of slacks in a hound's-tooth pattern. He looked like no Black Panther leader that John Morrissey had ever seen before, but of course—as Morrissey reminded himself—he had never been to Las Vegas before.

"Our program calls for more black brothers in the blackjack pit and on the roulette wheels," the Black Panther declared. " 'Out of the kitchen and into the casino!' is our motto."

"Right on," said the interviewer. "And our next guest, now appearing in a sensational lounge show twice a night at the Riviera, is one of the funniest dialect comedians who ever worked this wonderful town—"

Morrissey clicked off the set. He'd watched an endless succession of old movies and closed-circuit instructional films on gambling and amateurish commercials for the shops in the Mecca's subterranean arcade. But he'd thought only of Lise Christian.

A dozen times he'd picked up the telephone to call her room, and a dozen times there was no answer and he was relieved. After all, what could he say to her? That she was right about fate—and that he believed it was his fate to meet her, to fall in love with her, to sleep with her? That he no longer wanted to aim his Alfa toward New Mexico unless she was sitting next to him in the front seat? That her own peculiar passion had inspired a new passion of his own? No. She would laugh.

He glanced at his watch—in another two hours, they would meet for dinner downstairs and he would have to make conversation without blurting out his wild thoughts and reckless dreams. He would have to choke back the madness that she seemed to inspire in him. He would have to discipline himself to leave her alone.

"Lise," he said aloud. And then he picked up the telephone.

"Lise," he repeated when she finally answered. "I just wanted to reconfirm our dinner date. Is eight o'clock okay?"

There was a moment of silence and then he felt dismay when she said, "I'm very sorry, but I can't see you tonight."

"But you agreed—"

"Something came up suddenly," she said in a voice that was both urgent and distracted. "I have to meet someone at midnight for an important dinner conference."

Morrissey swallowed hard. "That's too bad. I really wanted to see you, Lise. I thought we could talk and—" He stopped himself. "I'm sorry, Lise. I understand."

"I don't think so," she said gently. "I came here to learn about my father. I've learned how he died and I have to do something about it."

Her voice rang with self-confidence and quiet purpose, but her words struck Morrissey as half mad. "Listen, what the hell are you talking about? You sound like a child—"

"I'm not a child," she said, "and I'm perfectly serious."

Morrissey fell silent. He found that he understood her meaning without understanding her words; she had taught him something about fate, and now he wanted to share hers.

"Can I help in any way?"

"No, but thank you. There's unfinished business, and it's something I must do by myself."

"Yes," he said. "It's your karma, isn't it?"

"Maybe."

"But I need to know whether there is a place in it for me," he said, forcing each word out and fearing all the while that she would take them as an insult.

She was silent for a moment. "I'll call you afterward," she said softly, hanging up.

Morrissey held the phone, listening to the bland drone of the dial tone, wondering how he would fill the hours until she called and replied to the question that she had left unanswered. Is there a place in your fate for me? he wondered again. And what is my own fate?

Next to the telephone lay the single five-dollar chip. Morrissey replaced the receiver, picked up the chip, and headed for the door. He did not know what fate decreed for him, but he knew where to find out.

The persistent ringing of the telephone next to her bed brought Lucille Sheaffer out of her dreams. Her eyes fluttered open, and she groped impulsively for the last body she remembered—Jack, the pit boss, the man who'd taken her straight and clean and free. But he'd slipped out of bed hours before, and now she was alone with the ringing of the telephone—and the fainter ringing of a dimly remembered dream.

She paid attention to the telephone call first. "Yes," she mumbled into the receiver, closing her eyes.

"Lucy? It's Jack."

She opened her eyes. "Oh lover," she purred, sounding like a whore with a smooth line but meaning every word of it, "that was real good. I mean, it was really good. When are you coming back for some more, lover?"

"It's time for business, Lucy," he said gruffly, and his words stung her deeply. "No more freebies, just paying customers, and let's get ready for volume business. After all, it's Saturday night."

"Okay, okay," she said, warning herself against the girlish giddiness in her belly. The pit boss was her pimp, not her lover; he'd taken her a few hours before because that was part of the business, not because he cared for her. And there were plenty of men who'd sweet-talk her and play house with her back in Denver. I'm here to make some dough, she reminded herself, not to fall in love. "Can I start working the lounge now?"

"Yeah, do that," the pit boss said. "But I'll be sending you players earlier than last night. First one should be around eight o'clock. So be back in the room before then, okay?"

"Okay," Lucy said. "And maybe when it's all over—"

Jack wasn't listening. He'd hung up.

Lucy closed her eyes again and tried to recapture the details of her dream. She could see her third-grade classroom back in Denver, but her kids weren't in their seats—the classroom was full of men, men with black suits and even blacker expressions, all lined up in the undersized children's desks like a jury sitting in judgment. The vision reminded her of a visit she'd paid to the school board when she was first hired as a student teacher—they'd all asked her questions, probed her past experience and present morals, and made her feel ashamed of herself despite her utter innocence.

But the dream was different. The men weren't talking. They weren't asking questions. They were just staring at her as she stood, chalk in one hand, at the blackboard in the front of the classroom. And, with a start, Lucy realized why they were staring.

She was naked. She was completely naked. And they could see every inch of her body. But they were staring at one inch in particular—a part of her body that was wet with other men's passion. As she recalled that moment of humiliation in her dream, Lucille Sheaffer flushed with excitement.

She reached down and touched herself. At least one detail of her dream was not just a fantasy. Her fingers touched her mound, and she realized with surprise that although hours had passed since Jack had satisfied himself between her legs—she was still wet.

It was the worst time to slip away, he knew, and it was the worst act of irresponsibility. But Moe couldn't help it. Lise Christian had asked him to do it, and he could not turn her down. Not tonight. Not after what she knew. And especially not after Moe learned where she would be at midnight.

Her page over the casino public address system had reached him in the blackjack pit where he was telling the pit boss how he was to handle the much-too-lucky-to-be-true Oriental player. According to the numbers, he was now $214,250 ahead of them.

"We should have told him to walk a hundred grand ago," the pit boss said.

"Too late for that now," Moe Black grunted.

The pit boss listened to instructions. First an undertaker was to be brought in. Every casino had at least one. These are unhappy men who smile at nothing, don't respond to small talk, and are lucky for the casino. Casinos, like players, believe in luck. When a dealer allows too many players to get too lucky, he is fired. The undertaker grinds them out. His deadpan and lack of response to queries, lack of appreciation for tokes (tips), seems to unnerve the player, who loses control of himself and whatever "system" he is playing.

If that didn't work, they were to do a thing rarely done. They were to send in a mechanic: someone who would deal seconds. The element of luck would be gone. Cards would be dealt by hand and so skillfully from the bottom of the deck that even the most savvy state casino inspector couldn't see or hear anything unusual.

Assured that the pit boss understood, Moe took the page. When he heard Lise's voice, he motioned the pit boss away and spoke softly into the phone. "Lisetta, are you ready to go to the airport now?"

"No, Mr. Black. There is a family debt I must pay off and you're going to help me. I want you to get me a gun."

"A gun?" Moe had almost laughed into the phone. "A gun?"

"A pistol. One that I can fit into a small handbag."

"But why—" He changed his tone to very serious. "Impossible, Lisetta. I wouldn't know where to find one."

"Don't treat me like a child, Mr. Black. You said you were my father's friend. You brought me all the way from Paris. Tonight I'm going to speak for my father. I'm meeting Mr. Everett in the private penthouse. At midnight."

"Somebody's pulling your leg," he said. "Someone is toying with you. Everett hasn't been out of his bunker in years. Years and years." But he knew even as he spoke that, incredibly, it was true. The old bastard would have seen her face on his television monitor. Now he would want to face her.

Then, quietly: "It's true, Mr. Black. I have a written invitation in my room. An invitation from Edward Roger Everett. And it asks me to meet him for dinner in the private casino at midnight."

Moe swallowed. "But why do you want a gun?"

"Let's call it protection," she said.

"Let me go with you," he offered. "I'll bring a gun, but I'll come with you."

"No, Mr. Black," she said. "This meeting I have to attend alone."

"Listen to reason, Lisetta," he pleaded. "Everett won't come. And if he did he wouldn't sit still and allow you to point a gun at him. He's received mysterious phone calls designed to frighten him. He has an army of bodyguards. He may think you are a threat to him. He'll bring his own people. Just like he did with your father—"

Moe fell silent, his stomach churning. He realized that if this phone was tapped, he had as much as confessed to making the calls. It could be an epitaph for him.

"A small but efficient pistol, Mr. Black," she said. "Bring it to my room, please, and you'll have done me and my father a great favor."

Moe nodded to no one in particular as he stood in a corner of the blackjack pit. "Yes, Lisetta," he said numbly.

Everything in Moe Black's being balked at her request: he'd always been a numbers man, not a shooter. He'd never carried a piece. He was brains—not muscle. That's what kept him alive in the old days when the boys played rough. A numbers man is not a fighter, and as long as he didn't carry a piece, the shooters would leave him alone. Yet he alone knew what he owed Bertinelli. His life. His wife's and daughters'. Bertinelli had intervened so many years ago when Mike Bellazio had threatened to destroy him and his family.

Moe Black, a man of substance and responsibility, a respected executive of the Mecca Hotel and the casino, was trusted by the bosses to remain on the job when it counted. And tonight it counted—the take was down by a quarter-million, and Moe's job was to win it back. Leaving the casino, even for a few minutes, was a breach of security, a breach of trust, a breach of honor.

Lise Christian's words repeated in his head—"Bring the gun to my room, please," she'd said, "and you'll have done me and my father a great favor." He'd heard the words before. He'd seen those eyes before. The soft request and the solemn promise: ". . . you'll have done me a great favor."

As Moe hurried through the casino and headed for his Cadillac, he wondered how the little girl, who'd never known her father, picked up the precise phrase that Augusto Bertinelli always used to seal a pact of honor with one of the boys: ". . . you'll have done me a great favor."

The boat bobbed up and down in its slip as the rippling waves from a passing speedboat rolled up to it. Instinctively, Alexander Tate scanned the open water around the docks. His eyes followed the speedboat and noted the two water skiers who were riding in its wake, swirling in a long curve around the lake, and then he returned to the delicate task that had consumed his attention.

Tate was aboard a twenty-two-foot fiberglass-hull powerboat that was docked in one of Lake Mead's private marinas. To all casual observers, it was not much different than the other pleasure craft that carried cute names in even cuter script on their bows: *Miss U-Bet*, or *Lost Wages*, or *Big Dick*. During the day, the boats would have been fighting each other for open space on the lake, tangling fishing lines and water-skiing towlines, gambling casually on the collisions that turned sleek speedboats into flotsam.

But now, in the late twilight of an August day, only a few stray boats cruised on the lake, and Alexander Tate was alone on the dock. All the better, he knew. All the better for the work he had to do for the old man. And then he picked up the needle-nose pliers and went back to work on the black box in the bow of the powerboat, which carried no cute name at all on its bow.

The black box contained a hypersensitive FM receiver, a compass and direction-finder, and a voice-activated tape recorder. When Tate finished wiring the unit to the boat's power supply, it would allow a lakeside sailor to monitor the conversations aboard the private yacht of the Mecca

Hotel—the 144-foot boat that rode at anchor two miles along the shore in the Mecca's private anchorage, near the dual towers that fed the waters of Lake Mead into the massive turbines of Boulder Dam.

Of course, when Larry Johnson had purchased the big yacht for the hotel, the old man had ordered a discreet visit aboard the yacht to install bugging equipment in the elegant oak-paneled bulkheads and the polished teak furniture. But the yacht on Lake Mead was out of range of the old man's master console in the bunker, and so Tate had been dispatched in a powerboat to trail the yacht on its midnight cruise. The black box in the bow would pick up the transmissions of the electronic eavesdropping devices, record the words exchanged by Larry Johnson and the Arab, and track the yacht during its lake cruise to stay within range.

Tate nodded crisply as he tested the power connections, the transmission and reception circuits, and finally the compass and direction-finder. Then he glanced down at his wristwatch: barely nine o'clock, and still twilight, but three hours away from Johnson's all-important dinner cruise with the Arab. Tate covered the black box with a fitted nylon tarp and then returned to the captain's chair at the helm of the powerboat.

He would wait for midnight. He wouldn't sleep, he wouldn't close his eyes, he wouldn't allow his mind to wander. He would only wait.

"Goddamn his tired old bones! Goddamn his senile old head!"

Lawrence Johnson turned the single sheet over and over again as if some message were hidden between the plainly typed lines of the memo from his secretary. But there were only the simple words of the simple message and nothing more. Johnson cursed aloud: "Goddamn the old man! Goddamn the old bastard!"

He'd returned to his office suite to find the sheet of

paper on his desk: Alexander Tate had telephoned from Mr. Everett's quarters to inform him that Mr. Tate would require the exclusive use of the private resturant and casino in the Penthouse at midnight. And that was the whole message—no explanation, no apology for the inconvenience, no hint as to why the old man's black manservant was to be given the run of the private casino on the busiest gambling night of the week.

But the insubordination of Alexander Tate irritated Johnson only superficially. What was far more disturbing was the sudden sign of life in the underground bunker after years of almost total silence. In the years since the old man had descended into his hole in the ground, Larry Johnson had never seen him and rarely heard from him. That fact was the crucial premise of his whole scheme—the scheme that would be carried out tonight aboard the hotel's yacht on Lake Mead.

Johnson thoughtfully crumpled the note into a ball and tossed it into the fireplace, where a fire now crackled in spite of the outside temperature of nearly 100 degrees. The air conditioner cooled off the suite, and the fire warmed it to a comfortable temperature.

If the old man starts paying attention now, Johnson warned himself, the whole scheme could collapse. The plan depended on Everett's total isolation, and on his refusal to come forth from the tomb he'd built for himself beneath the Mecca. Johnson's scheme, his future—no, his *life*—all depended on the old man remaining in the bunker, buried alive, silent as a corpse, locked in the crypt of his own madness.

And now that arrogant black bastard had come out of the bunker and started giving orders. What the hell was it all about, Johnson asked himself. A night of dice and booze and girls for the staff in the bunker? A little Saturday night blast for some men who hadn't seen a Saturday night in months? Yes, Johnson reassured himself. Tate must be treating himself and his black brothers to a night of pleasure in the Penthouse. Johnson thought, I'll bet the old man doesn't know a thing about it.

Well, he didn't need the Penthouse casino tonight anyway. So the take would be down for one night. Everything was primed, everything was meshing nicely, everything was taken care of. The Arab. The Senator. And the old man. It didn't matter if the nose-wipers spent a night in the private casino. In another few hours, Johnson vowed, they'd all be out of work and out of his life forever.

No, it didn't matter. What mattered were the words that he would exchange with the Arab aboard the yacht at midnight. And the words of the Senator's speech tomorrow morning. Yes, Johnson reassured himself as he stared out the window overlooking the sprawling Mecca Hotel, that's all that mattered now.

He picked up a desk phone and dialed the number to the backstage of the Oasis lounge. "Gimme the twins. Yeah, the twins—but I want the smart one. Belinda." And a moment later: "Belinda, you got the schedule straight for tonight?"

"Sure, sure," Belinda rasped, and Johnson knew that he was talking to the right twin. "Just 'cause I shake my ass for a living don't mean I can't figure out a scam—"

"Okay, Belinda," Johnson interrupted. "Just get yourself and your sister to the airfield by midnight. The Senator and Carne will be waiting for you, and the pilot knows where to take you."

"Listen, I've been out to the Mustang ranch before—"

"Just remember what happens after you get there, Belinda," Johnson said. "Just remember all the connections, okay?"

"Sure, sure, boss," Belinda said. "And don't you forget our bonus arrangement."

"Sure, sure," he said in a gentle parody of the stripper's voice. And then, smiling to himself, he hung up the telephone and allowed himself a leisurely pause at the picture window. The sight of a desert sunset was so damned beautiful, he thought, but the crazy old man in the basement never came out of his mole hole long enough to look. Well, you'd better hurry up before it's too late, he thought.

He'd turned down a plate of the strange food that the chef had prepared for the Arab—something with a lot of rice and lamb and a lot of lumpy things that Mike Adams couldn't identify—but now even the hamburger on the plate in front of him didn't seem appetizing. Mike hadn't eaten all day, not since the accident that spilled Carl Hagen all over a stretch of Vegas roadway, and still he wasn't hungry.

No, he wasn't hungry. Mike Adams was worried. At Bianco's quiet instructions, he'd gone directly from the sheriff's station to the Mecca's yacht on Lake Mead, where he changed out of his security guard's uniform and into deck shoes and white slacks and a sailor's middy emblazoned with the star-and-crescent symbol of the Mecca Hotel. The other members of the crew didn't pay much attention, and the chef had been damned friendly about the whole thing. But Mike Adams was a worrier.

Not about the evening's assignment—to eavesdrop on the dinner conversation between Lawrence Johnson and the Arab visitor and report what they said back to Louis Bianco. To make sure that the Arab didn't leave Las Vegas before Mike reported to Bianco. That would be fairly easy. But Mike couldn't keep his mind from remembering what Carl Hagen had told him before he died.

He hadn't taken the doctor's words seriously at first. It all sounded like the ramblings of a man who'd been too long at the gaming tables and swilled too much booze. Mike had seen that often enough. A down-and-out gambler who remembered that Edward Everett owned the Mecca and then demanded to see the old man himself. To ask for a loan. To threaten a lawsuit. Or just to start an argument. Drunk talk. Loser's talk. And that's what Carl Hagen sounded like. A tumor, a tumor that was a time bomb in the old man's head—no, it was all too crazy.

Until the doctor risked his life to go back to the Mecca —and lost.

That had shaken Mike Adams. He'd seen the maniacal drive in Hagen's eyes, the sudden strength as he tried to escape from Mike's grip and the car, and then the blizzard of dollars when he hit the roadway. If the doctor was busted and broken down, that was one thing. But if he was carrying a lot of dough, that was something else. And if he wanted to see Everett bad enough to throw himself out of a speeding car—well, that was beginning to turn Mike Adams around.

And now Mike Adams was confused. Who wanted to hear the bad news about the old man? Not Bianco—the doctor himself had told Mike's boss, and Bianco had just tried to ride him out of town. Not the old man himself— he was said to be locked away in the bunker underneath the Mecca, and nobody, especially a teenager in a security guard's uniform, could get past those oppressive-looking black bastards who protected the old man.

Mike thought about the strange, silent men who slipped in and out of the bunker from time to time, always unobtrusive and unapproachable. The only one he knew by name was Tate, the one in charge of the bunker. Yes, it was Tate who should be told the information that Carl Hagen had left behind with Mike.

And why shouldn't he tell Tate? Mike recalled the advice of the lieutenant at the sheriff's station—he ought to think about his future. He ought to steer clear of the hard-way boys like Bianco. And what better way to improve his future than to relay life-saving information to the old man himself? Mike began to feel a little better. Why, the old man might even reward him! A scholarship, maybe! Enough to forget about Louis Bianco and the job at the Mecca.

Yes, Mike told himself, I've got to do it. When I get back to the Mecca, I'll report to Bianco—and then I'll find Tate. And when I do, I'll tell him everything the doctor told me.

Mike Adams began to feel better, and he realized how

hungry he was. He looked down at the hamburger on the plate in front of him, and he realized how appetizing it looked. With four casual bites, he downed the burger and washed it down with two pulls from a bottle of chilled beer. And then he looked up at the chef, who beamed as he always did when someone so visibly enjoyed his handiwork.

"How 'bout another one?" Mike asked shyly. "I've got a long night ahead, and I need some energy to go on."

Lester shook his head stubbornly. "I don't want to do it," he complained, refusing to look at Pierce or Sato. "I just don't want to go back."

"You've got to go back. Just one more session and we're home free," Pierce said sternly, grabbing Lester by the shoulders and shaking him.

"Don't shake him," Sato called from across the room. "His back is hurting him, don't forget."

Pierce, annoyed, glanced at Sato. "Don't worry about the backache—I told him I can take care of it with an injection." He turned back to Lester. "You can do it, I know you can do it. It's just a matter of another hour or two, and I'll give you a double injection."

Lester shook his head negatively. "It hurts too much. I can't concentrate on the codes."

Sato volunteered, "Pierce, maybe we should get him to a hos——"

"Shut up," Pierce snapped. "Both of you shut up. We've got a lot of planning invested in this operation, and we're not going to blow it just because the two of you are bellyachers."

"We've already done good," Sato said. "I'm worried about Lester."

"Okay. One more shift," Pierce declared. "Maybe only an hour. Then we'll quit."

Lester stared at the other two men. The prospect of returning to the blackjack tables filled him with despair, but the cutoff time gave him new hope.

"Stay sharp on the codes," Pierce warned. "If I give you a double shot for the back pain, it means you'll have to stay very alert on the codes. You've screwed up a few times already, you know, and with big money on the table."

Lester winced as the needle went into his buttocks. Suddenly he felt excited, energetic, alive, even as the pain in his back diminished, lulled by the morphine cocktail in his bloodstream.

"Back to the casino," Lester announced, suddenly a prisoner of an urge as ancient as the gambler's curse, an urge that rendered all the sophisticated equipment—the sensors, the implants, the master computer, the microwave transmission circuits—completely and utterly useless. "Back to the casino."

He suddenly felt very good.

The shopping arcade stretched ahead of him like a glittering cavern of light, and shops lined the fluorescent-lit underground promenade. Morrissey walked along the arcade, scarcely noticing the furs, the string bikinis, the diamond-studded gold jewelry, the silk shirts, the hand-tooled leather shoes, all the fancy and costly temptations designed to lure back any dollars that might have been won at the tables in the casino upstairs.

His thoughts were not on the expensive shops, or the glamorous merchandise, or the elegant women and overfed men who strolled past him. Morrissey thought of only one thing—Lise Christian and her midnight rendezvous in the Penthouse casino.

He'd been driven from his own suite by a restlessness, a feeling of bewilderment that eroded his confidence in his understanding of numbers and probabilities while urging on him a bold recklessness, a sensation that now dominated him completely. As he wandered around the arcade beneath the casino, he fingered the five-dollar chip in his pocket and thought of Lise Christian.

So young, he thought. So sure of herself, if you believed the expression on her face. And yet so vulnerable, if you looked deep into her eyes.

His eyes fell on a sparkle of blue in one of the endless window displays along the promenade. Among the gold-coin belt buckles and diamond pendants and other jeweled paraphernalia, he spotted a tiny charm in the shape of a five-dollar Mecca chip. He stopped and stared. Rendered in gold rather than plastic, decorated with precious stones instead of bits of color, the charm was similar to the lucky chip in his pocket.

Morrissey went into the shop. The woman behind the counter glanced at his shabby clothes and sleep-rumpled hair, and her hands moved automatically to primp her elaborate coiffure. She sighed. The prices were scaled for winners, not losers, and the young man didn't have that winner's look, but who could be sure?

"Can I help you?" she asked.

"The charm in the window," he said. "The five-dollar chip—I want it."

"It's rather expensive, sir," she said, "but I can show you some gold-plated charms that are quite nice—"

"The one in the window," he repeated. "And a chain. A gold chain to go with it."

She moved slowly to the window and removed the gold-and-gemstone chip, laying it on a blue velvet pad next to a long gold chain. Then she sighed again. She was sure that when he heard the price, he'd ask for the gold-plated charms that she had offered in the first place.

"Three hundred and seventy-five for the coin. Eighty-five for the chain."

"I'll take them," he said.

Her voice warmed instantly. "Yes, sir," she purred, "and may I show you anything else? A watch, perhaps? Or some lovely cufflinks?"

"No, just the chip and the chain," he said. "Do you have a gift card?"

"Of course," she said, offering a tiny cream-colored

card and envelope along with a pen. Well, she thought to herself, I was dead wrong about this one. He might look like he's just come off the road with an outstretched thumb, but he's a winner. It just goes to show, she reminded herself.

She watched as the young man scrawled a single line on the card—"Since I couldn't be there . . ."—and then paused, debating whether to finish the thought. Abruptly, he dropped the card into the envelope, sealed it, and scrawled across the front: "Lise Christian." He handed it to the saleslady.

"And the room number, sir?" she asked.

"Penthouse four," he murmured. "She's in the Penthouse."

Morrissey reached back into his pocket and reassured himself by touching the lucky five-dollar chip. Until midnight, it was all that was left to remind him of the young woman's touch; until midnight, it was the only point at which their fates crossed. And until midnight, Morrissey would not know if their destinies intersected each other or had ended with their last meeting.

He turned toward the elevator that would take him back to the casino.

eight

The man in the expensive tuxedo signaled the pit boss with one upraised finger.

"Yes, Mr. W?" the pit boss asked.

Weston was giving the impression of being a man who was accustomed to close attention and dutiful nods, and he wanted others to see it. Not only the blonde who was playing blackjack with his chips, but especially the man on whose arm she leaned. Weston was the center of attention at the blackjack table, but it was the man with the blonde who held Weston's future and Weston's fortune in his hand.

"I'd like to extend my rim credit," Weston whispered curtly into the pit boss's ear. "Another ten thousand dollars."

That's all it would need. The whole Vegas trip had been designed to convince his companion to take a half-million-dollar position in Weston's failing machine-tool factory in Chicago. Too many years of skimming too much money for his own gambling jaunts had put him on the edge of the cliff, but this cigar-smoking angel could save his neck. So Weston had laid on the trip to Vegas, the flashy broad, and the all-night sessions at the tables to impress the investor with his wealth and savvy. He was down five thousand dollars, but a snap of the fingers would bring more rim credit and thus more persuasion.

"I am very sorry, Mr. W," the pit boss whispered back, "but we've called Central Credit and—"

Weston sat bolt upright. His face paled, and he seized the pit boss's arm in panic. "Uh, could I have a word with you—right now!"

Weston's companion looked up from the table and smiled. He'd never been to Vegas before, and he was mystified by all the obscure rituals that he had seen.

"Listen, man," Weston said, when they were out of earshot. "I need ten grand on the rim, and I need it now, and I don't want any goddamn backtalk."

"I'm sorry, Mr. Weston," the pit boss repeated. "But we've called Central Credit, and you know as well as we do that you have unpaid markers up and down the Strip for more than eighty thou. You haven't picked up anything from your last visit."

"But I don't owe you. Just the five grand."

"I got my orders, Mr. Weston."

"All right, all right," Weston said, wiping his brow and glancing nervously at the blackjack table. His companion caught Weston's eye and smiled again. Weston forced a return smile. "Listen, make it just another five grand then. I've got to keep playing for awhile."

The pit boss shook his head ever so slightly. "No more credit, Mr. Weston," he said sympathetically. "I just take orders."

"If you don't do this for me, I won't be able to pay back anybody," Weston said desperately. "I've got a big score riding on making a good impression on the man I'm with. And how is it going to look if I stand up and say, 'Sorry, no more cards, I'm busted out'?"

The pit boss paused. "I understand, Mr. Weston," he said, reaching into his pocket. "But I can't extend any more credit."

"Oh for Christ's sake, just one more hand. One more hand, that's all! Five hundred measly bucks."

The pit boss frowned. The cage had given a flat turndown to any extension of rim credit, but he was not a hard man. In fact, he was a very generous and sympathetic man. And he knew that it was good business to keep a high-roller coming back, even if he did sink into debt now and then. The pit boss reached into his coat pocket, took out a wallet, and counted out five one-hundred-dollar bills.

"Listen, let's call this a personal loan," he said. "The cage won't know about it. Nobody'll know about it. So go play your one last hand, okay?"

Weston pumped the pit boss's hand in abject gratitude, and stumbled back to the table. He smiled too warmly at his companion, and his companion smiled back.

"Maybe after one more hand, we can go to the lounge and talk business," Weston said, casually tossing the five bills on the table and asking for chips.

"Sure, we can *talk* business," the man replied. "But we're not going to *do* business, Weston. I don't do business with stiffs who have to borrow money from the hired help."

"Table sixteen is cooling off fast," the floorman whispered to Moe Black, who'd suddenly appeared in the craps pit, puffing hard and sweating like a man who'd been foolish enough to leave the air-conditioned comfort of the casino for the 90-degree heat of an August night. "I can pull the dealer and put another man on."

Moe shook his head. The trip from the Mecca to the

Sports Book had taken a short time despite the heavy traffic, but he'd spent a longer time seeking the old man in the cheap hound's-tooth jacket. They'd concluded their business quickly enough, but Moe was still distracted as he surveyed the action in the Mecca's casino.

He thought back to the conversation outside the back door of the Sports Book. "Ezra," he'd said earnestly, "I need a big favor tonight."

Ezra smiled, showing cigar-stained false teeth. He'd been a small-time bookie back in Jersey, an entrepreneur who had to be runner and bagman and shooter all at once, and he'd lost a few teeth along the way. "Favor, shmavor," Ezra said genially. "You want to know where to put your money on the next Cubs game? In your pocket, that's where."

"No joke, Ezra," Moe said, clasping the old man's shoulder with one hand. "I need a piece. A clean piece." He thought of Lise facing Everett and his bodyguards by herself.

Ezra frowned. The Three Blind Mice at the Mecca didn't carry guns. No one but the muscle carried guns.

"What's up, Moe?" he asked.

"Old business," Moe said.

"How old?" Ezra asked.

Moe said wearily, "Dead business that won't stay buried. That's why I need a gun."

Ezra clicked his false teeth contemplatively. "You and I are old men, Moe. Old men don't go around shooting people."

"Listen, be a *mensch*," Moe pleaded, and Ezra recognized the catch of hard emotion in his voice.

"Easy, easy, old man," Ezra said. "I can get you a piece or two if I have to."

"Sure, sure," Moe said urgently, "but let's do it."

Ezra nodded and extended his hand; Moe shook it solemnly. Then the two men turned and headed for Moe's Cadillac. A half hour later, Moe was back at the Mecca with a chrome-steel .25-caliber automatic in his coat pocket and an immense weight on his conscience. The little girl might as well put the gun to her own head instead of pulling it on the old man.

"Excuse me, Mr. Black," the floorman repeated, bringing him back to the casino and the bustling tables. "Should I pull the dealer on sixteen? It was cooking until some black dude dropped a bundle with everybody else's money riding on his point. Now it's empty."

"No, no," Moe said, waving toward the table where the dealer and the two stickmen stood idly. "Somebody will be along in a minute."

Even as Moe spoke, the swirling crowd deposited a new player at the empty craps table. Moe's eyes rested on the young man in the shabby suède coat as he dropped a chip on the table and picked up the dice.

"Seven," the dealer intoned in a bored voice. "A winner."

A moment later, the table was no longer empty. And Moe was no longer standing next to the floorman.

Linda Warner shifted her weight from one leg to the other, exaggerating the movement of her hips beneath the silky black dress that she wore, playing her eyes over the crowd that moved like a tide through the casino. Then she turned back to her bridegroom, who was hunched over the corner of a craps table with a stack of chips in his hand.

"Your sunburn seems a lot better now," she said with a sarcastic whine, but John Warner didn't hear. He'd signed another check at the cage, and now he dropped another chip on the come line.

Linda sighed and looked back at the crowd. She could see a half-dozen other women who stood in the center aisle of the casino, hanging loosely on players at the craps tables but drifting now then into the current of movement along the tables. She compared herself to the other women—and decided that she was a lot better looking than any of them. Great standup breasts, good hips. Good hair. All she needed now was a man who could appreciate them. If her bridegroom wasn't going to lay her, she was going to find someone who would.

She spotted the dark man in the gray suit, the one who was just leaving the baccarat table and heading down the center aisle of the casino toward the elevators. Dark hair, dark eyes, small build, expensively dressed, and walking like he knew it. Maybe one of those rich Arabs you're always hearing about, Linda thought. And she found herself wondering if what they said about Arabs making love was true. She knew a lot about lovemaking, but there weren't many Arabs in Dayton.

Her blue eyes met his dark eyes, and she turned away with a coy smile. Subtly, slowly, she detached herself from her husband and took a step into the aisle so that the man with the dark eyes would pass next to her as he walked by. Then she shifted her stance ever so slightly, throwing back her shoulders by a few inches, so that his elbow would brush her breasts as he passed.

"I am terribly sorry," he murmured as he collided gently with her.

Linda managed to stumble just a bit, and the man with the dark eyes caught her by the arm. "Are you all right, Madame?" he asked.

She thrilled silently at his exotic accent and his soft voice. "All this hustle and bustle," she said, trying to sound sultry. "Too many people, if you know what I mean." Then she smiled at him, a thousand-candlepower smile that she'd perfected back in Dayton. Now she'd see if it worked with Arabs.

He stared at her for a long moment, allowing the stream of people to ripple past him, and he began to raise his hand toward her hair. Yes, Linda thought to herself, he *would* like the blonde hair. Good hair.

"Excuse me, Madame, but are you alone tonight?" the dark man asked.

Linda exulted, throwing her chest out just a bit further, slinging her hip just a bit more, and glancing over her shoulder at her husband. He saw nothing. And she turned back to the man with the dark eyes. "Yes, I'm all alone," she confessed with a twitch of her carefully moistened lips. "And it's a lonely place to be—"

The dark man took another step closer. "Perhaps you would like company for awhile," he said. "My company, Madame."

"Well, yes, that sounds terrific," Linda said. Then, boldly, "I have to wash up. Do you have a room here?"

He nodded slowly, never taking his eyes from hers. He led her away from the tables. Linda glanced once more at the craps table, where her husband was whispering to the dice in his hands in a far more intimate way than he ever addressed her. And then she was followed by the dark man into the elevator.

"Are you a real blonde?" he asked as soon as the elevator doors closed.

She shivered with excitement. "Just wait and see," she giggled.

Jack spotted him first, and noticed the difference immediately. The quiet Oriental, who'd spent twelve hours at the blackjack tables with an expression of self-effacement and outright embarrassment, now rolled through the casino with a triumphant grin on his face. He nodded and smiled as he moved down the center aisle.

That's a winner, thought the pit boss. That's the look of a man who thinks he has his finger in Lady Luck's cunt. High, exuberant, expansive.

Jack had seen enough of them to know the outward symptoms of the gambler's passion, and he'd seen enough of them go broke again. He hoped the Oriental was itching to lose his bundle.

"Mr. M," Jack said softly, easing up to his side and

falling into step with him. "Can I do anything for you? Would you like me to clear a blackjack table for a private game?"

Lester shook his head energetically. "No blackjack," he said, riding the new eruption of excitement in this throat. "Craps! I'm going to play craps."

Craps! Lester rubbed his thumb against his forefinger as he'd done a thousand times since they'd arrived at the Mecca, but for the first time the gesture had nothing to do with the master computer back in their room. The black box upstairs was programmed for only one game—blackjack. The sensors and implants were there for only one game— blackjack. When he picked up the dice at the craps table, Lester reminded himself excitedly, he wouldn't be playing under the mute instruction of a box of wires and plugs. He'd be playing the only way that counts—he'd be playing all alone with his own luck.

"Craps," Lester repeated aloud, glancing along the row of craps tables and settling on a nearly empty table where the only player was a young man in a shabby suède coat. "That will be fine."

Jack steered him over to the craps table—at least this one won't win any more money from my section, he told himself—and whispered to the floorman in the craps pit. "A big winner," he muttered, gesturing at Lester with the slightest movement of his eyes. "He's holding two hundred plus of our money. Give him anything he wants."

The craps pit boss nodded. The routine was easy— keep the player loose with complimentary drinks, keep him distracted with beautiful women, and above all, keep him playing. As long as he keeps playing, the pit boss knew, the odds would whittle him down.

Lester smiled at the young man in the suède coat, and reached for the stack of red dice that the stickman had pushed across the table.

"Good luck," Lester Masaoka said to the stranger.

"Good luck," John Morrissey answered.

Ben Payne, loking for a table, heard the words, moved into a place just as the Oriental threw the dice. He called out a five-hundred-dollar wager on the pass line. The box-man nodded and called, "You can have a bet." Ben was back in the game. For his life, he thought. The point was six.

"Easy now, Bobby. Bend over, farther, farther! Bend over."

Bobby sighed to himself as he assumed the demeaning posture of a proctologist's patient, leaning over the edge of the desk in Louis Bianco's office. He felt Bianco's fingers fumbling with his slacks, pulling them down, exposing his buttocks to the chill air.

He sighed again. He had been buggered by the best of them since he arrived in Las Vegas—if you're a pretty boy dancer with a lot of ambition, you have to swing both ways now and then. And he'd be buggered again when he finished his assignment with Sally Martin and returned to his boyfriend, the macho blond in the wild animal act of *Salaam, Sultan.* But this was the first time that his boss had asked him to put out. In fact, it was the first time that Bobby Reed had detected anything but a cold lust for abstract power in Louis Bianco.

"Is this how you really like it, Bobby?" Bianco hissed in his ear. "Is this how you really get off?"

"Mmmmm," Bobby murmured, a neutral sound that could be taken for acute pleasure, or boredom, or anger.

"But you've been putting out for Sally Martin," Bianco reminded him.

"That's my job," Bobby said softly. He'd caught the dangerous edge in Bianco's voice, the cutting hostility in his touch, and he began to grow anxious. "I'm a pro and I do my job."

"Yeah, sure," Bianco grunted, backing away from the

slender young man but pinning him against the table with one hand against the small of his back. "But I'm getting the idea that you like your work too damn much."

"I don't know what you mean," Bobby protested weakly, fighting the panic in his voice, reminding himself to act like a trouper. "I diddle the old lady, that's all. Isn't that what you want?"

"Yeah, yeah, but she's not talking, is she?" Bianco said. "And meanwhile you're spending more and more time in the sack with her. And you're giving me lots of helpful suggestions, like letting her split with the money and forgetting about it."

"Hey, no heat—" Bobby began to say, but his words were cut off by a sudden stab of pain from behind. A sharp, cold stab that seemed to penetrate deeply into his body. "Oh my God!"

Bianco wheezed a short laugh. "You like to take it in the ass, don't you?" he hissed. "Well, take it, and enjoy it. All I have to do is pull the trigger to make sure you never take it again."

Bobby choked back the painful sobs that rose in his throat. You must not let him see you cry, he disciplined himself. You must not show him your terror. If he sees it, if he senses it, he will have won everything. Act like a trouper.

Bianco leaned into the young dancer's body with the loaded gun and waited to hear him whimper. "Listen to me, faggot, you find out where that dame is heading, or else I'm going to blow you like you've never been blown before. You're going to remember who you work for. And you're going to do exactly what I tell you to do. Aren't you, Bobby? Aren't you?"

"Yes," he said in a voice without volume. "Anything you say."

He grimaced again as Bianco ripped the intruding metal out of his body. The pain rumbled through his belly like molten lead, his heart raced and his lungs thirsted for deep sobbing that would bring oxygen into his constricted chest. But Bobby stayed cool, stayed under control, and rose unfalteringly from the table.

"No pressure, Mr. Bianco," he said with an easy smile that concealed an impossible humiliation. "Hey, no pressure at all."

Bianco smiled. Then he gestured toward a suitcase in the corner of his office. "That's full of newspaper, Bobby dear, all nicely cut into strips and bundled up like three hundred thousand dollars in cash. You're going to put that dough in Sally Martin's luggage tonight and take out the cash. Then you're going to put her on a plane tomorrow morning. And then you're going to tell me where she's going."

"You're going to have the old lady hit?"

"Not your business, kid."

"Yes, sir," Bobby said, walking stiffly toward the suitcase and then turning to the door. "No pressure, Mr. Bianco."

Bianco watched the young dancer with sublime satisfaction; he'd put the fear into Bobby, and now he could move on to other important matters. He saw only the hobbled progress of the dancer toward the office door; he did not see the snarl of anger on the dancer's lips or the fire in his eyes.

Ira Tuthill had it all figured out now. It would be easy.

He sipped at his third glass of Seven-Up and watched the peculiar mating ritual of the players, the pit bosses and the unattached women of the Mecca casino. Over the past hour or so, sitting primly on a barstool in the lounge, he'd managed to figure it all out.

A gambler would catch the eye of the pit boss. The two men would huddle together for only a few moments—that's all it would take, he told himself—and then the pit boss would go to the telephone. Ten minutes later, the gambler would slip away from the table and disappear into an elevator. And thirty minutes after that, he would return to the tables on unsteady legs and shining with the unmistakable glow.

Tuthill glanced at his watch—almost ten o'clock. He'd have to do it now if he intended to do it at all. Gertie's bus would return to the Mecca by twelve-thirty, and he'd have to be in and out of their hotel room by then. It would take at least an hour to do it right, maybe more than an hour, and Ira Tuthill intended to do it right.

After all, he told himself a thousand times, what was the harm? He was far away from home, far from the disapproving stares of the school board and the schoolteachers and the elders of the church. He was in a town where you could buy any dream, any pleasure, any form of abandon. And if he returned home without buying his dream, he might never have the chance again.

It was worth the risk, Tuthill told himself. In fact, the risk made it all the more exciting.

He took a deep breath and launched toward the black-jack pit. He climbed aboard one of the chairs at a slow table and pushed a two-dollar bet on the table. Cards flashed in front of him; ritual words were spoken; but Tuthill paid no attention, and a shrugging dealer swept away the cards and the bets. He lost twelve more dollars before he managed to catch the pit boss's eye the way he'd seen the others do it.

"I need a little company tonight," he whispered into the pit boss's ear.

"What?" the man demanded. "What did you say?"

"A little company," Tuthill replied in a whisper that was only a fraction of a decibel higher, flushing with deep shame and wondering if he would be able to ask the next question. The all important question that would mean the difference between an unredeemed act of adultery and a sublime fantasy.

"Sure," the pit boss said. "You staying with us? You want me to send someone up to your room—"

"Yes," Tuthill said, turning his head so that the pit boss could not see his eyes.

The pit boss rolled his eyes—Christ, the Saturday night crowd was full of weirdos. But it was part of the action, and the action was the job.

"Sure," he said. "Room number?"

"It's 1047," Tuthill croaked. His hand was shaking with the palsy of a fearful sinner, and he knew it. "Right away, please. I promise I'll be generous."

"Sure," the pit boss said, slipping away and picking up the telephone in the blackjack pit. "Lucy," he muttered into the telephone. "This is Jack. I've got a john for you, lover."

Morrissey watched the dealer stack thousand-dollar chips in front of the Oriental. Little wheels of gold—and lots of them. He felt a rumble of anticipation and a surge of adrenalin as the Oriental piled three thousand dollars on the pass line. Morrissey tossed a hundred-dollar chip on the don't pass. For once, Ben Payne hesitated. He had been playing a careful game. He felt he was in the presence of luck. He wondered who had it at the table. Earlier he had seen the young man in the suède coat. He remembered that. But here was the Japanese, full of emotion and excitement, feverish, maybe ill. Ben did something he had rarely done before. He waited, made no bet. He was down more than one hundred and fifty thousand, a prison term beckoned, and yet he was not desperate.

The Japanese threw a two. "Snake-eyes," a woman at the far end of the table said, and looked at Lester as if he had planned the Pearl Harbor attack.

Lester hardly cared. He loved craps, hated blackjack. Everything went at the craps table, bets within bets, every roll a new challenge. It was more exciting than counting cards, tapping out the codes, and following the computer's instructions on hand after hand. A faint pulsing in his fingertips reminded him that his two colleagues were waiting in the upstairs hotel room, waiting for the pulse codes, waiting for him to act as the robot programmer for the bloodless computer. Even now, the computer was transmitting a reminder code: *send data, send data, send data,* all spelled out in the sequences of pulse and pause in his fingertips.

Lester bet two thousand on the shooter. Morrissey almost lazily bet three hundred against him. Ben bet the pass line. The Japanese threw a six. "Six, the point six," the stickman intoned. "Who wants hard ways?" The Japanese rolled the dice hard against the far wall. They shook into a four and three. "Seven, line away," the stickman cried. "Pay the don't side."

Ben had lost, had chosen the wrong man, the wrong bet. Now the dice passed to the man in the suède coat. He waved them by. On an impulse, Ben called out, "Shoot good!"

Morrissey picked up the dice. The Japanese man bet against him. Ben Payne put fifteen hundred on the pass line and two hundred on eleven.

Suddenly there was a flurry of betting. A wave of special excitement gripped the table. John Morrissey felt for the lucky chip. He didn't even believe that stuff. And yet he found himself calling out "E-lev-EN" as he rolled. The dice scurried like tiny red animals, came up five and six. The roar rose from the table like a mushroom cloud of sound.

Lise Christian's eyes flashed, "Let me have it, Mr. Black," she said quickly, pulling him into the suite and shutting the door behind him.

Moe reached into the pocket of his coat and brought forth a thin package of oil paper and string. Slowly, carefully, almost surgically, he laid the package on the coffee table and unwrapped it. Lise watched nervously.

"It's a .25-caliber semiautomatic," he said solemnly as the last fold of brown paper revealed the silvery object.

"One round in the chamber, five more in the clip. And once you've pulled back the slide action, you can fire all six shots as fast as you can pull the trigger."

Lise nodded but did not speak, and neither of them reached out to touch the gun.

"It's a lady's gun, all right," Moe prattled nervously. "For a small hand. Lightweight, too. Easy to use. But not too accurate unless you're at point-blank range."

As if in slow motion, Lise extended one delicate hand toward the gun and closed her girlish fingers around the butt. Moe saw again how young she looked, how innocent, and again he felt like crying the tears of a father over his daughter.

"Listen, listen to me," he pleaded. "One second after you pull that little popgun on the old man, his muscle is going to open up with an arsenal. Do you hear me, Lisetta? You've got to walk out of here right now, I'm begging you. Do you hear me?"

Lise's eyes met his face. "I hear you, Mr. Black. But there's nothing else to be done now. Nothing else matters now."

"You're such a nice girl, Lisetta, you're so pretty. Don't you have a boyfriend somewhere who wants to marry you? Don't you have someone out there who cares for you? Think of him, Lisetta. Think of what he'll be losing."

She thought of her mother, dead. She thought of her father, dead on the orders of the very man she would be dining with in less than an hour.

And for a fleeting instant, she thought of John Morrissey.

Her hand went instinctively to the thick gold chain around her neck, the chain that carried a tiny bejeweled charm in the shape of a Mecca five-dollar chip. When she'd first opened the package an hour before, the bauble had struck her as both unattractive and gaudy. It was an example of the crassness of the town, the ability of Vegas to take anything of beauty and make it cheap and tawdry, the sudden devaluation of sexual hunger and physical beauty in a world that bartered them like dollar bills.

She would never wear a charm like the one Morrissey had sent her. In Paris, on the Riviera, in the Alps, the charm would be a disgrace if it wasn't a crude joke. But somehow the thought of the encircling gold chain around her neck and the chip of gold over her heart had been seductive, reassuring, fortifying. And now she touched the little charm for the hundredth time since it arrived at her suite, and she thought again of John Morrissey.

She fought against the emotional tug of the young man downstairs. Instead, she picked up the gun and palmed it in one hand as if she'd handled firearms all her life. Moe noticed the ease and experienced sureness of her grip, and thought of Augusto Bertinelli.

You are his daughter, he thought to himself. *Lisetta, you are truly his daughter.*

Linda Warner threw down the leather riding crop and drew up her knees in aching anticipation. The dark gentleman with the exotic accent had been kinky, all right, but she'd seen enough kinky scenes back in Dayton to keep her cool. After all, the guy just wanted a few swats on the backside with the stick, and she'd actually begun to enjoy the scene—the hissing of the riding crop as she brought it down on his bare flesh, the moans of pleasure intermingled with the groans of pain, and the incomprehensible muttering in some strange language that rose and fell like a song as she whipped him.

But now she was ready, she was hungry for him, and she pulled back her long legs so that he could enter her as deeply and powerfully as possible. "Hmmmmm," she moaned, running her fingertips up and down the soft skin of her inner thigh. "Let's get it *on,* let's go!"

The dark stranger glanced at her as if she were something he'd stepped on. He was on his feet, delicately wiping the blood from his back with a towel, grimacing faintly against the pain of new wounds on the old ones of the night before, but clearly enjoying it. Linda glanced between his legs and saw, to her horror and disgust, that the dark stranger had already spent himself.

"Hey, what about me?" she demanded, a bit too brusquely for a woman intent on seduction. "I don't mind playing your screwy game if that's what gets you off, but what about me?"

The dark stranger shot a quizzical look at the blonde woman with her hand between her legs on the bed. He retrieved his trousers from the dresser, where he'd folded them neatly to avoid wrinkles, and picked up the officer's swagger stick from the floor, inserting it carefully into the cloth panel that his Bond Street tailors had unquestioningly added to all of his suits.

"Hey, what about me?" Linda repeated, reminding herself to sound girlish and seductive. "I've been waiting for you to climb aboard—"

"That will be all," the stranger said quietly, slipping deftly into his jacket and straightening the arms and shoulders with precise tugs.

"That will be *all?*" she echoed sarcastically. "Well, that's a real pile of shit—"

He silenced her with a quick blow across the face. These heathen women, he thought, have absolutely no sense of decorum or dignity. And they speak the language of the streets. Then he softened a bit. At least she'd been a real blonde, and he couldn't fault her technique with the swagger stick.

"That was a love slap," he whispered as Linda raised a hand to her face, as if to convince herself that he'd really struck her. He reached into the breast pocket of his suit, removed his passport case, and dropped a thousand-dollar bill on the dresser. "If there has been misunderstanding, I'm terribly sorry."

Then he turned crisply, crossed the room, and slipped

into the corridor, leaving Linda Warner open-mouthed and far short of orgasm. The camel-lover had *paid* her for the kinky scene. He'd paid her—what kind of shit was that, anyway? What did he think she was? Linda raged silently, pounding the bed with small fists and forcing herself to cry in mewing, catlike sobs. He thought she was a *hooker*. He thought she put out for *money*.

But the effort toward outrage began to wear her out, and she abandoned the sobbing altogether while softening her blows against the unresisting bed. And then curiosity replaced outrage. She rose from the bed and tiptoed across the room to the dresser. Well, at least she could find out how much he thought she was worth.

Linda Warner gasped. A thousand dollars! Was it real? How could she know? She'd never seen one before. Maybe he was playing a joke. No, he was too serious.

A thousand-dollar bill! She clutched it in one hand and returned to the bed, positioning the other hand carefully over her mound of authentic blonde hair. If the stranger thought she was worth a thousand dollars in the sack, why was she horsing around with a middle-income insurance peddler who couldn't get it up or keep it up—not for love *or* money? She debated the question energetically while her forefinger worked with equal fervor as she closed her eyes. When she came, she squealed with delight and, even while coming, rubbed the thousand-dollar bill against her clitoris.

Jim Carne clutched desperately at the armrests of his seat. Senator Alan Simpson Harwell drank deeply from a highball glass of bourbon. And the twins, Melinda and Belinda, giggled at each bump and shimmy. But the pilot of the Mecca Hotel's private Lear Jet concentrated on the takeoff procedure, building the engine to maximum thrust, releasing the brakes, and shrieking toward the end of the runway.

"Christ, I hate small planes," Carne complained to no one in particular. "Give me a Boeing 747 with a pilot who's graying around the temples. Or even a 727 with a fighter-jockey who learned how to fly in 'Nam. But nothing smaller than a 727—that's my rule."

The strained effort at wit fell flat. Melinda was busy making eyes at the Senator and licking the corner of her mouth with a lascivious tongue; Belinda was staring into space, working out some nice steps for their act when they finally made the main showroom; and the Senator was already lost in an alcoholic stupor. So Jim Carne sulked.

The last-minute flight had been Larry Johnson's idea. Instead of yet another evening in the private casino, why not something more adventurous—a visit to one of Nevada's famous legal brothels in the outlying counties? And none was more famous than the Mustang Ranch, a castle of connected trailers and bungalows in Sparks, the wilderness of the Nevada flatlands, where just twenty minutes from Reno a man could choose his women and his drink and his pleasure and know that it was all legal. Joe Conforte's comfortable broads.

Well, Carne told himself, the Senator would soon have to absent himself from pleasure for awhile when his Mecca buddies were called to appear before an indignant Senate subcommittee. Of course, the Senator could read about the hearings from his Caribbean refuge, but he, Jim Carne, would be at the committee table from gavel to gavel, making sure that the corruptors in the empire of Edward Roger Everett were showcased before the whole country. So far, only Carne knew all the secrets and the interconnections, and only Carne could pull the foundation stones out that would cause the whole rotten structure to tumble.

Senator Alan Simpson Harwell would explode the first bomb tomorrow at the Mecca. Carne glanced again at the Senator—he seemed too relaxed, too at ease, too comfortable for a man about to betray his lifelong cronies in another few hours.

It didn't matter, though, and Carne knew it. There was no retreating. Jim Carne was there to see that the Senator followed the script down to the last word—and he had insisted on making the flight to the Mustang Ranch to make sure that the Senator didn't get lost between now and the morning.

Carne turned his gaze to the twins. Melinda was a giggler, a silly little girl, but Belinda struck him as someone more complex, more insidious, and maybe a little dangerous. Even as she stared blankly into space, Carne wondered what occupied her concentration so completely. He followed her eyes to the far side of the corporate jet's narrow passenger compartment, but he saw nothing special—only the circular porthole, the emergency exit door, and the bright red handle that operated it.

Lester Masaoka was angry. He didn't like the man in the suède jacket or the effete-looking black across the table. They were putting a jinx on him. He scowled at the scruffy stranger next to him, at the dice, at his diminishing stack of chips. The exhilaration that had carried him into the casino was gone, replaced by a hard, driving emotion somewhere between sexual passion and profound hunger. He lusted for a winning roll. He *hungered* for it. And the unbearable ache had returned to his back despite the injection. The pulse signals in his fingertips didn't help. He felt himself unraveling.

Ben had made a gradual, an encouraging, recovery. He began to feel his confidence returning. At first he had slavishly followed the man in the suède jacket who had almost absentmindedly bet the pass line only, playing fifty or a hundred dollars as though he cared nothing for the money, and was killing time. Numbers on which Ben would normally lay odds, suède jacket would ignore as though he knew something, knew when the dice would have long or short runs between making the point or sevening out. Oddly, the man held a five-dollar chip in his right hand but never placed it on the table.

A conviction grew in Ben's mind. The guy was a dice

mechanic; he could make numbers come up almost at will. Of course, he was betting small on the pass line. The person to watch was his accomplice, Ben thought, who would be betting heavily on the don't pass when the time came. Luck, Ben Payne thought wryly. He had almost been taken in. Suède jacket was an artist. He would bet with him until the switcheroo came, until suède jacket's confederate appeared and bet a pile on the don't pass. Then he, Ben, would be in at the kill. Five or six heavy bets on a sure thing would make him well, guarantee his freedom, give him another chance. He looked around the table trying to figure out who might be the confederate. Surely it couldn't be the Japanese. He seemed so spacy, so crazy, so full of animosity toward the suède jacket. The Jap was playing the limit. He was making crazy bets, the field bets—the all-time sucker bet and the propositions nobody ever tried. It wasn't him. Maybe the confederate was the quiet, unobtrusive man in the checked jacket who looked like a dentist on vacation, the heavy-set dowager who carried enough gold to throw the London market out of whack for a day, or the tough-looking Chicago in the white shirt.

Ben would find out. He looked at his pile of chips. Over five thousand. There was, with what he had dragged and handed to Selma, maybe forty thousand in the Gucci. Okay. I've got enough to make it back. I'll take it easy. But when the time comes, baby, he told himself, it will be winning all the way.

Morrissey watched the young man across from him, tried to read from his face the thoughts which were going on in his mind. The Japanese hated him, that was clear. But the attitude of the others was not so clear. Emotions were fogged at the dice table. His heart wasn't in it. It was Lise he wanted. He'd give back the money, the luck, anything for her.

Dinner was an ordeal. To Lawrence Johnson, it seemed never to end. The chef had prepared an elaborate feast of

Middle Eastern dishes, serving them with great ceremony and Western efficiency, and the Arab seemed to relish Johnson's discomfort at making small talk with a man who never answered a question directly.

And there was the new busboy, the big dumb one who looked like a football player and kept barging into the yacht's dining room with bottles of mineral water or fresh cups of Turkish coffee or other unwanted items. As the dinner stretched on into the night, the new busboy grew even clumsier, more flustered, spending more and more time in the dining area at such simple tasks as clearing the dishes and distributing scented hand towels.

If the kid hadn't been so clumsy, if he hadn't been so obviously embarrassed at his clumsiness, Johnson might have suspected that he was trying to spend as much time in the dining area as possible. He might have thought that the kid was trying to overhear as much of their conversation as possible. Johnson dismissed the possibility—no one would be so stupid as to plant a clumsy oaf like this kid.

The last dishes had been cleared, the last serving of coffee had been set on the table, and Johnson reached for the thin attaché case that he'd carried aboard the yacht and placed against his leg under the dinner table. When the Arab spotted the case, he allowed Johnson the single smile of the evening.

"And so we finally arrive at the real purpose of your kind hospitality," Sayd said.

Johnson returned the smile, though he suspected that the Arab had just insulted him. "Well, it took a little longer than I had planned, but it's all here now," he bubbled, clicking open the attaché case and producing a slender file folder. "All we need to agree upon now is the price."

Sayd nodded solemnly as he opened the dossier and paged through each document, pausing here and there to scrutinize a signature or reread a contract provision. Johnson studied his face and listened for each grunt or sigh; after all, he reminded himself, he'd done everything he could to prepare the scheme, and now it was up to Sayd. His whole future was contained in the folder that the Arab now held in his graceful fingers.

At last, Sayd looked up from the documents. Johnson hoped for another smile, but saw only the even expression of an experienced poker player.

"The signatures are very good," Sayd said. "Where were they done?"

A compliment. Johnson flushed with pride and a new sense of self-confidence. "Of course, you'll understand that I cannot reveal the identity of the man who prepared the documents," he said. "But you need have no fear at all—no court in the world would believe that those signatures were made by anyone other than Edward Roger Everett."

Sayd paused. "And I repeat, Mr. Johnson," he said icily, "where were the forgeries done? If you ask me to invest a considerable amount of money in your scheme, then I must know how secure the investment will be."

"The documents were typed here at the Mecca—I did them myself, and it took me weeks. I mean, literally weeks. I can only hunt and peck, you know." Johnson realized that he was stammering like a schoolboy, and tried to regain his composure. "I used authentic letterhead stationery of Everett Enterprises. I used a typewriter that is inventoried to the bunker itself. So there's no way in the world that anyone can prove that the documents weren't drafted in the old man's offices."

Sayd nodded. "And the signatures?" he repeated with a sigh. "Who forged Mr. Everett's signatures?"

Johnson paused and then shrugged. "An experienced banknote forger among my friends. He's done ten years in the penitentiary for counterfeiting. He was busted in Vegas on another funny money scam just three weeeks after parole. He wanted very badly to keep out of the can, and I used my juice to keep him on the street. He is very damned grateful, of course, and all I needed were a few signatures—"

"Where is he now?" Sayd persisted.

"Mexico City. With plenty of cash and the best Mexican passport money can buy. He's stashed, and he's safe."

"Can you locate him on short notice?" Sayd asked. "I need to know exactly where to find him."

"I really don't think that's necessary," Johnson protested. "These signatures are first class. He couldn't do any better—"

Johnson fell silent. He suddenly realized why Ahmed Ibn Sayd wanted to know the whereabouts of the forger; and he realized what fate might await the forger in Mexico City—a knock on the door at an odd hour, a dark stranger in the doorway, a bullet in the heart, and the secret of the forgery would be sealed forever. He shuddered.

"Well, then. Let us review the documents themselves," Sayd continued, removing a gold pen from his pocket and a leather notepad from his coat.

"A power of attorney signed by Edward Roger Everett, giving Lawrence Johnson the exclusive and unlimited authority to sell all of the assets of Everett Enterprises, including the Mecca Hotel and Casino.

"A letter of consent from Edward Roger Everett to Lawrence Johnson, giving his explicit assent to the sale of Everett Enterprises and the Mecca Hotel to a consortium of international investors consisting of certain citizens of the nations of the Arabian peninsula.

"A contract for the sale of all assets of Everett Enterprises to the Arab consortium, with a closing date exactly ten days from today, after which the sale becomes final and incontestable by all parties."

Sayd paused, and Johnson piped up: "And don't forget the last document—a contract between Edward Everett and Lawrence Johnson, naming me sole chief executive officer of Everett Enterprises and granting me a 20 percent interest in the profits of Everett Enterprises and the proceeds of any sale of the assets."

"Yes, of course—the payoff," Sayd commented. "I have dealt with Americans long enough to know that baksheesh is not strictly an Arab custom." He watched a flicker of embarrassment dance across his companion's face, and continued: "Only two matters remain to be discussed between us, Mr. Johnson."

"The price?" Johnson said eagerly.

"Yes, the price," Sayd said, "but our more important concern is that the forgeries will be discovered and the sale voided."

Johnson waved his hand in protest. "No chance whatsoever, I assure you," he said eagerly. "The old man buried himself in that crypt years ago, and we haven't heard from him since. I run the hotel and the business operations, and I deposit his earnings in one of two dozen bank accounts, and I send him reports that never get read."

"But certainly he would emerge from his quarters when the newspapers announce the sale of Everett Enterprises."

"That's the beauty, Mr. Sayd. That's the beauty of the whole plan. The old man has had a dozen reasons to come out of hiding over the years—lawsuits, subpoenas, Senate investigations, a dozen different reasons—but not once did he show his face. Just last year he lost an entire airline because he wouldn't answer a subpoena from the Civil Aeronautics Board. So you can be sure he's not going to come out of hiding now."

"And if you're wrong, Mr. Johnson?" Sayd probed. "If he decides to challenge the sale in court?"

"Okay, okay, let's say that he does try to challenge the sale," Johnson countered. "Unless he appears before the ten-day closing period, the sale goes through automatically. And then the only way to challenge the sale is to prove that the documents are forged. Now who is going to believe a babbling old fool like Everett? We'll just file some psychiatric testimony that says he's suffering from senile dementia and can't remember signing the documents. I'll provide witnesses to the signatures."

Johnson leaned forward across the table, consumed with his own enthusiasm and certainty. Here at last was the chance to gain real control of Everett Enterprises, to make the decisions that would make it a thriving international corporation instead of the plaything of a senile old man, to cleanse its operations of the hangers-on like Moe Black and Louis Bianco who were left over from the Bertinelli days. And here was the chance to make a money killing that would guarantee him luxury for the rest of his life.

"Yes," Sayd said in a contemplative voice. "Yes, it is a good plan. A good plan." He paused, and his voice took on a cutting edge. "Let us talk again about the price."

Johnson smiled carefully. "When we talked in Geneva two months ago, I mentioned a certain figure. You seemed to agree—"

"Out of the question now," Sayd snapped. "Your dollar has weakened considerably. Your exaggerated asking price values every asset at its greatest possible worth. And what discount do you give for the risk factor? How many millions do we deduct for that?"

"What risk factor?" Johnson demanded. "The deal is foolproof."

"Only in a world that is free of fools," Sayd said pointedly. "The transaction could be challenged, and if it is, then our investment is in jeopardy. So I believe that we are entitled to a substantial discount. I believe that three hundred and thirty million dollars at the current exchange rate is a fair price."

"Preposterous," Johnson sputtered. "You've cut it in half. The aircraft plant alone is worth that much. The research and development facilities, the merchant marine fleet, the mineral assets, the Mecca Hotel, the real estate holdings —we are talking about a billion-dollar package."

Sayd looked at the other man. "I will not insult you if you don't insult me," he said smoothly, slipping into the familiar role of camel trader. "You are asking me to take a terrible gamble. I am asking you to lower the stakes. Three hundred and thirty million is not bad for a couple of forgeries and a large risk."

"Four hundred million," Johnson countered, "and that's the lowest I'll go."

A crash of broken crockery disturbed the negotiations. The considerable bulk of the new busboy fell backward through the swinging door that led from the galley to the dining area, and he looked up with a sheepish grin at the two solemn men.

"Hey, I'm really sorry," he nearly shouted as he scrambled to his feet amid broken dishes and spilled sauces. "I'm really sorry, but I guess I'm just not a sailor—all this rocking and rolling is making me a little seasick."

"Don't be silly, Bobby dear," Sally Martin scolded, puffing between words as the costumers cinched her into the elaborate construction that would conceal her age and her shape for the audience at the late show in the main room of the Mecca Hotel. "You know how tired I am after a show, and I've already got tickets for tomorrow morning's flight to New York."

Bobby Reed forced himself to perform the warmup exercises for tonight's performance despite the burning pain that seemed to drill through his body—and despite the burning anger that seemed to blind his judgment. "Tomorrow morning is too late, Sally," he whispered forcefully. "We can catch the red-eye to New York tonight, and nobody will be watching."

"Watching?" Sally asked, shooing away the costumers. "What are you talking about, silly boy?"

"The money, Sally," Bobby said, abandoning the exercises and kneeling at her side. "What if they're watching you?"

"Don't worry, silly boy," she giggled. "I've been a courier for years. They trust me. Nobody watches me."

"Do you love me, Sally?" Bobby asked, seizing her hand and holding it tightly.

"Oh yes, Bobby, I love you, I love you so much."

"Then you've got to listen to me. We have to catch

that flight tonight. After the show, we can't even go back to our rooms—I'll get the luggage from your room and I'll have it ready as soon as we change out of our costumes."

"Why, Bobby?" Sally asked, becoming alarmed. "What do you know, Bobby?"

"Don't ask me why or how but Bianco suspects what you're up to."

"Rio," she said in a flat voice. "He can't touch us in Rio." She was studying the young dancer's face. Suddenly, she started to sob. "Don't betray me, Bobby. Please! I've come to depend on you—"

"Rio?" Bobby interrupted, repeating the destination insistently. "You've got us booked to Rio?"

She nodded.

"Okay, okay," Bobby said, suddenly distracted. "I've got something to do upstairs. And so I won't see you until our cue. But remember, Sally, we're leaving for the airport as soon as we come off the stage."

She nodded again, and continued to nod as the young dancer hurried out of her dressing room. His destination was the closet where the three hundred thousand dollars was carefully concealed beneath a false bottom, but he had to detour to his own dressing room first for the suitcase full of shredded newspapers that Louis Bianco had given him.

Lise Christian pushed tentatively at the door marked "Private Salon" and gasped involuntarily when it opened easily under her touch. She peered into the cool darkness, half expecting to see the old man or the bodyguards that Moe had warned about, but she was alone in the empty casino on the Penthouse floor of the Mecca Hotel.

As her eyes grew accustomed to the darkness, she could make out vague shapes in the shadows. A craps table, two blackjack tables, a roulette wheel, a baccarat table— each stocked with a bank of chips under locked glass but ready for action. A serving counter along one wall, with a neat row of covered containers and baskets of plastic-wrapped fruit, all of the food protected against stray bacteria like a sterilized bathroom glass in a motel room. And in the center of the empty casino, someone had placed two chairs—a pair of simple, injection-molded plastic chairs on stainless steel legs, each also covered with a germproof wrapping of plastic fabric.

I'm early, she thought. Maybe I should go and come back. Here is where she would face the man who had ordered her father's execution. His assassination. Why was she here? What curiosity drove her to this confrontation? She shivered.

She slipped the pistol from the slash pocket in her slacks and worked the slide action just as Moe had shown her. Then she allowed the clip to drop out of the butt, checking to see that it was full, and snapped it back.

She eased herself into one of the two plastic-wrapped chairs, listening to the unearthly crackle of the plastic under her weight. It was thirty minutes to the midnight rendezvous, and she wondered how far away the old man was at the moment. She wondered how far away from death she was at the moment. But she knew with certainty how far away from death the old man was.

Carne peered out of the window of the private jet as it screamed into a sharp banking movement and then straightened out over the unending blackness of the Nevada wilderness. Somewhere down there was the Mustang Ranch, but Carne would be damned if he could see it.

"Come over here," Belinda said coolly, patting the seat next to the emergency door. "They turn on the airstrip lights whenever a plane buzzes the ranch. A lot of ranchers fly their own planes to the Mustang."

Carne stared at Belinda for a moment. He didn't trust that easy smile or the inviting hand on the seat next to her. He didn't trust the sudden decision to leave the Mecca and fly to some godforsaken patch of desert just so the old man could get laid. Then the pilot banked sharply to the right and then the left, waggling the wings to signal for airstrip lights below, and suddenly Carne didn't trust the tiny jet.

"I don't like small planes," he muttered again, moving to the seat near the emergency exit and pushing his face hard against the porthole. As if by magic, a crucifix of light appeared on the desert floor, and he could make out the cluster of bungalows and trailers that were the Mustang Ranch.

"Do you see it?" Belinda asked, glancing over to see that the Senator and her twin sister were both safely in their seats, belted tightly against the sharp dive of the plane.

"Yeah, I can see it," Carne said. "But I wish to hell that he'd put me and the goddamn plane on the ground—"

Jim Carne, who was accustomed to having his way with U.S. senators, got only half his wish.

Belinda reached for the bright red handle of the emergency door and yanked hard, just as she'd been shown by Larry Johnson a few hours before, and then she planted both feet against Jim Carne's buttocks. She pushed with all the strength of an exotic dancer who rehearses four hours a day.

"Hey," he cried shrilly, clutching desperately at the emergency door. "God help me—"

But it was too late. The cabin was filled with an explosive current of air, which carried both Carne and Carne's last words out into the void of night airspace, sending him on a short trip from four thousand feet to ground zero. The pilot struggled to control the sharp bank and the steep dive; the Senator, who still held his highball glass, laughed heartily but hysterically; and Melinda, wide-eyed and open-mouthed, screamed in horror.

Only Belinda remained cool and composed. In fact, she wasn't thinking anymore about the "accident," the improperly locked emergency door, and the passenger who neglected to wear his seatbelt despite the instructions from the pilot. No, Belinda was thinking about the choreography of the new act that would replace Sally Martin as the finale of *Salaam, Sultan.*

Bad luck, Lester said to himself. The bastard is bad luck. He looked at the man in the suède jacket and Morrissey returned the look. Ben Payne caught it, too. Is this the moment? He signaled the boxman. "I want to raise my betting limit to five thousand dollars." The boxman looked at the pit boss, who nodded. Ben reached for Selma's hand, pressed it. "Give me everything in the Gucci," he whispered. It could be anytime now, he told himself. He felt like a million dollars. Better than cocaine. Better than cognac. Better than Selma at her most passionate moments.

Morrissey felt uncomfortable. He wanted to leave the table, yet something held him there. That was the mystery of gambling. That magnetism. That sense that you were playing a role in a drama—so large, so *cosmic*—that you couldn't quit. That would be the test. Leaving the table, the casino, Vegas, never to return, but quitting a winner. Did he have that kind of guts?

He rolled the dice. "Eight. Eight's the point," the stickman intoned. "Anybody for the hard ways?"

Morrissey placed twenty-six hundred dollars' worth of chips in front of the dealer. "I want all the numbers. Five hundred each on four, five, nine, and ten, buy the four and ten. Six on the six. Here's the vig," pushing another two green chips—fifty dollars—toward the dealer, who repeated the instructions aloud. The numbers, if they were rolled before a seven, would pay odds ranging from two to one for the four and ten down to seven to six for the six. John backed up his hundred-dollar pass line bet with two hundred behind. Then he began to roll numbers. Almost at will. Ben, expecting the don't pass ploy, got in toward the end, came out a little bit ahead on his bets. But he was confused. When would the don't pass ploy come?

Lucy Sheaffer knocked at the door of room 1047, and

imagined that she heard a faint voice from inside. So faint that she knocked again. The voice that invited her inside sounded stern but ghostly, and she shivered slightly before opening the door.

The room was dark, although she could make out a figure sitting in a chair facing the door—a figure wearing long rubber gloves, a rubber apron, and a surgical mask, all of which had been offered as free samples to delegates of the Funeral Directors Association convention by suppliers of undertaking equipment. And next to the seated figure was a coffee table draped neatly with a white sheet.

Lucy shuddered again.

"Come in, Miss," the figure commanded. "Come in and then turn around so you cannot see me."

Lucy hesitated. Jack had warned her that the next job might want it special, but she was beginning to worry about how special it might turn out to be. Still, it was three bills for the kinky stuff, and she was a working girl now. Bravely, she stepped into the room and faced the closed door.

"Listen very carefully, Miss," the figure said. "Please don't say a word. I don't want to hear your voice at all. Not now. Not later. Just don't say anything."

Lucy nodded. The room was chilled to the maximum capacity of the air conditioner, and her skin rippled with goose bumps.

"Now I want you to go into the bathroom," the man in the rubber apron continued. "You'll find five buckets of cocktail ice cubes on the sink. I want you to pour them into the bathtub, and then fill it up with cold water. As cold as you can make it. I want you to undress and sit in the bathtub for at least five minutes. Longer, if you can manage it. Then I want you to come out here, lay down on the table, and pretend that you're dead."

He paused. Lucy shivered. Then he continued: "Just don't do anything. Don't say anything. Let your arms and legs go limp. And don't worry—" his voice tightened with excitement, "—I'll take care of everything. You won't be hurt and I'll pay you well."

What the hell, Lucy said to herself. It was kinky, but it sure beat the work back in Denver. She could think of worse things to do in Las Vegas in August than sitting in a tubful of ice. She shivered in anticipation.

Although the old man never believed it, Alexander Tate was loyal. Once attached to an individual or a cause, Tate's loyalty was ferocious. But it was complex. Crimes against property—the embezzlement of gold coins, for instance—were not a violation of Tate's code of honor; they injured no one, especially not an old man whose wealth was almost beyond counting; and in fact it assisted his brethren in their holy mission to achieve self-sufficiency on the farmlands of Georgia and South Carolina.

His faith taught him discipline, self-control, and a love of orderliness in one's life and one's loyalties. He perceived no contradiction in his duty to preserve the life and fortune of Edward R. Everett and his duty to provide gold to his brothers and sisters for their survival. If he thought about these two facts at all, it was merely to explain to himself the fact that he was exacting a greater price for his services than Everett suspected that he was paying. In the end, Everett could have asked for no more loyal or dedicated a retainer than Alexander Tate.

Now, as the black man maneuvered the speedboat in the wake of the Mecca's yacht, he was driven by a single thought—to eradicate the threat that he'd overheard on the monitoring equipment. To frustrate Lawrence Johnson's plan to steal the old man's empire. Because if the old man fell victim to Johnson's schemes, then the flow of gold Krugerrands would come to an abrupt end. And Alexander Tate knew that it was up to him to stop the scheme because Lawrence Johnson had been correct about one thing—the old man would not venture forth from the bunker. Not to meet the young woman named Christian. And not to turn away the insidious challenge from the Arab named Sayd.

The yacht had been cruising in a neat oval around the center of the lake, coming within a hundred yards of the shore and fifty yards of the twin intake towers of Boulder Dam. Tate had shadowed the oval throughout the evening, following the direction-finder and keeping the powerboat within range of the bugging equipment on the yacht. He'd heard it all, and now he had to act.

Tate pushed the throttle forward, raising the noise level of the outboard engine but also increasing the speed, and within a few minutes he was closing in on the boat. The yacht was cruising slowly enough to allow an agile man to jump from the trailing boat to the deck of the yacht. And Tate, thanks to his extreme self-discipline, was an agile man.

But now Tate spotted an obstacle to his plan—one of the crewmen, a hulking young man in a tight-fitting uniform, was lounging on the rear deck of the yacht. A lookout or a bodyguard of Johnson's. Tate reached into the holster on his belt and pulled out the snub-nosed .38-caliber revolver that was standard equipment among the bunker staff. Its six rounds of hollow-point, low-velocity shells were designed to inflict the maximum damage on an intruding body without ricocheting dangerously around the enclosed spaces of the bunker. But even at the greater distances on the open water, Tate was confident that the .38 would do its work well.

The man on the rear deck cocked his head and listened to the sound of an outboard engine, but in the darkness, on the open surface of the lake, it was difficult to know where the noise came from. Tate pushed the throttle even further, closing on the boat even faster, and he smiled to himself as the clumsy oaf cranked his head back and forth, searching desperately for the sound.

And then the young man spotted Tate's boat. He leaned out over the water, trying to identify the craft or the man at the helm. Those wasted seconds allowed Tate to bring the powerboat within a half-dozen yards of the yacht. And then, in the split second before the lookout turned back to the hatch that led to the crew's quarters, Tate fired two silenced rounds in his direction.

The first shot grazed Mike Adams' head and spun him around in a dizzy pirouette; the second round smashed harmlessly into the polished teakwood trim of the yacht. But Mike was already on the deck, reaching for the sidearm that Bianco had insisted upon for the mission aboard the yacht, scrambling at the same time toward the hatch. Mike didn't know who was firing at him, but he knew that it didn't matter much now.

The black man at the helm of the powerboat pulled back the throttle and allowed his craft to glide alongside the yacht. A moment later, Mike heard the sound of a grappling hook crash to the deck and then crawl up the railing until it caught on a brass stanchion. The intruder would be over the railing in another moment, and Mike—despite the painful wound that oozed blood into his ear and over his sparkling white uniform—knew that he had to fight the attacker.

He struggled to his feet, holding the pistol in one hand and steadying himself with the other, and lurching to the railing. He tore at the grappling hook, trying desperately to disengage it, but the intruder had already pulled the line taut against his boat. Mike looked up, and suddenly he was face to face with a familiar black man wielding a snubnosed service revolver.

"Tate," Mike said numbly. In a flash, he recalled his earlier decision to bring the news of Carl Hagen and the old man's tumor directly to Alexander Tate; to warn Tate of the imminence of the old man's death if he were not treated for the cancerous time bomb; to redeem himself and perhaps reward himself by saving the old man's life. And so Mike repeated: "Tate!"

But Tate was over the railing and on top of him before he could utter another word. With a single powerful blow, Tate brought the butt of his gun down on Mike's head, stunning him into unconsciousness. Bracing himself against the railing, Tate levered the senseless body over the edge and into the water. Momets later, he saw that the security guard was being drawn slowly by the current toward the induction vents of the intake towers of Boulder Dam. That's where the dam's maintenance crew eventually would find him pinned lifelessly by the suction of the water against the steel screen that protected the intake system from precisely such flotsam and jetsam.

Ahmed Ibn Sayd was distracted by the heavy meal and the heavy bargaining, but the distraction did not dull his finely honed sense of survival. He sensed rather than saw the black face that passed the porthole of the yacht's dining area; his hand was on the pistol in his shoulder holster before Larry Johnson perceived the movement.

Sayd raised one finger to his lips. Johnson froze, and his eyes widened as the Arab withdrew the pistol from beneath his elegantly tailored suit.

"What the hell—" he started to say, but the muzzle flash and the muted snapping sound from the Arab's gun silenced his words in midsentence. Sayd fired once, twice, three times, each shot splintering the teak slats of the door that opened from the dining area to the rear deck.

Johnson sniffed the acrid stink of spent gunpowder; he studied the splintered holes in the slatted door, three ragged holes spaced out in a neat diagonal across the rectangular door; and he heard the shriek of wood against doorframe as someone on the other side of the door collapsed against it.

Sayd was already on his feet, working the doorlock and pushing the dead body to the deck with one delicate shove from a booted foot. With the meticulous care of a man who valued his wardrobe, he avoided touching the bloodied wounds on the black man's body; but with the care of a man who valued his life, he kept the barrel of his weapon pointed at the man's head in case a final shot was necessary.

It wasn't. Alexander Tate died with the first shot, which

pierced his heart and lodged against his spine, and the other two rounds simply perforated his corpse. Sayd listened for the sound of breathing; he checked for a pulse on the man's wrist and neck. Finally, he rose to his feet and replaced the gun in its hidden holster.

"Do you know him?" Sayd asked quietly.

Johnson's jaw worked silently for a moment before he found his voice. "It's the old man's bodyguard," he said. "Everett's bodyguard."

"And why would he be boarding your yacht with a drawn weapon, Mr. Johnson?" Sayd asked.

Johnson shook his head. "I don't know, I just don't know," he said. "But it doesn't mean a damn thing. Tate came after us, but the old man can't." He ventured a delicate kick against the hand that held the .38 revolver, knocking the gun from the corpse's grip to the deck. "There's nothing to stop us now, Mr. Sayd."

Lucy's teeth chattered as she climbed out of the bathtub. She'd heard a lot of advice from the pros about how to avoid clap, but no one had told her how to avoid a cold. And now she sniffled deeply and tried not to sneeze as she padded out of the bathroom and crossed the john's room to the draped coffee table.

She waited to hear his voice, another set of instructions, but he was totally silent. With a sigh, she climbed onto the table and laid back. Moving quickly and noiselessly, the john was next to her, breathing hard, wielding another sheet in the air until it settled over her like a shroud. When Lucy was covered from head to toe, the john rubbed his gloved hands together and wheezed in anticipation.

And then Lucy sneezed.

"Please," the john said reprovingly. "You're supposed to be dead, you know."

"I'm sorry," she said, sniffling deeply again. "But I'm so damned cold—"

"Shhh," he hissed irritably, stamping one foot like a

petulant child. "I told you not to speak. Don't speak at all. You're supposed to be dead."

Lucy nodded and fell silent, wondering what the john intended to do next. She heard a rustling sound, rubber against cloth, and then she felt his icy fingers at her head. Slowly, solemnly, he pulled the sheet from her body as a mortician undrapes a corpse before embalming it.

Holding her breath, fighting the urge to sneeze again, Lucy allowed herself to open one eye halfway. The john was still wearing the rubber gloves, but the rubber apron was pulled up to reveal a probing erection, and the surgical mask was pulled aside to reveal—

"Mr. Tuthill," Lucy blurted out. "My God, Mr. Tuthill!"

He peered closely at the face of his well iced hooker, and the color drained from his face. "Miss Sheaffer," he blurted out. "My God, Miss Sheaffer!"

"A member of the school board," she lectured him from her reclining position, not bothering to cover her naked body. "Behaving like a weirdo."

"A third-grade teacher," he lectured her right back, not bothering to conceal his growing erection. "A whore!"

They considered each other's pronouncements. Lucy shivered, but not from her ice-cube bath. Ira Tuthill shivered, too, but not from the chill of the air conditioning. The imminence of the forbidden pleasure, the imminence of the forbidden payment—Mr. Tuthill and Miss Sheaffer spent a long moment in contemplation of what might be lost and what might be gained and what, after all, was at risk.

"It's going to be three bills, you know," Lucy ventured in a meek voice. "No discounts on the kinky stuff just because I work for you back home."

"Shhhh," replied Ira Tuthill, working the zipper of his black mortician's suit with chilled fingertips. "You're supposed to be dead."

The old man needed another injection. He needed a

soothing bowl of the special soup that Tate made for him. But most of all he needed Alexander Tate. Midnight was only minutes away, and his battery of monitors told him that Lise Christian was waiting for him. Waiting for him with a silvery little gun in her right hand.

"Tate," the old man muttered into the intercom that connected his master control room to the kitchen. "I need you right away, Tate."

The speaker crackled with a different voice. "Mr. Tate has not returned, Mr. Everett," said one of Tate's assistants. "Shall I come instead?"

"Who are you?" he demanded crankily. Herbert or Norbert or Egbert—he could never remember their names; he could only remember Tate's name. And he could never trust the others; he only trusted Alexander Tate. But now Lise Christian was waiting for him, and Tate was nowhere to be found.

A betrayal!

The pain throbbed behind his eyes with new intensity. He slumped forward in his chair, letting his head fall against one of the television monitors, trying to fight back the pounding agony that filled his skull and threatened to explode it. But when he opened his eyes, all he saw was the young woman's image as she sat in the darkened casino.

Waiting for him.

But he could not go alone. Not without Tate. And Tate had betrayed him, left him alone, left him behind to face the ghost from the desert grave. Who would stand by him now? the old man wondered. Who would raise his hand in defense of the old man now? No trust, no loyalty, no enduring security despite all the precautions—the old man despaired. He should have learned from Bertinelli that the most trusted man is always and inevitably the betrayer. He should have remembered that the man Bertinelli most trusted in the world was the same man who put him in the grave.

Louis Bianco. And now the ghost was stirring in the grave, the old man was alone, and where was Louis Bianco?

"Bianco," he said aloud. "Bianco."

The voice over the intercom crackled into life. "Do you wish to see Mr. Bianco?"

"Bianco," the old man repeated.

"I'll see if I can locate him, Mr. Everett," a voice said soothingly.

Moments later, another voice materialized over the intercom. "This is Louis Bianco," said the familiar old voice in a tone of impatience and boredom. "Who's calling, anyway? Tate?"

The old man paused. He smiled to himself. And then he spoke. "I need you, Luigi," the old man said. "I need you tonight."

"We've got to do it," Pierce whispered to Sato. "We've got no choice."

Sato nodded. "He's going to pass out if we don't get him to a hospital and dig the goddamn wiring out of him."

"Yeah, yeah," Pierce mumbled. "And we're going out of here broke if we don't get him away from the craps table. But I don't want to call attention to us. We have to hold off."

"He can hardly stand up straight," Sato said. "He's gone bananas."

Lester Masaoka reeled at the edge of the table, leaning on the padded edge to steady himself, fighting the fever that burned in his head. Something was desperately wrong with the implants, but even more was wrong with his run of luck.

Watching the Japanese, his pallor and unsteadiness, Morrissey said kindly, "Listen, you ought to go upstairs and get some rest. You look very sick."

"Roll the goddamn dice," Lester said. "I've five grand that says you're going to crap out." Ben Payne paid close attention. This could be the signal; these two could be the best pair of actors since Bogart and Hepburn. He put five thousand on the don't pass. Suède jacket had rolled two sevens, an eleven, and made his point five times in a row. Morrissey kept his bet low. A hundred on the pass line. He rolled the dice, felt no energy, came up with a three. "Three, craps, three, the pass line goes. Pay the don't."

Ben was elated: *This could be it.* The Japanese asked if the table limit could be raised to ten thousand. That required a personal nod from Moe Black. But Black was nowhere to be found. The assistant casino manager said it was okay. The boxman announced the table limit and some telegraph in the casino seemed to bring crowds to the table. The stickman passed five dice to Morrissey, who chose two. Ben pulled Selma to a spot next to him. He bet ten thousand for himself on the don't pass and ten for Selma. Lester put ten thousand on the don't side, as well. The other bets did not seem to count. It was the two of them against Morrissey. The opposition was palpable. Lester out of his agony. Ben out of his need.

Morrissey kept to his hundred pass-line bet, threw another craps. A sigh went up as the players saw it. Except for Lester and Ben, who collected their winnings. Ben was now more convinced than ever that he was in on a setup.

The limousine turned sharply, pulling away from the performer's entrance of the Mecca Hotel. Behind the smoke-tinted glass sat an aging matinee star in tears and an ambitious young dancer in pain.

"Did you hear them, Bobby?" Sally Martin wept. "My God, the things they say: 'So fat! So old! So clumsy!' I can't stand it, Bobby, I really can't. It's killing me, Bobby, it's really killing me."

Bobby Reed wrapped one arm around her—a slender, muscular arm over a fat, flaccid arm—and comforted her. "It's just your imagination," he lied, always the trouper. "They loved you tonight, Sally, just like every other night." He paused to kiss her tear-salted cheek. "And tonight was the last night, Sally. We're not coming back here anymore. Not ever."

He fell silent, stroking her arm with one hand and making a hidden fist with the other. "We can't go to Rio," he said at last. "Anywhere in the world but Rio."

"Why, Bobby? It's a lovely place. I spent my summers there until 1954—" She stopped abruptly. "The year you were born, Bobby."

"We can't go to Rio because Bianco knows that's where you're going," Bobby said softly.

"How would he know?" Sally demanded.

"Shush," Bobby said. "I told you before. No questions. Listen to me. We can go anywhere in the world except the place where Bianco thinks we're going."

Sally studied his face in silence, and then she leaned against him. "Whatever you say," she sighed. "Whatever you say, Bobby."

He nodded but did not speak. Maybe Ibiza, he thought to himself, or one of the Greek islands. The three hundred thousand in the laundry bag would keep them comfortable, and Bianco's belief that they'd gone to Rio would keep them safe. And the suitcase full of shredded newspaper that he'd left behind in Bianco's office would repay him for the last insult that Bobby Reed intended to suffer.

"I love you, Sally," he said at last. And, for the first time, he did not remind himself to act like a trouper. "I love you."

Linda Warner stepped out of the elevator and headed directly for the craps tables, seeking her errant bridegroom. She promptly collided with a tall man wearing an open-necked tuxedo and an abundance of gold chains around his throat. He steadied her with a reassuring hug that lasted a moment longer than absolutely necessary, and she allowed herself to enjoy the hug with a seductive shiver.

"Sorry, little lady, but you'd better watch where you're going," the stranger drawled.

She peered up at his faintly familiar face, and then she squealed. "It's you. It's really you."

The stranger smiled. "I can't say that we've met, little lady, but that's my loss—"

"Oh yes, we've met," she giggled. "I'm staying in your room. Don't you remember—you gave me the key to your room when the front desk told us they didn't have our reservation." She shimmied a bit and giggled some more. "Gee, if it weren't for you, we'd be sleeping on a bus bench somewhere. I guess I owe you a big kiss or something."

He smiled. "Well, honey, why don't we just go upstairs and see exactly what it is that you owe me."

Linda giggled again. "Well, after all, it *is* your room," she said sweetly. And, she thought to herself, my big bold husband isn't going to wander from those damned craps tables 'til dawn—and I don't intend to spend the night by myself. "Let's get to know each other a little bit better."

"Yeah," said the stranger. "And let's use the back door tonight, okay?"

"Huh?" Linda asked. "I don't think I know what you mean."

"You'll see, honey," he said. "You'll see."

What Linda saw, thanks to the expansive mirror over the immense bed in the room, was her own naked body and her unmolested mound. The stranger, it seemed, wanted to use the back door in the most literal sense—and now she felt him beneath her, pounding harder and harder, grunting into her ear, while she wondered to herself when someone in Las Vegas would bother to knock on her front door.

Both Linda and the stranger were too preoccupied to hear the sound of a key in the doorlock or to see John Warner's face when he stepped into the room. They did not hear his exclamation—"Oh my-God-Jesus-Christ-Linda-what-is-doing-on-here?"—and they did not see him linger at the foot of the bed, staring unabashedly at the sight of his wife being buggered by a perfect stranger.

Slowly, as their bodies continued to writhe in harmony and he continued to stare at the sight, John Warner became aware of something stirring within his forgotten loins. A new hunger, a new sort of passion, a brand-new erection. Without taking his eyes from the bed, John fumbled with his trousers and then eased up to the vacant space on his wife's body.

"John?" she asked, shocked and pleased. "John, is that you?"

There was something wrong, Ben knew, and it was time to quit. Surely he had enough to cover the looted money at Volta Records. He had made it betting against suède jacket, betting on the don't pass. But the man he thought was a dice mechanic was making even more money betting the numbers. His rolls went for eight or ten numbers, and more often than not he would call off those bets, as he could, just before throwing a seven. The Japanese, he decided, could not be a confederate. He bet the don't pass with a steady and malicious glee whenever suède jacket rolled. But his other bets were crazy ones, and mostly losing. No, the Japanese was a random factor, Ben thought, someone who had just happened along to screw things up.

Morrissey was at least ninety thousand ahead. It was like a dream. He flipped his five-dollar lucky chip into the air and caught it easily in one hand. Arrayed in front of him on the craps table was a castle of chips, blacks and golds and greens, circular chips and rectangular plaques, an unimaginable fortune—and he was still winning.

Lester pushed another ten thousand to the don't pass. Ben bet twenty thousand on the don't pass. Morrissey bet ten thousand on the pass line. Easily, casually, as though the dice were the least concern in his life, he sent the dice dancing along the table. "Eight. Eight. The point is eight," the stickman said. Morrissey bet a thousand on the hard eight and in the next throw came up with two fours, eight the hard way. It paid off at ten to one. It seemed as though he couldn't lose. And yet, the yearning in his heart remained for the girl. He worried about her as he had never worried about another human being before in his life.

Pierce and Sato knew they had to move in. Lester was hysterical. If they didn't stop him, he'd blow the whole bankroll. He'd collapse any minute now and the implant would be detected by the hotel doctor or the emergency clinic at the hospital. The two men pushed through the Saturday crowds, edging closer and closer to the table where a dozen gamblers were letting their action ride with Morrissey. They'd watched Lester drop nearly a hundred thousand of their money. "Excuse me, excuse me," Pierce repeated, pushing with one shoulder through the crowd. Sato came in his wake. When they were within shoulder-grasping distance of Lester Masaoka, one of the hotel's security guards blocked their passage. "I'm a doctor. That's my patient at the table. He is a very sick man. He has to leave the table."

Lester looked up. "Excuse me sir," the guard said. "But this man says he's your doctor . . ."

"I've never seen him before in my life," Lester muttered. "Now leave me alone . . . I'm trying to gamble."

"But it's my money too," Pierce screamed. "Goddamn you, it's my money too."

The shift boss, who had been standing unobtrusively in the shadows, stepped forward and snapped his fingers. Suddenly a trio of security men had Lester firmly in tow and were half walking, half carrying him to the executive office. "You two had better come along as well," the shift boss said. The little parade was hardly noticed in the casino.

The players called for action. Morrissey looked at Ben Payne. Somehow, Payne thought, it was a contest between the two of them. As though there was only one measure of luck left in the universe. One or the other.

Morrissey's mind was not on the game; his thoughts were twenty-six floors away, in another casino where another game might be playing out even at this minute. And for the player in that game, not for himself, he raised the five-dollar chip to his lips and murmured: "Lise!" He put two thousand on the pass line. Ben Payne put five thousand on don't pass.

Morrissey raised the dice and rattled them casually. He felt a dread in the pit of his stomach. Some more important throw was being decided for him, in that other casino, his fate and his future.

Ben Payne willed suède jacket to crap out.

The dice came rolling down the green. Three. Craps.

Ben grinned. Morrissey's mind was elsewhere.

The door opened with a whoosh, and Lise's eyes widened in the darkness. As if in some solemn, slow-motion processional, a slight old man in an oversized wheelchair moved into the room, followed by a short, wiry man who kept one hand on the wheelchair and one hand at his side. Lise closed her fingers around the pistol in her purse. It rested in her lap.

"You are Lise Christian?" The words rasped tremulously through the darkened room, like the voice of a disembodied ghost, and they reached Lise's ears in a skin-crawling whisper.

She nodded, but she said nothing. Instead, she stared at the old man, trying to fathom his features in the semi-darkness. A gaunt, skeletal face. Pale, nearly transparent parchment skin. Long fingers that rapped sequentially on the armrests of the wheelchair when they weren't crawling over his face. And a pair of milky-white eyes that resembled the eyes of some sea creature that dwells on the bottom of the ocean.

"If you'll forgive me, I'd prefer to leave the lights off," the old man murmured. "Hurts my eyes."

Lise nodded again. The man who'd pushed the wheelchair into the casino had taken two steps to one side, and he now stood facing her from across the room. One hand was at his side, the other hovered near an open jacket. But she paid no attention to him. The old man, who seemed to shimmer in the darkness like an apparition, dominated her mind and her moment.

"You know, young lady, I knew your mother," the old man rasped. "Knew her rather well."

Lise stiffened at the old man's words. Moe had said nothing about Everett and her own mother.

"And, of course, I knew your father, too," he continued. A moment of silence passed, and then he spoke again: "Why did you come here? Did she send you?"

"She's dead."

"Your father, I knew him."

"He was murdered."

"Don't stare at me that way. You're giving me a splitting headache. Tell me why you came?"

She felt a strange sensation in her fingertips, as if her blood were speaking to her in some barely understood way. No, he's not gone, Lise reminded herself. He lives on in me, in my blood, in my fate. And my fate has brought me here to face my father's killer.

"Why won't you let me rest?" the old man asked. He appeared to be sucking in gulps of air.

"Did you kill my father?" she asked softly.

"Get out! Go!"

Lise observed the palsied trembling hands as they rubbed his forehead. His head began to nod compulsively, and his hands reached ineffectively to steady it. A long, low moan rose out of the old man's throat—a protest, a confession, and a half laugh. And then he managed to form the words: "Your Dago justice! I knew you had come to settle your grudge. So here—" he pointed a palsied fingers behind him, "—Bianco is the man who murdered your father. Not me. I brought him to you."

Lise Christian's eyes flashed in the darkness, and the figure in the corner recognized the ancient vengeance in the young woman's face. "Boss," he shouted, "who is she? What—" His hand reached into his jacket, but before it came out two shots in rapid succession broke the cold silence of the casino. Louis Bianco staggered forward, already dead on his feet, falling only when his legs collided with the draped craps table.

Lise looked down at the gun in her hand, and slowly realized that she hadn't fired it. Then she looked up as a small man in a dark suit stepped through the doorway of the casino.

"Mr. Black," Lise exclaimed.

He shrugged. "I could not let you do it, Lisetta," he said. "You're a lady. Ladies don't do things like this."

Lise raised the silver pistol to her shoulder. "He lied, Mr. Black. Mr. Everett said he had nothing to do with it," she said, leveling the gun at the old man's head. "You're a liar, Mr. Everett."

Her fingers froze as they touched the trigger.

Staring through the darkness, she saw that the man in the wheelchair had slumped over, mouth agape, eyes open but eyeballs rolled upward, his long fingers clenched.

"Don't shoot, Lisetta," Moe Black said quietly. "You don't have to shoot. There is no more need for killing."

Edward Roger Everett was dead of natural causes.

The dice bounced high over the green felt and fell back from the far wall. But Morrissey paid no attention at all. Instead, he clenched the lucky five-dollar chip in his hand—and he prayed. For the first time in his life, he prayed as if there were someone to hear his prayers. And then, as if in answer to those prayers, the elevator at the far side of the casino opened to reveal Lise Christian.

"Seven. Pay the front line. Don'ts away," the stickman announced. Ben had lost it back. He felt drained and cleansed. He had taken his bath. He turned to Selma. She reached into the Gucci and brought out the last five-thousand-dollar packet of hundreds. Ben pushed it back to her. "Keep it for the baby," he said.

The stickman shoved the dice to John Morrissey. "They're your dice," the stickman said.

"Not mine," Morrissey said, picking up his chips. "I pass."

He hurried across the casino floor to Lise Christian, and they stood facing each other silently for a full minute. Then he took one step toward her, and she slumped forward into his arms.

"I've been waiting for the moment when I could put my arms around you ever since I came to Vegas," Morrissey whispered into her ear, almost overcome by the sudden closeness of her body and the perfume of her hair. "I've been waiting to say I love you since I first laid eyes on you."

Tears formed in Lise's eyes. "Just hold me now," she whispered. "Hold me now, and there'll be plenty of time for us when we reach New Mexico. Our karma is ahead of us."

It was time for the shift to change. The dealer stepped back from the craps table and solemnly passed one palm over the other in Pilate's ancient gesture of handwashing.

Players drifted out; others came in to replace them, coffers full and hopes high. Like life, the game goes on. It is a twenty-four-hour game, seven days a week. Casino action continues whether you care or not; whether you're there or not. The game never ends.

"New shooter." The call hung briefly in the garish air. "New shooter coming out."